A BIGGER PRIZE

ALSO BY DENIS GRAY

Teardrop

Della's Deed

Lucky

Benny's Last Blast!!

A BIGGER PRIZE

DENIS GRAY

iUniverse, Inc.
Bloomington

A BIGGER PRIZE

iUniverse books may be ordered through booksellers or by contacting:

iUniverse
1663 Liberty Drive
Bloomington, IN 47403
www.iuniverse.com
1-800-Authors (1-800-288-4677)

ISBN: 978-1-4759-9385-1 (sc)
ISBN: 978-1-4759-9387-5 (hc)
ISBN: 978-1-4759-9386-8 (e)

Library of Congress Control Number: 2013909856

Printed in the United States of America.

iUniverse rev. date: 7/2/2013

"I just wanted to meet him."
Elegant Raines

PROLOGUE

Tugboats look just like pugnacious terriers. Of course they are neither hairy nor do they sport stubby tails, but they do look like they can beat up anything put in their way—even great battleships commanding the high seas. Indeed, it may be romanticizing it some, but this is the way it is in boxing, oftentimes taking a "pug" of a fighter and making him king.

Boxing and fighters have lived through hell together. They're mated like glove and fist, oftentimes making it impossible to tell one from the other or to feel where one begins and the other ends. It's a business after all, this business of boxing, and it's a business where boxers/prizefighters must fight for pittance or fortune. It's how all prizefighters begin, by fighting for pittance, small purses. It's just that some never get beyond it, to where fabulous fortunes await them like distant, glittering shores or a mariner's ghostly call.

Prizefighting is ancient and creaky, beginning with bare knuckles and staunch backs and granite jaws and marathon rounds of skilled but boring exhibitions. These were contests fought for sport, for the purity of young men's minds and souls—the human spirit.

Everyone who has a stake in boxing, from the promoter to the manager to the trainer to the fan, takes their lumps. But none more so, more seriously, than the boxer. No one has to have as much heart and soul as a prizefighter, who stands in the boxing ring with brute fists flying furiously at his head without the luxury of foresight—absorbing the punishment meted out to him, the blows from his foe and not beating in quick retreat, back down (unless everything is lost), out of the grasp of the smartest, cleverest of "tricksters."

Prizefighting crossed the Atlantic from England to America to crown John Lawrence Sullivan, a.k.a. the Great John L., and "Boston Strongboy," its king. From victory to victory, John L. stalked the American dream by rising from poverty, from a disadvantaged lot on the immigrant streets of Boston to being worshipped as a hero by ascending to the top rung of his profession through hard work and dedication and strong will—not to mention his gifts of courage and bravery and talented fists and rugged chin, which came to him not through mythmakers or the ink of poetic scribes.

Prizefighting is a natural sport in its simplicity (two men fight to see who is the better man) but complicated in its handling, in its shuffling of men as they try to prove who is what and who should be what in the eyes of the masses who wish for the glory of others, even if their own hearts would fall faint and far short of the mark if they were ever to duck their heads between the roughed ropes and seek the grand prize, the victory inside the ring.

It is the poor blacks and the poor whites who dream the biggest dreams. It is the poor blacks and poor whites who scuffle among themselves with huge ambition and noble cause. It is the poor blacks and poor whites who are locked in a titanic struggle to determine who is the better fighter in the ring (as in life), to determine who can strike the biggest blows for their race, leaving the foe disgraced and bloody as they claim victory for their own kind and achieve their own superelevation.

There are strange, odd, spooky things that happen in this quest for boxing glory. No one race is exempt; all races are guilty. It is only power that can cheat the deck, make the human contest dishonest, impure, and unequal in the end.

———

Leemore "Pee-Pot" Manners had a pretty pair of hands. Any honest man would say Pee-Pot knew more about boxing than any man alive—whether that man be black or white. He was a trainer of boxers, an ex-boxer himself. He lived in the state of West Virginia, once a part of Virginia until Virginia seceded from the Union in 1861, at the time of the Civil War, to join the Confederate States of America. West Virginia drafted a state constitution and, in 1862, applied to Congress for statehood. It was a state of tobacco crop and peanut crop and men who invested their time and sweat into the honorable profession of being farmers and toiling the land for commerce and industry—for bountiful product.

Pee-Pot Manners lived in Longwood, West Virginia, where it was hillier and oak forested than any other part of the state. In distance, the town of Longwood wasn't far off from Pee-Pot's home, just three miles north. Pee-Pot was looking at his sweet pair of hands and was mumbling like a man who lived alone but didn't give a damn who heard him, not even Gyp, his Labrador retriever, who was lying on a thick, royal-blue throw rug off to the right of his feet.

Pee-Pot had taken his eyes off the letter he'd read no less than four times. The letter was on his lap. Pee-Pot was looking down at his hands, and probably, it was being done unconsciously, unawares, but it was being done in direct response to the letter. Pee-Pot sighed. He'd never gotten a letter from a boxer before. He chuckled. He didn't know too many boxers who could write! Gyp, a beautiful black, looked up at Pee-Pot and then shut her eyes again. A short-handled grooming brush lay by Gyp's forepaws, the nylon bristles soft to a dog's rich coat.

What boxer I know would even be so much as interested in writing me a letter? Pee-Pot thought. The letter was because of Frank "Black Machine" Whaley. He was dead. He was an ex-fighter, an ex-pug, an ex-lightweight. Black Machine Whaley and Pee-Pot fought inside the ring fifteen times. Sometimes the match was billed as Pee-Pot Manners vs. Frank "Black Machine" Whaley, sometimes Frank "Black Machine" Whaley vs. Pee-Pot Manners. It was all according to how the poster maker felt on that particular day, Pee-Pot would often joke.

But it's how it was in boxing for the top-notch black fighters, fighting each other all the time, since they couldn't get, for the most part, the kind of fights they wanted against the top-notch white fighters. Frank "Black Machine" Whaley was a great fighter. Over the years, Black Machine and Pee-Pot staged spectacular fights up to a point, but beyond that point, their fights became dull, flat affairs. Their black fans were not getting what they paid for, for both simply knew each other's boxing skills far too well.

"Gyp, I'm gonna read this letter again. One more time. So don't you start counting. Making a mountain out of a molehill."

Gyp wagged her tail.

Dated March 14, 1946

Dear Mr. Pee-Pot Manners,

You don't know of me, but I do of you. This is through Mr. Frank "Black Machine" Whaley, sir. It is with great sadness that I report Mr. Whaley has died of a heart attack one week ago. He had this heart condition for a while. The heart attack was not something he did not expect.

It is why he informed me of you, Mr. Manners. I am a fighter of his, fighting out of the Whaley Gym. He trained me for the period of eight months, me recording twelve professional victories in the ring. He was ailing so. So he told me if anything should happen to him, that he would like for me to contact you, that you were the best trainer outside of him he could think of. He said I had great potential and that I should continue my training as was accorded me up till now.

I do hope you feel the same way, Mr. Manners. For I will make every effort in my power to make this happen if you are willing to take me on as your fighter. If you think my fighting ability is worthy of such.

Most gratefully,
Elegant Raines

PS. As of now, I am currently not in training session, even though I am still conducting my roadwork.

It's how all of this began, with the letter from Elegant Raines on behalf of Black Machine Whaley—in a sense, in the memory of Black Machine. It took little time for Pee-Pot to write Elegant Raines back. He was going to honor Black Machine and felt honored Black Machine would think enough of him to send one of his young (presumably) black fighting prospects his way.

Only, he hadn't made it easy on Elegant Raines, not in the least, since this wasn't Pee-Pot's style. If Elegant Raines wished to meet him, then he would have to find a way to get to him the best way he could. He made it very clear to Elegant Raines in the letter he mailed to him.

Dated March 19, 1946

Dear Mr. Raines,

It is with a heavy heart I received the sad news regarding Mr. Whaley. I am so grateful for your correspondence with me on his behalf. Him and me fought many a war in the ring together. Mr. Whaley was a great fighter of his time. He was a great friend of mine I wasn't always in contact with, but our friendship always stood for something.

Now for us. I would like to meet you. You have my address in Longwood, West Virginia. You just let me know when you are expected, and I will be here to greet you. I wish you well. And do keep up with your roadwork. It is a smart thing not to neglect for a fighter.

Sincerely,
Pee-Pot Manners

Pee-Pot's letter was then followed by another letter from Elegant Raines that read:

Dated March 29, 1946

Dear Mr. Manners,

I thank you for your cordial reply, sir, and I will be in Longwood, West Virginia, on any date you think is best I come. I will not let anything or anyone delay me. This is a satisfactory day for me.

Most gratefully,
Elegant Raines

PS. I am still not back in the boxing gym but am keeping steady at my roadwork.

Pee-Pot wrote Elegant Raines back, giving him the date of April 18, today, for him to come in from View Point, Texas, to Longwood, West

Virginia, to find out what kind of fighter he was. Or was Black Machine Whaley using the word "potential" more for effect than substance. Pee-Pot got no pleasure in subjecting Black Machine's motives to question or suspicion, but the boy was coming a long ways away to visit him—to either accept or reject for training.

The letter he forwarded to Elegant Raines offered him no directions for how to get to Longwood, only the time of day he expected him: midafternoon. Pee-Pot figured if this Elegant Raines boy wanted to train this badly with him (as his letters indicated), then his inner desire would guide him to his doorstep. It was the only pact he'd made with him thus far, at least.

Pee-Pot got out of the rocker. No firewood was burning in the chimney corner. The house was cool from rains hammering it from ten o'clock this morning until one o'clock this afternoon. Now the sun was breaking cleanly through the windows, soon to heat up the middle-aged farmhouse. But Pee-Pot wasn't anticipating this; he was heading for the kitchen to boil a pot of tea to take some of the chill off himself when, suddenly, he heard a loud knock on the front door.

Woof! Woof!

Gyp was up on all fours, alert and, apparently, ready for action; her nap, history—all but forgotten by her for now.

"Now quiet down, Gyp. Behave. You know I told you this morning who was coming today to visit us. Ain't a stranger to visit us. But this fighter sent by Black Machine Whaley."

Gyp still stood her ground though.

"Okay, then, sniff this letter so you can make sure it's him. When we get to the door. This Elegant Raines boy. He ain't a fake."

Gyp's nose did just that, sniffed the letter Pee-Pot held.

"Okay, Gyp, let's get to the door before he thinks nobody lives here. Uh, for we can see what the boy looks like for ourselves."

Gyp loped off to the door as Pee-Pot followed from behind.

Now Gyp was stationed at the door, looking up at the doorknob. Pee-Pot stopped to laugh at Gyp's preparedness, but after all, that was Gyp at her best, a purebred Lab, her bloodlines working to peak form.

Pee-Pot opened the door.

A face like a black pearl, Pee-Pot thought. *A face like a black pearl!*

"Mr. Raines!"

"Mr. Manners, sir!"

Pee-Pot and Elegant Raines shook hands at the door.

"Come in. Come in."

"Thank you, sir."

It was one big tan suitcase Elegant Raines carried.

"Glad you got here okay, considering the rains, Mr. ... well, Raines ... uh ..."

"Don't worry, Mr. Manners. It happens all the time."

Gyp came from behind the tall wooden door.

"I'm accustomed to ..." Elegant Raines was thrown off stride, so his speech stalled midsentence.

Gyp was sniffing Elegant Raines's right leg.

"Mr. Manners, sir, uh, she's not going to take a bite out of my leg, is she, sir?" Elegant Raines asked, smiling at Pee-Pot.

"No. She's trained. No, she's just making sure you are who you say you are. You ain't a mistake. She sniffed your letter a minute ago."

"Oh. The first one or the second one, Mr. Manners?"

Pee-Pot laughed, for he enjoyed Elegant Raines's wry wit.

Gyp's tail wagged.

"So you passed the first test, so I see, Mr. Raines."

Elegant Raines then, mentally, returned to the reality of his trip in from View Point, Texas, why he was in Longwood, West Virginia—to present himself to Pee-Pot Manners as a professional fighter of skill.

"And, Mr. Raines, you can leave your luggage right there. Parked where it is. No sense in you carrying it into the living room with us."

Now Gyp loped past Pee-Pot and Elegant, was back on her royal-blue throw rug, her head comfortably down on her forepaws.

Pee-Pot was looking Elegant up and down.

"You're tall, Mr. Raines. What ...?"

"Six feet, Mr. Manners," Elegant said eagerly. "Six feet even, sir."

"A middleweight."

"Yes, sir."

Pee-Pot was looking at Elegant Raines's broad-set shoulders now and his unusually large hands.

"How old are you, Mr. Raines?"

"Eighteen, sir. Had, uh, had a birthday in February. J-just recently, sir. February 18, Mr. Manners. "

Pee-Pot saw this young man filling out easily, comfortably, in time, becoming a heavyweight somewhere down the line.

"Sit, son."

It was a long wooden bench with a long one-piece cushion attached to its solidly constructed frame.

"Thank you, Mr. Manners."

Pee-Pot sat back down in the low-slung, high-back, wooden Rapson rocker. Pee-Pot saw Elegant Raines was trying to make himself feel at home, comfortable on the bench. He could well imagine the kind of trip it must've been for him to get from View Point, Texas, to here—the effort it must've taken. So he was empathetic to him possibly to a fault. Indeed, he would let him catch his breath, Pee-Pot thought, gain his bearings, satisfactorily.

Now Pee-Pot remembered what he was about to do before the knock on the door, and that was to boil water for tea for himself, the cold no longer really in him—excited, in a big way now, in seeing Elegant Raines in person, dressed in a gray suit jacket, matching trousers, a white shirt, and black tie. He was a handsome black boy. His hair was neatly cropped. To date, he'd had twelve professional fights, all ring victories, yet no scars or ring wars were visible in his delicately sketched face that presented an easy, gracious, winning smile. He was like his letters indicated: graceful and elegant.

"So how was the trip here? From View Point, Texas?"

"Oh fine, Mr. Manners. Fine, sir," Elegant said, seemingly snapping out of his thoughts. "From the time I left View Point, until now."

"Did the rain catch you?"

"No. No." Elegant smiled. "I seemed to be following it, sir."

"Chasing it, you mean."

"No, Mr. Manners, sir, I didn't have a mind to catch up with it. Not the way it was teeming out of the sky. No, not at all, sir."

Gyp's tail wagged.

"Hit us hard for a few hours. Early on."

Pee-Pot glanced at the dried-up mud covering Elegant's shoes.

"Got your shine dirty though."

Elegant looked down at his shoes. "Yes, they sure are, sir."

The sun was warming the big room, but Pee-Pot asked, "Cold?"

"No, Mr. Manners. I'm excited, sir."

"Nervous then?"

"Right, Mr. Manners. Yes. I am, sir."

"Well, I'm not—ain't gonna rush you through anything today. You've been on the road, traveling, and we're gonna give you every opportunity, chance, to catch your wind. Wouldn't be fair otherwise."

Elegant smiled.

"I want you to know, Mr. Raines, that this is as important to me as I expect it is to you."

"Yes, sir."

"I've spent my entire life in the fight game. And I respect it from top to bottom. The whole idea of the craft of it—the fight game. The learning that goes into it. Science, if you will."

"Yes, sir."

"To be a boxer. Not a puncher. A slugger. But a boxer. Know what you're doing in a ring. Inside it. How to think. Maneuver in ... well ..."

"You, you sound like Mr. Whaley, Mr. Manners. When Mr. Whaley talked about boxing—with such passion, sir."

Pee-Pot laughed. "Guess all us old-timers are the same. Put us all in one room and we'd—h-how was Mr. Whaley's funeral, by the way?" Pee-Pot said, leaning forward in the rocker.

"Very respectable and moving, sir. Mr. Whaley was very much loved in the View Point community, Mr. Manners. And a lot of fighters he trained from his past were in attendance at Mr. Whaley's funeral."

"Good. Good. I knew he would be sent off right. To meet his Maker. It's all any of us can hope for, I suppose, Mr. Raines."

Elegant locked his large hands together. "I, yes—it is, sir."

Pee-Pot thought about the last time he saw Black Machine, six or seven months back. Both had fighters fighting on the same fight card out in San Francisco's Cow Palace, and, at the time, he looked as fit as a fiddle, and he told him just that. He had no idea Black Machine was masking a heart condition that'd soon end his life.

But he would be as stoic about his health (even though he was in good health) as Black Machine about his if the shoe were on the other foot.

It would be the fighter in him trumping any rationale openly revealing his vulnerability, that something might defeat him. So he would like to respectfully think this was the same for Black Machine Whaley before he died.

Elegant, looking at Gyp napping, needed this respite. And he knew all too well Pee-Pot Manners was thinking of Frank "Black Machine" Whaley. Maybe not about the past fights they fought, had put themselves through, but probably about him in general. Frank "Black Machine" Whaley was a great father figure to him. He was a man who knew how to survive in a world that had been hostile toward him, restricted him, stunted him. To an America that preached freedom, emancipation for all its citizens, but was caught in the web of a terrible lie Black Machine Whaley knew about and Pee-Pot Manners knew about and he now knew about for eighteen years of his life. He had lived and seen things. These things were indelible, things that gave him nightmares, things that haunted him, things that almost practically killed him.

Now looking at Pee-Pot Manners, no longer looking at Gyp, whom he already liked (never mind the sniffing of his leg), inwardly, Elegant laughed, for he knew Pee-Pot Manners was probably bald-headed beneath his flat checkered cap. Pee-Pot Manners was a lightweight, all right, who stood about five five, at least seven inches shorter than him. He wore baggy pants (khakis), with a belt that looked like it could wrap his waist twice. He was brown skinned, not black complected like him and Mr. Whaley. He had a sweet, enduring face; but he wondered how he'd be, what his patient, sweet face would look like during a training session if his standards were not approached and then met.

"So you got a peek, small peek of Longwood?"

"Yes, sir."

"What you think?"

"Quite friendly, sir."

"Then you must've met Mr. Holloway. Chadway Holloway."

"Uh, yes, Mr. Manners. How did you know, sir?"

"Runs the general store. Generally, he's friendly. Not unless you're too late on your credit."

"Yes, he was quite friendly. He offered me a wagon and a horse to get here to the farmhouse."

"Was in his place seeking, asking for directions, were you?"

"Yes. I felt pointed to—"

"It being the biggest store in Longwood."

"Exactly, Mr. Manners. But I said no, thank you. I told him I was a fighter, so I needed the exercise, sir."

"He must've gotten a kick out of that."

"Yes, he did."

Pee-Pot stood and walked over to the window. The sun was still radiant, and then Pee-Pot turned. "I was just about to boil some water for tea before you got here, Mr. Raines. In the mood for some?"

"Yes, yes, uh, that'd be, be fine, Mr. Manners."

"And got some chicken sliced up. How'd that hold you?"

"Mr. Manners ... I ..."

Pee-Pot removed his flat checkered cap with the short bill and rubbed what was his bald head twice before returning the cap back to his head. "You're my and Gyp's guest until, of course, uh, we get this thing between you and me straightened out. Settled for us."

"Yes," Elegant said, nodding his head, swallowing hard, with difficulty. "Yes, Mr. Manners."

"So you're hungry then?"

"Yes, I am."

"I ain't talking about the three miles now. But the whole way from View Point, Texas, Mr. Raines. That whole trip you made in—to get here."

<hr />

All the rooms in the house were big, this big bedroom he was in being no exception. Elegant turned the oil lamp off. The room, soon, was as dark as him. And before he knew it, he was tossing and turning, and it had nothing to do with the bed. The mattress sagged and felt worn, but it was better than what he'd been sleeping on on his way in to Longwood. To put it bluntly, he'd been hoboing. It was the kind of financial shape he was in, certainly not able to afford a train trip like this one would cost him, so he hopped trains. He had to resort to hoboing, something not below him since he'd done it for the past eight years of his life.

When Black Machine Whaley died, after the funeral, the fighters in his stable, scattered like seeds to the wind—just like him. They were in pursuit of other trainers too. They were looking for new deals too. There was nothing in View Point, Texas, to keep them there but Black Machine Whaley, Whaley's Gym. They'd been farmed out to do menial jobs in View Point, jobs putting little pay in their pockets. Most of the fighters in Mr. Whaley's stable were young like him, after glory. There was no reason to lie or exhibit deception toward his goal, not even to himself. He was a fighter after glory. And he wanted the boxing ring, one day, to provide him this glory if he worked at it, dedicated himself enough to the pursuit of that ideal.

It was the pursuit of it, Elegant thought, shutting his eyes, and then reopening them. This is what thrilled him before falling asleep at night, the pursuit of glory, fame—to become somebody. If, as a black man, his life was defined by this, finding glory through boxing like Jack Johnson, a hero of his, then he accepted it; he made this possible for a black man. The twelve victories under his belt only encouraged him, gave him greater hope.

Even though Black Machine Whaley said he would not live out the year, he still held out hope, not until his health turned for the worse. He was mortified when he did die though but tried not to show it.

"Scared. That's what I was."

It was as if the world had pulled the rug from under him again. He couldn't, wouldn't equate his life with anyone else's; it's just that he was ridden with so much pain so much of the time. But being under Frank "Black Machine" Whaley's tutelage, his attention to him, oftentimes being called the teacher's pet by the other fighters in Whaley's Gym, he'd found, what he thought, the ideal setting.

It's why it pained him so much leaving View Point, Texas, for here. Him not knowing what he was going to get himself into but determined to find out. The past month had been lonely. The trip—he felt alone. Writing the letter to Pee-Pot Manners, of course, was the easy part. After Frank "Black Machine" Whaley's funeral, it was the first thing he remembered to do. He had to get back to fighting, to training, to fighting form—not just the roadwork.

Boxing was a tonic in blunting the feeling of being alone, Elegant thought. "When you have good days in the gym, you dream better, I think. At night. In bed." He had to laugh at himself, for it sounded like it could be true. But of course, a good day in the gym meant your spirits were buoyed. There was nothing like Black Machine Whaley saying, "That was a good workout, Elegant. You showed yourself good. Followed my instructions to the T, son."

"Praise. I love it. And Mr. Whaley lavished me with it all the time. Every day."

He knew he had a quiet but needy personality. He didn't mind being quiet but didn't like being needy. Needing praise. Affirmation! He'd fight it but had yet overcome it. He continued pointing to his age, youth, using it as a yardstick, an excuse, a crutch, that he'd outgrow it, wouldn't be dependent on it—that all of this would, eventually, work itself out. Only, it'd taken years in the making, and it couldn't be shaken off him like fleas on a dog.

His arms folded over his chest. Elegant laughed, for he pictured Gyp, whom he hadn't seen scratch her black shiny coat for fleas, a joy to watch, when wagging her tail at whatever she must've thought amusing in his verbal exchanges with Pee-Pot Manners.

"Mr. Manners does act like he likes me though. That I am not in any way an intrusion by my coming to Longwood to the farmhouse."

It certainly had to do, Elegant thought, with his relationship with Black Machine Whaley. To maintain their relationship over the years after their boxing campaigns was honorable, commendable. Black Machine Whaley never mentioned who got the better of the bouts, and he hadn't asked. He'd thought about asking but always stopped short of it. And then, after a while, it seemed unimportant to ask, as if he'd be trampling on sacred ground, something warmly shared between two great fighters of their time—and Black Machine Whaley had said Pee-Pot Manners was a great fighter of his time.

Elegant was scared about tomorrow. It would be judgment day for him—Pee-Pot Manners would judge him as a fighter. He would determine whether or not he would train him, keep him on course in attaining the glory he was in such desperate need of garnering.

He was born in Saw Mill, South Carolina. He was geographically closer to South Carolina than he'd like, closer than he felt comfortable with. View Point, Texas, had served as a better buffer between him and Saw Mill. *Yes, geographically,* Elegant thought.

He hated Saw Mill, South Carolina. He'd never go back to the place physically, for, mentally, he was always there. He was always a part of Saw Mill's black dirt, buried in it like a dead body, decayed, unable to rise again, and its waters too, murky, a graveyard of rootless, floating corpses of chalked bones. A harrowing thing happened to him there. At one time he ran from Saw Mill, South Carolina, for his life.

CHAPTER 1

Knock.

Woof!

"Y-y-yes?"

"I came to wake you, Mr. Raines. Me and Gyp."

Elegant's sleepy eyes smiled.

"Were you awake?"

Elegant felt embarrassed. "No. No, uh, Mr. Manners."

"The trip in, I suppose," Pee-Pot acknowledged sympathetically.

Yes, it must've been the trip, Elegant thought, presently forgiving himself.

"It's five thirty, Mr. Raines. Time for roadwork."

"Yes. Yes, sir, Mr. Manners," Elegant said, hopping out of the bed, off the mattress and onto the floor. "My roadwork!"

The oil lamp shot on, and Elegant, straightaway, made haste for the opened-out suitcase on the floor—to retrieve his boxing togs.

Jointly, Pee-Pot and Gyp walked from the bedroom door.

"You'll have your turn with him next, Gyp. Don't you worry," Pee-Pot said, patting Gyp's head. Gyp looked up, and her tongue licked Pee-Pot's hand. "See what kind of legs and wind the boy's got."

Elegant wanted to make a good impression straight off, and here he was making a bad one, even though the traveling did play its role in this early-morning predicament. Mr. Manners hit the nail on the head, but he still had to compensate for his mental lapse—find something, some opportunity in the day to make up for this morning. *Wow Mr. Manners,* Elegant thought. Wow him enough to make him forget about what happened, him knocking on the door, waking him up—a fighter like he was.

———

When Pee-Pot heard Elegant rumble down the narrow wooden stairs, he went into the icebox and grabbed the bottle of water, putting it on the short, square-faced, grainy kitchen table.

"Mr. Manners?"

"In the kitchen, Mr. Raines. In the kitchen."

"Yes, sir."

Pee-Pot was wearing his flat checkered hat. "Good morning."

"Good morning, sir."

"Now it's official."

"Yes, sir," Elegant said sheepishly. "Y-yes, it is."

"You look spiffy, Mr. Raines."

"Thank you, sir."

Elegant was attired in gray sweats, black boxing shoes, a white towel strung around his neck with part of it stuffed down inside the sweat top, and a blue knit ski cap.

Elegant saw the bottle of water on the table and knew it was for him. And in a bowl, on the table, was one apple and one banana.

They looked into each other's eyes, connecting, as it were.

"Thank you, Mr. Manners."

Gyp was at the kitchen sink, lying down on a big pink towel spread across the oak-planked floor.

Elegant took a big bite out of the apple, and then another, until he finished it off. He then peeled the banana, Pee-Pot reaching for the banana peel and the apple core.

"Thank you, Mr. Manners."

Pee-Pot disposed of the banana peel and apple core in the metal trash can by the squat, aged icebox.

When finished with the banana, Elegant picked up the bottle of water, and after two strong pulls from the bottle, it was empty.

Pee-Pot's fingers tugged the cap's bill. "Guess you're ready now, huh, Mr. Raines? For your roadwork?"

"I am, sir."

Gyp stood.

"Yesterday I confined you."

Elegant had no idea what Pee-Pot Manners meant.

"Come, Mr. Raines."

Gyp was standing at the back door.

Now Elegant caught on.

"You don't know what's in the backyard, not from the direction you came in yesterday morning. And from your bedroom, you just looked out at what you already saw. Same … from the living room. Your vantage point.

"And from the kitchen, I saw you kept to your manners darn, pretty darn good too. The whole time."

They were through the kitchen's back door and out onto the vast piece of property in back of the farmhouse. "All my land, as you might expect, Mr. Raines. Out to the start of the woods."

It was a breathtaking view to say the least.

"I know you said you were from New Town, Oklahoma, Mr. Raines, but nothing's like this part of the country. West Virginia. There's not a beautiful sunrise or sunset this land'll make you soon forget."

Pee-Pot turned back around to the house. "I built that house."

"Uh, I do carpentry too, Mr. Manners."

"You do, do you? Hmm … that's good to know. Have you ever built a house though, Mr. Raines, in your eighteen years of living?"

"I've helped on a few. But no, sir, not by myself, sir. For, for my own needs. Shelter, Mr. Manners."

Pee-Pot took two steps toward the house.

"I bought the property. Then built the house. Took two years to build it. Not bad, wouldn't you say, Mr. Raines?"

"No, not bad at all, sir."

"Back in 1915. How old were you then?" Pee-Pot teased.

"Uh, not, not very, Mr. Manners …," Elegant said, keeping in line with Pee-Pot's humor, outright teasing.

But none of the conversation had distracted Elegant from what was really on his mind, for in the distance there stood a good-sized wood-frame building, something the size of a rural schoolhouse populated throughout the South.

"Of course there was a house on the property when I bought it. A shotgun shack, nonetheless. But—"

"Pardon me, Mr. Manners …"

"Yes …?"

"But what's that, sir?" Elegant said, pointing his finger to the building Gyp was briskly walking toward.

"Come on then, Mr. Raines. We might as well follow Gyp. For I can show you everything there is on the property."

Pee-Pot and Elegant walked toward the wooden building. "It was the next stop on the tour anyways."

The building was about 175 yards in distance.

"Another one of my enterprises, Mr. Raines."

Mr. Manners had all the reason in the world to be proud of it, Elegant thought. And probably what was inside its charming wooden frame.

"Had a barn on the farm at one time. But tore it down. Was no need for it. For my purposes. So I used the wood from the barn to build … well … you'll see, Mr. Raines."

Gyp's tail wagged.

As soon as they got to the building, Pee-Pot opened its door.

"A gym!"

"Yes, Mr. Raines, a gym!" Pee-Pot said proudly.

"And a beautiful one at that, Mr. Manners!"

One ring, exercise mats, three speed bags, two heavy bags, and lots of room—it's what Elegant saw.

"I've got a gym in Longwood where I train my boys. But before any big bout, they get special attention out here, with me, Mr. Raines. Me and Gyp."

"This, this is great, Mr. Manners. Great," Elegant said. "A gym, sir. An actual gym."

"Longwood, the town, ain't but so busy, Mr. Raines, but you can meditate better out here. Concentrate better too for the task ahead. Let, uh, let me show you something, if I may." Pee-Pot walked over to a door that was a few feet to his left. He opened it.

"A bed bunk, Mr. Manners."

Then Pee-Pot opened the door adjacent to it.

"And a toilet too!"

"It's a recent addition, Mr. Raines. Before that, the fighters had to use the outhouse. Wouldn't let them in the house to use the bathroom. Uh, was real Spartan training."

Elegant looked over at the boxing ring and could well imagine himself in it. But knew soon, before the day concluded, that his wish would come true, would stare him smack dab back in the eye.

"I'm gonna have to go into town later, work with some of my fighters."

"Yes, sir."

"I was able to block out some time yesterday for you but not so today. There're a few fights on my plate coming due."

Gyp sauntered out of the building.

"Five miles," Pee-Pot said, looking up at Elegant. "Mr. Raines, right?"

"Right. Yes, uh, Mr. Manners, five miles, sir."

"And then we're gonna put you right in that ring there. Through your paces," Pee-Pot said, looking at the boxing ring along with Elegant. "For I can see what you know. What Mr. Whaley taught you in his gym."

That knocked Elegant back to today's reality, what was at stake for him, and fast.

Pee-Pot saw the anxious look on his face and was glad he'd put it there, for they were back to the business of the day, why Elegant Raines was there in Longwood, West Virginia, and why he was offering him hospitality, unconditionally.

Back at the gym's doorway, Elegant joined Pee-Pot, and then together they were back out onto the land on this cool but sunny April morning. Pee-Pot was looking over the lay of the land, and as he was, Elegant was doing deep knee bends a few feet in front of him.

"Since you don't know the course, Mr. Raines, what comprises five miles here, you'll run with Gyp."

"G-Gyp, sir!"

"She'll mark it off and guide you. Knows just what paths to take."

"S-she will!"

Gyp licked Pee-Pot's hand and then shot off like a bullet.

"Wait for me, Gyp. Wait for me!"

And so Elegant broke out after Gyp as Pee-Pot watched, Gyp slowing down, Elegant catching up, and then them running side by side.

"She'll keep a good pace. Hmm … the boy's got a good gait. Smooth. Very smooth looking."

Then Gyp left Elegant's side when about fifty yards from entering the woods, leading him by about four or five feet, about that far in front.

"Oh, five miles, they should be back in, oh, let's say … about thirty minutes or so," Pee-Pot said, glancing at his pocket watch.

⸻

Pee-Pot put the cup in the sink and ran water over it. He stretched his arms and then sat back down at the table. Every morning, as a matter of habit, he woke at five o'clock. His old boxing trainer, when he was a fighter, was Fly Mellon, a former black, top-notch bantamweight. He was a no-nonsense trainer (like him) who knew all the tricks of the trade. He'd taught him things he was still trying to master—it's how smart Fly Mellon was. The first thing he had him come to terms with, beyond the boxing skills and requirements, was that he was a black man in a white man's sport. From the start, it's what Fly Mellon emphasized in subtle and not so subtle language. He didn't want to wreck his dreams (it was not his interest) but didn't let them fly in his face either.

Boxing was a sport that beat men up physically even if they were the best defensive boxing exponent inside the ring, where they made their opponent look amateurish—even foolish at times. But for a black fighter, if he wasn't mentally strong, if he didn't know how to protect himself, or for someone to persistently teach him how (as Fly Mellon did for him), he could go mad if he truly believed there was such a thing as "fair play" in boxing, that crooked white men—invisible to him—didn't control his destiny; if they didn't beat him, win, every time.

It was a bitter pill to swallow but a pill he had to swallow for him not to lose his way, for him not to fall off the deep end as he saw so many black fighters do during his era, men meeting tragedy like blinded beasts, not bleeding from head shots or violent body shots but, instead, from too many damned daggers to the heart.

There were times when he felt too old for the game, the ups and downs, the trials and tribulations, the half wins and half victories. But when you are around other trainers, your peers in age and experience, you never brought up a subject or a feeling like that. You still spoke young, of tomorrow, of the latest fighter, prize you had. A Henry Armstrong or a Sam Langford. For boxing trainers, it's where the joy was—to work with talent, be around fresh legs and spirits.

Pee-Pot stood and walked off to the back door and then out onto the short back porch. He walked down onto the step below, stopped, only to linger there. His shoes making contact with the dirt, Pee-Pot raised his arm and looked at his watch.

"Gyp and Mr. Raines should be coming out of those woods any minute now." Then he looked at the gym. "They'll finish where they started off."

And when Gyp and Elegant emerged from the woods, Elegant was leading Gyp (for Elegant knew it was the original path they were back on). And they were dashing across the grounds with no strain but effortlessly, with fun, competitively, Elegant just a wee bit, a foot or so, ahead of Gyp but then, suddenly, Gyp sprinting to surge ahead, and then Elegant making a hard charge back at her; only, maybe, seventy-five yards more before each got to the building, Pee-Pot not knowing who was going to win between them, Gyp not ever (to his recollection) being challenged so seriously like this, but then again, Gyp sprinting, sprinting, her body seemingly whipping up the wind. Elegant's body unable to do the same, match another gear. Gyp beating him to the building by ten yards. Gyp barking and Elegant whooping loudly on the grounds.

Excitedly, Pee-Pot began hustling for the building. Gyp was still jumping up and down and Elegant with her.

Ten yards from them, Pee-Pot yelled. "If that wasn't a race, dammit! If that wasn't a race!"

Elegant bent over to expel air out of his winded body.

"I've never seen anything like it before. Never!" Gyp ran to Pee-Pot, jumping up into Pee-Pot's arms. "What about you, Gyp? You, girl!"

Gyp licked Pee-Pot's face.

Elegant stood up straight. He was back to breathing normally.

Gyp leaped out of Pee-Pot's arms and walked over to Elegant. She licked his hand. Elegant patted her head. "Thanks, Gyp."

Woof!

"First time, Mr. Raines. Gyp never had to run like that before. For home. Across the grounds like that. First time for her with a fighter."

That made Elegant feel particularly good.

"Nice to see that competitive spirit in her. She's still got it, Mr. Raines, all right. When challenged."

The gym door was still open, so Gyp walked away from them and then into the gym. Elegant had a feeling he knew what it had signaled.

Pee-Pot had carried a bottle of water out of the house. "For you, Mr. Raines."

"Thank you, sir."

Now Pee-Pot headed for the gym. Elegant tailed behind him.

"We might as well get this over with, Mr. Raines. I've already got a long day ahead of me."

"Yes, Mr. Manners."

Gyp was stretched out on the gym floor, a few feet from the ring.

"Strip down and let me take a good look at you, Mr. Raines."

This never made Pee-Pot feel comfortable. He often likened it to white auctioneers at slave auctions. But as a boxing trainer it had to be done. Only, he wasn't checking teeth or buttocks or anything to humiliate or to insult or degrade him or a race of people.

Elegant took the towel off his neck and then the sweat top, sweated T-shirt, and then the sweat pants. He stood in front of Pee-Pot in boxing trunks.

"You have a perfect middleweight's physique," Pee-Pot gushed while Elegant blushed. "I must say, Mr. Raines."

Of course Pee-Pot knew about the large hands Elegant Raines possessed, and the broad shoulders, but it was his muscled chest that was impressive, along with his muscled stomach and tapered waist. His legs were slender but powerfully curved.

Pee-Pot walked over to the gym's northern wall and then came to where Elegant was with a scale.

"One fifty-eight?"

"Yes, uh, sir. It's what I weighed for my last outing, Mr. Manners."

Pee-Pot put the scale down on the floor. Elegant stepped up to it and then onto the scale. The scale's needle headed north.

"One sixty-two … But of course with your boxing shoes on, Mr. Raines. Gotta give allowance for them."

"Of course, Mr. Manners." Elegant smiled.

Elegant stepped off the scale. Pee-Pot picked up the scale and then walked with it back over to the wall.

"You know what's next, don't you, Mr. Raines?"

"Certainly, sir, uh, calisthenics."

"Let's see in what order they're done."

Watching Elegant Raines go through his calisthenics, Pee-Pot took note of how coordinated he was. He offered no comment, just observation. And whatever Elegant did, the exercise he undertook, Pee-Pot always stood to the back of him, for in this way, there was never any sign of approval or disapproval from him either by body language, gesture, or eye contact. Elegant Raines was free to do what he wished today. He was in charge—full control of everything.

"T-that's it, Mr. Manners. I've completed, uh … uh my rounds of calisthenics."

Then Elegant looked at Pee-Pot for further instruction.

"This is your day, Mr. Raines. All yours."

"Oh …," Elegant said softly.

"So what's next?"

"Oh. Oh, next. Next. Right, sir. Next … the speed bag. Speed bag, Mr. Manners. Uh, next. Yes … next."

"Let me pick your mitts."

"Fine, sir."

"This'll do fine," Pee-Pot said, reaching down into the wooden bin, picking out some black mitts.

Standing in front of the speed bag, Elegant looked back over his shoulder at Pee-Pot and then turned back to the speed bag, positioning his body to it. Feeling comfortable and in balance, his fists struck the speed bag slowly and then picked up steam and then caused the bag to hop at a quick clip.

Elegant did this over a period of time and then stopped. He'd broken out into a handsome sweat. Pee-Pot handed him a towel, and Elegant began wiping off his neck and arms, both caked in sweat. He'd put his sweat pants back on, and they too were sweated thoroughly through.

Elegant was in front of the heavy bag. He began hitting it. And so this went on for a while.

When Elegant finished, knowing he was in charge, he said, "I'd like to go into the ring now, Mr. Manners. Shadowbox, sir."

He walked up the three wooden stairs at the side of the ring. Now in the ring, Elegant sighed, for it felt especially good to him—like home.

Slowly Elegant unlimbered his arms by shaking them out and then moving around the ring loose limbed, falling back against the ring ropes, acting so free, so exuberant. It's as if no one was in the gym but him, not Pee-Pot or Gyp, only him and his boosted energy.

He stopped, paused, and then gathered himself. Elegant positioned himself in the middle of the ring. His shadowboxing began slowly and then gained momentum. Elegant moved as though someone were inside the ring with him, not a phantom target.

This continued for a while before Elegant stopped. "Finished, Mr. Manners," Elegant said. His body was saturated with sweat.

Pee-Pot walked up the three wooden steps and then into the ring. He handed Elegant a fresh towel. "Mr. Raines, I must go into town. Longwood. To do my duties. There's that chicken in the icebox for your lunch. How's that?"

Shocked, Elegant showed it in his bearing and breathing. "F-fine, Mr. Manners, sir."

"Gyp'll keep you company for the day until I get back."

"Thank, thank you, Mr. Manners."

Pee-Pot stepped out of the ring.

Gyp stood. Pee-Pot walked over to her and petted her. She followed him to the door. Elegant hadn't begun wiping himself down with the towel yet—he was kind of staring at it—while he looked over at Gyp, who was out on the grounds and in front of the building wagging her fluffy tail.

Elegant figured he didn't have to see what Pee-Pot Manners was doing, probably heading for the dark, avocado-green Studebaker truck parked by the side of the house—the one he saw as soon as he approached the house yesterday afternoon.

Frustrated, disgusted, mystified, dismayed, Elegant threw the towel on top of the ropes. He bounded out of the ring and toward the door. When he looked up toward the house, Pee-Pot was getting into the short truck's cab. When he did, it's when Gyp barked and Pee-Pot honked the horn and the truck tracked its way off the farm property.

Elegant turned, for he couldn't be more upset than he was by what just happened between him and Pee-Pot Manners. This wasn't how he envisioned the day, of how it would unravel for him, in this shrill way. He didn't expect this kind of treatment from Pee-Pot Manners. It was shabby. It put him at a grave disadvantage. He was mentally exhausted, mentally wanting.

———

Elegant and Gyp were in the house. He'd left Gyp down in the living room, lying on her throw rug. Gyp was in and out of the house, independently, running in and out on her own, not completely ignoring him but keeping herself up with what appeared to be her daily routines.

When he got back to the house, he went straight to his room and then to the bathroom to bathe. It was a bath where he was able to keep his mind at a deep level of contemplation. His mind, for a while, transitioned between panic and alarm. And then when it calmed, it attempted to recapture every fine detail, nuance of the day, from the 5:30-a.m. knock on the door, to Pee-Pot Manners's last words to him. Everything was up for analysis, up for grabs—no stone to be left unturned, unexamined!

"What did I do wrong? What!" Elegant said from the bedroom window that looked down onto the side of the house, not the front or back. He even tried gaining clues from Gyp—it's how desperate he was, how tortured. Even while they had lunch together, him and her. While she ate out of her dog bowl and drank water out of the bowl at its side. Then coming to his senses, he felt utterly, absurdly foolish.

Then he began feeling sorry for himself by thinking of the sacrifices he'd made to get to Longwood from View Point, Texas. The arduous travel. He began to indulge in self-pity. But this is what he wanted, to be in the company of a great fighter and, what he knew, was a great trainer. For once he got in the ring today, became acclimated to it, was totally immersed in his shadowboxing, was when he heard Frank "Black Machine" Whaley in Whaley's Gym bark in his ears, tell him so many things. But mostly praising him. Singing his praises, making him more enthusiastic and keen and ambitious—that he could become the middleweight champion of the world despite his color, despite the system, despite the big odds stacked against him.

———

Pee-Pot was three quarters home.

The Studebaker's tires kicked up its usual amount of dirt off Hattersfield Road's dusty road. *Routine … everything's routine*, Pee-Pot thought. And routine conveniently translates itself into discipline. It's what makes for a successful life. There are so many ideas, philosophies, theories floating around as to what makes a successful life, and that was one of them: discipline.

What did he see in Elegant Raines today? He looked into the truck's rearview mirror and then chuckled: he didn't forget him—not for a second of the day. He worked with three fighters today, but anchored to his mind were all the pluses and minuses of Elegant Raines's early-morning workout.

He knew his silence, by saying nothing to him during the workout, had to jolt him. It never happens between fighter and trainer. Just to think of it, Pee-Pot laughed, is sinful! Silence sometimes is communication between a fighter and a trainer but not silence as severe or slanted as today's. But it's how he communicated his first day with a new fighter in his camp. A fighter in from a different camp, especially, who'd been trained under the guidance of a different trainer. His role was that of an observer, to observe just what the fighter had, the good habits and the bad, and to take mental notes of them and then, later, break them down to the fighter as clearly as they were originally noted.

He was going to have a lot to say to Elegant Raines, good and bad. He was a fighter with just twelve fights under his belt—whether they were wins or not. Henry Armstrong began his career with losses—so even great fighters lose, don't blaze out the gate as some ceremonial heroes to be worshipped. Even his own ring record didn't go unblemished, and he was still considered a great fighter during his time and age.

Of course he knew nothing about Elegant Raines, just his record and what he'd observed this morning in the ring. He didn't know what Elegant Raines thought of himself as a person, an individual—or as a fighter. He knew nothing about his ego or his willingness to learn—nothing of the two attributes.

But it is fire strengthening the metal that counts. It's the fire making the metal glow white-hot, brightly, shaping it in the cauldron, not the cooling air afterwards, after the heat, after the test. "No trainer knows anything about the kind of fighter he's got, not till the boy gets belted good to the chops. Is down on the canvas. See if he's gonna get back up. Has the guts to. Wants any more punishment." Pause.

"How about when he loses that first fight? What kind of thoughts invade him. What's he thinking? What's going through his mind then? The loss was a fluke? It's what happened to him. Or he's a fake, a plain fake? The biggest fake in the damned world? A damned fake, not a boxer!"

He'd had so many black fighters come and go on him he'd stopped counting, even try naming them. You have to live with that sour taste in your mouth—that maybe you failed some of them even if you talked to them like men, leveled with them, never held back your punches. Since there were some of them who he thought had the makings of a great fighter but, for one reason or the other, quit on him. There was Eddie Martin and Alonzo "Bullwhip" Fulton and Dorel "Classic" Page, to name a few.

"Yeah, I remember them. Oh do I, like it was yesterday," Pee-Pot said, soon to pull the truck up onto the farm property, the tire tracks grooved into the dirt.

"Thought they wanted it. Were all passion. No bull. Were hungry fighters."

But each fighter, eventually, lacked a quality. It was something they battled with—but couldn't seem to overcome. So it turns out to be each man's battle fought on an individual basis. What's inside him. How much guts and courage he has. As a trainer of fighters, it's one of the first questions Pee-Pot asked himself: how much valor and honor does my fighter have, since it wasn't something he could teach or the fighter train for. It only happens in the heat of battle, when the fighter fights. Only then was everything exposed, the negatives, became clear and concise and obvious.

"Where's he, Gyp, Mr. Raines? In his room?"

Gyp stood; she came over to Pee-Pot.

"I put him at odds. Guess he wanted an answer this morning, right … Well, he did want an answer right away. Who wouldn't. But life ain't always so predictable, now is it, girl?"

Gyp turned and then went through the kitchen and out the back door and then into the backyard.

Pee-Pot climbed the front stairs to the second floor. He saw the door was shut. He walked up to the shut door. "Mr. Raines, I'll take you on as my fighter."

Asleep, until now, Elegant hopped out of bed. He swung the door wide. "Y-you … Thank you, Mr. Manners. Thank you, sir!"

"There're things though that you and me gotta talk about, Mr. Raines. We've got to come to an agreement with."

"Y-yes, I understand, sir."

"Do you?"

Elegant paused, for he really didn't understand, not now.

By giving Elegant this apparent predicament, Pee-Pot attempted to clear it up for him. "But you will."

Pee-Pot stuck his hand out, and he and Elegant shook hands.

"I'll get dinner going for us. And afterwards, Mr. Raines, we'll discuss everything. The particulars as thorough as possible. Not during dinner though. Don't like to talk with food in my mouth."

"Me either, Mr.—"

"At my age," Pee-Pot laughed, "seems like food likes to stick to my teeth a lot. Just another one of Mother Nature's unpleasant tricks, I suppose. Got a lot of them up her sleeve."

———

"Now you wanna know what I saw today, don't you, Mr. Raines?" Then Pee-Pot sucked at food still in his teeth.

"Yes sir, Mr. Manners."

They were in the living room. Gyp too.

"Well, I saw a lot. A helluva lot. You've got speed and power. Power in both hands, not just one. You don't favor one hand but both. And that's awful rare in any fighter, an equal distribution of power. That you can knock a man out with either hand."

"Thank you, Mr. Manners."

"No, don't thank me, Mr. Raines—the boxing gods gave you that. That's a gift from God. It's something you don't have to pray for."

Yes, he did feel blessed at times, Elegant thought.

"And with someone with so much power, your hand speed's exceptional too. Is quite impressive. Is quite a package to have." Pee-Pot smiled. "Ain't thanking me this time, huh?" Pee-Pot smiled mischievously. "This go-round?"

"No, Mr. Manners," Elegant laughed.

"'Cause that's God given too." Pause. "You keeping score?"

Again, Elegant laughed.

"And talking about God, do you believe in him?"

"Yes, sir. I do."

"You're a religious person?"

"Yes, sir. I am."

"Practice it or just preach it?"

"Both, Mr. Manners."

"Call on him only when things get rough or—"

"He's my Father, Mr. Manners. I find comfort in his teachings. The Bible, sir."

Intensely Pee-Pot looked at Elegant. "Well said, Mr. Raines. Put."

"Thank you, sir."

"But back to boxing. Even if I did steer us from it."

"You did, Mr. Manners. Ha. You did."

"But what we do is dangerous, Mr. Raines. And I do believe it's good to believe in something when you go into the ring. To not only pray for your protection in the ring but the other fighter's too."

Elegant nodded his head.

"You and Gyp"—both looked down at Gyp lying on the royal-blue rug—"made you quite a pair this morning. Actually had to root for Gyp, cheer her on—you had her in such a bad way for a time there, Mr. Raines."

"But she was too tough for me, Mr. Manners."

"Like she is for all of them, you mean, Mr. Raines." Pause. "So your wind's good. And like you stated in the letter, you've been holding steady to your roadwork since Mr. Whaley's death. So this morning was certainly testimony of that."

"I thought it still important to do. Uh, my roadwork, sir."

"Your coordination is excellent. Saw that too. Right from the start." Pee-Pot removed his checkered hat, looking down inside it. "But you're not a perfect fighter by any means. Stretch of the imagination. No fighter is, Mr. Raines."

"Yes, no, yes—I mean, I know that, sir."

"I hope you do. Because the first thing I'm gonna change is your boxing stance. The one Mr. Whaley taught you."

"My, my boxing stance, sir?"

"And there's more. A whole lot more to this …"

Elegant squirmed in the chair, waiting for what was to come next from Pee-Pot Manners.

"I'm gonna break you down, Mr. Raines. Start with the basics. Make sure you understand everything I tell you and want from you piece by piece."

"Y-you mean—"

"We're gonna start from scratch. Like an amateur fighter with no fights. Ain't been in the ring till this day. 'Cause you're my fighter now. Not Mr. Whaley's. But mine. Not training in Whaley's Gym but mine. And I don't wanna miss anything in your technique. Or something that's there that oughtn't be. It's all gonna take time, patience, and discipline, Mr. Raines. Something, all three, I hope you've got—ain't shy of."

Elegant twiddled his thumbs. "I-I just didn't think, sir … I thought Mr. Whaley prepared me well. My preparation for the ring. F-fighting in the ring, sir."

"I didn't say that. But good or bad, I'm the one responsible for what goes on in the ring, not Mr. Whaley. You're coming out of my gym. Other trainers look at me. Judge me. Sportswriters. Can't, can't very well blame it on Mr. Whaley if Mr. Whaley's dead, Mr. Raines. Deceased, now can I?"

"No, you can't, Mr. Manners. That w-wouldn't be fair. No, no, sir. Not to you or, or Mr. W-Whaley, sir."

"So any new fighter who comes in camp from another camp is trained to my ways. My ways of doing things, my way of thinking—so there's no mistaking who trained him. I can't blame it on anybody else, and he can't either."

Elegant took a solid breath. He stood. "Mr. Manners, I'd like to take a walk, if I may, could, sir. If you don't, don't mind."

"Yes. You go right ahead. Do as you wish."

"Excuse me, sir."

Pee-Pot acknowledged him.

Elegant headed for the kitchen and then went out the back door. It was dark out.

Pee-Pot expected this. He'd already surmised from Elegant Raines's personality that he was a thoughtful person. And this was asking a lot of him, no doubt. But it was his reputation at stake, on the line, and it was going to be protected at all costs. Breaking down a fighter and then rebuilding him is a tedious process. It's no fun for either the fighter or the trainer—but necessary.

Just changing his boxing stance was going to be a huge undertaking. To take a fighter away from anything that is natural to them, that they feel comfortable with, is asking for trouble. It's probably the most devastating thing a trainer can do to a fighter—especially his boxing stance, the core from where everything else works, Pee-Pot thought. It was like destroying the Holy Grail.

But if Elegant Raines thought coming to him from another trainer would be easy, quickly, he'd found the opposite true, Pee-Pot thought. He knew Black Machine was a kinder, more gentle man than him. A man who heaped loads of praise on his fighters in the gym in ways to indulge them. Out on the road, he witnessed it many times. It was how Black Machine developed his personal relationship with his fighters. It was how he won over their trust and confidence in him.

It was not for him to judge Black Machine Whaley; it was only for him to say he was different than him. Every little thing wasn't subject to praise. Building a fighter, for him, was like building a machine; and what he was in search of, from his perspective as a trainer, was the final product. He'd already told Elegant Raines of his assets. Tomorrow, in the gym—if he consented to train with him—he'd discover his flaws.

Pee-Pot stood. "Gyp, you know where to find me when Mr. Raines gets back from his walk."

Gyp looked up at Pee-Pot and then lay her head back down on the throw rug.

Elegant was back from his walk. He came in through the kitchen and then wound into the living room.

"Hi, Gyp."

Gyp's tail wagged. She smiled at him.

"Guess we'll be running in the morning—if it's all right by you."

Gyp was up on all fours. She walked over to Elegant and he petted her. Then Gyp walked back to the royal-blue rug and lay back down.

Elegant sat on the cushioned bench. He looked around for Pee-Pot but then heard him coming downstairs. "Mr. Raines, you're back."

Elegant stood.

"You don't have to do that."

"I want to train with you, sir. I-I gave it a lot of thought. Plenty."

"Hoped you would. It's not gonna be easy what I'm asking of you."

Both sat.

"I really want to be a fighter, Mr. Manners. D-do whatever it takes."

"Then, I can do that for you. Take you in your mind where you, as a boxer, have never gone. This is what's gonna be most exciting about this arrangement of ours, Mr. Raines."

"Yes, sir."

"Studying and strategizing boxing. When we begin squeezing it, you see, getting the most we can get from it. Using our minds to full advantage and capital."

Elegant enjoyed how Pee-Pot Manners put that, how he creatively expressed that possibility.

"Of course some would say more is knocked out of your brains in boxing than is put in them."

"I know, Mr. Manners."

"I don't defend it. Uh, boxing. I really don't."

"Boxing, you don't, sir?"

"If I had a son, Mr. Raines, would I want him to be a boxer? Take up something as brutal, violent? Would you?"

"No. I wouldn't, Mr. Manners."

"Neither would I. So how can I defend it if it touched my life, personal like that. Powerful that way."

This was food for thought, Elegant thought—a lot.

Pee-Pot leaned forward in the creaky rocker. "So what do your parents think of you boxing, Mr. Raines? You taking it up as a profession?"

"I'm an orphan, sir."

"Your parents …"

"They're deceased, so I was placed in an orphanage by the ward of the state. O-Oklahoma, sir."

"Sorry, sorry to hear that."

Elegant twiddled his thumbs.

"No relatives to take you in?"

"No, sir."

"Oh."

This personal history, needless to say, was important for Pee-Pot to know, just how dependent Elegant Raines could be on him in this relationship they were about to embark upon. He'd had fighters in this kind of situation before, with this type of background, and it wasn't always easy dealing with it, the vicissitudes.

"But I've been all right with it, Mr. Manners, I—honest I have."

Pee-Pot wanted to believe him, he really did, but was wise enough to know that only time will tell—that and that alone.

"Anything else you wanna tell me about yourself, Mr. Raines. That I should know."

"No … uh … no, Mr. Manners," Elegant said.

"That's of note?"

"No," Elegant said, continuing to shake his head.

"Any brothers, sisters?"

"No, Mr. Manners. I'm, I am an only child."

Pee-Pot stood. "There's something else I wanna show you."

"You do?"

"Gyp, if you would do the honors by leading the way!"

Gyp's body sprang out of its rest position.

Into the kitchen Gyp led them, and off to the side of the kitchen was a basement door.

"Go ahead, Gyp. What's stopping you?"

Pee-Pot switched on the light. The three were on the stairs leading down into the basement.

Of course Elegant was wondering what was going on, for he knew there would be a surprise of some kind at the end of the rainbow or, in this instance, the stairs.

Another light switch was flipped on, and it was only a matter of seconds before Elegant saw a red three-by-five-foot wooden sign with black lettering over the door reading, "PEE-POT'S BARBER PARLOR."

"A barbershop, Mr. Manners!"

Gallantly Gyp's tail swished the air.

"I'm a barber too. But only by appointment." Pee-Pot chuckled, bragging.

There was a barber's chair, four regular chairs, a tall wall mirror, and barber tools; the room had excellent lighting.

"Gotta keep a few jobs juggling in the air, Mr. Raines, if you wanna keep a steady income for yourself."

"Yes, and that's something, well, Mr. Manners ... I can do a bunch, a range of things, sir. Jobs. To earn income."

"Don't worry, I'll get you a job. Don't have to worry about that for now. But first things first. I want you to work your way into my methods first. I don't want us to waste— well, it wouldn't be wasting time—but I want us to get out the gate fast on what we've got to do on the boxing front first. That's gonna be hard enough for you to concentrate on. What's ahead for us."

"This is nice, sir. Very nice, Mr. Manners."

Pee-Pot examined Elegant's hair.

"You about due?"

"Uh, yes, sir, you could—it must've grown overnight, sir."

"Then hop in the chair, Mr. Raines!"

"O—"

And then Pee-Pot whipped out a blue-and-white-striped barber's apron.

"'Kay!"

Elegant got into the white porcelain-constructed barber's chair with the brown leather seat. Pee-Pot continued his mastery. He snapped the apron and then wrapped it around Elegant. He tied it in the back into a neat, snug knot.

"See how you like it cut," Pee-Pot said, examining Elegant's hairline more. "So you don't have to—"

"Uh, but pardon me, Mr. Manners, uh, but not too short, please, sir."

"Oh no, I was gonna leave you some hair, Mr. Raines. Enough to brush, at least."

But suddenly, there was an acute tenseness riding through Elegant's shoulders, and Pee-Pot felt it. This amused him, for this felt like the first time he'd cut a child's hair, one new in his chair. He was going to tell Elegant to relax but then thought he had every right to feel nervous: he'd just have to prove himself to him—this maiden voyage, as it were.

Elegant Raines's reaction was a representative example of how it'd be between them as fighter and trainer, Pee-Pot thought, no matter his gold-plated reputation in the boxing game. Pee-Pot reached back to the back shelf for the hair clippers. It was gaining the fighter's confidence by him constantly, continually nurturing and pruning, building the fighter up from day to day in the boxing gym.

"Ready, Mr. Raines?"

"Y-yes, sir, Mr., Mr. Manners."

"I hate to brag, Mr. Raines, but I'm not only the best boxing trainer in Longwood, West Virginia, but its best barber."

"There're other trainers in Longwood, Mr. Manners?"

"Five. But there're eight barbers!"

Pee-Pot was slapping the pearl-handled razor blade against the thick, aged leather strap. "I set my appointments up one after another. So usually, I have three or four customers in here at a time. And we talk up a storm, Mr. Raines. Sample just about everything there is under the sun. But we always get back to boxing. It's in our blood. Men and boxing."

Elegant could only imagine the lively conversations in Pee-Pot's Parlor.

"Of course, everybody's got an opinion on who was the best fighter of their time or all-time." Pee-Pot smiled. "There's no referee in here, no one to separate us, so we really go at it. Don't hold nothing back."

"Mr. Whaley said Sam Langford never really got a chance, Mr. Manners. Even Jack Johnson wouldn't fight him."

"Oh, yeah, yeah, that." Pause. "He was tough all right. Langford. Tough. Hit like a mule. A hell of a wallop, Mr. Raines. But was too small for Jack. Don't think he could hurt him. Punish him enough. Not that there ever was a man who could. But Jack could hurt Sam. So Sam Langford couldn't beat him, even if Jack gave him a chance to fight him. Uh … was so willing."

Pee-Pot picked up the large scissors.

"Mr. Whaley said he, Jack Johnson, that is, uh, wouldn't fight other black fighters when he was champion, Mr. Manners."

Pee-Pot was scissoring Elegant's hair. "That's a fact."

"Why, sir?"

Pee-Pot stopped scissoring. He pondered. "Uh, I don't know why, Mr. Raines. I …" He was a part of that time, that era; consequently, he should know the answer to that question as to why, at least come up with some theory based on his connection to the boxing culture then.

"Uh … maybe, Mr. Raines, because the public didn't want it. Two black men fighting for the heavyweight championship of the world. Two black men reaching the top. Succeed like that." Pause.

"Bad enough there was one."

Pee-Pot kept to scissoring Elegant's loose ends until the scissors were put down on the back shelf. He grabbed the whisk broom, wiped hairs off the blue- and-white-striped barber's apron, and then swung the barber's chair around to face the mirror.

"I look great, Mr. Manners. Just great, sir!"

"I felt the tenseness in your shoulders before, Mr. Raines. When we started. But now I think I have a regular customer on my hands."

"You do, sir!"

Elegant was out of the chair.

Pee-Pot turned back to Elegant. "I can teach you, you know. The barber trade."

"Barbering, Mr. Manners?"

"Another skill you can tuck under your belt. Can't have too many."

"I'd like to give it a try, Mr. Manners."

"Then I'll teach you."

Elegant shook Pee-Pot's hand.

"I was the one who taught six of the eight barbers in Longwood. Couldn't cut everybody's hair. Only thing is, I'm always the guinea pig."

Elegant was puzzled. "What do you mean by that, sir?"

"I'm always their first customer, Mr. Raines!"

———

Elegant was in his bedroom. This time he was looking into a different wall mirror.

"Some job Mr. Manners did with my hair. Best haircut I've had—ever. The very best."

Elegant couldn't stop admiring the haircut, thus himself in the mirror. But then he froze up. "Cut Mr. Manners's hair? Me!"

The very thought made his skin crawl.

"I just might lose a boxing trainer," Elegant said, cringing. "It might mark the end of everything."

But in reality, he was good at most things to do with his hands. He not only liked boxing with his hands but practically anything at all to do with them. He was just a natural, he supposed.

"But at least, I want to give Mr. Manners the same excellent haircut he gave me. When I learn how to barber hair." Elegant walked from the mirror and to the suitcase still opened out on the bedroom floor. He would have to hang his clothes for now, for he was living in Pee-Pot Manners's house according to him. Pee-Pot took Elegant into his home.

Elegant had no idea how often something like this happened between Pee-Pot Manners and his fighters. He didn't bother to ask. He, for some reason, didn't want to know if Pee-Pot Manners was treating him in a special way. Or if everything was connected to Frank "Black Machine" Whaley's death, Pee-Pot Manners's ongoing homage to Black Machine Whaley manifesting. Elegant felt he couldn't overemphasize the point enough—Pee-Pot Manners's relationship with Black Machine Whaley, not his with Pee-Pot Manners.

Obviously, theirs was just beginning to bear fruit. And so far, Elegant thought, it was respectful on both ends. He wasn't being treated like a fighter by Pee-Pot Manners but like a man. Not like someone who was eighteen years old but like someone much older, much more mature.

Was it how he carried himself, had to carry himself the past eight years in order for him to survive, to keep his anger and pain from destroying him? Actually killing him, everything inside him, it was so deep, so toxic, so real. Was this what Pee-Pot Manners saw in him, instinctively. Or was it the letter, this determination to get to him, travel there with no questions asked, no inquiry on his part, of how to get to Longwood, West Virginia from View Point, Texas—that he would arrive on April 18 come hell or high water.

Wire hangers were in the closet, enough for the clothes in Elegant's suitcase. He went over to the suitcase. Some of the clothing he collected in his arms—careful that none fell to the floor.

Having hung his clothes, Elegant started putting his underwear in the short, tilted-to-the-left dresser. He'd have to wash some of the underwear tomorrow, Elegant thought, looking at them as he shut the drawer.

He got back over to the suitcase on the floor. He now held the King James Bible and then a tightly bound folio of Shakespeare plays. The Bible and the folio Elegant carried wherever he traveled. He was a religious person who loved reading. His father, Austin, couldn't read; but his mother, Selma, could. Both impressed reading upon him, telling him all the stories of the past, of slavery, of denial—of all the benefits of reading and writing, of writing your name and reading documents and papers of value not only for himself but for others.

He was proficient at reading, at retaining information and concepts and interpreting them well. This sprung from his thirst for knowledge, his ambition, his enterprise. He had a gift for learning coupled with his gift for fighting. For the present, his fighting had won out. As for Shakespeare, he loved *The Winter's Tale, Othello, King Lear, Hamlet, Romeo and Juliet, Macbeth,* and a slew of Shakespeare's poems—especially Shakespeare's sonnets.

He'd not read all of the plays but one day would. Actually, he'd seen some of the plays acted out on stage. This experience excited him. To see Shakespeare's characters actually come to life, to hear them speak the English language in such clear, crisp speech was particularly pleasurable. The costuming and staging of the plays were remarkable, far exceeding his poor, feeble imagination.

And as for engaging this intimately in a white man's world of sophistication and erudition, him, a Negro, just meant he was human, not subhuman. That Shakespeare wrote to the human condition, the human heart, to its chaos, tumult, and turmoil, no matter the skin color—whether the actor be black or white on stage. Only man's humanity had been plotted by Shakespeare and written by him as dramatic verse for execution for staged production.

No one taught him to think this way, with, one might say, such a liberal view and attitude as a black man. Maybe it was just the unqualified act of reading that had led him onto this path, of looking for human qualities within situations and then drawing lessons from them as the Bible was written to do by parables, by its storytelling. Maybe this is what was fed into his conscious thinking, to look at things beyond the drift of the color line, him being a Negro, limited in the physical world by his color.

He put both books on a table the size of a card table. Resting there, the books looked stately in the room, and Elegant was pleased. Having the anger, the pain he had, he'd always wrestle with the idea of his humanity. He was in the business of "hurt," as Mr. Whaley so plainly put it, Elegant thought. But he was still seeking redemption for the human race through his own clear sense of morality, mores, this ideal place, setting, he was seeking. He wanted to absolve the human race of its sins. This feeling was couched in his background, what drove him out of Saw Mill, South Carolina, and made him fear and then hate every white man he saw by age ten.

It was the farm. His mother and father's farm. It was there where he witnessed acts of violence too horrible for reasonable description. And it was through his own spiritual meditation, of looking into the future that formed him, his thinking, to take a leap of faith he was still yet sure he could fulfill or justify. Yet he knew he must in order not to regress. In order not to have to retreat back into dark, primitive, dangerous places still raging inside him.

Religion had helped him. Reading had helped him. Shakespeare had helped him. He would always prove himself smarter and better than what he thought he was, his violent impulses. The violent, emotional parts of him seeking revenge. The violent, emotional stretches to avenge, to—

"Stop it. Please, please stop it!"

He was happy where he was, in Pee-Pot Manners's house. Longwood,

West Virginia. For him to become a part of Pee-Pot Manners's stable of fighters. For him to work toward becoming the middleweight champion of the world. Nothing less would fulfill him or make the venture worthwhile but that. And soon he was to learn a new trade, barbering, as soon as Pee-Pot Manners found time in the day, he'd said.

Elegant was undressing by removing his shoes and then his socks, smelling them. His head drew back repulsed, like a wasp had stung his nose. But instead, it'd been the sock's pungency, so he knew what their future would be tomorrow: underwear and socks would be subjected to a thorough washing by tub and washboard.

Elegant heard Pee-Pot and stood when he got nearer his bedroom door.

Knock.

"May I come in, Mr. Raines?"

"Yes, of course," Elegant said, opening the bedroom door. "You may, Mr. Manners. Sir."

"Barefoot, are you, Mr. Raines?" Pee-Pot said, looking down and then back up.

"I just began undressing, sir."

"Looking forward to tomorrow, are you?"

"Yes, I am, Mr. Manners."

"I don't wanna say this to scare you, but I ain't Mr. Whaley, Mr. Raines."

"What do you mean by that, Mr. Manners?"

"I don't coddle my fighters."

Mr. Whaley did, Elegant thought. *He did.*

"If you're looking for that, tell me now. Because you won't get it from me."

"No, I don't, Mr. Manners, need any coddling, sir."

But he was needy at times. He did need a pat on the back, a good, kind word now and then—he wasn't indomitable.

"Just don't want tomorrow to get off on the wrong footing for us, when we really get down to work. My focus, I promise you, Mr. Raines, will be on you and a championship."

"Thank you, Mr. Manners."

Pee-Pot turned to leave but then turned back to Elegant.

"A boxing career is short. Unless you hang on till you're a shot fighter. Become a shell of yourself, Mr. Raines. A victim of the game."

As a fighter he was just beginning, Elegant thought, but was being spoken to as if he had sixty or seventy bouts under his belt.

"When I look at young fighters, I can't help but think how cruel this sport is to anybody who's put on a pair of gloves. It's heartless. Soulless. You can be on top, own a city, like an emperor, a king, then lose it all in one day. One fight. One defeat. And nobody wants you. Got no taste for you."

He wasn't going to be one of those shot fighters, Elegant thought. That wasn't going to happen to him.

"So, Mr. Raines, Gyp'll be at your door in the morning for your roadwork. As usual."

"She won't have to bark this time, Mr. Manners. I'll be up, sir. W-wide awake, ready to go."

"Same time."

"Yes, sir."

"Good night, Mr. Raines."

"Good night, sir."

Elegant shut the bedroom door. "I'm surprised Gyp didn't tell him," Elegant laughed. "We made that date as soon as I got back in the house from my walk in the woods."

CHAPTER 2

Gyp didn't have to bark outside Elegant's bedroom door at five thirty. In fact, Elegant politely opened the door for Gyp as soon as he heard her paws strike the second floor's hallway's floor. Of course Elegant was pleased to see Gyp as well as Gyp him. In fact, Elegant wondered what Gyp's life had been without him!

Elegant and Gyp, as soon as they'd gotten out of the woods, had made their dramatic sprint for the building, with Gyp winning out for a second straight morning pretty much by the same margin as yesterday's win. But Elegant vowed he wouldn't give up, maybe push the pace harder for the first three miles or so, wear Gyp down, and then outsprint her in the final 220 yards. It all may be about tactics, he'd thought—be all about outsmarting Gyp.

He'd been put through his calisthenics, Pee-Pot changing the order of them, and the repetitions, increasing some, decreasing others. And so both were inside the ring, going through the "daily labors," as Pee-Pot termed it. They were about ten minutes in, and Pee-Pot was vocal, his voice assuming a sharp, early-morning rasp.

"Look how you came out of that stance of yours. Where's your balance, Mr. Raines? You've got to be in balance. Your defense depends on it. Try it again."

"Yes, yes, Mr. Manners. Again, sir."

Elegant performed the same simple maneuver.

"And again," Pee-Pot said.

"And again." Pause.

"And again." Pause.

And Pee-Pot kept repeating the same thing over and over to Elegant until Elegant began to appear bored, dispirited.

"Am I boring you, Mr. Raines?"

"No, you, you aren't, Mr. Manners."

"I hope not."

"No, no, Mr. Manners."

"Because if I am, you and me can quit at any time." Pause.

"Your foot's wrong. The left one, Mr. Raines. The left one."

Elegant looked down at his left foot.

"It's gotta be planted like this," Pee-Pot said while showing Elegant. "You wanna move right, not left, out that position. It's the best defensive position you can attain after throwing a punch like that. Do you understand, Mr. Raines?"

"Yes, yes, I do. I do, Mr. Manners."

"Go on. Go on. Nobody's paying you to talk." Pause.

"Twelve victories, all by knockout—and you know nothing about defense. I don't know who you've been fighting, Mr. Raines. Who Mr. Whaley put you in the ring with, but some fighters fight back. Do know how to swing back. I don't care how good a puncher you are, hard you hit, you ain't anything without defense, Mr. Raines. Nothing, Mr. Raines. Nothing."

Fifteen minutes later.

"Tuck that chin in. That chin of yours in. Stop sticking it out. Into the air. Tuck it in, for the hundredth time, Mr. Raines!"

"Yes, sir. Yes, sir."

"Do it, Mr. Raines. Do it. Just do it. And don't be so damned polite about it!"

Five minutes later.

"You're dancing, Mr. Raines. I ain't teaching dance steps. This ain't dance school. I ain't a dance instructor, Mr. Raines. You're burning up too much energy. Plant, switch, move. Plant, switch, move. Backpedal only if you're trying to get out of trouble or you've got to clear your mind, refocus your concentration, Mr. Raines. Take a breather."

Two minutes later.

"Tuck that chin in. Tuck it in. Stop sticking it in the air. I ain't gonna say it again. Not again, Mr. Raines!"

The training session was a rough one. It was the toughest Elegant had experienced—the most frustrating. Nothing had prepared him for it—nothing. Pee-Pot had left but told Elegant to get back to what they'd been working on later in the day. "Let your mind cool down," were the exact words he'd used.

Still inside the gym, Elegant was lying flat on his back on the canvas, looking up at the ceiling, the old wood, as if its splinters were stars. He'd grab them and hold onto them. He wasn't tired; it was just that he really did need to cool his head.

Gyp was off on her own, but it felt more like she, intuitively, recognized he needed his privacy. Gyp expressed this to him in her own grand, self-assured way.

"Tuck that chin in! Tuck that chin in!"

It was ringing in Elegant's ears, Pee-Pot Manners's shrill, raspy voice. "Tuck that chin in!"

Elegant was bare fisted. His arm blocked his eyes. He shut his eyes and then opened them.

"I have to try harder. Harder. Yes, much, much harder," he said, standing. "Mr. Manners has made me think about this thing more than I ever had before. Boxing …"

When Pee-Pot got in from town that evening, he asked Elegant if he went over the things they'd worked on that morning, and Elegant, of course, said he had. Then when he attempted to elaborate on just what he'd done, Pee-Pot quieted him by saying he'd see for himself, firsthand, in the morning, during the gym session. This gruffness on Pee-Pot's part didn't go over well with Elegant. He was really beginning to feel like a subordinate, a second fiddle in this operation, something Black Machine Whaley never made him feel like during all the time of training with him in Whaley's Gym.

Certainly, he didn't want to begin feeling like a piece of flesh. He was willing to be reshaped as a fighter but not as a man. He wasn't willing to give up his dignity, something, up to this point in his life, he felt he'd justly earned. Last night almost felt like a sleepless, wake-filled night for him, full of tossing and turning and deep, troubled thought.

He'd been cast into the world of Pee-Pot Manners, he'd thought over and over. It was a very tight and controlled world. And it had to be in order for Pee-Pot Manners to operate at peak capacity, peak efficiency. He was the outsider who had to adjust to this new circumstance, for it would not flex itself in adjusting to him. It was just too inflexible to do that. There could be no oversight: Pee-Pot Manners was the teacher and he the student.

Thus, this, Elegant had concluded, was his duty.

⁓

"You ready, Mr. Raines?"

"Y-yes I am, Mr. Manners, sir."

And Elegant heard Pee-Pot walk down the stairs. He flung the bedroom door open.

He and Pee-Pot were going to town, the town of Longwood, together this morning, his third day in Longwood, West Virginia. He'd done his roadwork and gym work and was about to embark upon something, anxiously, he was looking forward to—stepping into the town's gym, meeting other fighters in the gym like himself.

When Elegant got downstairs, he heard Pee-Pot in the kitchen.

"Here I am, Mr. Raines. Fixing up Gyp for the day."

Food was in one of Gyp's bowls, and Pee-Pot was pouring water out the tap over the short sink, into the other bowl.

Elegant stepped over to Gyp. He began petting her.

When Pee-Pot looked over at Elegant and Gyp, he saw a sad expression fogging Elegant's handsome black face.

"Now don't feel sorry for her, Mr. Raines, because she's not going off to town with us. She loves being out here on the farm. On her own."

Pee-Pot put the water-filled bowl next to the food bowl.

"Uh, used to take her in with me. But it's when we used to have arguments, her and me. Right, Gyp?"

Woof!

"There're woods ringing the town, you saw them for yourself when you came in, Mr. Raines."

"Yes. Certainly, Mr. Manners."

"A town is just cleared land anyways. No matter where you go. Settlements, communities … Oh, but Gyp there, she's spoiled rotten. Only the woods in the back of the house, the hills, will do for her. Plus, at her age, Gyp doesn't like a lot of people around her."

Gyp walked them out to the truck. When they got in the truck was when she loped off toward the backyard and then from sight.

The dark avocado-green Studebaker was out on the bumpy, dusty country road. Hattersfield Road. Elegant wouldn't say riding on it was better than walking on it, but he and Pee-Pot Manners would get into Longwood much faster this way, surely, he thought.

This morning's workout with Pee-Pot was as tough on Elegant as yesterday's. But what was still at the heart and soul of his struggles was his boxing stance. This now was the crux of his problems: the rudder. Without it in place, nothing worked. Old habits kept cropping up, creating tenseness, plaguing his body in its attempt to unlearn something but compounding the problem more by its trying too hard. The rasp in Pee-Pot's voice, the constant corrections impeding progress on a scale Elegant did not comprehend but was sliding back and forth on like a greased wheel.

He would think the problem was corrected, solved, and then, like a phantom, it was back, recalcitrant, knocking whatever progress he thought he'd made back. And that in and of itself would cause him great anxiety, that his mind couldn't control his reflexes, that they couldn't keep up with the exacting, rapid changes required.

The truck's cab was quiet.

Elegant never felt in control. If Pee-Pot Manners was thinking, he certainly didn't want to interfere with that. How much of this morning's workout was on his mind? How much was he analyzing sitting at the truck's wheel. Pee-Pot Manners stiff, Hattersfield Road's bumps meaty, jostling him but otherwise stiff, cold, unappealing, suffering him only because he had to show him the town, building by building—at some point.

Gyp was what made Pee-Pot Manners human, now. Gyp, Pee-Pot Manners's relationship with her, Elegant thought. And about learning to cut hair from him, this new trade he would learn, it wasn't attractive to him now, to learn from someone like Pee-Pot Manners. The gym was enough—he didn't need the barber's chair too.

"Mr. Raines," Pee-Pot finally said, "there're things on your mind, aren't there? At this very moment?"

How honest should I be?

"Yes."

"You want me to say something about this morning, don't you? Your training session?"

"I ..."

"Out with it, Mr. Raines."

"Yes. Yes. I do, sir."

"Well, if I'm disappointing you, I wish I wasn't."

"This, this is very strange, very odd talk to me, Mr. Manners. In, incomprehensible to me, sir."

"Incomprehensible?"

"No, yes, but—"

"That book of Shakespeare of yours, I saw it out on the table in your room, and what I said's 'incomprehensible' to you?"

Again, Elegant felt embarrassed.

"It's incomprehensible maybe because it's not what you want, Mr. Raines. How you wanna be treated. Handled. Isn't it?" Pause. "You want a daily report on your progress. How you're doing from day to day with your workouts?"

Slowly, reluctantly, Elegant nodded.

"And you want me to talk about your workout not just in the gym but outside it too."

Elegant was unresponsive.

"Like now. Driving into town together."

"Yes, Mr. Manners. Yes, I do, sir."

"So I'm disappointing you, Mr. Raines."

"Yes ... yes, you are, sir."

"So I apologize for the disappointment."

He had broken it all down, Elegant thought. Eloquently. Efficiently.

The teacher. The teacher. All the time.

All the time. The teacher!

Longwood's short buildings came into view, a quarter of a mile off.

"Besides, it's your body, not your brain, that's not catching on, Mr. Raines. That's hindering you. You're smart enough. Willing enough. But you already know that. Figured that out, haven't you?"

The pickup truck drove right up to a wooden building with the wooden hitching post in front of it, which had a big white sign filmed in tall, dusty letters.

Pee-Pot's Pugilistic Paradise

Pee-Pot and Elegant stepped out of the truck.

"Here it is, Mr. Raines!"

Elegant's eyes brightened. Suddenly the morning sang.

"'Pee-Pot's Pugilistic Paradise.'"

Elegant had to say it, knowing it would spark his spirit.

"Built this building too. With some help. Had to get this one up fast to make a living. At the time, Mr. Raines."

Whaley's Gym couldn't compare to Pee-Pot's Pugilistic Paradise, Elegant thought. Whaley's Gym was a shack, made out of wood, board, and nails and sitting out in the middle of nowhere. Whereas, Pee-Pot's Pugilistic Paradise was a rugged, oversized hewn log cabin. It had length and width and height, and since the logs were squared, Elegant knew— from his craftsman experience—it was built for permanence. It looked like it belonged there where it was— nowhere else. It took blistered hands and skill to build such a gym as Pugilistic Paradise, Elegant further thought.

Pee-Pot looked over his shoulder; the gym sat behind a group of other buildings closely connected: a pharmacy, a general store, a dressmaker's shop, a beauty shop, and other such commerce.

"I'll show you around, Mr. Raines. Introduce you to folk, but I know you're eager to step inside the gym. See what it looks like from the inside. Not just outside."

"Yes, sir, Mr. Manners."

"Big enough, ain't it?"

"Yes, sir!"

"Come on, before you trip over your shoelaces!"

Even before going through the solid-wood double doors with the three thickly plated iron hinges, Elegant heard the sweet, familiar sound of music. Speed bags hummed in the gym's air.

They walked inside Pee-Pot's Pugilistic Paradise, and it was huge to say the least, with four regulation rings and equipment galore. Giant wooden beams supported the high ceiling. The beams ran horizontally, from the east wall to the west wall, and made for quite an impression.

No boxers were in any of the rings, but some were skipping rope or doing stretching on exercise tables and floor mats—so there was plenty of activity for Elegant's eager eyeballs. And he was beaming from ear to ear. For he was back in the gym with boxers whom he considered, of course, his brethren. Indeed, this was something he missed and most desperately pined for.

What he saw, Elegant held dear to his heart. It was as if everything was back on track, as things ought be—he had hoped for. Now any personal sacrifice he'd made up to this point to get to Longwood and any obstacles laid in front of him by Pee-Pot Manners as his boxing trainer seemed worth it. What could make him think any differently? He wanted Long View, Texas, Mr. Whaley's Gym to be a cherished thought; but at the same time, it was time to move on and make this new challenge work 100 percent for him.

The boxers began looking at him, this new boy, fresh face, in the gym, and he smiled back.

Pee-Pot was all business as they walked off to his office.

The office, surprisingly, to Elegant, was neat. No one could say that about Frank "Black Machine" Whaley's office, Elegant thought. There was a small desk with a Royal typewriter in its center with a felt green pad beneath it, a chair on the side, and a wooden bench like the farmhouse's, minus a cushion, against the wall. There was a metal filing cabinet against the same wall. The room smelled fresh.

"Sit, Mr. Raines."

Elegant glanced down at the chair he was standing in front of and then sat.

"This is where my days are spent," Pee-Pot said, sitting.

There were two windows on either side of the building, and the sun poured winningly through both.

Pee-Pot tugged down on his checkered cap. "This is paradise for me,

Mr. Raines. Even though the fighters and town folk call the gym the Pug, this is how I pictured my life to be a long time ago. After leaving the ring behind. The ring wars."

It's something Elegant hadn't thought of, and sitting there, it did surprise him—what he would do with his life, with himself when his fighting days were over. All he pictured, for now, was him, one day, becoming the middleweight champion of the world. He was single-mindedly focused, working hard toward one single, solitary goal: it was his lone horizon.

"So that sign outside on the building is no trick. No gimmick. This is my paradise, Mr. Raines. Pee-Pot's Pugilistic Paradise."

"I think it's w-wonderful, Mr. Manners."

Clasping his hands, Pee-Pot leaned forward. "Now listen, Mr. Raines, no boxing for you today. Uh, sparring."

"But, but I thought I would—"

"I'll tell you when."

Control. Control. I'm under his control!

"The fundamentals. The basics. That's enough on your plate, for now."

"Yes, sir."

Elegant didn't want to sulk—he wasn't going to!

"It's still gonna be the morning sessions. And your afternoon sessions are your own, for now."

"Yes, sir."

"It's how it's gonna be, run for a while, Mr. Raines."

"Yes, sir."

Pee-Pot rubbed at his chin. "I brought you in today to observe. Not to spar. Wasn't the purpose of your trip into Longwood."

"Yes, sir."

Pee-Pot stood. "So I'm gonna introduce you to the fighters out in the gym. So come, I guess they're all curious about you by now."

———

Elegant was introduced as a fighter to the fighters in Pee-Pot's Pugilistic Paradise but wasn't fighting. It was midafternoon, but it might as well have been midnight—the day felt so long. To be in the gym among boxers and not be able to box was like cruel, unjust punishment. It's what it felt like watching other fighters train. And when they sparred, he could well imagine himself inside the ring, vicariously being put through the paces. But it was Frank "Black Machine" Whaley doing the teaching, instructing him, not Leemore "Pee-Pot" Manners. And he'd been stuck in the gym since this morning. Pee-Pot hadn't shown him the town, Longwood yet. He hadn't introduced him to the town folk, locals as he'd promised.

The most he'd done, regarding Longwood, was tell him its population: about 1,200 people. An all-black town. A town that had no booming industry. But many of the town folk depended on neighboring mines for work and income. Then it was Pee-Pot working with one fighter, and then another. And he saw polished fighters and ungainly fighters, and he wanted to spar with any one of them—hit them. Slug them with his fists.

And Pee-Pot wasn't in the gym. He saw him duck out of the gym with his barber tools. And he didn't find it funny or amusing when it happened (Pee-Pot Manners not explaining anything to him), only more frustrating, actually, insulting. When he'd walked into Pee-Pot's Pugilistic Paradise he was aflame, but no pilot light lit in him now, no fire in his belly—it'd been extinguished.

Yes, he felt like a fool, and no one was engaging him. He felt like an outsider, a leper. He had to wonder, for the first time, if he saw a fighter (like himself) new to the gym, whether he'd take to him. How much time he'd spend with the fighter if he was doing nothing but taking up space and time, not engaged in the gym's spirit.

A fighter came into the gym carrying a brown leather gym bag. And he headed straight for Elegant.

"New, huh? Ain't you?"

"Uh, yes, yes, I am," Elegant said, shocked.

The young fighter stuck out his hand. He was cocoa brown complected. "Name's Tommie. Tommie Lathers."

"Elegant. Elegant Raines."

"Pleasure to meet you, Elegant."

"The, the same, Tommie."

Tommie Lathers was snappily dressed: cream-colored slacks, brown-and-white shoes, red crew neck. "A middleweight?"

"Yes."

"I'm a welter." Pause.

"So how many fights you got, Elegant?"

"Twelve."

"Wins?"

"Twelve."

"Any kayos?"

"Twelve." Pause.

"What about you?"

"Nine fights. Nine wins. Two kayos. Kinda pit-a-pat them boys 'round, man. Cute as hell—and ain't talking about my good looks neither," Tommie Lathers said, grinning from ear to ear.

Elegant laughed.

Tommie Lathers *was* good-looking. "Who brung you in?"

"My trainer died."

"Oh, sorry to hear that. Really is."

"His name was Frank Black—"

"Machine Whaley."

"Right. R-right," Elegant stammered excitedly.

"Was a lightweight like Mr. Manners."

"Yes."

"My daddy was in the ring with him. Fight botha them."

"He did!"

"Tommie Lathers. I'm a junior." Pause. "But I ain't finished yet, Elegant—Daddy lost to botha them."

"Oh."

"Mr. Whaley four times and Mr. Manners two. Said they was the best around. Said there was no shame in that. Losing to them. Said the fights was all-out competitive but said he lost them fair and square. No bad decisions come outta them."

"Is your father still—"

"Alive? No. Ain't alive. Momma neither. Daddy been dead over ten years. Seem just like yesterday though. For me. Same with Momma. But Momma been dead even longer than Daddy."

Tommie Lathers looked around the gym. "Love this old place. Only place to be. This old place."

"Yes, yes, I know."

There was a gold tooth in Tommie Lathers's mouth that flashed on the occasion of his wide, engaging smile, something, it seemed, Tommie Lathers liked doing: smiling a lot. "Gonna spar today? Show us what you got?"

Elegant wished he could be so light spirited as Tommie Lathers. "No, Tommie. Mr. Manners is teaching me *his* way."

"So you staying with him out at his farmhouse—training there?"

"Yes."

"How you like Gyp?"

"Love her."

"Man, all us fighters do. Whenever we get us a chance to see her."

"We do roadwork together, uh, every morning."

"How many's that?"

"Three."

"Mr. Manners's demanding."

Elegant shook his head.

"'Specially with new fighters coming in. Even though the old ones, you know, love him." Tommie shrugged his shoulders. "So I gotta go get busy, Elegant. Now just don't stand there copying my style, man, okay?"

"O-okay."

"You promise?"

"Promise. Promise, Tommie."

Then Tommie Lathers tapped Elegant on the shoulder, and then Elegant did the same, returned the favor. "Damn, Elegant, see why you got them twelve kayos, man—got you heavy hands. Lead in them bad suckers."

Tommie took off, and Elegant turned, looked toward the ring, and wished with all his heart and soul he could hit someone, anyone! As long as it was a fighter.

———

An hour later.

Pee-Pot was back in the Pug, back on duty with his fighters. Once back, he barely acknowledged Elegant. In fact, he'd brushed by him, tipping his head to him. Elegant wanted this day over with, done with—nothing more!

When Elegant watched Tommie Lathers spar, he saw an exciting young prospect in the making. Never mind Tommie lacking punching power, for his reflexes and maneuverability were exceptional. He was a natural mover and extremely strong for someone his size—about five feet eight. So with his ability to move, he saw how he leveraged his strength to his advantage, especially when choosing to move the other fighter around, spin him, or keep him in place using his strong shoulders. It was both fun and educational to watch Tommie Lathers put on an amazing show but not showing off, utilizing his fantastic skills exceptionally well—to what was for maximum effect.

It was inspiring to see. It lifted his spirits, somewhat. But when Tommie quit his workout, he had this helpless feeling as to what to do. Tommie had taken time to talk to him for a little bit. But he went back to the locker room to change out of his gear. He said he had to get back to his second job. One job he started at 6:00 a.m. until 11:00 a.m., and the other from 4:00 p.m. until 12:00 p.m. Elegant asked when he slept, and he answered, "Don't!"

Also, Elegant was hungry, since he hadn't eaten lunch. He didn't know if Pee-Pot Manners simply forgot or it was intentional. Lately, Elegant didn't know what to think of Pee-Pot Manners. He just couldn't size him up, and he was becoming a larger-than-life enigma.

Three rings over, there was some explosive hitting. It drew Elegant's attention like a bee to honey. And then Elegant turned his head, for Pee-Pot's office door opened, and out flew Pee-Pot with his case of barber tools in tow. He didn't look Elegant's way. He just possessed a rigid, determined, frowned look that he had to get to his next appointment, wherever that was in Longwood.

Elegant, normally, was of good humor, but with a starving stomach and imbalance, the topsy-turviness of his day, he had no patience nor tolerance for Pee-Pot Manners and his apparent "antics."

The closer he got to the third ring, the more he saw of this muscled monster of a fighter. He had to be five foot nine, charcoal colored, and powerful. He was a natural middleweight—had to be, Elegant thought, like him.

With his headgear on, sweat dripping out of it and his dark eyes peeking out, he did look menacing.

Elegant crept closer to the third ring. Then he stood transfixed, looking at this muscled behemoth's power.

"Name's Black Moon Johnson."

"Oh, I—"

"Ain't meant to sneak up on you like that, Elegant. Saw you was concentrating, man. But name's Black Moon anyways. Lives over in Monongalia County. Two towns over."

Elegant remembered some of the places he passed through on his way to Longwood, but that wasn't one of them: Monongalia County.

"Wants everybody to call him Black Moon, but I know the boy's real name ..."

Elegant looked at Tommie as if to say, "That is ...?"

"Oh, yeah. Yeah. Uh, sorry. Cecil Links. Uh, make him up Johnson. Don't know the devil why. Maybe sounds better. He's fifteen and zero. Hits like a pack mule. Fifteen kayos. Twelve first rounders. Comes right at you—like a bull. Straight ahead. Shit, hard as hell to avoid."

Black Moon Johnson was standing in the corner, his sparring partner in his. He looked down at Tommie.

"Black Moon."

"Tommie."

"Don't see you when you get in."

"Yeah," Black Moon grunted. Then he glared at Elegant. "Who you looking at!"

"You!" Elegant said, not backing down.

"Why I oughta—"

"Black Moon, cut it out!"

Black Moon Johnson was halfway out of the ring, his body through the ropes.

"Get the hell back in here!" Gaston Moore yelled, a trainer whom Pee-Pot had introduced to Elegant earlier and was working with Black Moon Johnson.

"'Nother time, punk!"

"Yeah, another time. Anytime, in fact."

"Come on, Elegant," Tommie said, grabbing Elegant's arm, hustling him away from the ring.

"Hold on to him, Tommie. So the boy don't fall."

They didn't leave the gym but walked inside Pee-Pot's office.

"Look, Elegant, I gotta get off to work. But listen, listen to me, don't mess with that boy. Out there. Don't need you no trouble right off the bat in here. The Pug, man."

"No, I don't."

"Enemies. Black Moon Johnson, how I gotta put it, uh, he's the big wheel 'round here. The gym. Most of them boys in here look up to him. When you hit like him, I guess it's only natural you do."

"Uh … sure."

"But liked your cool. How you was under fire. You the same in the ring, right, ain't you?"

"So far."

Tommie switched hands, taking the gym bag out of his right hand and shifting it to his left. "So I'll be seeing you tomorrow?" Tommie said, shaking Elegant's hand. "Right?"

"Tommie, I-I don't know. Mr. Manners didn't' say. Say one way or the other."

"No?"

"No."

Tommie took a long exasperated look at Elegant, dropped his head, and then opened the office door.

"Look, Elegant," he said, turning back to Elegant, "just do the best you can with the situation, man. Do that. Stick to that. Shit."

Tommie shut the door.

Now what? Elegant thought. Mr. Manners's not here and Black Moon Johnson … He didn't even want to think about what happened between him and Black Moon Johnson out on the gym floor a few minutes ago. Elegant plopped down in the chair. He was steamed. He was miserable— just miserable.

"Am I whining? I don't want to whine."

Elegant crossed his arms and stiffened his back and swore he could stay like this, frozen in place like this until Pee-Pot Manners got back from wherever he was in Longwood.

It was about fifteen minutes later when Elegant got up to use the bathroom, opened the door, and walked out onto the gym floor. Hearing the explosive sounds, Elegant knew Black Moon Johnson was still sparring. But he wouldn't look in his direction. Without deviation, his eyes looked straight ahead. Elegant was out of the bathroom but decided not to go back into Pee-Pot's office, opting, instead, to go over to a vacant speed bag. Elegant stared at the bag and then said to himself, "What the heck." He began hitting the bag bare-fisted but lazily, lifelessly. He was doing this only because he wanted to do something physical, but if he really could, he'd be drilling the heavy bag—it's where his real mood was.

Elegant didn't see him, but he stood behind him.

"So that how a sissy hits a fuckin' speed bag."

Elegant's right hand missed the bag, but he didn't turn, having recognized, by his voice, who stood behind him.

"You ain't got fuckin' nothing to say!"

Elegant said nothing.

"Thought you was a punk. A fuckin' punk!"

Black Moon had the gym's attention.

"Ha. Still scared to say something, huh!"

Elegant was still lazy in hitting the speed bag.

"What you, the teacher's pet!"

Elegant turned, squaring his body off to Black Moon Johnson, face-to-face with him. "I'm not anybody's pet."

"Look like one to me. A scared fuckin' monkey!"

Red streaked through Elegant's face.

"Don't fuckin' like you!"

"The feeling's mutual," Elegant said, turning back around to the bag.

"Boy, I oughta smash your fuckin' face—"

"Black Moon! Black Moon! Get back over here! And leave that boy alone!"

Black Moon banged both gloves together.

"You better watch your fuckin' step 'round here, man!" Black Moon said under his breath.

"Get back over here, Black Moon. I can't leave you alone for a damned second!"

"Coming, Mr. Moore. C—just got me some advice to give the new boy you was telling me 'bout."

"That's Mr. Manners's boy. He'll do the advising. Mr. Manners. Not you!"

"Just 'member what I said, boy," Black Moon whispered again. "Don't forget. For there ain't gonna be no fuckin' trouble 'round here for you ..."

When Black Moon left, Elegant stared at him from behind, and it was the first time he really wanted to hurt another fighter and bad.

———

Elegant was still a stranger to Longwood, West Virginia, and Pee-Pot had made no apologies for his actions. He'd taken no responsibility for what he'd done today. But Elegant was holding him accountable. Six o'clock. They'd been in the truck for only a few minutes. Outside of the gym, there wasn't a person he knew in Longwood. Not one shopkeeper knew him by name, no one.

Maybe he should've been more independent, Elegant thought, gone around town and introduced himself. Only, how would Pee-Pot Manners have taken a liking to that. First, him being out of the gym and, second, him taking it upon himself to do what he did since he was, needless to say, under his supervision. He was under his thumb, pressed under it; he just had the freedom to run in the mornings with Gyp—even though that too was charted to specification.

"So you met Black Moon Johnson today, did you, Mr. Raines?"

"Black Moon John-Johnson...?"

"Deep into your thoughts were you, just now."

"Yes, Mr. Manners. I—"

"Was told by Gaston Moore that you and Black Moon didn't hit it off so hot."

Elegant was going to defend himself. He didn't care how the story was relayed to Pee-Pot Manners by Gaston Moore. "It wasn't me, Mr. Manners. I had no argument with him."

"You're a fighter, ain't you, Mr. Raines?"

Why, what, what's that to mean? Elegant asked himself.

"Am I confusing you, Mr. Raines?"

"Yes, yes, you are," Elegant said softly.

"He, uh, Black Moon Johnson knew about you before I brought you into town today. He knew you are a middleweight." Pee-Pot's eyes shifted over to Elegant. "Same weight class. Same division. Same competition." Pause. "Same breed."

The truck was slowing down, and it's when Pee-Pot braked the truck on Hattersfield Road.

"So what do you think about it, Mr. Raines?"

Maybe I'm too young for this, Elegant said to himself. All of this. Too unwise, my lack of experience showing, or maybe it's instincts, animal instincts, what it takes to be a fighter.

The truck hadn't moved. Pee-Pot was still waiting for Elegant's answer.

"Seems Black Moon understands, but you don't, Mr. Raines."

Pee-Pot started the truck back up.

Elegant grabbed Pee-Pot's arm before he could shift the truck back into gear.

"I don't want to win the fight now, in the gym, Mr. Manners. It doesn't count for anything. But in the ring. Where ... w-when it does, sir."

Pee-Pot was stunned; he just stared at Elegant for the longest.

Elegant couldn't've been more pleased to see Gyp when she was at the side of the house, wagging her tail at them. If circumstances were different, he'd yell out "Gyp!" at the peak of his lungs, but really, he had no right to—it'd be inappropriate to, yes, given the current dreary circumstances.

He got out of the truck before Pee-Pot, and Gyp was wagging her tail. She didn't move from the spot. Only when Pee-Pot got out of the truck did she run toward him.

"Gyp," Pee-Pot said. "Did I cut a lot of heads today, Gyp. What do you say, Mr. Raines?"

"Yes, yes, you did, sir."

After Pee-Pot petted Gyp, Gyp went over to Elegant and licked his hand.

"Hi, Gyp."

As soon as they got into the house, Pee-Pot told Elegant what the routine would be. So Elegant went up to his room and shut his door. As soon as he got in the room though, he paced the floor. He was aware he'd missed out on his two-workout day. It bothered him. He was starved. But after eating, he'd asked Pee-Pot Manners if it was all right he went into the gym to do his second workout. He never worked out on a full stomach, but it didn't matter; he just felt cheated that he was going to lose a full day's training.

"But suppose Mr. Manners doesn't grant me permission."

To defy him, he felt, could cause friction, something, indeed, he didn't need nor want.

"S-so I'll do it in my room. Some of it in my room. It's just that I'll have to be, keep quiet. Make sure I'm, that I'm extremely quiet when I do it."

This was uncomfortable for him, plotting, scheming—thinking of doing something behind someone's back. He was an honest person, not deceitful or untrustworthy. His word meant something, it stood for—

"I'm treating this, all of this as if it's a crime!"

He aborted pacing the floor. He sat on the bed. "I'm going batty. I'm not thinking like I should … l-lately."

Maybe after dinner he'd forget about it. Just come up to his room, lie on the bed, read the Bible, quell his appetite for working out if it meant this course of interrogation he was putting his mind and intentions through.

He was in the gym today and couldn't box, hit someone. He was in a gym today and was bullied, targeted by its gym bully, its kingpin, and all he could do was act like a fighter; but no one in the gym knew what he was—a good fighter or a bad fighter or a mediocre fighter. This was the first impression of him and he stunk the gym out, lost any respect he could imagine to gain, bring to himself, his first day in Pee-Pot's Pugilistic Paradise.

It was Gaston Moore who kept the bully off him, not his fists, not him challenging Black Moon Johnson to get in the ring with him, or to fight right there, where they were, by the speed bag—let everyone find out, see for themselves who Elegant Raines was, what kind of fighter he was.

"I'm a fighter," Elegant said, standing. "Not a chump. Not a punk. Elegant Raines is a fighter."

After his brief confrontation with Black Moon Johnson, once Black Moon got back into the ring with Gaston Moore and he, himself, quitting the speed bag, did it feel inadequate in context, in the high stakes the thing between them was pitched to, walking into Pee-Pot Manners's office, closing the door, maybe stabilizing the opinion he was low, short on guts, courage?

"If I could write a letter … just talk to someone."

But it was a part of this isolation he was going through, this new life he'd taken on, and more and more he felt like it was beginning to overwhelm him, knock him back, his dreams losing their zing and zeal.

There was no one to write, to quiet his suffering. Mr. Whaley was dead. He wouldn't be in this predicament if Mr. Whaley wasn't dead. If there was anyone who he could write, it would be Frank "Black Machine" Whaley. But how can you write a dead person? Elegant thought. How nutty does a person have to get?

CHAPTER 3

Elegant and Gyp ran in the woods, deep into its interior where the land kept climbing, building onto itself from one shelf to the next, staggered, elevating, ascending, spiritual-like. He and Gyp ran like partners, in unity—like equal animals sharing each step with magic breaths winding through their chests and out their mouths, both relishing the next step, the next advance, Gyp's four legs stretching, Elegant's two legs extending, it being the only distinctive difference between man and dog in their grand run, how they looked, not what they felt, each slipping into nests of shadows from the tall oak trees slanting downward across the glistening gray-steel creek. It was a creek's water so clear and clean a human hand might spoil it. A creek's reflection a painter might paint in lively conversations of colors onto his white, plain, blank canvas. This was sublimity tested, unsterile, alive—sweet in the bones of the ancients, the native tribes of the ancestors.

And when Elegant and Gyp emerged from the woods, the great West Virginia mountains were the backdrop, at their backs, sat in the early morning's satin-gray mist, enshrouded from horizon to horizon with each hill rolling like gentle armies of brown broad-backed mountain bears padding lightly the silent, misted ground.

They didn't race for the building—Elegant and Gyp this morning— see who would get the upper hand, for today the land's beauty was winning the race. They couldn't inhale enough of the land. They didn't want to rush the run or fail to enjoy the natural wonders of the wind or how their feet traveled over the dark earth or the unlocking of the morning's secrets, making Gyp breathe lighter and lighter into it while heading for home, the building dead away—trapped in their sights.

"Good run, Gyp. Good run!"

Pee-Pot stepped inside the gym.

"It was a good run," Pee-Pot said. "Mr. Raines and Gyp have an understanding of each other. A good understanding now between them."

This was the fourth day for him and Elegant Raines, and how would he rate his progress? About as well as could be expected for any young fighter who was going through what was a complete destruction of his former self. It was akin to building a new person with the object of still being human but with a new personality. But he couldn't be saddled by that, Pee-Pot thought—he had a job to do and he was going to do it no matter what it took for him to finish it.

He took no pleasure in another man's pain, and he saw the pain in Elegant Raines, the pain to please, the pain in failure, the pain in not knowing how far his hard work would take him—the unknown, the mystery. But in the boxing ring a fighter has to look pain straight in the eye, endure it, understate it—sore hands, sore ribs, bones that cry out each time they're hit, they are punished, but he keeps swallowing the pain like a tablet (his blood many times), hoping it will dissolve; and if it doesn't, then it's only the mind that conspires with the spirit. It's what a great fighter needs, spirit, Pee-Pot thought, spirit. And Elegant Raines had plenty of it up till now. It was carrying him through this arduous ordeal, his "remaking" of himself.

"Oh, there you are, Mr. Raines. Thought you and Gyp got lost."

Gyp moseyed over to her usual spot on the gym floor.

"No, sir. Gyp was a little, uh, playful, sir, so I—"

"Thought I heard her barking. And … so let's get busy, Mr. Raines. Down to business."

"Yes, sir."

"Keep on our time schedule."

"Yes, sir."

Pee-Pot really liked the energy he felt in Elegant Raines's body this morning. Sometimes he, the trainer, would produce this kind of energy and sometimes the fighter. It appeared the fighter would this morning—or already had, Pee-Pot thought, correcting himself.

"There's old ground and new ground we're gonna cover this morning, Mr. Raines. It's gonna be a long day. A good day, Mr. Raines, for us."

———

Elegant was in his room, and it hadn't been a good day in the gym between him and Pee-Pot Manners—not even close. It'd been an awful day, and he didn't know who to blame—himself or Pee-Pot Manners. There were the looks of dismay and disgust, these small insults coming from Pee-Pot Manners. The hand slaps to the boxing gloves, to his arms, when he did something wrong.

The rasp. The rasp. Always the rasp!

He was coming back in from town, from the gym, early today, but didn't say why but that he would talk to him. A fear shot through him at the time, immediately—was he being dumped? Was it over between them, him and Pee-Pot Manners? Had he lost another boxing trainer? Would he have to start all over again from scratch?

He didn't have time to ask anything; he was in the bathroom when it happened. It was a knock on the bathroom door from Pee-Pot Manners, and there was a politeness offered, but then the message, and then him, Pee-Pot Manners, leaving the floor.

Elegant snatched the Bible off the table.

"How much more can I take? God, how much more can I take of this!"

The Bible gave him faith in things, told him, explained to him he must have faith in things. That God's at work, that He's always at work, at the center of the universe. And that He won't fail you at a time of crisis, when things are at their darkest, bleakest—is this one of them?

Elegant put the Bible to his head and shook his head: he wanted to keep his faith simple. He wanted it to warm him and keep him protected, for there would be no more troubles to deal with, not after thinking he'd found another ideal setting to be in, where he'd have someone to take care of him, make a home for him and make him feel welcome.

What had gone wrong between them, and how would he pay? And where would he go now, turn to now?

"S-should I pack now? Just leave this damned place. This damned place!"

Why couldn't he just spar with someone, hit something, as a fighter, show his value? He didn't know how to wile away the next few hours, what to do inside his room, the gym—a second workout? No, it was out of the question, he thought. There was no more peace in the gym for him but self-doubts and setbacks and disillusionments and unfulfillments.

"I-I don't want to leave. I don't want to leave. The, the farm. H-house. But if I have to, I will. I will!"

———

Later.

"I'm back, Mr. Raines. From town. May I come in?"

"Yes, sir, Mr. Manners."

Pee-Pot entered Elegant's bedroom.

Elegant was standing over by the small table.

Pee-Pot rubbed at his chin. "You haven't been in your room all this time, have you?"

"In, in fact I have, Mr. Manners."

"Is there any worry, concern you're having, Mr. Raines? About us and our situation?"

"Yes. Yes, Mr. Manners, there is."

"It's the pace, the progress, every day you want to ask me the same questions I won't answer. You want to force answers for."

"I'm, I'm young, Mr. Manners, at, at all of this. Af-after all." Pause. "But I'm looking for rights."

"Rights? You have none. I have the rights, Mr. Raines. I do, not you. Nothing's clearer. Couldn't make it any clearer. In my gym, Mr. Raines, you have no rights."

This was as bold and arrogant a message that could be issued to Elegant, and it angered him and marginalized him, what he thought, more than before.

"Now, why I'm here, Mr. Raines. I apologize for my rudeness this morning in talking to you while you were in the bathroom. Behind the door."

Elegant still hadn't recovered from Pee-Pot's remarks; he was still angry, resentful, hurt, licking his wounds.

"But I'm not used to telling people of my comings and goings. Not in the house—not for a long time now."

Why should he care what Pee-Pot Manners was saying to him? He had no "rights," no say in anything—he was just a damned fighter!

"Then I remembered you were here. Uh, staying in the house with me ..." Pause. "I'm going outta town, Mr. Raines, for the next few days. Up to New York. Coney Island, Brooklyn. Black Moon Johnson's got a fight up there. So I'm leaving at"—Pee-Pot glanced at his pocket watch—"one, uh, one o'clock."

It was eleven thirty-five.

"By train. Gyp's taken care of, foodwise. Water, I'm sure you can do that for her. Fill her bowl when it's low."

"Yes."

"Well ... that's about all ... Oh, and the icebox is stocked with—"

"When can I pay you, Mr.—"

"You need a job to do that, Mr. Raines."

"Then when can I—"

"I told you when. I told you I've got a job lined up for you in the brickyard. Locally. Just gotta take you over there when I feel it's time."

"But I feel, I feel uncomfortable involved in this kind of arrangement, Mr. Manners. I'm, why, I'm a man, sir."

Pee-Pot's back turned to Elegant.

"So it's where I'll be the next few days, in New York. So I trust you'll keep up the same training routine I've set up for you, Mr. Raines."

Only, Elegant had bigger thoughts on his mind.

"I want to fight, Mr. Manners. I want a bout. I'm, I'm ring rusty, Mr. Manners ... sir."

Pee-Pot pivoted sharply. "Don't you cross swords with me, Mr. Raines. How easy do you want this on you? A cakewalk in the park?" Pee-Pot continued to stare at him until Elegant extended his hand to him.

"Have a safe trip, Mr. Manners. S-sir."

"Thank you."

The two shook hands.

"Good-bye, sir."

"Yes, good-bye, Mr. Raines."

Elegant escorted Pee-Pot to the door.

When Pee-Pot left the bedroom, Elegant closed the door behind him.

———

Three days later, Pee-Pot was back in West Virginia, making his way home from a side trip to Martin County, Kentucky. Black Moon Johnson registered a devastating knockout over Newsome Frazier, an old wizened and tested vet who'd never been knocked out, never mind off his feet. Frazier was knocked out in the second round. Black Moon chased him around the ring, cornered him, and then thundered him with shots that would cripple an ox.

For Pee-Pot, it was a spur of the moment thing, going off to Martin County, Kentucky, continuing on the train, Black Moon and Gaston Moore getting off. Maybe it was more of an urge. His brother, Totter "Biscuit" Manners, lived in Martin County, Kentucky. He'd been ill, and he hadn't done enough, being the younger brother, to keep up with his health. It was just the two Manners boys. They were close when young but had gone their separate ways. Biscuit was a jockey. During his heyday he was the best jockey on the horse-racing circuit, winning the most prestigious of all the major races during the era: the Kentucky Derby.

Pee-Pot wasn't a witness to it, but Biscuit's description of the run for the roses by him aboard Night Hound in the derby's homestretch was enough to make your toes curl. It was a blazing final run and finish. It had to be since Night Hound was still hanging back in the pack into the final turn. "Rovel him up!" Biscuit said he heard Filch "Pushcart" Simmons, Night Hound's trainer, yell powerfully above the screaming crowd from the rails from at least one hundred yards away (and it meant Biscuit should dig into his mount, Night Hound, up to the rowel heads of the spurs).

Well, by the time Biscuit got Night Hound to the front, to the lead horse, Proud Pilgrim, the two horses had felt the cut gut whips and steel spurs still spurning them on. Running side by side, Proud Pilgrim stumbled and Night Hound crossed the finish line, beating Proud Pilgrim by less than a foot.

Twice more Biscuit won the Kentucky Derby on different mounts.

But the first win was a milestone, one he'd talk about like it was run just yesterday. Often Pee-Pot thought how any of them, at their advanced ages, would survive without their golden memories. The crash of celebrity and success that still burned fast in them.

Biscuit lived alone in a farmhouse like Pee-Pot's. He was a good-humored man who owned a dog that he purposely named Butter. Thus, Biscuit and Butter. All previous dogs had gotten the same treatment. This, Biscuit's longstanding joke. On this trip to Martin County, Pee-Pot was displeased by Biscuit's visible frailty. Except, Biscuit was a stubborn man, one who was set in his ways—mirroring Pee-Pot. Biscuit said he was doing and feeling fine, that there'd be no eulogy for him—surely—not anytime soon. In 1937, nine years ago, he'd lost his wife, Edna, to natural causes. They were the proud parents of Edwin and Christine. His children lived out of state.

Pee-Pot had parked the Studebaker in the town of "Five Hundred" in the county of Wetzel County, West Virginia. It was a town on the right shoulder of Longwood. Longwood didn't have a railway station, rail lines, so everyone went into Five Hundred for the train.

Pee-Pot was driving back into Longwood from Wetzel. Wetzel was roughly six miles outside Longwood. Of course Elegant Raines had been on his mind for the past three days. He was out at the house, just him and Gyp. A fighter who wanted to spar and fight a professional boxing match because he was "ring rusty" (and it was true). A fighter with special gifts who he was asking to have a gift of patience as an attribute, even at his young, tender age.

If he looked back at his and Biscuit's youth, he'd see Biscuit as a black exercise boy for horses for the Prescott Farms in Louisville, Kentucky—one of the most prestigious racing stables of the South. Then Biscuit, at fifteen years old, a jockey for Prescott Farms. And him, at age sixteen (he was three years younger than Biscuit), a professional boxer. What's patience for the poor, for anyone scratching out a living? Elegant Raines was thinking down the road when he could take on eight or nine fights over a five-month stretch, making it possible for him to put money in his pocket. This cold reality he recognized all too well.

"I know I'm asking a lot from Mr. Raines. But it's for his improvement as a fighter. To give a him a better opportunity in the future. I ain't trying to take food out his mouth. A living in the ring from him."

But how was Elegant Raines interpreting his actions. A young man hell-bent on making something out of himself. The drive, the hunger, it was swelling up in him. It is the most difficult thing for him, a fight trainer, to control—Elegant Raines's "hot pursuit." It's something he wanted to see in Elegant Raines, yet ironically, he was asking him to tamp it down as if there was an on and off switch.

"It doesn't work like that. But it's gonna pay for him down the road. He's gonna see the benefits, the rewards for sticking with me. For not giving up on me. Even if it's gotta be my way or no way. He doesn't see eye to eye with me." Pause.

"I'm one pain in the rear end!"

The pickup truck pulled up onto the property on Hattersfield Road, and straight off, Pee-Pot sensed something was wrong. He could smell it like a dead raccoon in the attic. Where was Gyp? She heard the truck; she always heard it when he came in from out of town, from off one of his road trips. She'd be outside wagging her tail like wild, 150 yards away before he even got to the house.

Pee-Pot parked the truck. He was scared to death. He really was scared. He'd lost Cora. Now Gyp too!

The compact suitcase stayed in the truck as Pee-Pot slammed the truck cab's door as he ran toward the back of the farmhouse.

"Gyp! Gyp!" He just had to check the back of the house first—he thought maybe Gyp was in the gym with Elegant Raines or they were out in the woods, maybe running again. Yes, running. Running!

"Gyp! I'm home, Gyp! I'm home!" He ran farther out from the house. "Mr. Raines! Mr. Raines! Gyp! Gyp!"

He stood there terrified. It was midafternoon, and what he smelled wasn't diminishing but growing.

"I, they're not in the gym. They're …" Pee-Pot turned back and looked at the farmhouse.

If the problem couldn't be solved out here, maybe it could be solved in the house. In the house, Pee-Pot thought. But then, before entering the house, Pee-Pot looked out on the land that lay before him one more time.   He turned and then ran like an old man who'd just cranked up his body to run fast, but it could charge up only so much as Pee-Pot labored onto the back-porch steps.

It's when he heard Gyp's first whine and then her second.

"Gyp! Gyp!"

She was standing at the front of the kitchen table. Her fluffy tail drooped.

"I was worried sick. Sick. Just … w-why didn't you answer me!"

A third time Gyp whined.

It's when Pee-Pot spotted a white sheet of paper lying atop the kitchen table.

"What is it, Gyp?" Pee-Pot said, quickly approaching the table.

Gyp moved off to the side.

"Dammit, Gyp, what's happened!"

Gyp just stood there depressed.

He picked up the sheet of paper

Dear Mr. Manners,

I am not ungrateful for what you have done for me the past few days, but I cannot continue in this way. I find it most troubling I cannot reach the conclusions you have reached about my training under your tutelage. I wanted to use the word "wise," but I do not know. This is the first time I have had a chance to express myself. To craft my opinions, and I do not wish to be unkind or unpleasant with you.

I have left your home grateful. You took time with me. Fed and gave me board. I fell in love with Gyp. I have no regrets, none here to voice. I am disappointed. I am that. But I will try my luck elsewhere. Where, I do not know. But I know you wish me luck. And I hope I find my luck in another town. In another place.

It seems I do not know how to end this letter unsentimentally. I hope you hear about me one day. As a prizefighter. As a great champion. That our paths might cross. And that we might shake hands when we do meet. To mark it as time spent together.

Sincerely yours,

Elegant Raines

"What ... what a beautiful letter. What a beautiful young man."

———

In bed, Pee-Pot tossed and turned. He couldn't sleep tonight but had tried to buck all odds—tried. But it made no difference: he was worried about Elegant Raines, his fighter. This shock of shocks was not expected, that he would leave like he had. The letter was thoughtful, as polished as he was, Pee-Pot thought. It's what had impressed him most about Elegant Raines from the start and now his sense of thoughtfulness, depth of character, and personality.

Pee-Pot didn't know if ... yes, he had to say Elegant Raines was born with that quality in him, it was inherent. Just like he was born to be a fighter, he showed that quality too. It's always the chin though, if he had a glass jaw, it's something he didn't know. But courage, he had it, even though someone might say he chose a cowardly way out, wrote a letter, didn't stand up to him like a man. But Elegant Raines did it his way, Pee-Pot thought, gracefully, intelligently, thoughtfully, respectfully—without confrontation.

"The boy's a real gentleman. It's what he is. What I admire about him."

The letter contained all of his disappointment, frustration, by the very fact of his restraint in bringing it all to the surface, for if he had, he would've been emotionally trapped, emotionally vulnerable, and he was trying to hold on tight to his emotions, along with his dignity.

"It's another thing I liked about the boy."

It was something else he displayed right off, Pee-Pot thought—dignity plus pride. Both were great assets for a fighter to have, especially in the brutal business of boxing: to know who you are as a person first before that of a fighter. Boxing had lost its purity to build character, a young man's character, not when the devil's money got into the mix.

But Pee-Pot knew that was a whole other story, not something fresh like what he was dealing with tonight. He enjoyed Elegant Raines. He enjoyed him as a houseguest in his home. He'd been a perfect houseguest: respectful, courteous, responsible. The sad part was that he didn't know where he was going. Right now, it was a long shot. *A damned long shot!* Pee-Pot thought.

He was out there somewhere wandering, looking for a trainer, because he, in a sense, had failed him. He had to swallow that bitter reality, live with it. Frank "Black Machine" Whaley had picked the wrong trainer for Elegant Raines.

"I was the wrong trainer for the boy. I was a bad choice. Black Machine did a good job, but he still didn't build the machine right. The smallest parts have gotta be built right so the whole thing won't fall apart."

It's not that Black Machine didn't know that, Pee-Pot thought, it's just that … He couldn't speak for Black Machine Whaley, for another man, he could only speak for himself. And it's who he was with Elegant Raines—himself, Pee-Pot Manners. And as a trainer, he had to impose his will on his fighter, just like Biscuit did on his mounts.

"They've got to know who's boss. In charge of them at all times. There's nothing pretty about it. There's one boss, not two. Can never be two bosses in the ring."

He left him alone with his trade for those two days. He left him alone with instructions on how to become a better fighter. But the man in him rebelled. The pride in him, telling him he was better off the old way, not the remodeled version. After all, he'd posted twelve victories in the ring, all by knockouts. He was looking for progress of course but not to be recast.

"I lost a great fighter. The makings of one."

Pee-Pot wished Elegant Raines all the luck. The best of it. If things worked out well for him, he was certain he'd see him as a prime middleweight contender somewhere down the road. He still had Black Moon, who was a great young middleweight prospect in the division but limited. He couldn't build him into the kind of fighter he was on the way to building Elegant Raines into for the simple fact Black Moon didn't possess the physical skills or intelligence, mental capabilities Elegant Raines did. Those two assets alone would serve him splendidly in the ring.

So it would be of no surprise for him to hear of or for Black Moon to go up against Elegant Raines at some future date. They'd had one confrontation and Gaston Moore claimed that one. But that was outside the ring, Pee-Pot said to himself, not inside the ring where even Elegant Raines was smart enough to know—when it counts for something.

———

Elegant was camped out under the moon and stars.

Elegant was still in West Virginia, only a different part. It was Wilmer, West Virginia. One day of travel away from Longwood, and he was hoboing again. He had just a pittance of money in his pocket to make do. He was in an open field; his suitcase, the pillow for his head. He'd been thinking.

"Why did I do it!"

Tears welled in his eyes—to the point of streaming onto his cheeks. And now there was regret in him, plenty. The letter he left for Pee-Pot Manners didn't speak of regrets, but that was then, not now, for now, he had plenty. He'd lost one day of training, of honing the skills Pee-Pot Manners said he needed in the boxing ring to succeed, and it'd felt like a million. Tomorrow would count too, only it would count for nothing. He'd be traveling. There wouldn't even be roadwork for him tomorrow.

But it was the pain of losing Pee-Pot Manners affecting him, like it'd been with Frank "Black Machine" Whaley, of losing a good man, an ex-fighter who was on the side of the fighter, who wanted to do the right thing for him. His examination of Pee-Pot Manners was over: he was a man who believed in his methods, concepts—and who stood by them. He wasn't an enigma as he'd once perceived him but a man who'd figured things out perfectly and simplified it practically to a point of arrogance.

"I questioned it. I had no right to. It's what my mistake was. I questioned Mr. Manners's method. To the point of asking not only when I would spar again under his tutelage but when I'd fight again. Have a professional bout. Get back in the ring because of my—"

Elegant was going to say it but blocked himself. "Ring rustiness." Ring—

"Mr. Manners didn't care about that. Any, any of that. Just the fundamentals. The basics. Making certain I paid attention to them. Were put in proper place."

He could shudder at his ignorance or innocence—he didn't know which. And why couldn't he blame it on his youth. Why wouldn't he? But he wouldn't. He knew Mr. Manners would if he cared to be charitable with him, overlook what happened. But it was hard for him to accept, to fall so far short of something, to look at it all wrong and then react to it and then embarrass yourself with your impetuousness, your puerile actions, gaining only disadvantage, not advantage.

It was a cool night. He was lying on grass, and the dirt wasn't warm. His body was warm. It had to be his emotions boiling over. He was looking for and to tomorrow morning.

"Gyp. Gyp."

When he went down to the kitchen, she didn't get up—there was no reason for her to. But then when he put the white sheet of paper on the table was when she rose as if sensing something was wrong (for him, it really was spooky). What could he say to her when he pet her and then walked out of the kitchen, Gyp at his side, winding through the living room and then out into the hallway of the house, and at the foot of the stairs sat his suitcase (what his head was now lying on).

Gyp whined and it broke his heart.

"All right, girl. It's all right. All, all right, Gyp."

But it wasn't, and he knew it, and so did Gyp.

He pet her again, Gyp's forehead.

"Good-bye, Gyp."

He expected her to kiss his hand, do at least that, but she didn't. Maybe, he thought, quickly, she was in a state of shock, something like he was that it'd gotten that far. But maybe too she was angry at him

But he opened the front door and then paused for a second or two and then closed it and walked away from the farmhouse and was too scared to look back, for it would've taken great courage to look back at the house; he was just too scared to.

From the ground Elegant was looking up at stars he'd hope he could catch onto like luck, but that would be too easy, the ride. Life's grain and fiber would only continue to test his metal. It was something he was feeling more and more each day: that the journey, his journey to find the true essence of Elegant Raines was just beginning, setting itself in clear motion; and he, independent of any paternal, wise council, would have to remain reliant upon his own instincts and native intelligence.

That too sounded courageous but he was so scared. He was so afraid of his future. For there would be no more early-morning runs with Gyp.

This would be lifelong, stretch into eternities. This was not a small regret, incidental, but a big one, significant.

———

Two days later, Gyp was still moping and Pee-Pot was worried. She was eating but just enough food for the day. He'd seen this before with Cora, something that lasted for weeks. Gyp was out of the house, on her own, and he was waiting for barber customers to come by the house (by appointment) to barber their hair. This would be an animated group: Josh Barnes, Lyle Pete, Willie Jenkins, and Wilbert Jenkins. They all had an opinion on everything, and each tried, in earnest, to outtalk the other as if the loudest, most boisterous of the bunch won the argument—hands down.

Pee-Pot, emotionally, was in the mood for them today. He always enjoyed their company, but today it felt like it might be a blood transfusion for him, to inject new life in him. He was suffering—sure he was. Elegant Raines had dug himself into him too, not just Gyp. It was odd. He'd seen fighters come and go, so this was not new, unfamiliar territory for him. But Elegant Raines did have that something, that charisma, that something in his blood that was hard to forget or fully define.

Tommie Lathers, for the second day, at the Pug, asked about him. And for the second day he'd lied, hadn't owned up to the fact Elegant Raines had quit him, outright quit him. All right, maybe even at his age his pride had been hurt, maybe that was it, his pride—he'd concede as much. But it did go deeper than that. It couldn't be as simple or egotistical for him in admitting to Tommie Lathers Elegant Raines had quit him. Maybe he hadn't given up the ghost that he was no longer his trainer. He just wasn't ready to accept that cold, hard fact. He had to think back, scratch his head to when he'd lost a fighter of his potential. Who from the start had the signs of greatness written all over him.

———

The four had been down in the basement, in the converted barbershop for a couple of hours. They'd start their bull sessions by talking about everything under the sun (not unlike any Longwood, West Virginia, woman worth her knitting yarn at a knitting party). But the conversation would soon turn on a dime, flip over to boxing exclusively.

Pee-Pot was strapping his razor, about to shave Willie Jenkins.

"Does he have that gleam in his eyes, Wilbert?" Willie Jenkins asked Wilbert Jenkins, his identical twin.

"Looks like I'm about to lose a twin brother, if it's left up to Pee-Pot, Willie. Eyes look like the devil holding a razor."

The men laughed.

"Still say he lost to Black Machine Whaley though. The fight, that night. 'Cause I was there!"

"Watch out, Willie, Pee-Pot's about to let that razor get friendly with your throat," Josh Barnes joked.

"I wouldn't cut him, Josh. What, spill blood on my basement floor?"

"Me and you, Willie. Say Black Machine beat him. So that's an opinion of two," Wilbert said.

"Twins," Lyle Pete said. "I thought you two was separated at birth! By a doctor and a nurse for starters."

"We were, Lyle, but when you dress alike all your life, it's damned near impossible to think for yourself."

There was additional laughter.

"Was a hell of a fight," Josh Barnes said. "Those two put on. Back and forth. Back and forth."

"Thought I lost it too."

"You did, Pee-Pot!" they said in unison.

"Even though I had Black Machine down in the seventh."

"First time in all your encounters. Black Machine hit the canvas. With you being a big hitter for your weight class."

"First time," Pee-Pot repeated. "Black Machine had a rock hard jaw."

"Only he was down and up. Was a flash knockdown," Lyle Pete said. "Got right back up on his feet. Back in the battle."

"Right. Black Machine wasn't hurt. Tried going to the body, sap his legs, but he wasn't having any of it."

"He wasn't the greatest defensive fighter going. There was, was he, Pee-Pot?"

"Right, Wilbert. But he was—"

"So busy all the time, like a buzz saw—"

"You had too much to think about in keeping your own defense intact. Careful you didn't let it slip. He was such a great offensive machine."

"Because he'd make you pay, right, Pee-Pot?"

"Right, uh, right, Josh."

"He was a battler, all right," Lyle Pete said.

"Was why when you said he passed on, was a blow to us," Josh Barnes said. "Hearing it."

"So how's my shave looking?" Willie Jenkins asked.

"Thought of how time just sails by," Josh Barnes said. "Gotta meet in a barbershop to have a good time nowadays."

They laughed.

"Pee-Pot hasn't cut you yet, Willie, unless you'd know it by now!" Josh Barnes said.

"Oh, now somebody answers me."

"Working on a delay switch."

"Uh, by the way, Pee-Pot, Chad Holloway—"

Pee-Pot cringed.

"Told me the other day there was a boy, said he was a fighter, come to town. Was inquiring about you," Lyle Pete said. "Said he directed him out here. To the farmhouse."

Pee-Pot stopped shaving Willie Jenkins, and the little bit of lather still on his hands he washed clean from the small basin of water directly behind him.

"Offered him a horse and wagon but the boy said he'd walk out. Needed the exercise. Chad said the boy had the build of a fighter and all too. Tall, smooth-skinned. Real handsome looking."

Finally, Pee-Pot would have to speak of Elegant Raines, honestly, not dishonestly as he'd done with Tommie Lathers. He would finally get this thing off his chest at least for himself, if not for Gyp.

"The young man got here, all right. Was his destination, all right," Pee-Pot said, looking at everyone, not just Wilbert. "And yep, it's just what the boy was: a fighter. A boxer. And a damned good one at that."

Pee-Pot was in the final stages of shaving Willie.

"Here we are talking about Black Machine Whaley, and it's through Black Machine the boy came to Longwood looking for me."

"How?" Wilbert asked.

"Black Machine was this boy's trainer before he passed."

"Really ..." Josh Barnes sighed.

"Told him to get in touch with me, which he did." Then Pee-Pot examined Willie. "Finished, Willie."

Wilbert Jenkins was next, but Willie hadn't left the barber's chair nor Wilbert his. "By letter. Uh, wrote me a letter. A nice one. So we wrote back and forth. So he came to Longwood to audition for—"

"By the way," Josh said, "what's the boy's name, Pee-Pot?" Pause.

"Elegant Raines."

A hush fell over the basement.

"Elegant Raines?" they said in unison.

"Like that boy already," Lyle Pete said.

"With a name like that—Elegant Raines," Willie Jenkins said.

"Wilbert, uh, you're next in the chair."

"I know that, Pee-Pot. After all these damned years—what, you gotta tell me?"

Pee-Pot removed the barber's apron from Willie, and when Wilbert sat, he wrapped the blue-and-white-striped apron around him.

"He ran in the mornings with Gyp."

"You took him on then," Josh said.

"You bet. Speed. Power. Coordination. Agility. Intelligence. I took him on."

"So where's he, this Elegant Raines boy? Out here, in town, or—"

"Neither, Josh. He left me."

"But I thought you said—"

"I know good and well what I said, Willie," Pee-Pot said, nettled. "So you don't have to tell me."

"He—so he was that good, Pee-Pot."

Pee-Pot shook his head at Josh's astute remark.

"So it's why we didn't see Gyp when we came in?"

"Right."

"Since you say she ran with the boy."

"What weight class, Pee-Pot?" Lyle asked.

"Middleweight. Tall. Broad shouldered. Six feet. Rangy. Could blow up to a heavyweight easy. He's just eighteen years old."

"Might grow an inch or two more too. His growth rate ain't over yet either," Willie said.

Pee-Pot didn't want to think about the possibilities—he didn't. This confession was helping him, but still only so much.

"He's been gone two days. But feels like much more."

"You're not putting, placing the blame on yourself, are you, Pee-Pot?" Josh asked, his eyes squinting painfully up at Pee-Pot.

"You know how demanding I am, all of you." Pause. "Was asking Mr. Raines to start from scratch. He'd had twelve bouts under his belt. As a professional fighter. Twelve knockouts. I was asking to remake him."

"Tough. Tough thing to do," Wilbert said.

"For anybody to want to change anything, not with that kind of success rate," Josh said, "going for them." Pause.

"There was no argument between you and him before he—"

"Left him with Gyp, Josh. When I went off to Brooklyn, uh, New York for Black Moon's fight, I came back to a letter. Mr. Raines is a young gentleman. Has pride, class, is intelligent—uh, dignified."

"Feels like I know him now," Josh said. "This boy. Elegant Raines."

"Sure does," the other three said.

"It's no wonder … wonder why you and Gyp miss him. Elegant Raines sounds special. A special package delivered to your doorstep, Pee-Pot," Josh said.

"But Black Moon's on his way up for you, Pee-Pot," Wilbert said cheerfully. "In the same weight class."

"Told us he fights up in New York in another week," Willie said. "Black Moon's gonna do you and Longwood, us, proud one day. Bowl himself right into the middleweight picture before we know it. Then, Pee-Pot, then you'll be on top of the—"

———

Josh Barnes drew Pee-Pot off to the side of the house. The other three men were busy petting Gyp, who'd finally appeared.

"You'll get over this, won't you, Pee-Pot?"

"Oh, yeah. Oh yeah, Josh."

"Just a fresh wound."

"Yes." Pause. "Wish I could change."

"Don't we all at our ages."

"So damned stuck in my ways."

Josh laughed. "Come on now, Pee-Pot, a trainer's nothing but a parent. In so many ways—am I on the mark with that?"

"Ha. True. You're right."

"And you know how our parents were with us. When we were little."

"Wouldn't yield ground to a bull moose."

"That's right. If you broke a rule that was law in the house."

"Discipline."

"Most of us colored folk have known it all our lives, Pee-Pot—an iron hand in the household."

They'd all come in one car, Lyle Pete doing the driving. They were pulling away from the house. They were waving back at Gyp and Pee-Pot like always.

"See you in two weeks!"

Gyp's tail wagged.

"Feel better. What about you, Gyp?" Pee-Pot said, looking down at Gyp.

Gyp's tail stopped wagging.

"Well, I guess we can't take it out on the world."

They climbed the house's front steps and onto the porch and then into the house. When they got into the living room, Gyp laid down on her royal-blue throw rug and then yawned, shutting her eyes.

Pee-Pot sat down in his rocker, paused, and then lay his head back on the hard wood.

Suddenly, the house felt lonely again.

CHAPTER 4

It was after nine o'clock and Gyp leaped to her feet—she was wagging her tail.

"What's wrong, Gyp? What's gotten into you—"

Knock.

Pee-Pot was startled.

"Why ain't you barking!"

Ordinarily, Pee-Pot would go into the kitchen and get his shotgun, but looking at Gyp, he decided to trust her, that whoever was at the door was someone Gyp knew—not a stranger.

Gyp was already positioned at the front door, wagging her tail, but Pee-Pot stood back from the door, still somewhat wary. Actually, he was waiting for another knock, but it didn't seem forthcoming.

Gyp was pawing the door.

"Okay, Gyp. Okay. Gonna get to the bottom of this." Pause.

"Who is it?" Long pause.

"Mr. Raines, Mr. ... Mr. Manners. Mr. ... Mr. Raines, sir."

When Pee-Pot opened the door, there Elegant stood in the dark, blending in it, his broad shoulders accentuating his tall silhouette.

"G-good evening, Mr. Manners. G-good evening, sir."

"I don't know what to say, Mr. Raines. I-I'm speechless."

Pee-Pot turned and walked away from the open door.

"But come in. You don't have to stand there like that."

When Elegant entered the farmhouse and closed the door, Gyp, who was behind the door, came to him; she began licking his hand.

"Gyp. Gyp."

But then Elegant saw the sternness in Pee-Pot's walk into the living room.

And even Gyp's exuberance was squashed.

Elegant walked into the living room with the suitcase. He did not look unruly but didn't look a thing like he'd looked a few days back when he first walked into Pee-Pot's house.

Pee-Pot sat in the rocker. Gyp didn't return to the rug on the floor.

Elegant put the suitcase down and then walked up to Pee-Pot. He stood in front of him.

"I was wrong, Mr. Manners. My actions, sir."

Pee-Pot's eyes looked up at Elegant, but he said nothing back to him.

"I'd like to apologize to you, Mr. Manners." Pause. "I handled the situation poorly. Very poorly, and I regret it, sir."

Pee-Pot hadn't taken his eyes off Elegant.

"I mentioned luck, Mr. Manners, in my letter, sir. But my luck was here, sir. Right here, sir."

Pee-Pot sat in the rocker, impassive.

Elegant couldn't say anymore, even if he had to: his courage had run out.

Finally, Pee-Pot broke the silence.

"There's still a room upstairs for you, Mr. Raines. Nothing, in that regard, has changed."

Elegant picked up his suitcase and began leaving the room. When he reached the staircase, Pee-Pot said, "There's food left over from tonight's meal, Mr. Raines. I know you must be hungry."

"Thank, thank you, Mr. Manners. I am, sir."

When Elegant got into the room and shut the door, he didn't bother to turn on the light. He just punched the air with his fist. It did him no good—he was still emotionally overwrought.

Now he hunted for the oil lamp in the room, not the overhead light. He turned the light on. He looked into a narrow, confined lens of light. He was glad to be back in the house, in the room, not because it was shelter but because it felt like home.

The big room was brightening.

Elegant sat on the bed, and even with his perfectly conditioned body, he felt alive in it. Just approaching the farmhouse on Hattersfield Road, the beating his body took, the pounding of his heart, each step producing more fear inside him, it ... It was the same fear he tasted in his mouth but under much different circumstances. That fear was controlled by the spectacle of violence ... This one by the unknown: Pee-Pot Manners's tolerance of him.

Tonight, at least, he wouldn't cry. At least he wouldn't feel empty and hollow tonight. At least both could be effectively ruled out tonight.

―――――――

Elegant looked down at the bed and knew he was the last to make it and sleep in it. He was probably the last one in the room. The letter, after all, was left on the kitchen table—not in the room. Still looking down at the bed, he felt exhausted. He was wearing dark brown pants, a blue dress shirt, and a blue tweed sports jacket. He dropped down on the bed. He was dead tired.

―――――――

Pee-Pot was having difficulty sleeping. He was being burdened by how, in the morning, he was going to deal with Elegant Raines, clear this whole matter up, since he was the leading figure in it—an older man whose life experiences were being called upon by a younger man for confident guidance through the thickets and thorns.

Pee-Pot knew Elegant Raines hadn't come out his room either to eat or bathe or use the bathroom. It'd been about three hours he'd been in the house. Of course he had to be sleeping—it was the only conclusion for him to logically draw.

"The boy did look beat. It's been a rough few days for him. Hoboing. Out on the land on his own."

This is so unexpected—not that he expected another letter from him if he did change his mind and came back. But Gyp knew it was him right off. But him ...

"I can't figure that part out."

Maybe it had something to do with Cora Manners. It was that longing for her, wanting her to, unrealistically, come back from the dead. To yearn for something only to be crushed by it in the end, the thought, putting your mental state under such incredible stress, disadvantage. Maybe it's what Cora, his wife's murder had done to him.

Then Pee-Pot heard Elegant's room door crack open and Elegant begin to walk down the hallway and to the stairs.

"W-what's he doing?" Pee-Pot said in a whisper. "The boy ... Where's he going, to the kitchen to—"

But Pee-Pot heard the house's front door open and then close.

"He's not running away again, is he!"

Pee-Pot scrambled out the bed and then heard Gyp whine. In shock, Pee-Pot just held his head in his hands.

Elegant had rounded the house and was in the backyard. He walked past the back porch and out onto the field of grass and patchy dirt.

Gyp came out the house's back door and onto the porch. She stood there for a few seconds and then walked down the stairs and stood in the yard watching Elegant descend downward in the dark.

Elegant reached the gym and touched the wood and let out a sigh that would howl if he were a wolf. He walked inside the building. There was a shaft of moonlight shot through the window, and he used it to guide himself. He was at the door, opened it, and then closed it behind him.

He was in this small room and turned to the bed. He stood over the bed and then sat on it and then stretched his body out on it. He was down there, in the gym, because he didn't feel worthy of staying in the house. The feeling crept over him and then persisted—he couldn't sleep. It was at this point when he began thinking he should sleep elsewhere, not in the house. Was it punishment, self-inflicted punishment? Guilt for what he'd done? And he must be punished, for Pee-Pot Manners certainly hadn't punished him—meted out some kind of justice to him.

Often he'd wish his mind wasn't so complicated, but conflicted by so much from ten years old, it was. There was this huge complication and conflict in him he couldn't resolve no matter his every effort. He wanted it to go away but he couldn't forget everything. He mustn't forget everything. Those vile horrors were a key to his life, his survival, to who he was; they must continue to torture him, keep him a prisoner to that past, chain him in like leg irons or things that can't be hurled into the night.

When did he decide to come back? When? When he could no longer take another step forward away from Longwood, West Virginia. When it hit him in the stomach so hard it almost bowled him over, that he'd made a mistake, that there was so much more to learn from Pee-Pot Manners—that there was so much more for Pee-Pot Manners to teach him.

There was nowhere else to run off to then when it became that lucid to him.

Elegant began to ease back, relax, try to release his tension. If only he could envision tomorrow, maybe give it a positive spin, mold it into positive thought, it might calm the waters.

Whine.

"Gyp!"

It'd startled Elegant.

And Gyp whined again.

Elegant shot up to his feet.

"Go away, Gyp! Go away!"

Gyp whined a third time.

Elegant stood at the door, refusing to open it.

"Go away. I said go away …"

———

Elegant was up. He'd slept hard. He couldn't remember much, whether or not—

"Gyp! Gyp!"

Woof!

Elegant dropped down on the floor and began hugging her, rolling on the gym floor with her.

"Gyp!"

Woof! Woof!

"Oh, you're the best friend I've ever had, Gyp. The best friend I've ever had, girl!"

Gyp and Elegant were out the building, heading for the house. When they got through the back door and into the kitchen, it was quiet, and then Elegant heard Pee-Pot in the basement, and so did Gyp—her ears had perked. Elegant was petrified and thought it better he not go down in the basement but to his bedroom. Gyp tagged along, both running agilely up the staircase with him.

When Elegant got to his room, Gyp parked herself outside.

"Be right out, Gyp. After all, you are a woman … You don't want to see me undressing, naked, now do you?" Elegant said, shutting the door.

Minutes later when Elegant came out the room, Gyp sprang to her feet. The two were off and running. And then within seconds they were on the back porch, looking out onto the land.

"Ready for our run, Gyp?"

Woof! Woof!

"Five miles. Five miles. Remember five miles, Gyp." Pause. "We can't make up for lost time."

And off they charged into a satin-gray mist for the woods, the tall oaks, the creeks and climbing hills, and to see if their wind had been shortened, cheated, paled by the lost days.

———————

Pee-Pot wouldn't say this wasn't timed out, but it was, so to argue to himself any differently, he'd catch himself in a big, fat lie.

Gyp and Elegant were out the woods, racing for the building, Pee-Pot, as usual, watching them. When he got to the building, Elegant bent over and then looked up at the farmhouse. It's when Pee-Pot turned and began walking for the dark avocado-green Studebaker parked at the side of the house. It's when Gyp shot off like a bullet and began barking. Pee-Pot opened the truck door and then turned to Gyp. Gyp jumped into his arms.

"You're such a good girl, Gyp. Such a smart girl."

Gyp's tongue licked Pee-Pot's face.

"I knew last night he wasn't running away again either," Pee-Pot said. Gyp sprang out his arms. "When I came to my senses. Mr. Raines's got too much character for that."

Pee-Pot got in the truck and took off.

Woof!

And then Gyp sped off like a bullet, running back down the hill to Elegant.

Elegant and Gyp were back in front of the house and then back inside it.

"I …" Elegant was speechless.

There was a table setting on the kitchen table: plate, glass, eating utensils. Elegant smelled the food on top of the stove. All he had to do was heat it. He was really, really hungry. He hadn't eaten since yesterday afternoon. He'd been running on adrenaline since then.

"But first things first, Gyp."

He hadn't had a bath since the day he left the house, so that was really the priority of the day, Elegant thought—soaking his body in a tub, and especially after his early run.

Gyp moved over to her bowl of water. Her long tongue began lapping the water, and then she moved off for the living room.

Having soaked in the tub and eaten breakfast and washing his and Pee-Pot's dishes, Elegant knew what he had to do: get back to the business of boxing, back to where he and Pee-Pot Manners had left off—the last few things he'd taught him.

Elegant didn't have to call out Gyp's name. Gyp was right in front of him, leading the way. He thought of Pee-Pot Manners: their communication was so much better.

<hr />

Pee-Pot was back from what he'd dubbed his mission. It was an early-morning mission, but it had to be done for all parties concerned: him and Elegant Raines. Pondering a lot last night, he realized it was time for a change in Elegant Raines's daily routine. He was going to provide for that change. He'd keyed it.

It was early afternoon. He had every confidence that Elegant Raines had done his gym work after he'd eaten. And if he didn't know it or not, being out the gym, on the move, as it were, unable to train, contributed to Elegant Raines's restlessness, his nerves being on edge last night. He was really beginning to prove himself to be a fighter, Pee-Pot thought. It's these symptoms that plague a fighter when he's out the gym too long, when his training's been broken and he doesn't feel he fits into anything, not the things that blow you up, that passion, that desire, the need to feel the fire.

Elegant was in his room. He was reading the Bible. In fact, he was memorizing a Bible passage, Psalm 118: "The stone *which* builders refused is become the head *stone* of the corner." And Psalm 119: "Turn away mine eyes from beholding vanity; *and* quicken me in the way."

They were short, easy-to-learn passages, but both dealt so effectively, spoke so directly to what he'd been through. Psalm 118—"But that stone would become the headstone"—is something he truly believed in now. And Psalm 119—"Did he have this kind of vanity in him, and if so, it had to be expunged, purged from him for he could be set back on a path of humility"—at least it's what the passage meant to—

Knock.

"Mr. Raines, I'd like to meet you in ten minutes. If it is all right by you."

Elegant's body shook. "Y-yes it is, Mr. Manners. S-sir."

"I will meet you down in the gym."

"Yes, sir."

Elegant knew there was going to be a meeting, a showdown—whatever one wished to call it—inevitably with Pee-Pot Manners. Honestly, he couldn't tell you if he wanted it to occur upon his immediate return to the farmhouse or this afternoon or in ten minutes, as it was now determined. He looked down at Psalm 120 and then closed the King James Bible, for there was no passage in it for him.

Maybe, Elegant thought, he had been fortified enough for what had to be the crisis point of his and Pee-Pot Manners's relationship.

Gyp was neither in the house nor in the gym when Elegant got there, only Pee-Pot, sitting on the ring's apron, his back against the ropes, an empty chair in front of him, Elegant fully appreciating it was placed there for him.

"Good afternoon, Mr. Raines."

"Good afternoon, sir."

Elegant began walking toward the chair. He kept total eye contact with Pee-Pot, until he sat.

"You know what we have to discuss, Mr. Raines," Pee-Pot said, not beating around the bush—something that was never his style anyway. "Why you took off from the house. Uh, training."

"I was frustrated, Mr. Manners."

"And so was I, Mr. Raines." Pause. "By your performance." Pause. "It told me either you lacked confidence in my methods or thought yours and Mr. Whaley's better." Pause. "Which was it, Mr. Raines? Or would you say one could plainly substitute for the other?"

Elegant saw plainly what Pee-Pot Manners meant. "I had a lot of time to think, Mr. Manners."

"I'd say you did."

"It's all I did. And I realized, when I kept picturing what I was doing in this camp, things I rid myself of, and the things replacing them—that I was better, Mr. Manners. A better boxer. That I had improved as a fighter, sir. My defense. My footwork. Things Mr. Whaley really didn't work with me on. Emphasize."

"They were glaring flaws in your boxing arsenal, Mr. Raines. Not small items. I would not want to look down the road one day, when they were exposed, taken advantage of by another fighter of greater skill, and think I didn't do anything, take the proper action to correct them.

"If you fail in the ring, Mr. Raines, I fail along with you. If you take too many blows, then I do too. I want you always at your best. What about you?"

"Oh yes!"

"That's what this is all about, Mr. Raines. Preservation. Self-preservation in the ring. No matter how good you are or how fearless you are—and you are good, Mr. Raines. Damned good. But it ain't gonna help you one wit if you don't know what you're doing or how to do it when you need to—now is it?"

"No, sir."

"Now let me set the record straight of what's a trainer's biggest fear: his fighter getting damaged. Or killed in the ring by too many punches."

For the first time, Elegant saw how deadly serious this was. It just wasn't how Pee-Pot Manners's voice sounded but how his hands had explained things too, hands that had been in ring wars and knew the truth of his words.

Pee-Pot removed his checkered cap, looked down into it, took his hand, wiped it along its inner band, something a person would do if the hat were ringed with sweat on a hot day in Longwood, which this day, at this hour, wasn't.

Elegant sat in the chair too and readdressed the symbolism of him sitting down on the gym floor and Pee-Pot Manners sitting above him on the gym apron: Mr. Manners, the teacher; him, the student.

"What's your attitude now, Mr. Raines?"

"I'm going to try harder, Mr. Manners. At everything, sir."

"Was that what you did today during your training session without me?"

"Yes, sir. It was."

Pee-Pot came off the ring apron. The way he angled his body and walked facing the wall, it was as if Elegant wasn't there.

But now Pee-Pot paced the floor, keeping his posture correct, maintaining it, but pacing a small area, not the entire length of the floor. Pee-Pot's hands were out in front of him, and they were coupled together, tucked under his chin, but his head erectly stationed.

Possibly, after two minutes of this pacing, Pee-Pot walked over to where there was another chair and dragged it across the floor—not picking it up, something he could've done if he'd chosen, doubtless to say.

"I'd like you to know more about me, Mr. Raines."

Elegant felt honored.

"I want you to know some of my trials and tribulations. Things to come and go in my life —for you can have a better understanding of me. Who Pee-Pot Manners is, Mr. Raines."

Pee-Pot sat next to Elegant—to the right of him.

"Suddenly, this has become important to me."

"Thank you, Mr. Manners," Elegant said.

"I just don't know what I'd do without Gyp, even though she suffered as bad as me when, when my wife of thirty-four years, Cora, was murdered."

"Murdered!"

"Yes, murdered."

Elegant turned to Pee-Pot, and in each corner of his eyes, what he saw were strains of sadness from what was his past.

"Let me tell you what happened ... It was six years ago, Mr. Raines. Gyp was two years old w-when Cora Madison Manners was murdered in Montgomery, Alabama. Was in Alabama to visit her sister Oleatha in Crenshaw, Alabama." Pause. "She was gunned down. Shot dead."

"But why, why, Mr. Manners!"

Pee-Pot leaned back and looked up at the ceiling; his eyes remained moist.

"It was a train robbery. Cora, Mrs. Manners, from how it was reported, put up a fight, a s-struggle for her pocketbook, and was shot dead."

Elegant became more panicked.

"Something she would do. My Cora. Oh, undoubtedly. But I wish she hadn't. God, how I wish."

"Did ... did they—"

"Find the killer ... murderer?" Pee-Pot asked, agitated, his hands falling into his lap. "No, Mr. Raines. The answer's no. There was no investigation of any kind. None. Why a white man shot her. Even a thief gets Southern justice if he's white in Montgomery, Alabama, Mr. Raines. Got white skin.

"F-figured, what's a black woman doing resisting a white man, even if he's robbing her at gunpoint. Southern justice, Mr. Raines. She was a nigger—nothing more—who deserved being shot. Killed. Murdered. I ..."

Pee-Pot charged to his feet.

"If, if it didn't leave me bitter, Mr. Raines. Bitter and hateful. If ... if it didn't, Mr. Raines. Since Cora's been dead!"

Pee-Pot sat back down, and it was as if his eyes had folded back and sorrow sagged him.

"Poor Gyp," he finally said. "She took it so hard, Gyp did."

Elegant was feeling his own pain, his own tragic past knot his stomach and his throat.

⁓

The first horror he witnessed. The second horror he saw, but was hidden, heard the screams, the pain ... then knew the harrowing consequences when they mounted their horses and took her off with them ... bloodied, savaged ...

"I, there were pictures of her in the living room. I had pictures of her on the walls, tables. Like it was a shrine for her, Mr. Raines, for my Cora." Long pause.

"But Gyp—she would whine. Whine so." Then Pee-Pot laughed. "Like she would when we first got her, Mrs. Manners and me. When she was but a pup. Whine at night. Come up to the bedroom door, when it was shut, and whine."

Elegant smiled through his pain, his grief.

"How, it's how she got her name ..."

"Gyp, Mr. Manners?"

"Gyp. Yes." Pee-Pot smiled. "I told Mrs. Manners one night that that dog was gipping me outta my sleep."

Elegant laughed.

"So I said to Mrs. Manners, 'That's it, Cora, Gyp. Her name's Gyp from now on. After tonight.'" Pause. "Me and Mrs. Manners just spelled it g-y-p, not g-i-p. That's all. To make it different."

"What, sir, was it before, Mr. Manners?"

"Oh, uh, Lucy. Something like ... yes, Lucy. It's been so long, nearly forgot. Guess me and Mrs. Manners were just plain lazy at the time with the name."

Then the mood switched back to somber.

"What was I saying about, about—"

"The, uh, pictures, sir."

"Yes. Those pictures. Pictures of Mrs. Manners. Mrs. Manners's pictures would cause Gyp to whine." Pause. "So bad. How do they know they're dead? Dogs, Mr. Raines? When? What strikes a chord in an animal to know without any verbal communication? To know tragedy when it strikes as well as we do ... human beings?"

Pee-Pot puzzled his forehead as if adding further mystery to the trenchant question.

"Well, she knew all right. Right off. She just didn't know how she was killed. But Gyp knew, and after a while—it's why she doesn't come into the bedroom ..."

Elegant waited for some sort of explanation.

"You'll never see her go into my bedroom. When she's on the floor. Uh-uh. Mrs. Manners's is in there, Mr. Raines. Her pictures. All of them. She's everywhere, Mr. Raines. In that room of mine." Pause.

"So that's some of my story I wanted to share with you today. Actually, a big part of it. You just can't break free of your past, let it go—it just dogs … follows you to the end."

Elegant wouldn't expect Pee-Pot Manners to say anything different.

Soon, Pee-Pot's spirits lifted. "But I have a surprise for you today, Mr. Raines."

Indeed, Elegant was surprised.

"Y-you do, sir?"

"I do, Mr. Raines. Do I!" Pee-Pot glanced at his watch. "Let me see, I think in about another three or four minutes!"

Elegant was excited now because Pee-Pot was—and he'd never seen this kind of excitement from him before.

"But first, warm up. Do your calisthenics, Mr. Raines. Get yourself in tune."

"Yes, sir, Mr. Manners. Yes, sir!"

As spirited as he'd ever been in the gym (this one, at least), Elegant began his exercises under the watchful eye of Pee-Pot.

Minutes later.

Woof! Woof! Woof!

"Our invited guest must be here, Mr. Raines. Has arrived, if Gyp's not mistaken. Her scent hasn't been thrown off track."

"He is, Mr. Manners?"

"Now who says it's a 'he,' Mr. Raines?"

"Oh," Elegant grunted, putting the final touches on his stomach crunches.

But then both looked toward the door, for Gyp had barked one more time, but it was not from a distance (presumably the house) but outside the door.

"Mr. Lathers!"

"Mr. Manners!"

"Tommie!"

"Elegant!"

Woof!

The moment had finally arrived. It was a big, big moment for Elegant: finally, he was going to spar with someone, and that someone, of course, was Tommie Lathers. They were gloved and wearing headgear and protective cups.

Externally, Pee-Pot looked relaxed, but internally it's where he was nervous. He had to appear relaxed; it was his job as Elegant Raines's trainer to appear this way, but inside he was anxious: he wanted to see what Elegant Raines could do against someone like Tommie Lathers, a master boxer/technician.

Tommie's body was sweated since he'd engaged in exercise too.

Pee-Pot was in the middle of the ring. Elegant and Tommie were in their respective corners. First Pee-Pot would let them box and then begin working on things with Elegant. It was the sole purpose of today's sparring session.

"Okay, men, let's get to work."

They came out their corners. With Tommie being a welterweight, he was expected to be quicker than Elegant, a middleweight, in terms of hand and foot speed since Tommie's rapier-quick jab was on beautiful display.

Soon, Pee-Pot was both surprised and pleased by how Elegant was adjusting to Tommie's zesty jabs by smartly employing his defense in picking them off (some of Tommie's jabs were getting through though) at a reasonable rate. Pee-Pot didn't say anything to either fighter; he just kept out of their way both physically and verbally. He was sizing things up, assessing them. His eyes were definitely getting their money's worth.

After eight, nine minutes of this loose, free-spirited, unsupervised sparring, Pee-Pot intervened.

"Now let's work on some things, men. I saw some infractions that need working on." Pause. "But how does it feel to be sparring again, Mr. Raines?"

"Great. Really great, Mr. Manners."

"It's the hardest thing for a fighter to do," Pee-Pot said, Tommie and Elegant giving him their undivided attention. "Going as long as you did without, ha, hitting somebody, Mr. Raines. All along, I've understood that. How that felt for you."

"Good thing for me it was light hitting," Tommie said.

"Yes, good thing for you, Tommie," Pee Pot laughed.

———

"This is yours, Tommie, really!"

"Sure is, Elegant. Man, sure is!"

Elegant and Tommie were standing beside a 1941 Ford Super Deluxe Convertible, which was about eight feet to the left of Pee-Pot's truck.

Tommie kicked the white wall tires. "Yes, this here's mine all right, Elegant. One hundred percent."

Elegant thought the Ford car looked like a burgundy red doll. The strips of chrome were shiny, the bug-eyed headlights, the hubcaps, the metal skirts covering the back wheel; the whole car was spiffy, ashine. But what about the—

"H-how's it so shiny, Tommie?" Elegant looked out onto Hattersfield Road. "I mean—"

"Wait a second. Got you your answer, Elegant. So don't scratch like a match, man. Your head or nothing of the kind!"

Casually, Tommie walked around to the car's trunk. He opened it.

Elegant didn't see what he was doing. The trunk's hood blocked his view.

"Now see how it works, Elegant? Got four more of them in the trunk!" Tommie held onto a clean white towel. "Dusted the car off when I got here, that's all."

Elegant was laughing.

"Not with this towel. Uh-uh, see that for yourself. This one … it's gonna be dirty after I get to my job. Days after it rains 'round here, can't do nothing with the mud. Tires. Fenders. Gotta plain wash it then. Hose it down like a hog."

"How long have you—the car is yours, isn't it?"

"Cash on the barrelhead. Paid for it." Tommie put the towel back inside the car's trunk, shutting it. "Elegant, know much about cars?"

"No."

"It's a 1941 Ford Super Deluxe Convertible. Five years old, sure, but runs like a gem, man."

"I bet."

Then Tommie took a quick peek at his watch.

"Would think 'bout taking you for a spin but gotta get outta here. For my next job, man. On tap."

"Oh, right, Tommie."

"But'll spin you 'round in it one day," Tommie said, opening the car door, sitting like a proud peacock on the white seats. "Soon."

"You look great behind the wheel."

"Same as you was in the ring today, Elegant. Shit."

"I did?"

"Mr. Manners was hard on you, but from what I seen up to now, shit, you the best middleweight Mr. Manners's got."

Tommie charged the engine and then looked at Elegant.

"See how you looking. Queer at me. Thought maybe was skipping over Black Moon Johnson or something. Forgetting 'bout him, wasn't you? That boy?"

Elegant said nothing.

"Well, ain't. You'd crop Black Moon's ears back. That's what you'd do to that boy. And it ain't got nothing to do with me not liking him." Pause. "You just a better fighter," Tommie said, shrugging his shoulders. "I know that, the whole Paradise gym gonna know that soon. Soon as Mr. Manners lets you train at the Pug and not out here on the farm."

Tommie's car was rolling away from the house.

"See you, Tommie. Tomorrow!"

"Sure thing, Elegant. Sure thing!"

Gyp dashed out the house.

Woof!

"Gyp, Gyp, okay, Gyp!" Tommie said. "Okay!"

Gyp wagged her tail and her tongue hung out her mouth.

"Boy, we've had a good day, haven't we, Gyp? Haven't we?" Elegant was petting her. "One of the best days of my life."

And then out the house popped Pee-Pot. "Guess you're gonna get that shower going, Mr. Raines?"

Elegant's sweatshirt was soaked through with perspiration.

"Yes, uh, I was, sir."

"Don't let me detain you then."

"No, no, sir."

Pee-Pot was chuckling at the back of the truck; only, hidden from Elegant. "Going to town. Back to the gym—then off to cut Mr. Olden Jeff's hair. So dinner's gonna be—"

"Mr. Manners, sir," Elegant said, his hand anchored gently to Pee-Pot's arm, "may I cook dinner tonight, sir?"

"You, you wanna do that, Mr. Raines? Cook?"

"Yes, if you'll allow me, sir."

"Uh, of course—if that's what you'd like."

"I know what's in the icebox."

"So I'll be in by seven thirty. How's that?"

"Fine, Mr. Manners."

Then Pee-Pot took two steps and then turned back around as Elegant was about to round the house. "The house is still gonna be standing, uh, when I get back, won't it, Mr. Raines? Ain't gonna be burned down to the ground?"

"No, Mr. Manners. No, not at all, sir."

Pee-Pot got in the truck. Then the truck was on Hattersfield Road.

Woof!

Elegant stood at the back door waiting on Gyp. She turned the corner of the house. "Coming in, Gyp?"

Gyp wagged her tail and then darted in the opposite direction, out onto the grounds.

Elegant laughed. "This is one of the best days of my life. It is. It is …"

CHAPTER 5

It was two weeks later, and Elegant was still out at the house, not the gym, sparring with Tommie Lathers. They'd developed a friendship, Tommie Lathers and Elegant Raines, up to now that was quite special. They were kicking themselves around like old shoes. And Elegant had ridden in Tommie's 1941 Ford Super Deluxe Convertible three times. The second time Tommie handed Elegant a white towel out the trunk, and both got busy wiping off the dust-laden car. The whole time they laughed like mad.

As for Elegant and his training, Pee-Pot couldn't be more pleased with how things were progressing. Elegant promised he'd try "harder," and he was (not that Pee-Pot had had any doubts he wouldn't). His power was explosive, frightening; it was pure punching power. It was something Pee-Pot marveled at. And with his improved boxing stance (up to 80 percent to 85 percent), he was able to generate greater power, more of it (it allowed him to "turn his punches over" better too).

Pee-Pot and Black Moon Johnson had gone back up to New York for a match—Coney Island, Brooklyn, again—and Black Moon dispatched his opponent in two rounds, a knockout (it was supposed to have been better, stiffer competition for him).

Also during this time, Pee-Pot put barber tools into Elegant's young hands and began teaching him the barber trade. He was teaching him how to shape a head or hair with the patience of Job—at least he'd told Elegant as much. The test for Elegant would come after Pee-Pot's New York trip with Black Moon, once they got back to Longwood.

The guinea pig, or "subject," as Pee-Pot called him (Pee-Pot decided this time it wouldn't be him) was one Mr. Leroi Patchett, a ninety-one-year-old man with a mane of fluffy white hair, who would take the opportunity to get a free haircut whenever and wherever he could. And, of course, the haircut would be free of charge. At his advanced age, Mr. Patchett was still quite fussy about his hair, still gave Pee-Pot one devil of a stare if he cropped too much hair off since Mr. Patchett was dating a ninety-eight-year-old widow, Mrs. Myrtle T. Lyons of Longwood, and she did find pleasure in running her fingers through his fluffy all-white hair during his many and frequent visits to her home on Carson Road, just two roads up from Hattersfield Road.

And Elegant was cooking more dinners for him and Pee-Pot (hadn't burned down the house yet!). Out of a seven-day week, he'd cook an average of three meals. Of course there were leftovers. So they simply had to be reheated. Pee-Pot looked forward to Elegant's cooking, testimony to just how good Elegant cooked. His skill with pots and skillets.

"So Black Moon knocked Trooper Davis out in the second round, Mr. Manners."

"That he did, Elegant."

Elegant relieved Pee-Pot of his suitcase. Gyp was there by the door, thrilled to see Pee-Pot—as always.

"So much for a test, sir."

"Oh, it'll come," Pee-Pot said wearily, somewhat tired from the New York trip. "There's always someone out there. Pep and Saddler, Joe Louis and Max Schmeling. There's always someone to test a fighter—especially a young fighter—Elegant, on his way up the rung."

"Yes, sir."

Gyp stood in front of Pee-Pot. He bent over and hugged her around the neck.

"Missed me, huh, did you?"

Gyp licked Pee-Pot's face. Pee-Pot straightened himself.

"So how's your training been going?" Pee-Pot asked as he and Elegant advanced into the living room.

"Just fine, Mr. Manners."

Pee-Pot looked down at his rocker. "Now it's your turn to say you missed me."

Elegant laughed.

Pee-Pot laughed too before sitting in the rocker.

"By the way, Mr. Manners, are those matches in Coney Island, uh, well attended, sir?"

"Are they. A loud, noisy, rambunctious arena up there. Like most of them. But up in New York, I've never seen so much smoke in an arena or heard so much cursing, profanity in one place. It's exciting. Very exciting for fighters. The whole atmosphere up there."

What Pee-Pot said generated excitement in Elegant, and Pee-Pot saw his eyes aglow.

"It's what it's about, Elegant. The crowd. The people. Putting on a good boxing exhibition for the fans every time you lace up your gloves. Giving them a good fight. Getting them out their seats. Rousing them up to a high level. There's nothing like it."

Elegant was more excited.

"You start in the small arenas, for you can fight in the big ones. It's all a part of the package. Bigger package." Pause. "And ... by the way, how's Tommie?"

"Fine, Mr. Manners."

"He's been showing up to the farmhouse as scheduled?"

"Of course, sir," Elegant said assertively, as if Pee-Pot were somehow suggesting differently.

"Uh, didn't mean to ruffle your feathers any, Elegant."

"Oh, I'm sorry, Mr. Manners. I apologize, sir. But Tommie's my friend."

"And a good one at that."

"The best, sir."

"You and him been out on the road again in that car of his? Pulled out that towel trick of his on you?"

"Ha. Yes, sir."

"That car could embarrass a ten-carat diamond ring."

Elegant figured it had to be the shiniest car in Longwood, even if he'd only been three miles south of Longwood and maybe one mile north (the stretch of road he and Tommie and the Ford covered).

"So what are we dining on tonight?"

"Oh, I prepared—"

"But before we get to that ..."

"Oh ..."

"Tommie's not coming out here anymore to—"

"Tommie's not, but Mr.—"

"Let me finish. Let me finish now, Elegant." Pee-Pot leaned forward in the rocker. "Because you're going into the gym. Pee-Pot's Pugilistic Paradise, the Pug, tomorrow with me."

"I-I am, sir? I am!"

"Well ... not exactly."

"No ...?" Elegant said as if his curiosity were choking him.

"I figure three miles in the morning, through the woods with Gyp. Gyp'll figure it out." (Gyp wasn't in the living room with them.) "And then three miles into town, on your own."

"Great, Mr. Manners. Great!"

"Just hope Gyp doesn't complain any," Pee-Pot laughed.

"So do I, Mr. Manners."

<hr/>

"Just glad you didn't let the new arrangement upset, uh, bother you, Gyp. This morning."

Gyp and Elegant were sitting on the staircase. Gyp's grooming brush was in his right hand. He'd stroked Gyp's black coat numerous times by now, something Gyp simply loved Elegant and Pee-Pot to do—even though Pee-Pot, of late, didn't seem to have time for it, whereas Elegant did, doing it a few days a week.

"Mr. Manners says it's temporary anyway. Said it's not going to stay this way, Gyp."

Elegant got up to put Gyp's grooming brush back in the living room. Then Elegant returned to the vestibule.

"Well, it's time for me to get, uh, well, ready. Jog into town, Gyp."

Gyp, whose body was still lying in a prone position, alertly sprang to her feet.

"Gyp, I'm gonna miss you. We haven't been separated like this in a while. In quite some time."

Woof!

"Now come on, Gyp. Don't make it any harder on me than what it already is."

Woof!

"Come on, Gyp, have a heart."

Gyp licked Elegant's hand.

"There you go, Gyp. There you go, girl."

They were out at the front of the house. Elegant bounced up on his toes.

"So I'm gonna take off, all, all right?"

Woof!

"Okay, Gyp … Here goes!"

And off Elegant sprinted, and about twenty yards down Hattersfield Road, he turned while he backpedaled and waved back to Gyp. Elegant did that for about ten yards and then faced the road again.

"It's not the same without you. Out here. I feel it already. I really, really do."

———

Elegant was in town, and his one visit to town had been enough, for he knew where Pee-Pot's Pugilistic Paradise was without a map or compass. And then again, the town of Longwood was but so big, and the gym was tucked behind two other taller spruced-up buildings. Or maybe Elegant didn't have to be as smart as you might think to find Paradise.

But he was standing before it and was red cheeked, standing as solidly as a West Virginia oak. In a sense, he felt he'd finally arrived; his boxing career was perking again, back on course.

When Elegant entered the Pug, plenty of activity greeted him. The smell of it lit Elegant's nose. If you could think of sweat as perfume then that was the case for Elegant—no matter how pungent. From across the gym, he saw Pee-Pot. He was going to call out his name but caught hold of himself; instead, he said to himself, *What do you think you are, a big deal or something? You're just another one of Mr. Manners's fighters, and right now, Mr. Manners is busy with one.*

Just because he was privileged to live in his farmhouse, was sheltered, fed, bedded, and worked in the gym out there, it didn't privilege him to think he was so important he could stop another fighter's training session.

Some of the fighters seemed to take notice of him from before. They were friendly enough to nod at him. But some seemed to turn their noses up at him or openly snub him. Or was this his imagination? The last time in the gym, after all, it'd been rough on him, the Black Moon Johnson affair. Maybe first impressions were sticking out like a sore thumb and, as they say, are lasting.

Sort of in no-man's-land, Elegant didn't know what to do, so he walked over and looked at the picture on the wall of Kid Norfolk, a fighter who was born in Norfolk, Virginia. Black Machine Whaley spoke of him, one of the great black fighters of his era who began fighting as a middleweight and worked his way up to become one of the most feared light heavyweights in his division.

The picture on the wall was the same one in Mr. Whaley's photo album, Elegant thought. Kid Norfolk fought Sam Langford, Black Machine told him, and was knocked flat inside of two rounds. He also fought Harry Greb, the great white fighter, losing once (disputed) in Pittsburgh, Greb's hometown. But in 1924, at Mechanics Hall, Boston, he won in the fourth round on a foul (Greb hit Norfolk after the bell).

Mr. Whaley certainly knew his boxing.

"Elegant!"

Everything in the gym seemed to stop.

Elegant looked to his right.

"I see you got here!"

"Yes, Mr. Manners ... I-I'm here, sir."

"Been waiting for you, son."

The gym was still quiet, eavesdropping.

"Glendy-Boy, you keep doing what I instructed you, okay?"

"Yes, Mr. Manners."

"Straight from the shoulder. Don't loop the jab."

"Yes, sir."

Elegant was still standing by Kid Norfolk's photo.

Pee-Pot made his way out the ring.

Seeing Pee-Pot was heading his way, Elegant met him halfway, just beyond his office.

The gym was active again.

Pee-Pot slapped Elegant on the back.

"So you didn't trip over any live snakes in the road on the way over, huh, Elegant?"

"No. No, I didn't." Pause. "But it did feel lonely running without Gyp at my side, Mr. Manners."

"Like I said, Elegant, this won't last. This arrangement of ours is only temporary."

"It's what I kept repeating to myself on the way in, sir."

"So let's get you going. Right this way ..."

They were at the back of the gym. The last time Elegant was in the gym, he'd been in the back to use the bathroom. He'd passed by the lockers and wanted to feel like a fighter, how the fighters back there felt, in front of the lockers, but had to suppress that feeling. But not today!

"I set it up for you, Elegant. Put a sponge, soap, and elbow grease to it. Locker number fifteen."

"I really like it, Mr. Manners."

"Well, it's yours, so you'd better!"

Elegant opened the metal locker's door. "My old one, sir, uh, at Mr. Whaley's gym, creaked."

"This one did till this morning. Before I plied it with oil."

Elegant looked down at his gym bag (Pee-Pot brought it in with him in the truck this morning). Then he looked up at the clean towels, three of them.

"You ready, son?"

"Yes, sir."

Pee-Pot stepped up to him. "Just don't try to impress anybody out there in the gym today, Elegant, when you get out there."

"Uh, no, no I wouldn't do that, Mr. Manners. I'm not here for that."

"Good."

Pee-Pot shut the locker's door and then handed Elegant the tiny key. Elegant smiled and then locked the locker.

"I want you to do one thing before you spar with Tommie today."

"Yes, Mr. Manners ...?"

"Strip down to your trunks. I want everybody in the gym to see what a fighter's body looks like."

Elegant was flattered.

"Just do the speed bag. That's enough."

Elegant nodded his head.

"How's that coming, Glendy-Boy? You're not looping it, are you?"

"Elegant!"

"Tommie!"

All heads in the gym turned to Tommie. He ran over to Elegant, hugging him.

"A big step up, ain't it, huh?" Tommie said, looking around the gym.

"I couldn't wait for this day to come, Tommie—to be honest."

"Know you can't," Tommie said wistfully. "But as usual, man, gotta catch up with you."

"Yes, as usual," Elegant teased.

"We gonna put on a show today. Show these boys in the gym how we was doing it back at the farmhouse, you and me. Right, Elegant?"

"Right."

"Yeah, man, this joint gonna be in for a shock!"

Once again, Elegant felt flattered. If this kept up, he might have to check his hat size, he thought. But it was food for a hungry man, a starved man, for he was hungry to show himself off to other fighters—make this a prince of a day, a day like the gym would not soon forget.

"So I'm off and running," Tommie said, hustling ahead and toward the locker room. "Be back in a blink."

Elegant looked around the gym again. He felt engaged with it.

<hr />

Tommie, as usual, lived up to his word. He was back in the gym in a shot. He was spinning through his full range of exercises. While Elegant waited, he skipped rope. He was quite good at it but was no match for a dandy like Tommie. Tommie was a master at skipping rope. He dazzled you. If he had a tin cup, it'd overflow with coins.

The gym seemed to sense what was happening. It seemed to be in the rapid-fire rhythm of it. Excitement always boiled hot whenever a boxing gym anticipated the "new" guy, the "new" fighter, "mystery" fighter in the gym. A gym has pride, wears it on its sleeve like a coat of arms. A boxer saying he came out Pee-Pot's Pugilistic Paradise in Longwood, West

Virginia, meant something, rendered him quick prestige in a swath of Southern boxing arenas. He might not be regarded as a top-notch fighter or even a talented one, but at least he was a well-schooled one.

There was a vacant ring, and Pee-Pot moseyed over to it. Elegant stopped skipping rope and made his way over to the ring where Pee-Pot tested the ropes.

Elegant's sweat top was pasted black with perspiration. Pee-Pot turned to him. To be honest, he was as anxious as Elegant for the unveiling of his new "star student" (it's what he thought of Elegant) to the gym.

"I'll call Tommie over in … looks like he's about ready to spar."

Elegant looked over at Tommie, whose forehead was pasted with sweat.

Looking intensely at Elegant's sweat top, Pee-Pot said, "You didn't forget, now did you, Elegant?"

"No, Mr. Manners."

Elegant bounced up on his toes.

Minutes later.

"Tommie."

Pee-Pot had not only alerted Tommie but also the gym.

"On my way, Mr. Manners."

Once the boxing gloves were laced, Tommie and Elegant were to spar in full view of the gym's fighters.

"This is different," Elegant said in a nervous whisper to Tommie. "F-for us. Is-isn't it?"

"We got us a audience, that's all, Elegant," Tommie whispered back. "Us a full house in here."

Tommie and Elegant were in the ring with Pee-Pot. First, Pee-Pot laced up Tommie's boxing gloves. When done, Pee-Pot winked at Elegant.

Pee-Pot was holding Elegant's gloves. Elegant stepped back from him and into the middle of the ring. Off came the sweat top. Elegant's black body's upper torso, the broad shoulders and muscled back, were slicked down with sweat and bulged with power.

The Pug fighters gasped.

Pee-Pot laced up Elegant's boxing gloves.

Butterflies fluttered in Elegant's stomach. But at least it's where he wanted to be, he thought.

"So let's pick up where we left off yesterday," Pee-Pot said. "Oh, I'm sorry, pardon, pardon me, boys, I meant, before I left for New York for a few days."

Both bit down hard on their mouthpieces and then grinned wide as the moon.

In the middle of the ring, Tommie and Elegant met, and there, on display, was that remarkable grace in Tommie's physical movement. His noted jab, quick and steady, kept Elegant at bay despite Elegant's height and reach advantage. But Pee-Pot was teaching Elegant how to cut the ring off against a speedy, shifty boxer with this kind of boxing style. And to drive him to the ropes, somewhere he didn't want to fight from, against the ropes, not planted in the center of the ring where he could control the fight, thus pile up points.

Thus, this was strictly a defensive session for Elegant, and the other fighters in the gym sensed as much. Collectively, they turned their attention from the ring's action (Pee-Pot continuing his silent study of Elegant) and back to their own.

Elegant was picking off roughly 60 percent of Tommie's jabs with his arms and gloves. But this wasn't scintillating action, nothing like Tommie and Elegant hoped to ignite, especially so Elegant, who Pee-Pot still hadn't permitted to let loose his big guns (fists) either in this gym or the farm's gym. Elegant really wished to hit someone, even if it was Tommie. He was a welterweight, agreed, but he was a fighter, and he was inside the ring with him; and it was the danger, Elegant thought.

He and Pee-Pot were at a new stage in their relationship in many good, positive ways but not yet in the gym. If it were Black Machine Whaley, in Whaley's Gym, he'd be hitting people in the gym on a regular basis. He'd be making the gym shiver from his guns. While, granted, he was learning so much more from Pee-Pot Manners than he did Black Machine Whaley, he was still at odds with Pee-Pot Manners's methodology on this one point: him not being able to express himself as a fighter in this method, in this most primal and barbaric method—of just hitting someone, nailing him with a good shot while sparring, in training.

But it was not for him to rock the boat. It was for him to continue to listen and learn from Pee-Pot Manners, continue to give 100 percent of himself, grow at Pee-Pot Manners's rate, not his—it was the lesson being taught to him by Pee-Pot Manners. But chasing Tommie around the ring, from corner to corner, exerting pressure on him, he sensed Tommie's disappointment too, them stepping out from under the seclusion, veil of the farm, to the gym, did seem like his shackles would finally be broken, that he'd be free to execute some of his firepower in the ring.

Tommie and Elegant were in a clinch. "Hey, what's going on?" Tommie whispered. "Shit, thought Mr. Manners was gonna let you clobber me by now, Elegant. What I was thinking?"

"Me too," Elegant said, quickly breaking the clinch. "Me too, Tommie."

Pee-Pot didn't hear what they said but responded anyway. "No talking in there. This ain't a town meeting!"

Tommie's eyes laughed; so did Elegant's.

This kind of sparring lasted for a while, not until Pee-Pot said, "Roscoe, could you come over here, please."

Roscoe Turner was big and brawny—a mauler, not a tap dancer like Tommie. The gym's eyes were set on Roscoe Turner's back, his chest, his face.

"Yes, Mr. Manners, sir."

He was a heavyweight with a weight problem. He had no real boxing talent but was tough and could take an excellent punch from anybody. He had the respect of the fighters in the Pug because of his chin.

"I want you to spar with Elegant Raines here, Roscoe," Pee-Pot said in greeting him.

"Yes, sir."

Roscoe Turner climbed into the ring.

"But first, let me introduce you two." Pause. "Roscoe Turner, Elegant Raines."

Roscoe Turner had a big pancake smile, and he walked up to Elegant, hugging him. "Glad to meet you, Elegant."

"The same here, Roscoe."

Tommie was out the ring. He was sweating as well as Elegant and Tommie since Roscoe had been two rings over, shadowboxing. Tommie knew this would now be Elegant's time to open up, become offensive minded for a change.

And Elegant, looking at the size of Roscoe Turner, surmised this too, that he'd finally been freed. That he, now, could express the essence of Elegant Raines in the ring.

Pee-Pot walked up to him. "You can do what you want with him, Elegant. Feel free to."

"Thank you, Mr. Manners."

The gym now belonged to Elegant and Roscoe Turner, for Roscoe Turner was no longer smiling but knew what his job was. To fight Elegant Raines, to go all out, to find out what kind of fighter Elegant Raines was for the sake and good standing of Pee-Pot's Pugilistic Paradise.

Tommie smacked his gloves together. He knew Elegant was going to put on a spectacular show!

Now it would be Elegant's speed and power, his jab, and Roscoe Turner attempting to cut off the ring to neutralize Elegant's speed. It was Elegant executing the jab, sinister and straight, bouncing it off the top of Roscoe's rugged headgear. Being a brawler, Roscoe Turner collapsed both arms over his chest and then threw roundhouse punches at Elegant's head that Elegant slipped. But Roscoe, at times, was able to press and then force Elegant into the corner and wail away. Elegant covered up, mentally relaxing himself, letting Roscoe do all the work until he tired. Once sapped of his energy, Roscoe backed off. This allowed Elegant to skirt out the corner. Then it was back to the middle of the ring. Not until Roscoe's energy recharged enough for him to mount another serious attack by pushing Elegant back into the corner again.

This was an all-out war the gym was now intimately connected to. Roscoe was back to pressing his attack, orchestrating it with greater aggression, meaner intentions. His objective was to rough Elegant up. He had pressured him up against the ring ropes and cracked him with a short, compact blow. Roscoe smothered Elegant and then grabbed the ropes (something illegal) to lock him in place. Using all of his weight, he leaned on him. But Elegant, using his strength, pivoted Roscoe around to maneuver him into the same corner he'd left.

With fists no longer aimed at his headgear, Elegant's jab smashed Roscoe square in the face. Roscoe grunted. Then came a vicious body shot that drew Roscoe's full attention. Elegant doubled up the next body shot. It made Roscoe's right arm flag limp as a rag and his body fold into sections. Now Elegant hit him with an overhand right that the world should've heard if it didn't, for it dropped Roscoe Turner to his knees, and he toppled, fell backward onto his back and flat to the mat.

———

"You should've seen it, Gyp. You should've been there today!"

Elegant and Gyp were in the kitchen. Elegant was cooking the meal. He was joyous. He'd walked home from the gym. He and Pee-Pot weren't to keep the same schedule since Pee-Pot had the gym responsibilities along with his barbering business in town, so there was no sense in Elegant hanging around the Pug just to get a three-mile ride home in the truck—not a country boy like him.

"It isn't my best punch, Gyp. But it was good enough today."

Woof!

Then Elegant turned from the stove and faced Gyp. He began demonstrating to her what he'd done today to Roscoe Turner, why the guy was out for two minutes, why Pee-Pot had to call for the smelling salt, why Pee-Pot didn't expect that display of punching power, so sudden and merciless.

"Roscoe was heavy, Gyp. A load of a man. But you probably know him. Right? Right?"

Woof!

"But you've never had him lean all that weight on you on the ropes, Gyp. Not like me. He's big and strong. But, okay, clumsy. His footwork's not the best. Uh, sharpest, Gyp. But heavyweights aren't known for their footwork. Billy Conn, maybe, it's what Mr. Whaley said. But he's ... okay, okay, Gyp, I'm excited. Excited ... by ...

"But when he hit me in the gut with that punch of his, and it hurt, did it ... And I knew then he meant business. So I really got serious then. I knew I had to make him respect me then, Gyp."

Then Elegant slowed down. "I saw the opportunity, then took advantage of it."

Gyp's tail wagged.

Elegant turned back to the stove and upped the flame under the skillet. He was worried for Roscoe Turner even though, again, he hadn't hit him with his best punch but, still, one good enough to knock him cold. The

Pug went wild, and he needed that. Every fighter wants the respect of his peers, and one punch did it, one punch against a rugged chin did it.

He was frying ham, and there was a jar of honey. When it was ready, Elegant was going to glaze the ham with the honey. He could've skipped home from the gym this afternoon, not jog. His head was in the clouds.

"Gyp, Gyp," Elegant said, turning back to Gyp. "Oh, you should've been there today!"

Elegant poured the grease out the skillet and into a can of solid grease and then put the can of grease back into the icebox. Then, next, Elegant began setting the kitchen table. He paused.

"Maybe it's good to wait on things, Gyp. Not rush things too fast." Pause. "It's another valuable lesson I learned today."

It was so much sweeter this way, Elegant thought, to be challenged by new situations and then be able to produce positive results. He'd been struggling to reconcile his thinking with Pee-Pot Manners's, but gradually, he was beginning to see the wisdom in his ways, his integrity in sticking to his principles and not waver from them even if it meant crisis or confrontation. He was a man who was living a life of grandeur, Elegant thought, Pee-Pot Manners, and all it could do was rub off on him, sharpen his intellect, his outlook on life.

Today was a winning day for him, crystallized by what he'd done to Roscoe Turner, who, when he got to his feet, finally said, "What hit me, man? A-and what round?" And practically everyone in the gym laughed, for they saw he was all right, his eyes clear and shining.

Today was no mistake, Elegant thought. God had a hand in it. Had a lot to do with it. And he was thankful.

The table was set, and Elegant kneeled down on the floor and put his face in front of Gyp's, and she licked it.

"Because of you, Gyp, I'm in the best shape of my life. Running through the woods in the morning. Breathing in all this fresh air. The cleanest air in the world is in those woods, Gyp. It's the best place in the world to train. It's the environment, these West Virginia hills. Longwood, West Virginia."

Pee-Pot was in the truck, and his head was swimming in a sea of delight. He knew he had a catch before today, but after today, there was no doubt. With more hard work and dedication, Elegant Raines could well become the next middleweight champion of the world. And, in the process of getting there, make the world stand at attention and take notice. For he did have that something special, that aura about him. And he had that composure, that comfortableness in the ring that was innate, natural, came with no expectations, was just there, Pee-Pot thought.

He was glad he put Elegant in the ring with Roscoe Turner, through the paces with a tough fighter like him, a fighter who'd been tested in gym wars and pro fights, whose record was shoddy, who wouldn't win a championship because he'd never be good enough to get big fights, who wasn't worthy of them. But you could trust his heart and his chin—they'd proven dependable and sellable.

He had an announcement to make to Elegant, one to really make his juices flow.

"I think I'm just as eager as you, Elegant. My britches are on fire too. Yes, they are!"

Gyp's ears perked. Elegant heard the truck enter the yard off Hattersfield Road too. Tonight's meal sat on top of the stove.

"Ham," Pee-Pot said, entering the kitchen.

"Ham, sir."

"Smelled it from the back. Hi, Gyp." Pee-Pot looked at the table. "You know you're spoiling me with this. More than I deserve."

"That's all right, Mr. Manners."

Pee-Pot put his arm around Elegant's waist and guided him over to the kitchen table. Pee-Pot sat opposite Elegant.

"But before we eat, let's talk, son."

"Yes, sure, uh, Mr. Manners."

"We've been on a slow boat going to China, I know."

"B-but I realize the wisdom in it now, Mr. Manners."

"Thank you. Hoped you would. But youth's got energy, doesn't have time for patience." Pause. "Don't worry, I was once in your shoes. So nobody has to tell me the feeling."

Now Elegant was beginning to wonder what this was leading to, for him, for them.

"I'm gonna put you in the ring again."

"Y-you—"

"A pro fight."

"Are!"

Woof!

"Come on, Gyp, how'd you get into this conversation between me and the boy?" Pee-Pot laughed.

"Thanks, Gyp. Thanks for the support. Encouragement."

"I've already worked it out for us."

"Y-you have, Mr. Manners?"

"Three weeks, June 15, in Morgantown, Virginia. At Fame Arena."

"Yes." Pause. "Where you and—"

"Where Mr. Whaley and I put on some boxing exhibitions, son. Some stirring, sterling boxing exhibitions," Pee-Pot said, his heart beating a mile a minute.

Elegant stood. "Are you ready to eat, sir!"

"Wash my hands, and I'm raring to go!"

Pee-Pot was one foot from out the kitchen but turned. "The jab is what did it to Roscoe Turner, you know, Elegant. Not the body shot or the overhead right. But the jab. The first shot that shocked him."

No, I didn't know that, Mr. Manners, sir, Elegant said to himself.

And then Elegant was going to ask Pee-Pot who he was going to fight, the opponent, for the fighter was not mentioned, but decided he'd let Pee-Pot get upstairs and wash his hands since he was so eager to sit down and eat the glazed ham in the pan. He would get around to asking him that question later.

———

Tommie had just come out the bathroom when he spotted Black Moon, who'd just gotten in the gym. Black Moon was unlocking his locker.

"Guess you don't have to be here yesterday to get the news, huh, Black Moon?"

Black Moon's head twisted. He glared at Tommie. "Yeah, I got it. So what!"

"Elegant Raines knocked Roscoe Turner on his ass, man. Mean, out, Black Moon!"

Black Moon opened his locker.

"So you have you yesterday off."

Black Moon didn't answer right away.

Then he said, "When you knock a fuckin' punk out in the second round, your trainer give you the day off. Something ain't gonna never happen to you. Hell, hell—bet on that shit, boy."

"No, I'm afraid not, Black Moon. Shit, you right. I pitty-pat them boys silly, like I always say. But I ain't lost a fight yet. To nobody in the ring."

"You ain't fought nobody. I'm the only fighter Mr. Manners take up to New York. None of you bums down here. Don't wanna stink out the arena up there in Brooklyn. Where me and him go."

"Oh, you the star all right, Black Moon. Of the Pug. Not till 'nother boy comes 'long."

Black Moon's body swung around to Tommie. "Break that fuckin' punk into. Break every fuckin' bone in his fucking face!"

"Sure, Black Moon. Sure. Too bad you wasn't here yesterday. Seen him yesterday like the rest of us."

"Why I gotta see him!"

"Didn't say you gotta, Black Moon, just said, 'Too bad you wasn't here.'"

"All I gotta know, he seen me. And I scared the living shit out that boy. 'Fore I leave the gym."

Tommie smiled into Black Moon's angry charcoal-black face.

"You used the right word, all right, Black Moon …"

"W-what!"

"Scary."

"What you mean!"

"'Cause it was scary, scary as hell, man …"

"What, man, what!"

"The scary-as-hell punch Elegant Raines tag Roscoe with. Knocked the boy silly with."

Black Moon's eyes looked like two black moons.

Tommie knew Black Moon and Roscoe Turner had sparred on occasion, with Black Moon always coming out on top, battering Roscoe Turner, hurting him, but never knocking him down or, of course, out.

"It was scary all right. Sca-ryyy ...," Tommie said, tugging on both ends of the towel draped around his neck and then walking back into the gym with Black Moon suddenly speechless, seemingly not willingly but involuntarily.

Later.

Elegant was still working out. But hidden to everyone was Black Moon sneaking peeks at him. Usually Black Moon's concentration was superb but not today. Gaston Moore had realized why.

Elegant was sparring with a light heavyweight, Jimmy "Slender" Jones, who was a few inches taller than him. Slender had exceptionally long arms. In fact, he was like a spider with arms—arms a fighter could very well get tangled up in if they didn't know their way around the ring.

The good thing about the Pug, about training in Pee-Pot's gym, was you never knew what kind of fighter's style you might encounter next. There was always something new to learn, to study, to challenge you to find ways to overcome it, counteract it; and with Jimmy "Slender" Jones, it was his network of arms.

Pee-Pot was enjoying this, watching Elegant try to figure out what to do with Slender Jones like so many others before him. And he could hear Elegant's clever mind ticking, not afraid of Slender's power (he had a dynamite left hand, leveraged it, and turned it over well) but what it would take to climb the tall mountain.

But now Slender Jones had to worry about Elegant's head feints, ones Elegant had studied, observed, and learned from Tommie. They were ones he'd kept working at in the bedroom mirror when he shadowboxed and now was using on Slender, throwing Slender's timing off, making him arrhythmic, making him pause and think. The worse thing to do in the ring if it's all a fighter's doing, thinking and not reacting.

It's why one head feint did it, and Elegant negated those long spidery arms. He'd gotten under Slender's defense and sent him crashing to the canvas. Slender groaned like he'd been shot, but it was one shot to the rib cage why he was sitting down on his rump, had spit his mouthpiece out and groaned as loud as a whale.

The gym was set abuzz again by what Elegant just did to Slender Jones, the abrupt, brutal execution and cunningness of his attack.

Any gym is built on gym lore, the stories circulating out of it. The Pug had pages full. Elegant wrote one yesterday and added a new one today.

And going through some more paces, Pee-Pot said what he always said to his fighters.

"That's it for today, Elegant. We'll get back at it tomorrow." Then he cuffed Elegant around his neck. "You've got to stop roughing up my fighters. 'Cause nobody's gonna wanna spar with you if you keep this up."

Elegant smiled. "I think I'm still a little anxious about everything, Mr. Manners. At the moment, sir."

"I think you're right, son. Seems like I kept you away from red meat too long."

Pee-Pot unlaced his gloves and then tugged them off his hands.

"Thank you, sir."

Pee-Pot trotted over to another ring to work with another fighter.

Tommie ran over. He was about to take off for work.

"Keep thinking how lucky I am ..."

Elegant was unwrapping tape from his left hand.

"How's that, Tommie?"

"Shit, Elegant, don't try to outpossum the possum." Pause. "I mean I can take me a good shot. But that's only welterweight and lightweight. Not middleweight. Not that kind of power. Shit, Elegant, you could pulverize a horse!"

"I told Mr. Manners that I guess I'm excited right now."

"You gonna create a shortage of sparring partners in the gym who gonna wanna spar with you. That's for sure."

"It's what Mr. Manners said. Uh, cautioned me about. But I—"

"Including me. Me ... just might add my name to that list."

"Not you, Tommie. You wouldn't desert me, would you?"

"Just don't make me one of your victims then!"

Both laughed.

"Look, Elegant, 'fore I leave for work, want you to watch out for Black Moon, that boy, okay?"

"How come?"

"Seen the boy looking at the whole thing. Shit. 'Specially after what you done to Slender Jones just now."

"Oh."

"Black Moon have him a helluva time with him. I mean with Slender's style. Probably beat him on points if they was really to fight. For real. But it just that Black Moon can never figure the boy out. But you done." Pause.

"See you learned them head feints from me though."

"Darn tooting I did!"

"Could've worked my way into his defense like that too, Elegant. But ain't got the punch to finish the deal. It's where you and me is different."

Tommie took hold of Elegant's hands.

"Power." Then he looked at his hands. "Putty."

———

Tommie was out the gym, but what he'd said about Black Moon lingered with Elegant. But he didn't want trouble from Black Moon. A gym is supposed to be family—it's what Black Machine Whaley always impressed on him, preached in Whaley's Gym. Even though he did have trouble with one fighter in View Point, Texas, but one day that fighter left the gym to not return.

Elegant had unwrapped his taped hands. Now it was his job, he thought, to keep his mind focused on June 15, the date for his pending fight in Fame Arena in Morgantown, West Virginia. Before his previous twelve fights under Mr. Whaley, it was something he never had difficulty doing—concentrating—which, indeed, was a good virtue. This was most serious, for any new fight, any new time in the ring, since the risks were ever present.

A shower was the first thing he'd do and then dress and then get back to the house—home sweet home. He was loving his routine. It'd begun to feel great, exquisite. He loved it, living a defined, structured, disciplined life again. Back to where he'd been with Mr. Whaley minus living with him. He lived with three other fighters then: Johnston Graves, Benny "Beantop" Mines, and Sid Robertson.

"Great session, Elegant."

"Thanks. Thanks. Uh ..."

"We ain't met but glad to meet you. Make your acquaintance though. Name's Eddie 'Windmill' Sawyer." Windmill Sawyer extended his hand. "So just call me Windmill and I'll call you Elegant."

"Nice to meet you, Windmill."

Windmill was heading back out to the gym and Elegant into the locker room.

Black Moon hopped over the top rope and onto the floor. His body barreled straight ahead. It was not something in the gym that was unusual— him hopping the top rope with such a quick, sudden burst of energy.

Elegant was retrieving a fresh towel out his locker. There were two other fighters standing in front of their lockers, one on either side of the room.

The one to Elegant's right motioned to him.

"Hey, man, like what you done out there in the gym with Slender!"

"Hell, J. J., what the fuck this punk do!"

Elegant turned to his left: he was staring at Black Moon.

"Figure out something you couldn't!"

The other fighter on the other end of the locker room guffawed.

Elegant tried to be the peacemaker. "L-look, I just want to take a shower. I—"

"This ain't nothing, the gym. Kid play. Ain't no championship won in no gym. In two fuckin' day's work," Black Moon snarled. "This boy ain't done nothing."

"Why can't we get along? B-be friends? I haven't done anything to you. And you've, you've certainly done nothing to me. We're just fighters. Fighters in the same gym."

"Fuck, you hear this here boy? Shit he gotta say!"

"He's right," J. J. Ellison said. "Black Moon. The boy's right."

Black Moon smiled. "Ain't got no friends. A bully. Call me they friends 'cause they scared shit of me. When I be little, put a knot on they heads big as a fucking marble. Now I hit 'em. Chop they fuckin' heads clean off they fuckin' shoulders now!"

Elegant was stripping down.

"Told you what you was 'fore: A fuckin' teacher's pet."

Elegant put the protective cup in his locker.

"Staying out there on the farm with Mr. Manners. What right you got staying out there for? H-his house for?"

"I was a fighter of Frank 'Black Machine' Whaley. He was my trainer in View Point, Texas. Whaley's Gym. Mr. Whaley died."

"So, s—"

"Mr. Whaley and Mr. Manners fought in the past, were friends. So, so I was recommended to Mr. Manners before he died by Mr. Whaley's words that, that I put into a letter to Mr. Manners."

"So you a boy who know to write!"

"Damn, you can't!" J. J. Ellison said.

"Don't mean nothing," Black Moon said. "What I need writing for? Ain't nothing need to write down that can't say to nobody. And I telling you for a second time, Raines, you better watch your fuckin' step 'round here, boy."

Elegant took off his boxing shorts and his penis hung.

"I don't like you. Gonna kick your ass. Bad!" Black Moon's body blustered.

Elegant was naked, barefoot, and had his towel and a worn-down bar of soap.

"Gonna be the first time ... gonna kill somebody in the ring. F-first fuckin' time."

Elegant walked past Black Moon Johnson.

"An' it gonna be you, Raines. You. Fuckin' you!"

Elegant walked through the bathroom and into the shower.

Black Moon walked down to Elegant's locker, opened it, and then slammed it shut, making the metal locker shake. "He a coward. All y'all gonna see. When I get him in the ring. Gonna fuckin' see for y'allselves!"

———

Since Pee-Pot had three heads to cut in town, he wasn't in the gym with Gyp and Elegant this morning. They'd done their roadwork. In fact, Gyp had introduced Elegant to a new route, a new path of hills and trees and creeks and a muddy swamp guarding the land too.

They were outside the gym, the morning clear and mild and as serene as a cricket before it chirps in its odd but natural way, rubbing its legs together with a host of other crickets in their self-indulgent cacophony of conductorless morning music.

"Gyp, thanks for the new run. Adventure this morning."

Actually, Gyp was stretched out on the ground, on her back. Elegant was stroking her stomach, her four legs pointed skyward. Gyp's tongue hung out the left side of her mouth, and her eyes looked blissful.

While doing this with Gyp, Elegant was still troubled by what'd happened in the gym yesterday afternoon with Black Moon Johnson. He really felt Black Moon Johnson had pounced on him, ambushed him, that he could only lose in a situation like that, him having a nonconfrontational personality, disposition. Such confrontation was natural for someone of Black Moon's disposition; he was just inherently aggressive.

To kill someone in the ring, why would anyone want to do that? Elegant thought. It was a sport, nothing more. Had Black Moon Johnson ever seen a person die? Had he?

He had. Not in the ring ... And it's never a blur to the memory but burns with an ungodly fever that consumes you and—

"That's it, Gyp. We've got to go inside the gym. If Mr. Manners saw us out here, I don't think he'd be too happy with us. Not at all."

Gyp rolled over and got up on her feet.

Gyp walked in front of Elegant.

"I-I can tell you, Gyp." Pause. "Yesterday wasn't so hot in the gym. There's this fighter named Black Moon Johnson. Black Moon Johnson, Gyp, he doesn't like me. Not at all. In the least bit."

They were off by the ring. Gyp sat upright. Up on her haunches.

"I don't know why, I ..." Elegant looked more passionately toward Gyp. "Yes, I know why. Full well why. I'm a threat, pose a threat to him, Gyp. It's why."

Gyp was still looking brightly at him.

"I guess he's jealous of me too ... I don't know. I really don't want to say that. Who knows, Gyp."

Elegant walked over and picked up the jump rope off the floor. "Mr.

Whaley, he said the gym's supposed to be like, you know, Gyp, family. I'm glad I have Tommie, but I don't know about the rest of the fighters. How they feel about me s-so far."

Elegant thought about it last night. He didn't want to be divisive, some fighters in his camp, others in Black Moon's, since he realized everyone in the gym today would know what happened in the locker room, the fireworks—even if his role was faint. He had no idea how it was reported, what was said and how.

Elegant untwisted the jump rope. "This is it, Gyp. Being in a gym. It's heaven. Like you and me in here together. Just the two of us."

Gyp's tail wagged.

"I mean it really is, Gyp." Elegant, it seemed, was about to jump rope. "But the gym in town, it doesn't feel that way for now. Maybe soon. In time it will. But definitely not now. Not like out here."

Elegant began jumping rope.

Gyp stretched out on the floor, watching Elegant's moves.

───

"Elegant, I heard."

Tommie'd just gotten in the Pug. Pee-Pot, he was in his office. Elegant had been working out with the medicine ball but was taking a break.

Tommie put his arm around Elegant's waist.

"Let's go outside." Tommie looked around the gym. "Though everybody's gonna know why."

They were outside the gym, standing in front of the Ford, when Tommie leaned against its side door.

"Hop in."

Both got inside the car.

"So how you taking it? What happened yester ... and the gym today, how they taking it?"

"Well, as for me, I don't like confrontation. And the gym, up till now, the gym's never been warm to me, Tommie. Since I've been here."

"Outsiders, Elegant. Nothing but. Always been problems with outsiders coming in the gym."

"That's it, Tommie? Or is it me?"

"Ain't nothing to do with you. The Pug is what it is," Tommie said, looking at the long, log-built building. "Don't make no sense thinking Black Moon Johnson got that much say so over it." Pause.

"You tried staying out his way like I told you 'fore, right? To do, right?"

"Right."

"But it's hard to. Damn. Know that. That boy ain't gonna let you. Just ain't. Push you—"

"I was at my locker."

"Heard you was glaring at—"

"Glaring at him!"

"Know it's a bald-faced lie soon as I heared it. From the start. Know you ain't like that, Elegant. Never do nothing, no shit like that. But Black Moon says you was."

"But there were two ... a guy named J. J. and the other fight—"

"Don't matter. They gonna let him say what he want, man. Ain't gonna jump on it." Pause. "'Sides, it 'tween you and Black Moon anyways. Them boys don't have no stake in it. The bigger this thing 'tween you and Black Moon get, the better. You see what I'm saying, Elegant? Shit."

"Uh-huh."

"It's Black Moon's version, all his, whether people trust him or not— and it gonna stay that way. For now."

Immediately Elegant knew he had to live with that. He immediately saw he had no power, that Black Moon had won the first round.

"Let's you and me get back in the gym, 'fore, shit, we get both our heads handed to us by Mr. Manners."

"Oh, right. Right, Tommie."

Lightning quick, they were out the car, shutting the doors.

"But how you, uh, how you gonna handle Black Moon today if he tries getting under your skin?"

Elegant frowned. "It's ... Tommie, it's been something I've been thinking about too."

"And ...?" Tommie was looking up at Elegant, was all eyes and ears. "Ain't, you ain't got no answers yet, huh?"

"I just hope he knows we're both fighters, and it's in the ring where we should settle this. The score, Tommie, if we have to."

"Damn that was sweet, sweet, Elegant, how you just said that, man!"

"Well, it should, shouldn't it?"

"Right. Yeah, damned right it oughta!"

But then what Tommie said returned them to reality. "But not with Black Moon. Ain't gonna be with no Black Moon Johnson. That boy."

Elegant was in Pee-Pot's office. Pee-Pot was standing behind him. He'd been standing behind him longer than what Elegant thought he ought to. He turned around to Pee-Pot.

"Mr. Manners, what's wrong? What are you doing behind my back, sir?"

"I'd say you need a haircut, Elegant."

"Oh, that's all, sir?"

"Yes, we'll do that tonight. Cut your hair. After supper."

"Thank you, sir."

"And talking about barbering, since we're on the—"

Knock.

"Oh, come in, Tommie."

"Mr. Manners, sir, how do you know—"

"By my knock, Elegant. My knock, man. It's special. Right, sir?"

Pee-Pot pushed the Royal typewriter on the desk to the right and then looked Tommie up and down. "Tommie, when was the last time you fought?"

"A-a month ago, Mr. Manners. Back. April—"

"When would you like to fight again?"

"Uh, you know me, sir. Every week if I can get in the ring with somebody. Was up to me, sir. Or every few weeks like you and my daddy done. The old fighters."

"I know that, Tommie. But times have changed, son. It's a new generation."

Tommie was in his boxing togs.

"Well …"

Pee-Pot's eyes were beaming, and Elegant and Tommie took furtive glances at one another as he eased to his feet.

"How would you like to fight on the same card as Mr. Raines, on June 15?"

"Me and Elegant? Me and Elegant on the same fight card!"

"Why, it's what I said, Mr. Lathers."

"Elegant! Elegant!"

As soon as Elegant hopped out the chair, Tommie smothered him, and then it looked like they were bear wrestling one another across the office floor, and it was no telling who was winning.

"Fame Arena, here we come, Elegant. Fame Arena, here we come, man!"

"Yes, Tommie. Yes!"

"Of course I been fighting, uh, most my pro fights been fought there," Tommie said snootily, releasing Elegant.

"So," Elegant said, putting his arms around Tommie's shoulders, "you can tell me all about the place then. Fame, Fame Arena then, Tommie."

"Okay, you two lovebirds," Pee-Pot said. "Out in the gym, Mr. Lathers. And as for you, Mr. Raines, you ain't through for the day either. Let's get to work."

And when they opened the office door, who was lying on the floor by the wall near the stretching table with fighters surrounding her but Gyp.

"Gyp!"

"Gyp!"

"Gyp!"

Up sprang Gyp.

"Of all the strange … W-what are you doing here, Gyp!" Pee-Pot said.

Gyp came over and licked the back of Elegant's hand.

"Gyp …," Elegant said.

"Don't tell me she's getting lonely out at the farmhouse," Pee-Pot said. "S-suddenly."

Gyp lay back down.

"Must be," Tommie said.

"Without Elegant," Pee-Pot said with a toothy smile.

Shyly, Elegant smiled.

"But we've got work to do, Gyp," Pee-Pot said, patting Gyp's head. "Tommie's on the same fight card with Elegant June 15. Set it up."

Tommie then patted Gyp's head.

Then Pee-Pot and Tommie marched off together and then split, Pee-Pot heading for ring number two and Tommie heading for the exercise mat.

Elegant kneeled and cuddled Gyp.

"I know why you came, Gyp. I know why. Thanks. Thanks a lot."

Then Elegant marched straight ahead, shoulders pulled back, for ring number two. Then a nasty thought came to mind: did Gyp come from the house to take a bite out of Black Moon Johnson? He was lucky he wasn't in the gym yet. Then devilishly Elegant laughed—just to himself.

CHAPTER 6

June 15

Morgantown, West Virginia, was one of West Virginia's large population centers. On this "large population" map in West Virginia, you'd find Charleston, West Virginia; Huntington, West Virginia; Parkersburg, West Virginia; and Wheeling, West Virginia.

The Monongahela River snaked through Morgantown charmingly like a typical Southern day. It was a curvaceous, pretty pearl of a river, one fat with history (1794's Whisky Rebellion) and folklore and bass and kingfishers, navigable, flowing northward to Pittsburgh and joining with the Allegheny River to form the Ohio River—the mighty of the mighty United States rivers.

Morgantown was not Longwood, not by anyone's stretch of the imagination. Everywhere it was transparent, especially its architecture. Morgantown's downtown district, after many years, was designed, esthetically, to please the rich with imposing, ornate building structures. It was the railroad, this practical hub of transportation, that first brought industry and a population boom and jobs and economic capital and well-being to a downtown, through most of the nineteenth century, that had been as small and quiet as a West Virginia field mouse.

Modest downtown buildings by the early 1900s gave way to Romanesque and Queen Anne structures. This progressive climate produced over four hundred buildings of bracketed eaves or carved stone columns. It was the biography of Morgantown, its progression through the forward thinking of its city fathers and planners.

Elegant had never seen a city like Morgantown, West Virginia—its splendid, refined architecture. At the house this morning, he'd bid Gyp good-bye, asking her to wish him luck. Four made the train trip to Morgantown: Pee-Pot, Gaston Moore, Tommie, and, of course, Elegant. Whenever Pee-Pot boarded a train, overtly, his body trembled. Gaston Moore and Tommie were used to this, so when Pee-Pot trembled in front of Elegant, he apologized to him by bringing up Cora Manners, how much trains still affected him after six years, emotionally jarring him with the memory of Cora Manners's murder on the Crenshaw, Alabama, train.

By the time Pee-Pot seated himself on the train, the trauma appeared, to Elegant, to have passed.

They were staying in a black boarding house. It was one of a few on the outskirts of Morgantown's downtown district where black fighters bedded when in town. With no trains running out of Morgantown by the time Elegant fought his bout tonight, they'd leave in the morning. Elegant and Tommie would bunk together. Pee-Pot and Gaston Moore, the same.

Traveling by train, it'd been a fun trip down. There was great rapport between everyone. If either fighter was nervous, it didn't show. But it'd be different once in Fame Arena, especially after smelling the first drop of liniment.

"So this is Fame Arena?" Elegant said, standing in front of its bracketed eaves, its classical carved stone columns.

The four stood admiring the building's graceful lines.

"Don't let it fool you any. It was once a burlesque hall, Elegant. Burlesque shows. Built a bigger burlesque hall a block north of here," Pee-Pot said. "They're still doing a heck of a business—so they tell me."

"So they go from feathers and fans to gloves and trunks, huh, Mr. Manners?"

"Never thought of it quite like that, Tommie," Pee-Pot said. "But I guess it's safe to say that."

"So it's this way, Elegant. The fighters, we gotta enter through the back door," Tommie said.

"Paying customers through the front." Gaston Moore chuckled.

"Our throng of admirers," Pee-Pot said, topping things off.

Once theater seats were removed from Fame Arena's floor, a ring set up in the middle, and chairs placed to surround the four-squared ring from either side, Fame Arena was able to accommodate 450 people. Boxing was always a popular ticket in town, and like most beginnings in small and big Southern fight towns similar in moral code and custom and culture to Morgantown, it struggled with its image. Fistfights were staged on docks (stealthily) and dank basements and back alleys and beer joints. Boxing was subjected to ignominy, disgrace, to public humiliation; to wrath, outcry and censorship. It wasn't a sport but, instead, unsavory, a growing cancer in America's morality, its moral fabric. And therefore, it should be banned from society.

Thus, Fame Arena reflected a different time, a different stage of society's acceptance—of a public's view. The building had been willed over, in a curious way, to the boxing crowd, reflecting tangible change and progress in a town, by now, priding itself on such ritual and practice.

Entering through Fame Arena's narrow back door with Pee-Pot, Tommie, and Gaston Moore, Elegant's chest swelled. He didn't have to guess why. He knew it was because he was a fighter and was going to put in his hard labor and his metal to a test tonight. And that was why, for him, boxing had its glamour, its aura, its estate. It was majestic like many of Shakespeare's plays, Elegant thought, appealing to the emotions, one individual fighting what seemed the world on his terms, by his own marvelous intuition and ingenuity.

"Step right through here," Tommie said, stepping aside.

"What's—"

"Our dressing room, Elegant. Where we can throw up if we wanna, and nobody's gotta know it."

Even with other fighters in the big dressing room, Tommie completely ignored them. You'd think its door had a Private Only sign nailed to it, that it was reserved exclusively for him, Pee-Pot Manners, Gaston Moore, and Elegant Raines.

"Gas, I'm going out and look for Ambrose Felix. See in what order the boys go on tonight. So they're all yours."

Gaston Moore was tall and sleepy-eyed but would see things in the ring sometimes even Pee-Pot missed. "So babysit them is what you mean, Pee-Pot."

It was to be a ten-card fight night, with Tommie going up first, the fourth fighter on the fight card, and then Elegant the fifth. When Elegant was told the order, he was upset. He wanted to be out in the boxing arena rooting for Tommie, to watch him in action. Not that it didn't bother Tommie, but Tommie was smart enough not to want to upset himself or Elegant, for he told him he could walk out in the arena with him, be an aide-de-camp. This cheered up Elegant.

As a fighter and now a trainer, Pee-Pot had been in this building so many times he could tell you how many wooden planks were on the floor, and nails too. But he was really beside himself for tonight's match, this first time out the gate with Elegant. Even he, after so many of his own fights under his belt and the trainer in hundreds more, had difficulty sleeping last night. He was a victim of anxiety and anticipation. When was the last time he'd lost sleep in anticipation of a fighter's fight? he'd questioned himself.

"Tommie, time to go on."

Gas Moore had sweated Tommie good, and Tommie threw a few more lighting quick jabs, bobbed and weaved, and said, "I'm ready, sir! Bring that boy on!"

"Okay, let's get out there," Pee-Pot said.

Tommie loved hearing that: "Okay, let's get out there."

Elegant didn't know what to say when he joined Tommie at the dressing room door, but his eyes popped out when he got out into the arena, loving everything about it, its character and charm, thinking about how many fighters its walls had seen and judged, and it would spy down on him the same after Tommie won his match and he stepped into the ring to fight.

They were at the ring's apron. Tommie was just about to head up the side steps, when he grabbed Elegant around his neck and they hugged.

"I ain't gonna knock the boy out, Elegant, so you gonna have to wait back in the dressing room a while. But the boy, if he ain't gonna look like a piece of sausage once I get done with him."

Elegant watched Tommie's head duck between the ropes, and then he was in the ring. Elegant looked at the boxer who was in black and wondered if he knew he'd worn the right color for his own mourning.

Elegant took one more look out into Fame Arena and saw it was near capacity. Gas was in the ring with Tommie, Pee-Pot a foot or so from Elegant.

"Just keep yourself loose back there, Elegant. Keep that sweat on you. And I'll be back for you. All right?"

"Yes, Mr. Manners."

Pee-Pot tugged on his flat checkered cap and then turned toward the ring.

Back in the dressing room, after ten minutes or so, Elegant heard a rousing chorus of cheers and wished with all his heart he was out in the arena with Tommie. He knew he must be putting on a heck of a show by the crowd's cheers. But he still had to concentrate on keeping himself loose, limber, and ready for his match.

———

Later.

Tommie burst though the dressing room door.

"I won, Elegant! I won!"

"Tommie!"

"The guy, you don't wanna see his mug, what I done to him!"

"I'm sure, I'm—"

"But look, let's get out there!"

But Pee-Pot did come for him, for Pee-Pot was in the hallway. He looked at Elegant and saw he did just what he told him—not that he had any doubts.

"How do you feel, Elegant?"

"Fine, Mr. Manners."

"Now since this is our first time together doing this, remember like I told you in the gym: I do all the talking and you do all the listening—not unless there's a question I ask you between rounds. Needs an answer for."

"Yes, sir."

Tommie got Elegant's robe, handing it to Pee-Pot, who draped it over Elegant's broad shoulders and then knotted it in front.

"Okay, let's get out there."

Tommie, who was unmarked from his fight, was walking proudly behind Elegant, extending his arm to his back as if guiding him. But once they got to the ring apron, Pee-Pot took over for Tommie. He began kneading Elegant's neck muscles.

"Elegant, it's all yours, man. Just fight your fight, and everything'll be all right. Okay?"

"Okay, Tommie."

Tommie stood outside the ring, below Elegant's corner.

Gas greeted him when he got inside the ring. Then Elegant looked over to his opponent, who stood shorter than him, as most middleweights were. He hadn't taken off his robe yet, but he was well built. Elegant didn't know this fighter's name until this morning, when Pee-Pot let him know it was Bowie Ferguson, a tough fighter with a spotty ring record only because he changed trainers like a dirty shirt. But he was a talented fighter, twenty-two years old, with an excellent chin and good boxing skills and a decent punch.

In fact, he'd wanted to train under Pee-Pot but he turned him down because of his track record with trainers, and so Bowie Ferguson said one day he'd learn to regret it. It was a prediction Pee-Pot was sure he'd try to fulfill tonight by making Elegant Raines his ring victim.

Pee-Pot really didn't know Elegant's prefight habits, whether he had any, and if so, he'd pick up on them for the next fight. But he was watching him, saw he liked to look out into the arena but more up to the building's rafters, not at the fans. He was throwing light punches into the air and jigged his feet as if in a pattern but really wasn't displaying much nerves, even though Pee-Pot knew they were there, for there was no secret about fear, any fighter's fear, when first entering the ring.

Bowie Ferguson kept his head down as his trainer worked his neck muscles, but his head rose when he and his trainer and second were motioned by the referee to the middle of the ring.

And as soon as Bowie Ferguson and Elegant joined the referee for ring instruction, Bowie Ferguson's eyes burned into Pee-Pot's as Pee-Pot did everything he could possible to avoid them but couldn't. He'd never had a young fighter like Bowie Ferguson do this to him before, disrespect him like this, and without saying, he didn't like it.

Of course Elegant and Gas noticed what was happening too, this vendetta Bowie Ferguson seemed to be waging against Pee-Pot.

Then as they turned to head to their respective corners, Bowie Ferguson winked at Pee-Pot, saying, "He ain't making it past round two!"

Pee-Pot walked with Elegant back to the corner, unknotted the robe, and ducked out the ring but stood on the ring apron. Elegant bent his head down, and Pee-Pot whispered in his ear, saying, "Just do your best, Elegant. And between rounds, we'll take it from there."

Elegant shook his head.

Then Pee-Pot slipped the mouthpiece into Elegant's mouth.

Clang.

Both Elegant and Bowie Ferguson moved out their corners with matching eagerness.

Both had conventional stances: straight up with a slight bend in the knees for flexibility and maneuverability. Ferguson was the first to jab, and Elegant's head slipped it, and then he threw his own, which Ferguson's head slipped. Ferguson tried building a body attack, which Elegant repelled and then tied Ferguson up.

Feeling Ferguson's strength, instantly, Elegant was aware he was the stronger of the two. That he had superior strength to that of Bowie Ferguson's and knew it would be his edge over him. He didn't let the referee break them but broke the clinch himself, jabbing out of it, hitting Ferguson with two ringing shots to the head, which Ferguson took well.

They were in the middle of the ring, and Elegant had trained himself to hear only one voice in the ring: his trainer's. He wouldn't listen for Tommie's voice or a fan's voice, just his trainer's voice, Pee-Pot Manners's voice, totally isolating it.

Ferguson lunged at him, and Elegant chopped down on him with an overhand right, and Elegant saw his legs wobble; but quickly, Ferguson strategically backed off, out of Elegant's punching range, and then smirked at Elegant. But Elegant moved forward, going after him, making him backpedal, and without throwing a punch he'd bullied him into a corner. Ferguson's corner.

Bowie Ferguson fired a punch at Elegant that Elegant ducked. Then Ferguson fired off another one that Elegant ducked; only, this time, he hit him with a power shot to the heart and then flushed him with a power shot to the head.

This punch dropped Bowie Ferguson.

The referee started the count, and Bowie Ferguson was back up on his feet at the count of eight. He was glassy-eyed but was still willing to fight with the referee and his corner in honoring his commitment.

This was the part Elegant never enjoyed in the ring, found pleasurable, dismantling another fighter. He'd wished the one punch had done it, had knocked Bowie Ferguson out for the count, for he wouldn't have to do something unmerciful, savage, to another human being. But he had this talent, this gift in his hands, and he was a fighter, and there was this momentary lapse in time when he could give this pause and reflection while Bowie Ferguson leaned against the ropes groggy headed but willing to be punished more for his courage, for his unwillingness to give up—quit.

Ferguson held his gloves high. But at best, he was offering a futile attempt to protect himself. Elegant was tossing light jabs at the high gloves, not murderous ones, not thunderous ones; but then he hit Ferguson with a big body shot, and his body crumpled, and it became a quick descent to the canvas, Ferguson's body now sprawled out on Fame Arena's bleached canvas.

And lying there as Bowie Ferguson was, he wasn't going to stand to beat the referee's count—not twice in round one.

The following day, Pee-Pot parted company with Elegant, Tommie, and Gaston Moore. They all headed North while he headed farther South. He was back on the train, going back into Martin County, Kentucky, and off to visit his brother Biscuit Manners. This was another opportunity for him to sponsor this visit to Biscuit. More and more guilt was setting in that he wasn't doing enough with Biscuit's health now failing. And, of course, Biscuit couldn't train up to Longwood, not in his weakened physical state, so he'd sent Elegant back to the house and was doing his duty but also trying to show his love in the only meaningful way he knew, by visiting him.

Biscuit never knew he was coming to Martin County to visit, but for Pee-Pot, that was the joy of it, surprising Biscuit, making him feel he was thought of. That he was always on his mind.

Pee-Pot looked out the train window.

The train was still in West Virginia, the Mountain State, and no matter how old and tired his bones got, he never tired of looking at them, Pee-Pot thought, making him feel there was a paradise beyond the next high hill.

Last night was like paradise. He had a euphoric feeling watching Elegant in the ring, executing his boxing skills practically to perfection, destroying the young and game Bowie Ferguson. Just for a man to get back up after taking a hit like he did is testament enough that he is a fighter, never mind his ring record or whether he wins or loses.

It's never a pretty sight to see another fighter destroyed, Pee-Pot thought. But to see how it's executed, sometimes, can be extraordinarily exciting. To see it performed skillfully, expertly, each punch serving a purpose, an intent, can be thrilling. And it's what he saw Elegant do in Fame Arena last night, make each punch thrown at Bowie Ferguson count for something.

So far, he'd have to rate Elegant Raines the smartest fighter, to date, he'd trained. Tommie, he'd been around the gym his entire life, so his talent relied on instinct and absorption of what he saw and then adapting it to create his own distinct style.

Elegant, on the other hand, thought through a move, a maneuver intelligently, of why he was doing it and then, through his unique talent, made it look natural, instinctive when executed. The conversion from Black Machine Whaley's training to his was now complete.

Pee-Pot wanted to see Biscuit so badly. He told Elegant not to go into the gym until he got back, to train out at the farmhouse like before. Elegant didn't seem to understand, but he knew about Elegant and Black Moon, the jealousy on Black Moon's part, and didn't feel secure enough that Gas could handle the situation if it ever got to the point where it ignited.

Once Black Moon got wind of Elegant's success, he'd explode. He had to speak to Black Moon, sit him down and have a heart-to-heart talk with him. He had to be reined in. He mustn't ruin the Pug's chemistry. It's what he'd impress on him. But even he couldn't control a personality of someone like a Black Moon Johnson's. His was a natural, aggressive personality. He came from Monongalia County, but it's like he came from nowhere, had no connections to anyone or anything. He was single-minded, single-focused—as hungry a fighter as any fight trainer could mold.

All Black Moon wanted to do was fight. When given a day off, the way he reacted, it's as if he'd die if he were not in the gym. He wanted to be king of the gym and was. And Black Moon didn't know, just yet, Pee-Pot thought, what Elegant Raines's role would be in him maintaining his kingship.

There were good fighters in the Pug, but from bantamweight through heavyweight, there were none with world champion potential—just Black Moon, Elegant, and Tommie. Tommie could outbox anyone, and since he was strong at his weight class and could take a punch (not that he took many) and stayed in tip-top shape, potentially, he could become a world champ.

But it was Elegant Raines and Black Moon who were in the same weight class, middleweight, coming out the same small gym situated in Longwood. Who, Pee-Pot predicted, would be on a collision course, whose heads, in the future, would knock.

Pee-Pot sighed, still looking out the train's window, onto the landscape.

He wanted to see Biscuit, but Pee-Pot had, ostensibly, used this train trip into Martin, Kentucky, as a kind of tonic too, as a way of clearing his head. There was to be a bumpy road ahead. This was the first time, as a trainer, he had two top prospects in the same weight class. It marked the first time there'd be a "gym war," literally, in Pee-Pot's Pugilistic Paradise. Today he'd found a temporary solution to stave off an explosion. Next, he'd have to find a long-term one.

———

Two days passed. Pee-Pot was expected. He'd called Elegant to let him know he was coming in today from Martin County. For Elegant, that was a first, and if it didn't make him feel especially good, Pee-Pot's gesture. Being out at the house, becoming such a big part of Pee-Pot's life, while Gyp's company was excellent, he missed Pee-Pot a lot.

And now there was something he was really beginning to miss: church. Now that he was settled in Longwood, Elegant felt it high time to find a church to worship in. In View Point, Texas, he'd found one, a church he was happy with—so it'd turned out. This would take priority; it would be important for him to explore what church in Longwood would suit him, for he was sure to find one.

Gyp was out of the house. He was cooking brook trout for supper. He looked down into the skillet and then laughed. Tommie drove to the house yesterday and told him how Black Moon reacted to his win in Morgantown.

"I knew he wouldn't be pleased. How much he wanted me to lose."

Tommie said Black Moon Johnson said the usual things he'd say about anyone he hated, but the look in his eyes was "really, really scary, Elegant," something Tommie said he'd never seen before.

Elegant said he wasn't going to think about Black Moon. That he'd get beyond him—only he couldn't. He felt as if he were in this vise with him, and it was tightening.

They were natural rivals. They had to be. It's just that he wasn't playing his role right. He just didn't want to hate anyone, something he already had, hate. He was carrying it in him for someone else even if he could only remember his face and his laugh—that piercing, shrill, hideous, bloodcurdling laugh.

He was glad Gyp was out of the house. He lifted the skillet to stop frying the brook trout, even though the fish sizzled, and the sound it made when it did that ... And he put the skillet on another hot plate on the stove for it to cool even though he didn't turn the fire off the plate it'd left. He made his way over to the kitchen table. He sat and dropped his head, burying it into his arms, crying, more glad Gyp was outside romping the grounds for she wouldn't see him in this kind of pain and despair, letting it boil over in him in ways predictable—what he knew all too well.

Elegant's head thrust back as if jettisoning the pain (if he could), turning it on itself, against itself, for he was throbbing with it, the memory of his past, what he came from and out of. It was hurting him not like a fighter's fist or Black Moon Johnson's fists or anybody's fist could.

It's why in the ring he felt impervious to pain, was stoic when encountering it, for to hate someone and not be able to hate them for what it was they did, to keep running farther and farther from them so to live, so to survive, so to give yourself a chance, was pain but burden too. It crossed the line into hating yourself for being a coward, gutless, even at age ten, having this kind of perception of yourself for not standing up to fight and die a death no matter how violent—something giving your life personal honor.

Up on his feet, Elegant returned to the stove and the skillet of fish, putting it back on the other hot plate. He hadn't lost that much time. He still felt uncomfortable with his thoughts. Tommie had figured things out for him before he did himself, why Pee-Pot told him to train at the farm's gym and not at the Pug. Tommie said he sensed it was because of Black Moon. And innocently, he said he had no "quarrel" with him, and when Tommie stared incredulously at him was when he wanted to cram those words back down inside his mouth as fast as they'd come out.

Tomorrow he'd surely be back in town, in the gym. Black Moon would come after him. He'd make it his business to. The thought was discomfiting. If only he could stop thinking of the gym as a holy place, where he'd found himself, his courage—Elegant Raines. If only he could alter his way of thinking, he'd be better served. He knew reality was what would equip him better, more clearly, accurately for the task ahead that would be formidable enough for him to handle.

"It's either I was exceptionally hungry or your cooking's getting better these days, Elegant."

"I don't know just how to answer that, Mr. Manners."

"There didn't have to be an answer forthcoming, I was just thinking out loud."

"Oh."

"Now don't feel embarrassed. If anybody should, it should be me—for thinking out loud."

They were in the basement, Pee-Pot's Parlor. Pee-Pot was sitting in the barber's chair and Elegant in a regular one. Pee-Pot crossed his leg.

"You didn't ask about my brother when I got in."

"I-I didn't think it proper I, that I should, Mr. Manners."

"Why not?"

"I-I was worried for you, sir."

"For me?"

"I didn't want to bring it up unless you did. Since you said your brother was doing badly, sir. Healthwise. It might be bad news."

"Elegant, you don't like bad news, do you?"

"No, sir. Most people don't."

"But you, especially you, son."

Elegant hesitated before answering. "I just don't take well to it, sir. I don't know why."

Pee-Pot was going to press Elegant some more but decided to drop the subject since something told him Elegant did know why but was unwilling to get to the root of it no matter how much he might press him.

"I had a wonderful time with my brother ... But I always do. But it's not easy seeing his condition. I want nothing more than to say I'm ready for his death, prepared for it—but I'm not."

Elegant hadn't, at his age, experienced waiting out death, or had been on a "death watch" for a relative, someone dear to him. He'd only experienced the suddenness of it, the brute force of it, striking without warning, any regard. Compassion was there, of course, but not the empathy of knowing that feeling, for what he saw, when young, was quite different—was shocking.

"I don't want to see him die, that's all there is to it, Elegant."

Pee-Pot covered his eyes, and Elegant was glad he was there in the room with him. Maybe before he had Gyp and would carry these emotions and agony of his from Martin County, Kentucky, back home and talk them through with Gyp. But maybe to share them with an actual human being, a person, someone who was beginning to care a lot for him—even if Gyp loved him—was better for him, at least he'd like to think it was, Elegant thought.

"Hope you don't mind if I make it more of a habit, Elegant," Pee-Pot said, his eyes tearing. "Hopping on the train now and then. Going off to Martin County."

"No, why of course not, Mr. Manners."

Pee-Pot's back straightened. "How's it feel to have a few more dollars in your pocket, by the way, son?"

"Great, sir."

It was a small purse, the fight at Fame Arena, but it's all Elegant was earning, expected to earn, small purses.

"They already want us back."

"They do, Mr. Manners!"

"And the sooner the better. Called Ambrose Felix yesterday, uh, the one who books everything in the Fame—and he was excited about us. He's always loved Tommie so wants to do another double bill with us. Keep it going. The fans were put out by you. Damned near crazy about you, Mr. Felix said."

Elegant did recall that part after the fight, the fans' warm vocal adulation—but during the fight, it was that one voice he heard, that single, solitary voice—Pee-Pot Manners's.

Pee-Pot coughed, clearing his throat. "You start with the fans, you know, Elegant."

No, Elegant didn't know that.

"Getting them on your side means a lot for you. Exciting them. Having them root you on."

"Confidence, uh, Mr. Manners."

"That, and when things ain't going so hot, like you'd like in the ring, a lot of times they can reverse them, the tide. Pull the win out for you. Particularly ... if you hit the canvas."

"Oh."

"They can get you off it. Back up on your feet. Seen it happen so many times, son, I've stopped counting. There's so much to this game. So much to learn."

Didn't he know it. Didn't he!

"Now talking about money in your pocket ..." Pee-Pot sounded as if he were going to shift the conversation entirely. "How about we put a little extra, let's say, in yours."

"Y-you're going to finally let me work, Mr. Manners? Work, sir!"

"Yes, sir. It's what we're gonna do!"

Elegant stood and emphatically shook Pee-Pot's hand. "Thank you, Mr. Manners. Thank you. Uh, when do I start, sir?"

"Soon as you want. But I've ... uh, you've gotta choice to make on it, Elegant. What job to pick."

Elegant stepped back from Pee-Pot. "I do, sir?"

"Told you when you got here you could work in the brickyard."

"Yes."

"Well, I should've said the brickyard or the lumberyard at the time. Given you a choice. Two jobs to pick from."

"Oh, right. Right, Mr. Manners. Sir."

"So which is it, Elegant? The hours are the same. Eight o'clock to four o'clock. So you ain't gonna get cheated in the paycheck. Either way you decide on it." Pause.

"And it'll be good training when you do. In the afternoons. For everybody, Elegant. Everybody."

———

Pee-Pot was upstairs, said he was going upstairs to get something, something he wanted to share with Elegant. So for Elegant, this was a good time for him to reflect on what had just transpired between him and Pee-Pot Manners in particular.

"I knew it would inevitably happen. But the timing of it. Or was it to happen, regardless?" For the key word that stuck out in the whole conversation on the subject of him working was "everybody."

"And it'll be good training when you do. In the afternoons. For everybody, Elegant. Everybody."

Who was "everybody" but Black Moon, no one else. Black Moon quit the gym by three thirty, so he'd be out the gym by the time he arrived. He wanted to say thank you to Pee-Pot at the time, but this was a nuanced gesture, one which was being handled with delicacy, "white gloves." But there was recognition of this escalating problem, Elegant thought. And as he kept winning victories in the ring, it would grow.

"I know one thing," Elegant said, sneaking a sly grin between the words, "we'll never be on the same fight card together. Black Moon and me."

So far it was him and Tommie—and it was perfect that way!

"Elegant, I'm back."

"Yes sir, Mr. Manners." Pause. "Records, sir?"

"I know you've noticed the Victrola down here. Out on the table."

"Yes, I have."

"Well, it's for these and a whole bunch more I got upstairs in the room. The Dixie Hummingbirds. Heard of them?"

"Oh, uh, yes, Mr. Manners."

"I've got two of these," Pee-Pot said, walking over to the Victrola on the table. "This one and the one in the room upstairs."

Elegant, up to now, hadn't been in Pee-Pot's bedroom—it was kept private. Pee-Pot seemed to know when to open and close the door according to Elegant's whereabouts in the house.

"So," Pee-Pot said lifting the Victrola's arm, "I'm gonna play you something special to me. And when I say that, I really mean special to Mrs. Manners. The name of the record is … just let me play it. Play if for you first."

The record came on, and the six voices of The Dixie Hummingbirds sounded like they'd brought heaven to Earth with the lightness of their sweet voices singing each note with spiritual love and devotion to a real Jesus, whom they didn't seem to be talking about but personally knew.

When the record stopped, Pee-Pot and Elegant seemed to be at a loss for words, until Pee-Pot said, "Have you ever heard anything like it, Elegant? Ever?"

"No, sir."

"Was Mrs. Manners's favorite song and mine too, before she was murdered one year later. 'I'm Leaning on the Lord.'"

Elegant realized it had to be the song's title, so it didn't surprise him.

"But then when she was murdered, Elegant, I-I …"

Pee-Pot not only played one record but two. Pee-Pot's hands no longer shook when he lifted the second record off the platter.

"'Wouldn't Mind Dying.' That song, it's how I felt inside. I did. Oh how I did. Should've been 'I Want to Die,' the title. And the second song was 'Where Was Moses.'"

Both songs were emotionally charged.

"I play my records when you're sleeping, son."

"I am a sound sleeper, sir."

"I know. Found out. And it's not the sad records I play anymore. I played you those to let you know how I used to feel. I still play 'I'm Leaning on the Lord' but later records of the Hummingbirds like 'Jesus, I Love You' and, oh, some others along the way."

"They're all sung by the Dixie Hummingbirds, Mr. Manners?"

"Every single one of them. Can't get enough of them. Not for the life of me. Messengers from God. There're times when you've really got to suffer to be healed. Really go down to the bottom of the well to be changed."

This was the ideal opening, Elegant thought—just like when he saw one inside the ring against an opponent.

"Mr. Manners ..."

"What, Elegant? Sounds like you're making a declaration of some kind."

"No, not really, sir. But I'd like to go to church."

"Church? Why, church. I'm a member of The Body of Christ Church," Pee-Pot laughed. "I do backslide from time to time. But who doesn't ... Uh, I guess I'm in one of those phases now."

"Is the church near here, Mr. Manners? Near the farmhouse, sir?"

"Oh, a mile outta town. Southwest. Fowler Road. It has a strong, powerful minister and congregation there. The minister's been at its helm for over twenty years. Pastor Embry O. Loving. Yes, by now, twenty or so years as pastor at its helm."

"Do, do you mind, Mr. Manners?"

"No, of course not, Elegant. We'll make it for this Sunday, in fact. I'm well overdue for the Body of Christ Church. Guess Pastor Loving'll be glad to see me out, Sunday morning, besides."

Elegant missed church a lot, but in a new environ, a new community, he'd taken things at a gradual pace—something which he did in View Point, Texas too, when he first arrived.

"So that's settled. Just hope Gyp recognizes me with a shirt and tie on—yes, sir, it's been that long between Sundays for me."

"Don't worry, Mr. Manners, Gyp'll still know your scent."

"Why it was how you were introduced to her, wasn't it?"

"Yes, it was, sir."

"Pee-Pot Manners and Gyp. We've both got ourselves some nicknames, don't we, son? Some nicknames." Pause.

"Yours is a Christian name, isn't it?"

"Yes, Mr. Manners, it is. Elegant Theodore Raines, sir."

Pee-Pot squirmed somewhat in the barber's chair he'd returned to. "So I guess I have to tell you another secret of mine."

"Yes ... Mr. Manners, what is it, sir?" Elegant said, coaxing Pee-Pot, who'd gone silent.

"This nickname of mine. Pee-Pot. How I got it. 'Cause my birth certificate officially reads 'Leemore Edgar Manners.' Exactly."

"Yes, you do, Mr. Manners. Uh, have to tell me, sir."

"Oh, uh, well ... Ha ...," Pee-Pot began uncomfortably. "Well ..."

CHAPTER 7

It was 7:51 a.m.

"Elegant, Mr. Miller, your new boss."

Angus Miller was a big, thick-bodied black man. He looked like a person who'd own—with five of his brothers—and run a brickyard: Miller Brothers Bricks. Yes, it's what Elegant chose, the brickyard over the lumberyard—thought it a bit more manly for a fighter.

Angus Miller shook Elegant's hand, and it was as if he were trying to squeeze blood from the very veins of it either to test his own strength against that of Elegant's (a fighter) or to show Elegant he was the more powerful of the two.

Inwardly, Pee-Pot was amused, for Angus Miller even did this to his bantamweight fighters on their first day of work at the yard.

"Nice having you aboard," Angus finally said. "Hope you like to work and work hard."

"Yes, I do, sir."

"'Cause we got plenty of it in the yard."

Angus Miller's nose was thicker than most. His teeth white, spacey, and chunky. He was in overalls, a hat, a blue-sleeved T-shirt, and dark-brown lumberjack boots knotted snugly at the ankles. His dense, wooly beard began a little ways below his Adam's apple and then raged across his face like a forest fire.

"Would think Pee-Pot bringing fighters from the gym to work here in the yard, there wasn't gonna be a lazy one in the crop. Was opposed to work."

Pee-Pot grimaced. He knew all too well what was to come next.

"But some was as lazy as the sun setting. And there ain't nobody who ain't seen that sight. Was all of them lazy down to their last bone an' muscle."

"I won't be one of them," Elegant said, looking anxiously at Angus Miller and then at Pee-Pot. "Not me, Mr. Miller."

"No," Pee-Pot said, shaking his head. "Ain't a thing you've got to concern yourself with, Angus. With this boy. With my boy Elegant here."

They were standing in the middle of the huge yard of trucks, bricks, and men. All the buildings were brick. The kilns where the brick was fired had six tall soot-blackened stacks sticking out their brick structures, shooting black smoke skyward and then disappearing into the mist in a quiet drift.

"Well, then come along with me and let me show you around, uh, then. See how everything goes. Works here in the yard."

While leading Elegant off with him, Angus Miller glanced at the top of Elegant's hatless head and then turned to Pee-Pot.

"Get the boy a cap in town, Pee-Pot. For his hair don't get singed. You know how dangerous this work out here is. Working the kilns," Angus said, pointing to one of the kilns to the left of him. "Better the hat than his hair burning. The hat you can take off, but the hair … ha …"

"Will do, Angus. Elegant, what's your hat size, son?"

"Uh, you don't have to bother, Mr. Raines. I can buy one in town when I come into the gym later, sir."

"Okay. See you later in the gym then."

"Yes, sir."

"Well … come along, Elegant," Angus said. "Let's see … uh, get you acquainted then."

"Yes, sir."

"You're in good hands, Elegant."

"Yes, Mr. Manners."

Pee-Pot headed for the dark avocado-green pickup truck.

"How lucky can one man get? Don't have a son, but I've got one now. Good as you can find. Anywhere. Anyplace. Thank you, Black Machine. Thank you."

Now there was real balance in his life, and Elegant felt blessed by it—home, family, a job. Working in a brickyard was hard work all right, but he was young and up to it. He had all the energy in the world, brimmed with it, and he couldn't wait to get to the gym to do his training and then get up tomorrow and do his roadwork in starting the entire process over. They had a shower room at the Miller plant, and he'd taken one. It was four fifteen in the afternoon, and he'd have to walk a mile into town and then, of course, look for a working man's cap and then get to the gym.

Elegant was outside the plant, looking back at it. He'd been treated well, he thought, Angus Miller right down to the full complement of workers had treated him like one of them. Then Elegant's mind switched back to the shower he just took at the plant: *I'm going to be the cleanest person in Longwood. A shower after I jog, one after work, and one after my gym work. And I might take a bath out at the house just to relax—that, I don't know about yet.*

Elegant walked into the gym, and scanning the floor, he didn't see Pee-Pot, so he walked into his office.

"Elegant!"

"Tommie!" Pause.

"Tommie, what are you still doing, doing here!"

"Man, let me look at that Applejack you got first. You sporting!"

"Like it?"

"On your head, you betcha!"

"Mr. ... uh ..."

"Squires."

"Yes. I'm so excited, I forgot his name. At the store. Who I bought it from."

"Worked you hard out there, huh? Angus Miller," Tommie laughed, "and his brothers. The Miller brothers, don't they?"

"Just what I need." It's when Elegant looked at Tommie and then up at the clock. "Uh, but, Tommie, Tommie, why aren't you at work?"

"Was gonna come out in the car for you. Pick you up, Elegant. But figured ... a mile? Mile out?"

"Right."

"If you was from up north, maybe. But … Oh, 'bout … Was waiting on you. Mr. Manners told me everything. I'm on a clock, but you know, it don't matter—they look the other way as long as I make up for it."

"Oh …"

"Which I'm gonna do."

Elegant tugged at the Applejack's bill and then removed it.

"H-have to get used to this darn thing."

"Oh, and if you looking for Mr. Manners, he's out cutting hair. Figure I was waiting on you so said to do your usual till he gets back. Got Mr. Patchett on the docket today."

"I gave him a haircut—"

"A free one, you mean to say," Tommie laughed.

"Right. Had a feeling his hair grew fast—"

"Even at his age!"

They laughed.

"Shit, it's great, ain't it," Tommie said, hugging Elegant, "us going back into Fame Arena together to put on a show. Boxing show, man."

"So Mr. Manners—"

"Let me know 'bout it, all of it. Man, Elegant, we gonna be a one-two combination," Tommie said, throwing just that, a one-two combination. "Elegant Raines and Tommie Lathers, outta the Pug, Pee-Pot Manners's gym in Longwood, West Virginia. Oh yeah, oh yeah—hell yeah!"

"That's right, Tommie."

"Conquer the South, then the North, then the East, then the West. You and me, Elegant, gonna be the most fantastic team in boxing. Going places!"

"Why not, Tommie? Why can't we!"

"It's why … it's why …"

"What?"

"Ain't gonna let nobody break us up. That's what."

"What do you mean by that?"

Tommie shifted his weight. "'Cause when I get to the factory today, gonna shorten my work hours. Instead of from four o'clock to twelve, gonna be six to twelve."

"Why?"

"Ain't it obvious, or do I have to hit you over the head with a brick.

One of Angus Miller's bricks. Shit! You ain't training, 'less I'm in this here gym training with you."

This news didn't fly well with Elegant. "But that's two hours of work, Tommie. You'll be missing. Of pay. Of lost pay every day."

"Won't, ain't gonna miss it. Just mean I gotta spend less. Keep a better ... closer eye on my loot, which I oughta be doing anyways," Tommie laughed.

"Thanks, I—"

"You do it for me, I know, if the shoe was on the other foot. So the way I look at it, I just beat you to it."

Elegant felt so good inside, further loved.

Now Tommie looked up at the clock and then at his watch, like it was going to tell him something different. "Ten to five. They give me a hour. Nothing more. It's a four-minute drive. So let me get outta here. Shit!"

"You're sure they'll let you cut back hours?"

"Yeah. They love me there, Elegant. Alla them. Don't wanna lose me. Keep them boys loose. Have a good time, for nothing don't get boring." Pause. "Just gonna be less of me, that's all."

———

"Gyp, you're sure you don't want to go with Mr. Manners and me?"

"To church? No, that's not Gyp's style, Elegant. Never been. Not on a Sunday."

Woof!

"Sunday's just another day for Gyp—if you ain't noticed."

Elegant and Pee-Pot stood by the Studebaker and dressed in three-piece suits. Elegant was toting his Bible, and Pee-Pot his.

"We'll pray for you, Gyp," Pee-Pot said, getting into the truck before Elegant. "How's that?"

Elegant walked to the back of the truck and pet Gyp.

Both were in the truck. The truck was out in the road.

Woof!

"See you, Gyp!"

"See you, Gyp!"

Woof! Woof!

The truck was approaching the Body of Christ Church on Fowler Road.

It was a white wooden church as so many Southern churches are, with a tall golden steeple, multicolored stained glass windows, a slanted roof, and white magnolia bushes flanking the wide white porch steps leading up and into the Body of Christ Church.

As far as Elegant was concerned, the church's exterior looked like it'd been scrubbed down with soap, water, and a brush; it looked so sparkling clean. *Maybe*, he thought, *I'm the cleanest person in Longwood, but the Body of Christ Church is the cleanest building in Longwood—by far.*

There were a few cars and trucks and wagons, but most of the church folk heading into the church were on foot. It was a beautiful day for walking, and maybe this was usual, conventional for this type of Longwood day.

"It's a beautiful sight, people going into a church on a Sunday morning, ain't it, Elegant?"

"It is, Mr. Manners. And it's going to feel good joining them. It's been a while for me, sir. In church."

"Well, I don't know how long 'ages' is in regard to time, we tend to use it so regular … but it has been ages for me."

Ten o'clock was the church service, and it was nine thirty-seven, and there didn't seem to be any rush in the air. Elegant was feeling the peacefulness of the moment, how he wanted to feel, a manifest grace and elegance and self-satisfaction before entering the Body of Christ Church, into the house of the Lord to pray and to confess to the sins of the accrued weeks of turmoil and tensions and inconsistencies, first with Pee-Pot and then his internal unrest, strife, disdain for Black Moon, tipping almost into hatred of him for how he talked to him in the gym, not forgetting those words, not purging them out his mind but hearing them echo as if he were on trial to forgive him, as a Christian, a man of faith and God—to pray for Black Moon with neither malice in his heart, mind, soul, or fists.

The brown-stained oak pews glistened. The church was three quarters full, but with folk still quickly gathering, it'd probably be filled in a matter of minutes. The church's interior was big and open with maroon carpeting leading from its center aisle forward to the nave and then to include the pulpit. In fact, there were two tall pulpits on either side of the church. In the background, a long brass pole draped in maroon crush velvet, with large globular brass knobs on both ends, ran the length of the pulpit area's floor. It was an area reserved for the choir that had not yet marched out from the choir loft and down the aisle and trumpeted the official beginning of the church service with big, brassy sounds for Jesus.

Pee-Pot and Elegant were sitting way back in the church. Their sight lines were unblocked by the great numbers of huge-sized flowery hats worn by the women of the church. Both were lucky in this regard. But not yet knowing the characteristics of his surroundings, Elegant, soon, was enveloped by fragrances of sweetness that had nothing to do with the church's setting or the flora and fauna on the grassy grounds but with the women of the church—as if they'd, this very morning, collectively met at the river's bank and bathed lovingly in the blue Sea of Galilee.

So accustomed to the fragrance, Pee-Pot hadn't reacted to it; instead, he thumbed his Bible open and studied scripture. Then he put the bulletin there on the page as a marker, for the bulletin had indicated it would be the first scripture read by Pastor Embry O. Loving during the service.

"It's such a beautiful church, Mr. Manners."

"And we're all proud of it. Pastor Loving doesn't have to plead or pray for money—we give it willingly. There's a lot of goodwill in this church. Good folk in here."

The congregation stirred, and Elegant looked over his shoulder, to the back of the church—the middle aisle.

Pee-Pot's head cranked backward. "That's him, Pastor Loving."

Elegant was looking at a tall, erect-postured black man. A man as dark as him. A man in a plain, black, neat robe who wore glasses, who was smiling as if he'd sat down with Jesus, John, and Peter and had a breakfast of fish and a loaf of bread and then broke the bread in half, feeding it to the poor with deep love.

The choir stood behind him, three rows deep.

"This is a call to worship," Pastor Loving announced. "We praise his name with *jubilation*!"

The congregation stood. It's when the Body of Christ Church choir burst forth with song. Pastor Loving and his assistant pastor, Pastor Joseph Green, made their way down the long aisle. The choir blended into two abreast.

"That's Pastor Loving's daughter, Francine Loving, in the middle there," Pee-Pot said.

"She's beautiful, Mr. Manners."

"You should see the other one, Gem Loving. She's a college student. School's out, so she's probably off doing something. She's always doing something for somebody. Going off on Christian retreats."

Just how pretty could this Gem Loving be, Elegant thought, if she was prettier than her sister Francine Loving, whom he was still looking at. He'd dare not try to imagine, Elegant further thought.

———

Pastor Loving was standing at the front door of the church. Church service was over, and he was performing the functioning duty of greeting his flock. He was doing it with, what appeared, genuine enthusiasm and spunk.

"Mr. Manners, I thought I saw you when the collection plate was passed!"

"Cut enough heads this week to afford church this morning, Pastor—"

"And who's the handsome young man beside you?"

"Elegant Raines, sir," Elegant said as Pastor Loving hugged Pee-Pot.

"Glad to meet you, Mr. Raines," Pastor Loving said, shaking Elegant's hand.

"He's a fighter of mine."

"I kind of unified the logic of the two of you together … Sister Jaleeza … Now don't you go anywhere. Mr. Manners, please … uh, Sister Jaleeza's been under the weather, so just let me touch her hand in prayer."

Pastor Loving did this, and now with the receiving line having thinned, his attention rebounded to Pee-Pot and Elegant. "Now, your home, Mr. Raines?"

"I'm from Oklahoma. New Town, Oklahoma. But, uh, uh, came in from View Point, Texas, sir. My trainer died." Pause. "Frank 'Black Machine' Whaley, Pastor Loving, sir."

"Uh, boxers, fighters, forgive me, but as Mr. Manners knows, I know little about them, Mr. Raines. But may God bless him and keep him well."

"So of course," Pee-Pot said, "I'm Elegant's trainer now."

"You carry a Bible, son."

"Yes, sir."

"Hmm ... the King James Version."

"Yes, sir."

"So you brought religion with you from View Point, Texas. Is that it, Mr. Raines?"

"I did, sir."

"You really got him going this morning, as well as me, Pastor Loving."

"It, it was a wonderful sermon, sir."

"Thank you," Pastor Loving said, pressing Elegant's hand. "So you've settled into Longwood now, Mr. Raines?"

"Quite comfortably, sir."

"Staying out at the house with me, Pastor Loving."

They were off the church porch and down the steps and on the grass.

"You and Gyp, you mean, don't you, Mr. Manners? Mustn't leave Gyp out of the picture."

"Me and Gyp. That's right. She won't let me."

"How is Gyp, by the way?"

"I'll let Elegant answer that one since they do roadwork in the morning together. At five thirty."

"We run in the woods, Pastor Loving. Behind the house, sir. Uh, five miles every morning. Yes, at five thirty, like Mr. Manners said, sir."

Francine Loving was exiting the church with her girlfriends. They'd formed a neat huddle over by the white magnolias. They were busy ogling Elegant but not from where either Elegant or Pee-Pot or Pastor Loving could see them.

But then angling much more to his right, Pastor Loving spotted them and what they were doing.

"Girls, and particularly you, Francine, can find something better to do with yourselves, I'm sure, than just standing there giggling."

"Yes, uh, yes, Papa."

"Yes, Pastor Loving. Sir."

"So off with you now," Pastor Loving said as if he were shooing pigeons.

"And, Francine, aren't you supposed to be helping Sister Higginson with her Sunday cooking this afternoon?"

"Yes, sir. I'll head home now. And o-over to Miss Higginson's, sir."

"Thank you," Pastor Loving said reasonably. "Francine."

But when Pastor Loving turned his back, Francine kept her eyes trained on Elegant, she and her girlfriends. Lightly they giggled this time, sure not to draw additional attention to themselves.

"I guess Francine will be off to college before we know it, Pastor Loving. Like Gem."

"We're going to try to get her off to Howard University. Matriculate there like Gem. My old alma mater. Talk her into it. But, uh, as it stands now, she's toying with Spelman College down in Georgia."

"By the way, where is Gem?"

"Gem, oh, Gem ... on a Christian retreat, where else, Mr. Manners?" Pause. "She can't ... no, I'll do myself even better—she won't sit still. That girl, not Gem. Those two girls of mine couldn't be greater contrasts, even though they're a year and a half apart in age. Gem's so serious, and Francine so playful. Whimsical—"

"You mean to say driven. Gem's driven."

"Are you driven, Mr. Raines? Regarding your boxing?"

"Yes, I am, sir."

Pastor Loving shook Elegant's hand. "Welcome to Longwood, Mr. Raines. And the best of luck to you."

"Thank you, Pastor Loving."

"And Mr. Manners, do say hello to Gyp for me. She's such a special dog."

"Sure will."

Then Pastor Loving turned and walked back into the church.

Pee-Pot turned to his right. "That's Pastor Loving's manse, the one over there, Elegant."

It was a two-level finely built structure.

"It's just him and the girls. His wife, Helena, died three years ago. Oh, how she was loved by everybody in this community. Forty-two years old, Elegant. Forty-two years old. Tuberculosis. Had barely lived."

They were nearing the truck.

"This community really rallied around Pastor Loving. His loss was our loss. To lose a woman like Helena Loving was ... well ... it was heart wrenching." Pause.

"When I lost Mrs. Manners, it was Helena Loving who helped me in ways I will never forget. Even came to the house and cooked meals for me. Gyp and her became fast buddies ... those two, all right."

Pee-Pot looked down to Pastor Loving's manse with what seemed a measure of pride.

"He's raising those two girls of his beautifully. Even though Gem is just like her mother."

Pee-Pot and Elegant were on the opposite sides of the truck, passenger and driver sides.

Opening the door, appearing as if he was about to get in the truck, Pee-Pot stopped. "Elegant, why don't you come with me? I'd like to show you something. Yes, son, come with me."

Pee-Pot took Elegant's hand. Then after a few feet, he released it. He walked out of the dirt area and onto the grass, heading for the back of the church. Elegant saw what was ahead of him and what to expect.

Shortly, they stood in front of Cora Manners's headstone, reading:

Born May 3, 1878–Died August 10, 1939
IN LOVING MEMORY—A HEART OF GOLD

Flowers were at the base of the headstone.

"I come out once a week, Elegant," Pee-Pot said, touching the flowers. "Would've come with flowers. But I don't usually come out with anybody. Sometimes Gyp, but it's still hard on her. So I don't force her."

Pee-Pot removed his hat. "I'll bring some fresh flowers for her. Cora ... Mrs. Manners tomorrow."

Then he walked away, going about ten feet. He stood in front of another headstone.

Elegant walked over to join him.

"Helena Loving."

"Yes, Mr. Manners."

There were fresh flowers at the base of Helena Loving's marble headstone.

"Such lovely, remarkable women, Elegant, only a few feet apart. Heaven right here on Earth." Pee-Pot kept mumbling, shaking his head.

———

Two weeks later, Elegant got to see Tommie fight on a fifth-round stoppage of Mike "King of Hearts" Williams. Tommie opened up bad cuts above both his eyes. It was an excellent victory for Tommie. Williams was a young up-and-coming prospect too.

It was another ten-card fight night at Fame Arena in Morgantown, West Virginia. It was another near-capacity house. Tommie was the third fighter on the boxing card, Elegant the seventh. Gas, Elegant, and Pee-Pot were on the floor, beneath Elegant's corner.

"Make it short, okay, Elegant," Tommie whispered in Elegant's ear. "Hit that boy so much. Wanna get back to the boarding house to rest my arm."

Elegant wanted to laugh but restrained himself; it was something he'd never do just before entering the ring—laugh.

The fighter he was to face tonight was out of the rough-and-tumble fight town of Pittsburgh, Pennsylvania.

After Elegant got into the ring, Jimmy "Ironhead" James moved into the ring too.

From behind Elegant's corner, Tommie laughed at him, thinking Ironhead James and his iron head don't know what's about to hit them like a sledgehammer.

"He's a tough customer—it's all I know about him, Elegant," Pee-Pot said while removing Elegant's black robe.

After the referee's ring instructions, Elegant was back in his corner, and Pee-Pot slipped the mouthpiece in his opened mouth.

For a boxing trainer, if they'd never seen the fighter his fighter was to face in the ring, they'd have to rely on a network of other trainers who were willing to share information—then they could get a good take on the fighter's style, their strengths and weaknesses. But this wasn't the case with Ironhead James—Pee-Pot only knew he was a "tough customer."

Tonight, Elegant's body felt excellent.

Clang.

When Elegant came out his corner, his black back shined with sweat.

Ironhead James was squat and compact. He was built along the lines of Black Moon Johnson but shorter. He had short arms, so immediately, Elegant thought James couldn't outjab him, so he zinged him with a jab and then another. These were hefty jabs, hard as concrete, jarring Ironhead's head back each time he was hit.

Again and again Elegant hit him with the jab, disrupting any rhythm Ironhead hoped to muster. Now Ironhead James was trying to block the jabs. But resorting to head feints and displaying exceptional footwork and patience, Elegant's jabs were still able to break through Ironhead's failing defenses.

The fight fans in the Fame were oohing and aahing, for it was that kind of exhibition of boxing skill and power from Elegant.

The right side of Ironhead's head was already swelling, was as lumpy as a bag of fruit. And then there was another loud-sounding jab to his face to augment the lumping. And then there was a jab from Elegant that was quickly followed by a sweeping uppercut, and this punch knocked Ironhead backward, his wheels (legs) guiding him into Elegant's corner. Elegant pursued him by shooting another wicked jab down to his solar plexus and then back up to his head while edging closer to him.

Squaring his shoulders to Ironhead, standing tall and balanced, his feet in the right position to generate proper power, Elegant bashed Ironhead's body with a left hook and then, seeing his eyes deaden, Elegant delivered a short right-hand cross flush on his chin.

The referee began counting the ten count out over Jimmy "Ironhead" James accurately.

———

Pee-Pot didn't make his way into Martin County, Kentucky, to see Biscuit this trip but promised he would his next visit to Morgantown.

Everybody was back in Longwood—him, Tommie, Gas, and Elegant. This was the day after the fight in Morgantown. They'd trained back. He'd been back in the farmhouse for a few hours. He'd taken a nap and was back on his feet, about to put on his shoes, about to cut hair down in the basement for the usual gang: Lyle Pete, Josh Barnes, Willie Jenkins, and Wilbert Jenkins.

Was he ever pleased with both Tommie and Elegant's performances last night. Tommie was really moving along quickly. It's great to have a big punch in any weight division but something not necessary in the lower weight divisions, welterweights on down. Tommie didn't have a big punch but knew how to punch. He could literally beat another fighter up, Pee-Pot thought. He could pound and batter his opponent into submission with his relentless attacking style and his above-average conditioning. He was born to fight. Just like his father, Tommie Lathers Sr.

It's why he was so hopeful for him. Only, he knew a dirty little secret about Tommie, something that hadn't surfaced as a problem yet. But it had worried him from the reports he'd gotten, of late, from a few Pug fighters. Pee-Pot was surprised he hadn't taken action, hadn't sat down and talked to Tommie about it. Maybe it was because the "problem" hadn't affected Tommie's daily training or ring performances if that was a safe rationale to apply.

He was keeping an eye on the situation. He didn't want to panic yet, make a mountain out of a molehill.

Looking at last night, at Elegant, once again, he had proved he was the most intelligent, efficient fighter he'd ever trained. Last night, inside the ring, he did things with such precision, execution; it truly was a remarkable performance he'd witnessed.

"Gas," he'd said to Gaston Moore, "Elegant's got it all in there."

"I think so too," Gas replied. "A year from now, I think we'll be echoing the same praise."

It was just sinister the way he took apart Ironhead James, Pee-Pot thought. In a way, unfair when a fighter of Elegant's caliber is that good, that talented. It was just odd though how Elegant retreated from the corner as soon as Ironhead James met the canvas, Pee-Pot thought. How eager he was to stop fighting. Appearing as if in no way did he want Ironhead to get back up so he'd have to hit him again, deliver another punishing blow. There was this cryptic, perplexed look in Elegant's eyes—for he always tried to learn as much as possible from his fighters, to see what he could see in their most unguarded and private moments in the ring.

For the life of him, Pee-Pot knew Ironhead James wasn't getting up off the canvas, so he could study Elegant like this, in finding Elegant, his disposition, in the ring, more and more curious. Turning Elegant into a curiosity—in many ways—a puzzle. What was his nature? Did he carry the Bible into the ring? Was he a Christian inside the ring as well as out? Did he really want to hurt a man? Couldn't tolerate to see but so much of that person's pain if he hurt him beyond some measurable, acceptable level, some human, decent level he'd morally adjudged?

Boxing is such a psychological sport, Pee-Pot thought.

A fighter's psychological makeup is at as much risk as his courage. But fear, no, he hadn't seen fear in Elegant yet, especially fear of what another man could do to him, only in what he could do to another man.

"I don't … I ain't blowing this thing up," Pee-Pot said. "What I've seen, I … It's accurate and consistent."

It was Elegant's background, and he knew but so much of it. His parents being deceased. And there being no relatives to take him into their home or life, an orphan of the state (basically a ward), a difficult life. But his life only reflected a rooted reality, Pee-Pot thought, in Southern and Northern communities for black folk. He could line ten black people up, and six to seven out of the ten could tell Elegant Raines's story in some similar, if not familiar, detail. So by coming to him the way he did, there was no reason for him to dig too deeply into his past, tie up his psychological résumé.

But after last night he was more curious about him. Not what Elegant did, for he saw what he did to a man, but what he needed to know now was what Elegant felt about what he did to another fighter after destroying him inside the ring.

Elegant had waited for Pee-Pot to come upstairs. It was 9:10 p.m. He heard him out on the landing, so Elegant opened his bedroom door.

"Mr. Manners, sir, may I see you for a minute? In the room, sir."

"How long you been waiting for me to come up, Elegant?"

"Oh …"

"Gladly."

Elegant stood off to the side of the door until Pee-Pot got in to the room.

"Should I sit?"

"By all means, Mr. Manners."

Pee-Pot laughed into his hand and then sat. "Is this serious, Elegant?"

The reason why Pee-Pot asked was because Elegant, probably, unconsciously, had paced back and forth across the floor and seemed he was ready to do it again.

"Serious …? Yes, a little, sir."

"Oh, then, I'd better straighten my back and not slouch."

Pee-Pot's intent was not to trivialize the situation, but he also knew it couldn't be but so serious if related to Elegant.

"Mr. Manners … I am a man."

"Uh, what's that to mean, Elegant? Of course you are. Who said you weren't?"

"Oh, nobody, Mr. Manners. But … uh … but …"

"Elegant, this is rather most unusual between us. Do you want me to twist your arm, son?"

"Uh, no, no, that's not necessary, Mr. Manners. N-not at all …" Pause. "Really, though, sir, I should've said I'm a young man … and, well, I like girls, Mr. Manners."

"Well, I hope you do, Elegant!" Pee-Pot said after that heartfelt declaration and admission by Elegant.

"So … Tommie, Tommie has invited me out with him next Friday night, Mr. Manners. To go over into Inwood with him. Meet some girls, sir. Over there, uh, sir."

A chill ran through Pee-Pot, and it wasn't because of Inwood or because of girls, but because of what it was reported to him by the Pug fighters what Tommie did in Inwood. But how in the world could he say no to Elegant. How could he restrict a young man of eighteen who wanted to go out and have fun, meet girls—he should have that privilege and opportunity.

"Is, is it all right, sir?" Elegant asked, his voice quavering. "Would you want me to, Mr. Manners?"

"Why, of course. Why would I stand in your way? On, on something like this?"

"Phew ... I don't know, know, Mr. Manners. Tommie's going to drive us there. In his car. Just him and me, it seems, sir."

"That would be nice, Elegant."

"I don't feel cooped up here, Mr. Manners. Uh, just the opposite. I—"

"You don't have to explain yourself any more than what you have, Elegant. The key word in all this, of course, was, 'young man.'"

I guess it was, Elegant said to himself. *Yes, of course it was.*

Pee-Pot stood and then walked up to Elegant, touching his shoulder lightly. "Just have a good time in Inwood. You deserve it. For what you've done."

Elegant felt goose bumps prickle on his skin.

———

Pee-Pot was back inside his room. He was glancing through stacks of records. He had the oil lamp's light on, so the rest of the room was pretty much curtained in darkness. He'd carried some of the records over from the cabinet in the room. He had records of The Golden State Quartet of Norfolk, Virginia, and The Famous Blue Jay Singers of Birmingham and Jefferson County but was looking at a Dixie Hummingbird record, one he was surely going to play on the Victrola tonight, when he was certain Elegant and Gyp were asleep.

There were nights when he just needed to be soothed, to be taken back to a better time, to a time when everything was okay; a time he took for granted—not until tragedy struck. His thumb stopped at another record he was going to play on the Victrola tonight. He knew what Elegant requested tonight was inevitable—just a matter of time.

"You mustn't forget your spring times. No. Uh-uh. When you were young, Pee-Pot. Out fooling around with girls."

No matter how strict the times, there were always loose girls. And any young man who wanted one found them. And he found them when he was young, plenty of them, when sex mattered as much as anything, taking a backseat to nothing.

Now it was going to be a matter of how much influence Tommie was going to have on Elegant or how much influence Elegant was going to have on Tommie next Friday night, Pee-Pot thought.

"But that's foolish of me, foolish of me to think that way," Pee-Pot said, chiding himself, setting the records aside. For Pee-Pot knew, of the two, Tommie had the more dominant personality. That if anyone was going to rule over anyone, it would be Tommie over Elegant—even if he didn't want to put it in such stark terms, a context, as rule. But when you have a dominating personality like Tommie Lathers's, it's the end result.

Pee-Pot shut his eyes. His eyes were tired. He'd had a long day. Maybe, at his age, they were beginning to merge, catch up with him.

"No," Pee-Pot said, rubbing his eyes, "ain't gonna be that easy. Make it that easy for ol' Father Time. I'm gonna fight to end of the line. I'm a fighter."

Energetically, Pee-Pot hopped off the bed and got into his fighting stance. He winged a punch and then another and then bounced up on his toes.

"Oh, if Elegant could've seen me. If he could've but seen the old Pee-Pot Manners in his heyday."

Pee-Pot took one last crack at his opponent's jaw.

"He would've seen a marvel in the ring. Nothing less than a marvel."

CHAPTER 8

"Shit, Elegant ... man, it was like Mr. Manners was sending you off to war. Ain't just kidding neither."

"I know."

"We just going over into Inwood. Not no foreign land, ter-territory, man."

Still in Inwood, the car was bouncing along on a rather uneven, bumpy road.

"It's a good thing Gyp understood," Elegant laughed.

"Yeah, one wag of her tail, and we in like Flynn."

"Tommie, that's the first I've heard that."

Tommie laughed. "Don't know, Elegant, picked it up from somewhere."

"What's it mean?"

"Who knows, it just fits, don't it?"

"Yes. Yes, it does. Does."

"See. See."

"Right. Right."

"It's all you gotta know. If it fits or not."

Tommie was coolly dressed, wearing a striped newspaper cap, an open white shirt, short sleeved, high-waisted pants (with suspenders), and brown cordovan shoes.

Elegant sort of mirrored Tommie, the exception being, he was hatless.

It was 8:20 p.m.

"Gonna meet some hot girls tonight, Elegant—and I do mean hot!"

I'm all for it, Tommie! Elegant said to himself.

"Know you ain't a ..."

"No. No, I'm not a virgin, Tommie. Not that."

Tommie's hand slapped the steering wheel. "Yeah, like I said, know you ain't a virgin!"

They laughed.

"But it's been a while you been here, in Longwood."

"Hasn't it, Tommie!"

"But one night out with me, and well ..."

Elegant knew Tommie didn't have to fill in the blanks.

A little later.

"Well, we just left Longwood and crossed into Inwood."

"I thought the air changed, felt a lot different."

"Ha. Pretty colored girls in alla Virginia—but they got some of the prettiest girls 'round here. Not that we gonna run into a bunch of preachers' daughters."

Elegant knew what Tommie was getting at but didn't quite know why he used that expression.

"'Cause Pastor Loving got some gorgeous-looking daughters. Francine Loving—but 'specially Gem. Gem Loving. Know you and Mr. Manners got off to church the other Sunday. So you got an opportunity to see Gem Loving."

"Uh, no, no, I didn't, Tommie."

"You don't!" Tommie had said it as if a crime had been committed.

"Pastor Loving said she, uh, Miss Loving was on a Christian retreat."

"Oh, yeah—so one of them again, huh? Man, she just so straitlaced. Gem Loving. So straitlaced." Tommie said that as if it were a crime too. "Oh, I don't mean it any like that, Elegant—'cause everybody in town loves Gem, Gem, man. She's got her a heart of gold. But when you as beautiful as her, shit. If I was gonna get married—which I ain't ha ... not on your life—Gem Loving's gonna be the one. For sure. Quite definitely. Without a doubt. Gem Loving."

And Elegant was convinced of Tommie's sincerity—he really was.

"But wait till you see her. Your eyes gonna pop out on your lap. Or, shit, Joe Louis hit you with an uppercut while your hands was down!"

Elegant laughed.

"Look ahead, Elegant. Look ahead!"

And it wasn't as if Elegant had to so much look but listen to the honky-tonk blues, how it was churning up a beehive of activity out front of a jook joint named Angel's Corner as the 1941 Ford Super Deluxe approached the building dead-on.

"You can dance, right, Elegant?"

"Sure can."

"Just come out with a new dance 'round here. In Inwood. The Crocodile Crawl, but you don't wanna do that one. Touch that!"

Off to the left of the Angel's Corner was where the cars and the wagons were; Tommie parked the car there.

"Okay, Elegant, let's take in, gulp in some air, 'cause it might be the last time tonight we gonna, might get a chance to."

Elegant gulped in some air, and so did Tommie—and then laughed.

"Let's go!"

"Okay!"

Together they hopped out of the Ford.

When they circled around the front of the building, Elegant could really see things clearly, this one body of motion. Of young folk bodies writhing to the music, teenagers his age, and there were beautiful black girls galore.

"Shit, what I tell you, Elegant. What I tell you! Tommie Lathers don't lie!"

"No, you don't, Tommie!"

"Not for a dollar. Not for a quarter. Shit, not for nothing you sock in your pocket!"

Heads turned.

"Hey, Tommie!"

"Tommie!"

"Hey, everybody!"

Then Tommie turned to Elegant. "Let's get inside."

When they got inside Angel's Corner, this barn-sized place was teeming with young folk.

The live eight-piece band consisted of two female vocalists and one male. The male vocalist, in a three-piece powder-blue suit, sat while the two female vocalists, adorned in pink and green cocktail dresses and long earrings that practically dragged the stage floor, sang. Even in this backwoods honky-tonk, they sang like both were inspired by every blues singer who ever sang to keep tomorrow from knocking at their door.

"Oh, I forgot to tell you, mention when I asked you if you can dance, Elegant, that I'm the best dancer in these here parts, man."

Elegant let out a howl of a laugh. "Says who, Tommie?"

"Got the cash to prove it. Well, actually, spent all of it by now. But I won me so many dance contests they thinking about banning me next!"

"Tommie!" one of the four bartenders behind the bar shouted.

"Tommie's here!"

Tommie acknowledged everyone like he was standing in the ring, waving to his legion of fans. Even some of the band members waved at him—and both female vocalists. And it was as if the drummer had hit the cymbals extra hard (it's what it seemed to Elegant) to further announce Tommie's heroic arrival at Angel's Corner.

But then some heads began turning Elegant's way—from the female population in Angel's Corner—and Elegant didn't mind the attention, not in the least.

"Yeah, bait them like honey, Elegant. Bait them babes like honey. Shit," Tommie said, snapping his striped suspenders.

And in a flash, as if he were in the ring again and his reflexes super, Tommie's hand flashed cash. "Scotch and bourbon on the rocks, Lonnie!"

"Already started pouring, Tommie, when I seen you come in!"

"And what about you, Elegant? Same thing?"

"No need to, Tommie. I don't drink."

"You don't?"

"No."

Tommie pinched his fingers apart. "Not even a little?"

"Not even a—"

"What about beer?"

"What about your friend there, Tommie?"

"No, no, uh-uh, Lonnie. Nothing for him, just my—"

"Usual," Lonnie said, pushing the two whiskey glasses on the bar toward Tommie.

"'Scuse me, Elegant."

And then Tommie gulped down the glass of bourbon first and then the glass of scotch second.

Then Lonnie pushed two more glasses with the same liquor content Tommie's way, and Tommie repeated himself.

"Now I'm ready to dance, Elegant. Get out there on the dance floor. What about—"

"Me too."

"Just grab a girl and twirl her 'round the worl'. Shit, certainly is 'nough of them, ain't—"

But then someone was tapping Elegant on the shoulder, and he turned, and then Tommie looked behind Elegant's back.

"Hey, whatta you say, Tammi-Ray?"

"Oh, hi, Tommie."

Then a pretty young lady with tangled hair and sweaty skin snatched Tommie's hand.

"Come on, Tommie. You owe me a dance. From last week!"

"Okay, Elegant, you on your own. Damn, Fredericka here's like a alligator, man!"

"So, that's your name? Elegant?"

"Uh, yes. Yes, it is"

She was short and quite cute.

"You heard mine then," she said shyly.

"Yes."

"Tammi-Ray." Pause.

"You're tall and handsome."

"Oh, thanks."

"No bother."

She had a drink in her hand and then eagerly drank it down, not like Tommie but close. She turned to her left, and left the glass on the bar.

"I'd like to dance with you, if you'd like."

"Oh, sure … sure thing."

"Basically, I'm shy, but you're so handsome, Elegant, that …" And then she grabbed Elegant's hand.

She was leading Elegant to the dance floor that was a few feet away, and Elegant, since she was in front of him, was able to catch a good, clear look at her backside and saw she was built from the ground up, as the saying goes—with buttocks round as an Arkansas moon and packed tight. Elegant wasn't missing a wrinkle in her dark-blue skintight skirt. Her waist was narrow; Tammi-Ray had an hourglass figure.

Everyone was slow dragging, so Tammi-Ray and Elegant joined them. Of course Elegant wasn't able to alter his center of gravity, but Tammi-Ray lifted her body up neatly to him to receive the full, maximum effect of the lazy, indulgent grinds and thrusts of his hips.

Elegant didn't know how he felt, not having a girl in his arms for so long. He'd had sex in barns and behind bushes and even in beds (a few times). He started with sex at fourteen and now, of course, was eighteen. He never forced a girl to have sex with him—not to do anything they didn't want to do.

"You dance nice, Elegant."

"Thanks."

"Real nice." Pause.

"When you gonna call me Tammi-Ray?"

"I'm sorry, I didn't know I hadn't."

"It's all right. You're proper, aren't you?"

"I really am sorry, Tammi-Ray."

Tammi-Ray held Elegant tighter to her—if that was at all possible. Elegant shut his eyes; he wanted to take his mind off everything.

When the band switched over to a new song, the male vocalist singing it, Elegant opened his eyes and saw Tommie back over at the Angel's Corner's bar, and it was the same routine as before: Tommie with two whiskey glasses and both being drunk down and then two new glasses of whiskey and them being drunk down. Elegant didn't know what to think now.

Another girl ran up to Tommie, shouting out his name, grabbing his hand, and Tommie was back out on the dance floor. Elegant shut his eyes. The slow drag, the tempo hadn't changed. He and Tammi-Ray's body were still locked skin tight, and sweat was dampening him. It began to drip from his hairline and onto his forehead, and Tammi-Ray had her head buried in his lower chest, and she moaned a few times, and she did feel good to him too, but he wouldn't dare touch her buttocks, her backside, even though it seemed she wanted him to, but he kept his large hands in the small of her back, a back that was strong and supple.

The band was about to transition into a new song, when a young man with a checkered jacket—tall, curly haired, sporting a goatee, light skinned—ran over to Tammi-Ray.

"Hey, how 'bout it, Tammi-Ray ... what you say? You ain't dancing with him all night, is you?"

"Baron—"

"Come on, girl, the band's 'bout to jump one!"

He snatched Tammi-Ray's arm. She was about to protest, but Baron grabbed her around the waist, so off they flew.

Elegant was heading for the bar, when—

"Not so damned fast. You ain't getting away from me that easy!"

And before Elegant knew it, he was in the arms of this big-bosomed girl who already had him corralled.

"Honey, baby, my name's Big Maylene, and I'm able to do anything you want me to do to you!"

Elegant laughed. "My name's Elegant."

"Tommie! Tommie!"

And it's as if the ocean had parted since everyone cleared room on the dance floor for Tommie.

"Tommie's doin' it! Tommie's doin' it! The Crocodile Crawl! The Crocodile Crawl!"

And Elegant had to see this for himself. And Big Maylene appeared just as eager to too. Both got as close as they could get to him outside the ringed circle.

And Tommie and a long, thin, spidery-shaped girl were stretched out on the dance floor, on opposite ends, their noses meeting in the middle, inches apart, but their bodies doing these wild, strange, odd-looking but rhythmically sensible contortions, like dancing, gyrating crocodiles minus scaly tails, their eyes locked in fierce, ritual combat, one seemingly daring the other to come up with a better move or gesture—a better way their bodies could maneuver themselves, something even more primitive, primal, and fun.

"Tommie! Tommie!"

Everyone in Angel's Corner screamed.

He was putting on a show, Elegant thought, just like he did inside the ring.

Time had passed in Angel's Corner, and Tammi-Ray had found her way back to Elegant. She whispered something in his ear. Elegant nodded his head.

Tommie was with a tall, wild-eyed girl, and when he saw Elegant and Tammi-Ray leaving the dance floor and the song was yet over, he caught on …

"Come on, Annie, you and me got something to do."

"Oh yeah, Tommie!"

"Hey, Elegant!"

Elegant stopped in his tracks.

When Tommie got to Elegant, he walked him off to the side of the bar.

"Pardon us, ladies."

"You …?"

"Yes."

"You know how to drive, don't you?"

"Sure, Tommie."

"Here're the keys. Just slide the car off 'bout hundred yards, just 'fore you hit the woods. That's all."

Tommie turned to Annie.

"Shit, come on, girl! I got plans for you!"

"I know, Tommie, I know!"

The four walked out Angel's Corner together. When they got to Tommie's car, Tommie tapped Elegant's shoulder.

"Uh, sorry, Elegant …" He had his hand out.

Elegant handed Tommie the keys. Then Tommie went in the rear of the car, opened the trunk, and then shut it and came back around to the side of the car, and they all laughed, for Tommie was carrying a blanket.

"We ain't doing it in the car tonight, Annie!"

Annie grabbed Tommie's hand, and they headed for the back woods.

Elegant looked down at Tammi-Ray, and even with this slight interruption, they still looked steamy. Elegant opened the car door for her. Then he got in the car. Elegant drove the car about a hundred yards ahead, at the edge of the woods, and parked it there—just as Tommie had told him to do.

Tammi-Ray leaned toward him, and they began tongue kissing right away—something they hadn't done in Angel's Corner.

Now Elegant was touching her buttocks, and her hand was moving up his leg and toward his crotch.

"T-he backseat, Elegant ..."

"I-I know."

He leaned toward the door. But she grabbed him one more time, smothering him with kisses until they disengaged.

She got out of the car, and so did he. They were about to enter the rear of the car, when Tammi-Ray turned around to Elegant. She hiked her skirt all the way up to her hips and then got into the backseat, lying back on it comfortably. Tammi-Ray slipped her panties off.

Elegant's penis was hard and stiff.

———

It was after two o'clock in the morning, and Tommie was laughing like a madman. And the car kept weaving. And he kept telling Elegant he could drive the car back to Longwood blindfolded if he had to—if necessary.

"Elegant, Elegant, I don't know what to say 'bout you. Shit. Don't, man, don't!"

"What, Tommie?"

"'Cause, shit, she a party girl, yeah, all right. But she don't give it up on the first night. What h-her reputation is 'round here in, in Inwood."

Elegant wasn't going to try to play the Casanova role in front of Tommie or that he was a great charmer, seducer—he just figured he and Tammi-Ray hit it off, and they wound up in the back of Tommie's car and had sex.

"Shit, Annie, just gotta buy her one drink, and the girl'll go in the woods with anybody!"

"I bought Tammi-Ray a drink."

"She ain't no hog or nothing 'bout drinking. On drinking, man. She likes to dance more than she likes to drink anyways. An okay young lady ... De-decent and all."

Elegant agreed with Tommie's assessment of her.

Tommie had his head back on the car seat, and with the bumps coming fast and furious, the car hitting them, seemingly, not missing any, Tommie's head was bouncing up and down at will.

"Usually leave Angel's Corner after three, Elegant. But w-wasn't gonna get you home too late. Gotta think of Mr. Manners. You living there. W-with him." Pause.

"Did, did, uh, he … he ask you anything? 'Bout you drinking or anything, Elegant?"

"No."

"W-what 'b-bout me?"

Elegant's head turned sharply to Tommie. "Uh, no. No, Tommie. No."

Tommie didn't respond; his head just kept bouncing up and down.

"N-need my weekends, Elegant."

"Of course, Tommie. Of—"

"Shit, need me relief from everything."

"The way you work and all."

"We young. Young, man. Young as hell, Elegant. Always got responsibilities c-crammed down us. Ain't but a routine after a while. B-but one day it's gonna grind us down. Right down to nothing."

"Uh, I know."

"It's why I gotta get someplace in the ring. You … no, no, man—I must, must really be drunk bad. Bad. Ha. Not, not someplace, I don't mean no someplace—but world champ, Elegant. W-world champ.

"I love boxing. Like my father loved it. Shit, but I wanna make money outta it. Travel the world. Make money. Live good. I don't wanna wind up with nothing. L-like that." Pause. "Ha ha ha."

Instantly Elegant knew Tommie wasn't laughing hysterically, the gold tooth in his mouth gleaming, because of what he'd just said, laughing at his dreams, but because he was drunk, had drunk too much liquor in Angel's Corner tonight.

Just down the road from the house, Hattersfield Road, Tommie'd become more talkative, talking faster, undoubtedly aware the time with Elegant was shrinking.

"W-we go into Huntington in a week and a half, Elegant. Radio

Center Arena." Pause. "It's gonna be packed to the gills. They know me there, all right."

Radio Center Arena was in Huntington, West Virginia. It was an active fight town, with solid, knowledgeable fight fans.

"And you're headlining."

"Weeeee!"

One thing about out in the country, rural living, Elegant thought, you sure don't have to worry about waking up anybody. Maybe an old frog in the mud somewhere, but other than that, you were free to get away with pretty much anything you liked, sonically.

"When Mr. Manners told me that, Elegant, they want me as a feature after my last bout at the Fame, man, hell if I was a flame, woulda burned myself!"

Tommie hadn't sobered, but at times during the ride, Elegant did feel as if Tommie could drive blindfolded from Inwood to Longwood. But there were times when Tommie pressed his foot down on the accelerator and the car sped up, and then he'd ease his foot off the accelerator, making the ride home ragged.

They'd reached the house.

"We here, here, huh, Elegant?"

If it wasn't for the moon casting its pale glow on it, the whole house would be covered in darkness.

"Thanks for a great night, Tommie."

Elegant turned and hugged Tommie.

"Got many more to come, Elegant. Tammi-Ray, she just for starters. Bunch of girls was asking me 'bout you all night. Who you was."

"See you Monday," Elegant said, getting out of the car.

"Oh, yeah. Gonna work like a beaver Monday. Ain't gonna disappoint not one fan of mine at Radio Center Arena. Uh-uh …"

Elegant was out of the car.

Tommie turned the car in the road, and except for the car's back tail lights, no other lights shone out on Hattersfield Road.

———

The next morning, Gyp and Elegant came out of the woods.

Elegant hadn't done any roadwork, so he and Gyp hadn't done any running this morning. Elegant didn't do roadwork on Saturday or Sunday (his two days off). He didn't work at the brickyard on Saturday or Sunday either. He wanted to work on Saturday but was a five-day hire at Miller Brothers Bricks.

But on Saturday morning, Elegant had a different routine Pee-Pot had devised for him and his training: chopping wood. And it's what he was doing, balancing in his arms a five-foot-tall bundle (at least) of chopped wood across the grounds with the ax lying horizontally across the top of the wood. Elegant was fast-stepping, keeping his back straight, positioned, doing this for about a quarter mile, the muscles in his arms bulging, and Gyp by his side like she didn't have a care in the world, skipping blithely along in the morning's sun.

There wasn't just one spot on the property where there was a woodpile but several. And Elegant headed for one of them.

"Gyp, we did all right for ourselves this morning."

Woof!

While Elegant chopped wood, Gyp snoozed. And when Elegant said it's time to go, Gyp, like always, sprang to her feet.

Gently, Elegant put the wood down on the ground and then slapped his hands together. "Done!"

Then Pee-Pot came out of the house.

"Quite a stack, Elegant. A good stack you're carrying there."

"Thanks, Mr. Manners. This is good for me, sir. I really do enjoy it."

"As long as you got Gyp there keeping an eye on you."

"Good old Gyp."

"You and Gyp can come in now. I know you're hungry."

"Are we, Mr. Manners!"

Woof!

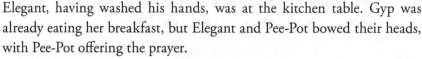

Elegant, having washed his hands, was at the kitchen table. Gyp was already eating her breakfast, but Elegant and Pee-Pot bowed their heads, with Pee-Pot offering the prayer.

"A-men."

Even with him getting in late last night from Angel's Corner, Elegant was up at his usual time, five thirty. So it meant he got less than three hours of sleep. It hadn't affected him one way or the other. He did his usual—wiped his eyes and then hopped out of bed. He hustled on his clothes and then went downstairs for Gyp. And then out they went, into the woods, as usual.

Gyp, having finished eating, went out the kitchen's back door.

"So you and Tommie had yourselves a good time in Inwood, at Angel's Corner, last night?"

"Yes, we did, Mr. Manners."

Elegant's knife sliced into the plump sausage.

"Around people your age."

"Yes, sir."

"You know I was young once."

Elegant looking directly into Pee-Pot's eyes saw a twinkle in them. It's when both laughed.

"Of course you were, Mr. Manners."

Pee-Pot was scooping eggs up onto his fork.

"Sometimes I think young people like you, though, think otherwise, Elegant. Forget that fact. If it wasn't for photographs, old pictures taken of us when we were young, you'd think we came into the world with gray hair or bald headed or wrinkles."

"Right, right, Mr. Manners," Elegant laughed.

"It's how I used to think. When I looked at somebody my age now. That it's how they must've arrived here on Earth."

"No, no, I don't think that way, Mr. Manners. Honestly. Not at all, all, sir."

Pee-Pot could always tell when a fighter of his had sex the night before. Even if Elegant hadn't told him he and Tommie were going to Angel's Corner, he would know. It would be in the gym, in the training session the next day. It would be in their movements, reflexes—even if it was temporary, would pretty much dissipate by session's end. But in this instance, he had an advantage—he knew Tommie took Elegant to Angel's Corner in Inwood. He knew its reputation. Why Tommie took Elegant there—and to do what there.

"I was asleep when you got in."

Elegant hoped he was. "Uh, yes, Mr. Manners. It was well after two o'clock."

Pee-Pot's fork speared the hash browns; they were chunky cuts. "Was dead asleep."

"Yes, sir." Pause.

"Dead asleep."

Elegant looked up from his plate, in a way, to study Pee-Pot's face, honestly. He wasn't in the habit of hearing him repeat himself like this.

"You got back safe—it's all that matters, Elegant. Tommie got you back last night ... safe and sound from Inwood."

He knows! He knows!

Pee-Pot was looking earnestly at Elegant, and he saw tenseness in his face. "Yes, Elegant, I know." Pause. "Known for some time now that Tommie drinks. It's gotten back to me in one form or another."

Pee-Pot leaned back. "Know it's on the weekends. Strictly. It's not done, uh, during the week—so as to interfere with his training. Get, uh, uh, in the way of his training—unless I-I wouldn't tolerate it, any of it. Let him get away with it. Not, not in the least."

Elegant realized his role was to listen—simply that.

"But I do tolerate it, even at that. Treat it like it's harmless. And I don't know why," Pee-Pot said. Pause. "See, I haven't stepped in. Counseled him any, in any way about his drinking, not since I found out—and it's been going on this way. On the same track. What's wrong with me!"

He threw the knife down onto the kitchen table.

It's the first Elegant had seen Pee-Pot Manners really upset like this.

"I don't separate my fighters from reality."

Elegant didn't completely understand.

"Just fighters. Just boxers coming to the gym—then disappearing till the next day. Their life's not just in the gym but outside it. Most of it's outside the gym. So I can't separate the two. Ain't but one reality to deal with." Pause.

"Am I making myself clear, son?"

"Yes. Yes, you are, sir."

Pee-Pot took a deep breath and then half smiled. "Our, I know our food's getting cold. So ..."

"Yes, yes, sir."

But Elegant knew this wasn't over, that nothing had yet been settled regarding the matter.

And when Elegant finished eating, and Pee-Pot the same, Pee-Pot cleared the table, put everything on the kitchen counter, and then rejoined Elegant back at the table as Elegant sensed he would.

"This has weighed heavily on me. Tommie. If it was just not on …"

"Weekend, the weekends, Mr. Manners?"

"Yes. It's on the weekends. Doesn't take account for the rest of the week. Like the boy has it under control. By, by all appearances."

Elegant could see how things counterbalanced themselves.

"I just don't know, son. Can't make sense out of this." It's when Pee-Pot's face drooped. "You don't know this 'cause Tommie never talks about it, but you might as well, Elegant. Tommie's father died from liver problems. Drank himself to death. Deliberately so."

Truly, this caught Elegant unawares.

"I just hope it ain't in his blood. Hereditary. Maybe it's why I ain't… haven't gotten into it with him. Gone on about it. Don't, I don't want to scare him. Preach to him. Don't want to accuse him of anything. Or make him think things would turn out like Tommie Lathers Sr. for him. Have him bear his father's cross."

Elegant gathered his thoughts. Suddenly Tommie's drinking problem had blown up into a big one, not what he thought he saw last night.

"So for now, I stand by and say nothing. Like a man in the mirror— silent." Pause. "J-just look at him as a fighter in that way. That he comes into the gym sober every day. Doesn't show any effects from his drinking in his boxing."

"No, no, he—"

"'Cause if he did, Elegant, I'd see it. I know I would."

"Yes, Mr. Manners. Of, yes, of course, sir."

"I-I wouldn't miss it. None of it."

Elegant simply nodded his head.

———

Pee-Pot was washing the dishes, and Elegant was in the backyard looking out on the grounds, looking at how evenly they sloped and then rose— something like life, he thought. Between last night's revelations and today's, it was more than what he expected. When things like this, of a serious nature, happen, you're rudely shocked. And he had the shock of last night in him and, now, this morning's shock.

He walked away from the house. Through the back door, he still heard the dishes clicking against each other, and he didn't want to hear anything but the morning, its light breath, not whispering but soothing—fearlessly alive. So off to the side of the farmhouse he walked, toward this huge clearing of land, something he neither did on his own or with Gyp: walk in this direction, yield to it such importance.

But he did, and when he reached a certain spot, a small sinking in the ground, he stopped and looked up at the sky and felt Pee-Pot's guilt, how guilty he'd become because of Tommie's situation, how it was eating away at him; and even for someone as wise, filled with wisdom as Pee-Pot Manners, Elegant thought, he didn't know in which direction to turn, the right path to take.

For what he was doing now was be the passive observer. And during his short stay with Pee-Pot Manners, he knew that went against his grain, his natural instincts. And he knew him as fighter through the eyes and language and history of Mr. Whaley, how he described Pee-Pot Manners, the fighter, in the ring, aggressive, relentless, "a tiger of a fighter."

"This is really tormenting Mr. Manners. A-a lot, I ..."

Elegant knew what he was about to say, where his mind was, what it'd been thinking all this time, of talking to Tommie about his drinking. Of talking to him, which, in turn, would be him talking to Tommie not only on his behalf but on Pee-Pot Manners's behalf.

"Tommie and I are close enough that we can talk. I know that."

He'd just have to pick his spot, the right, perfect opportunity, Elegant thought. To do this his timing needed to be impeccable. If in any way it sounded calculating, this was not his intent. He just didn't want Tommie to be put at risk, not in the ring or out.

He wouldn't make a separation either (it was essential not to); it was one reality: fighter / man / human being. It's what he and Pee-Pot Manners wanted to integrate regarding Tommie's drinking, in looking at his life and determining it was slightly out of balance, off center, and that he must see it as clear-eyed as them, with the same sense of worry and urgency and caution.

CHAPTER 9

On Tuesday, Elegant was off work. He'd just left the Miller Brothers Bricks brickyard. Routinely, he was still doing three showers a day and occasionally soaking in the tub when he really wanted to give his muscles a special treat. These days with money in his pockets (not a fortune, mind you), there were occasions when he wanted to spend some of it on something—not feel he was hoarding it, putting all of it under his mattress or a board in the floor.

So now when he saw Pee-Pot ran short of something, the cupboard was practically bare (Pee-Pot was always so busy), he'd shop in the general store in town and buy the necessary foodstuffs. It's why he was in the general store today, having greeted Chadway Holloway, a person who consistently exuded small-town charm, friendliness, and courtesies.

There were eggs he and Pee-Pot needed. At one time Pee-Pot said, when he operated the farm as a farm, there were chicken coops in the backyard. And the chickens had full range, and Gyp had full range; and when Gyp was in a mischievous, playful mood, she'd have the chickens squawking like crazy, put them in an uproar, their wings flapping like wild geese, and he and Cora Manners would laugh like crazy at Gyp's antics, even though at times, Pee-Pot said, they would side with the chickens, who weren't always so sure of Gyp's motives.

Knowing the store well, Elegant headed down the aisle for bacon and avocadoes. After gathering these two items, he paused and thought, *Hmmm ... what else do Mr. Manners and I need? Hmmm ... let me—*

"Gem. Gem. I heard you was back in town, Gem!"

Elegant stopped dead in his tracks this time.

"Gem. Gem. It can't be Gem Loving, c-could it!"

"Yes, Mr. Holloway. I returned home yesterday, sir."

"Heard that too. Caught wind of it. The whole town should know by now. By golly, Gem!"

Gem Loving, Gem Loving, Elegant thought. The famous Gem Loving of Longwood!

He had to get some flour, but it could wait, couldn't it? Wait for Gem Loving. Bread, bread—oh, he and Mr. Manners needed pumpernickel bread too ... But just maybe a peek, me taking a peek, that's all, that's enough, right? Right!

"That's all today, Gem?"

"Yes, Mr. Holloway. Francine only forgot the ginger—"

"This time."

He had to see her before she left Mr. Holloway's store!

"Oh, it's all right. Her mind's on so many things."

"But not yours, Gem."

"But we're not in competition, Mr. Holloway, Francine and I."

"Now ... no, Gem. But you don't forget nothing. And don't try to pass it off on her being young and playful, Gem, 'cause Francine's only a year and a half back of you."

There she is!

But Elegant was looking at Gem Loving from the back of her, not the front.

"Elegant, how you ... uh, 'cause you got a serious mind, Gem," Chad Holloway said, turning back to Gem Loving as if he must. "On them gorgeous shoulders of yours. Just born to get things ... Elegant, oh, I'm sorry."

And Gem Loving turned her head in Elegant's direction, and it's when Elegant went weak in the knees, and fast.

"Elegant, come on over and meet, let me introduce you to Miss Gem Loving, Pastor Loving's lovely, beautiful daughter."

"Y-yes, sir, Mr. Holloway. Yes, sir."

Elegant put the basket he carried from the brickyard down.

"Gem Loving, Elegant Raines."

"Good afternoon, Mr. Raines."

"G-good afternoon, M-Ms. Loving," Elegant said, removing and then tipping his Applejack cap at Gem Loving.

Elegant and Gem Loving shook hands.

Elegant put the Applejack back on his head.

"Ms. Loving, uh, Gem, just got back off that Christian retreat of hers, didn't you, Gem?"

"Oh," Elegant said.

"Just yesterday, in fact." Pause. "Elegant's a boxer, Gem."

"Oh, are you, Mr. Raines?"

"Yes, Miss Loving."

"Trains under Pee-Pot Manners. Guided him off there to his house when he got in. Soon as he stepped into Longwood, didn't I, Elegant?"

"Yes, sir. That, that you did, sir."

"From where, Mr. Raines?"

Her voice was so wonderful, so charming, Elegant thought. "View Point, Texas, Miss Loving."

"Now don't tell me you've heard of it, this place, View Point, Texas, when I know I haven't. Not for a day in my life. And I've lived longer than you, Gem, by a long shot."

"No, oh no, Mr. Holloway. Not at all, sir. Not View Point, Texas."

"Even though it wouldn't surprise me any if you did. Not at all. Uh-huh, Gem. Smart as you are." Pause.

"And, uh, Elegant's doing quite well, is quite successful for himself in the boxing ring, Gem. I might add!"

She was tall for a girl, no less than five feet nine. She was as dark complected as Elegant. She had straight black hair and wore a dark-blue bonnet and a long blue skirt and a white-and-blue-checkered blouse and smiled with refinement and high culture and maturity and divineness, Elegant thought.

"Elegant's undefeated, in fact. Uh, in the boxing ring."

"Mr. Manners and I attended your father's church, Miss Loving. We were told you were on a Christian retreat, ma'am."

"For eight days, Gem. And everybody in town was counting them too!"

Then Gem Loving turned and saw Mr. Holloway was handing her her change.

"Thank you, Mr. Holloway."

"No, this town ain't the same with you gone, Gem. When you go off to college. That Howard University of yours in Washington, DC. Might as well fold Longwood up and throw it in the Allegheny River!"

Gem Loving blushed.

"Since you was a tot, you've ruled this town, and you know it. Was the cutest little girl, Elegant. Just like Francine too. But this one here … being the oldest, stole our hearts without a doubt. Know it wasn't fair for Francine, no fault of Francine's … but …"

Gem Loving turned around. "It was so nice meeting you, Mr. Raines."

Elegant removed the Applejack cap again, tucking it in between his armpits.

"Yes, t-the same for me, Miss, uh, Miss L-Loving," Elegant stammered.

Gem Loving turned to Mr. Holloway. "Good day, Mr. Holloway."

"Yes, good day, Gem. See you in church Sunday. Oh, will I!"

Then Gem Loving turned back to Elegant. "Good day again, Mr. Raines."

"Yes, good, good day," Elegant said.

When Gem Loving left the store was when Chadway Holloway let loose a huge, numbing sigh. "Oh … to be young again. And I don't mean that in a rude, inappropriate way, Elegant, not at all."

"Yes, sir."

"To marry, Elegant. Just a perfect girl to marry."

Elegant wasn't looking at the door but beyond it—to wherever Gem Loving was.

"Oh, sorry I interrupted you there, Elegant."

"Oh … oh, it, it's all right, Mr. Holloway, sir." Pause.

"So you go ahead and get—"

"I forgot what it was now, Mr. Holloway."

"Ha, Gem'll have that effect, kind of effect on you. On most boys, when they first hang their eyes on her! And, oh, you can put that hat of yours you got tucked between your armpit back on your head—"

"Uh, uh … my—"

"Now that Gem's gone!"

Elegant entered the Pug. His eyes were fogged over. And who was the first to greet him? Tommie.

"Y-you seen her. D-don't you? Don't you, Elegant? Shit, don't you? Don't lie!"

Elegant's eyes were still fogged over, and he appeared in a mental haze.

"S-saw who, Tommie?"

"Gem Loving, that's who. Gem Loving. The one and only Gem Loving!"

"I ..."

"Heard she come back in town. Come in yesterday."

Then Elegant got better control of himself. "Yes, yes, she, I ... she did."

"Come on, Elegant, shit, snap outta it," Tommie said, snapping his fingers about a half foot from Elegant. "Snap outta it, man!"

"Right, right, Tommie. Right. Snap out of it."

Tommie laughed. "Shit, 'nother victim. How many do ... It's a good thing Gem don't keep count. Probably don't even know what she does to us boys 'round here. Good as she is. Just got a heart of gold. Can't help it if she's so damned pretty though."

"Yes, yes, uh ... I, I guess not."

"Hey, Elegant, you gonna get over it. Maybe by next year!"

That seemingly snapped Elegant out his daze. "Ha. Right, right, Tommie."

Tommie looked at the basket.

"Been shopping for you and Mr. Manners, huh?"

"Uh-huh."

"What, running low out there?"

"Oh ...," Elegant said, looking down into the basket, "bread, bread, I forgot Mr. Manners's pumpernickel bread and, and flour!"

"So that's where you met Gem—in Mr. Holloway's store."

"Uh-huh," Elegant said, nodding his head as if he'd gone practically speechless.

"So the bread and flour got lost 'tween you negotiating your charms on Gem, or her on you, and shopping?"

"R-right, Tommie. Right."

"God help you, Elegant. Man. God help you!"

Tommie, of course, was in his boxing equipment.

"Hurry up and gear up, Mr. Casanova!"

Then Elegant walked off with Tommie shaking his head in amusement. But instead of going into the locker room, he ducked into Pee-Pot's office to drop off the basket and then was out the door, when Tommie snatched his arm.

"W-what's wrong, Tommie?" Elegant asked concernedly.

"I forgot to tell you ..."

"What?"

"Black Moon."

"Black Moon?"

"Yeah, don't let me hold you up or nothing, Elegant."

Briskly, he and Elegant began walking. Elegant was greeting a number of the fighters in the gym.

"The boy was acting nasty all day."

"Tommie, I don't need to know—"

"Yes, you do. Yes you do, Elegant—since you why. Reason why. 'Cause of it."

"Me!"

They were in the locker room.

"You, Elegant. You. Shit, nobody but you. And I got it from a good source, man. Damned good one."

"I don't even see Black Moon ... him anymore, Tommie. During the day. I'm not in the gym when he is. Our paths d-don't cross."

"Don't have to. Makes no difference. He jealous as hell, Elegant. Jealous, envious as hell 'bout you and Mr. Manners."

Elegant didn't see this coming but knew enough about Black Moon Johnson to expect something like this.

"So today everybody in the gym's feeling it. The way Black Moon was acting."

"B-but I can't worry about Black Moon, Tommie," Elegant said, opening the locker. "It's ... that's the reality."

Tommie patted Elegant on the back.

"Was hoping you to say something like that. Hoping so. Ain't your doing. Worry neither. You come here as a great fighter and happen to wind up out at the farmhouse. Living with Mr. Manners. Happen natural … like."

Elegant began undressing.

"Black Moon wants to fight you though."

"Fight me!"

"It's what he told one of his boys. In the ring, outside—say it don't matter any to him."

"I-I don't want to fight him," Elegant said softly. "N-not unless it's in-inside the ring."

"It's gonna happen, you know that, Elegant? You and him?"

Elegant agreed.

"Black Moon don't care if it's inside or outside the ring to settle the score."

"But I don't have a score to settle with—"

"Ain't how the other boys 'round here seeing it, Elegant. They fighters, man. Hungry to see who's best, you or Black Moon. For them boys, ain't nothing to it than that."

Elegant realized this, even though he was not of that mental mind-set. If you're a boxer, he thought, you fight inside the ring, not outside it. His emotions were controlled, channeled inside the ring. It was a job, nothing more. Outside the ring, you could be fighting for your life.

"Elegant, uh, uh, you went mum on me."

"Oh, oh, Tommie, I'm sorry."

"Sorry, but just thought I better let you know what's going on 'round here, man. In the gym these days."

"Thanks."

Tommie was walking away. "And hurry up. Mr. Manners got you and me sparring today. I guess he wants me to teach you a coupla new tricks. Maneuvers, man."

Elegant laughed but then went right back to thinking of Black Moon, of an enemy (it's how Black Moon posited him, so he must posit him the same) he never bargained for, imagined, but there he was—graceless and bold, ready to protect and maintain his sacred turf.

Time had marched backward if, indeed, it had ever marched forward, to his and Black Moon's initial and only argument: who would hold dominance in the Pug. Who would survive under the conditions created by circumstance or fate, to be more episodic, Elegant thought, in keeping with Shakespeare, the plays he read and admired, the language and diction of the evolving human, his emotions and intellect and savagery and sophistication and warlike, combative tendencies, instincts and personality in the throes of fulfilling a destiny that sometimes was ruthless and wounding and, other times, noble and heroic and superior.

"There are so many levels to human conflict. Our spirits. So many levels to study."

Reading made him smart, intelligent. It made him question and requestion, analyze and reanalyze situations. Elegant shut the metal locker's door, now fully dressed for gym work, for his daily war out in the gym. To be in shape for his upcoming fight in Radio Center Arena in Huntington next week, fighting on a card Tommie was headlining, was up on cloud nine about.

Black Moon wanted him to fear him (this repeated theme). But the only thing Elegant feared was his past. And if he feared the past then, of course, it stood to reason he feared himself. Black Moon was insignificant; every fighter he fought in the ring was. He had to keep that fear of the past in him in order for it not to win in a larger sense, in a much larger, broader context. He always had to feel this fight was winnable, that each day was a fragment, piece of the same existing battle within him, that the enemy didn't change its face, that it fought with the same ugly demeanor, venal character—that it was never over, never defeated, that time didn't arch forward, free the soul of recollection but gathered moss at its feet, deepened its will, stood, unequivocally, still.

On Friday of the same week, it was two fifteen in the morning when Tommie and Elegant were in Tommie's car, crossing out of Inwood and into Longwood. Tommie was drunk.

For Elegant, it wasn't Tammi-Ray tonight; she wasn't at Angel's Corner, and he didn't know why. But he had sex with a girl who went by the name of Raven in the rear seat of Tommie's car.

Tommie had sex with a different girl too, not Annie, who was at Angel's Corner, all right, but a girl named Selena. But tonight, Tommie went back into the backwoods for a second time with another girl, her name, Elegant didn't know. All week he hadn't broached Tommie's drinking. Elegant didn't know if the timing was ever right or it was just him. But definitely, it sat heavy on his mind.

"D-don't know if you know it or not, Elegant, but I made me two trips to the woods tonight," Tommie quipped, leaning over to Elegant while driving the car, tapping Elegant's shoulder.

"No, I knew, Tommie. I saw you when you went back out again."

"Always do that …"

"Do what?"

"Have, have me sex with two or three girls a week or so before a fight."

"You, you do?"

"Yeah. Shit, Elegant, it relaxes me. Somehow. Don't know why. But it do."

"You know what they say about a boxer having sex before a match …"

"Know. Surprised Mr. Manners let you out the house. Shit. But maybe it ain't gonna be that way for the big matches you fight. The real big ones that come 'long. When everything gotta be perfect."

"Can't take any chances."

Even in the dark, Elegant felt Tommie's eyes.

"D-did you think I-I was perfect, Elegant?"

"P-perfect, no, I—"

"Just like alcohol, t-that's all. Taste of it. Crazy about t-the taste."
Pause.

"My daddy died from it, but you know that by now without me telling you any, right, right …?"

"Yes."

"Mr. Manners got 'round to it by now. I know."

"Yes."

"When?"

"After last Friday night."

"And it ain't no secret to nobody that he knows 'bout my drinking too, don't he?"

"Yes."

"Was part of the same conversation," Tommie said, shaking his head.

"Yes. At the breakfast table, Tommie. That morning."

"Don't, hell, don't want you talking outta school, Elegant—"

"No, no, it's all right," Elegant said, taking Tommie's arm and then quickly releasing it. "There's nothing to hide. Mr. Manners and I love you."

"Thanks."

Silence.

"He ain't said nothing to me. Mr. Manners all this time. I ... think Mr. Manners 'fraid to."

Silence.

"Think he thinks he ain't gonna be able to stop me. Ain't, ain't gonna be able to, to, Elegant."

That remark stunned Elegant.

"He tried—Mr. Manners tried getting Daddy to stop but can't. Daddy can't do it. Shit, he just can't do it, Elegant!"

Tommie braked the car. Elegant grabbed him and held him as Tommie cried into his chest. "Shit, shit, s-sorry, Elegant. Shit. Sorry as hell, man!"

"It's all right, Tommie. It's all right."

Elegant let go of him.

They just sat there in the car, in the middle of the road.

"Ain't, ain't cried like, this way since ..." Tommie wiped his eyes and then rubbed them.

"I don't drink 'cause of Daddy, my daddy though, though, Elegant. Don't get it wrong or nothing. Don't have nothing to do with Daddy. Swear, man," Tommie said.

His head fell back on the car seat. He breathed sporadically. "It, it don't."

Elegant believed him. There was no reason for him not to, Elegant thought.

"Y-you smart, smart, Elegant. W-what is it, Elegant? What is it I got?"

"Your chemical makeup."

"That's it, that's it. That gotta be it," Tommie said, starting the Ford back up. "My, my chemical makeup. Make ... I don't wanna die. Daddy done. Boxing. Not getting to the top. But I will. I wanna live. Ain't gonna fall short like Daddy.

"I-I mean ... it ain't like he don't try, don't. Things just don't go his way. That's all, Elegant."

They were panicked words out Tommie's mouth. But it was about being a champion, about wearing the crown, about a black man being recognized in a white man's society, about a lot of exotic, unmitigated things like that.

———

Elegant and Gyp were in the backyard.

Elegant had groomed Gyp with the grooming brush but now petted her. They'd been in the woods. Elegant had carried the ax and chopped the wood and carried the wood back and added it to last Saturday's woodpile.

"Oh ... you're such a good girl, Gyp."

He'd mentioned Gem Loving to Gyp, and Gyp's bark was about the loudest he'd heard to date, so if that wasn't vocal support for her then Elegant didn't know, had no idea what was. But that was but one aspect of it, the fun aspect of it, not last night when he was with that Raven girl, had sex in the backseat of Tommie's car with her, for it tortured him then and now, as if he'd betrayed something dear to him: his dignity and self-respect.

Woof!

"Sorry, sorry, Gyp."

Elegant had stopped petting her.

"My mind, it wandered off elsewhere."

It was Gem Loving, Tuesday afternoon's encounter, meeting her—it's why he was so confused last night and again this morning. It's why he felt so cheap and undignified and shameful. His feelings were no accident. It was why he was reluctant about going out with Tommie last night, but he didn't want to disappoint him, to have him feel, suddenly, they were doing something wrong when he was all for it, was hopeful it'd turn out like it had, meeting a girl, having sex with her; it was his plan for last night too.

But last night he felt dirty while having sex with Raven, as if Gem Loving had met the wrong person, and word from Inwood would track back into Longwood, and opinion would be formed of him leading, ultimately, to Gem Loving's ears.

Gem Loving. Gem Loving. I'm fascinated by her.

Gyp rolled onto her back. Elegant stroked her stomach. Then Gyp, seconds later, rolled over onto her side, stood, and then walked out into the sun and lay down.

Elegant was still in the shade, befuddled, for that had never happened between them, Gyp doing what she'd done.

"So I'm that boring, am I, Gyp? To you."

Then Gyp laid her head on both her forepaws.

It's when Elegant realized his feelings had somehow permeated him in such a way Gyp had felt them. That it was the kind of love and closeness they had. That it was no mistake Gyp wanted him to have this space to himself to think. That there was something going on, disturbing him that even chopping wood this morning couldn't fix.

Gem Loving had permeated him, all right. But what was most unsatisfying, displeasing, was not knowing if he had any effect on her. It's the imbalance he felt. It was the situation he was in. He felt anxious.

———

"Your gym work, as usual, Elegant, is sharp, son."

They were in the living room.

"Thanks, Mr. Manners."

"No fight's taken lightly. But this is no step up in competition for you next week at Radio Center Arena."

"No, uh, it isn't, sir?"

They'd had breakfast, and Elegant washed the dishes, and when finished, Pee-Pot called him into the living room.

"No. It's just to continue to keep you active, Elegant. Sharp."

"Oh."

"I'm working on a fight for you though. What will be a big step up. Something you're ready for."

This is good, Mr. Manners's confidence in me, Elegant thought.

"How's it feel me saying that?"

"Great. Just great, Mr. Manners."

Pee-Pot rocked in his Rapson rocker. "We've come a long way together in a short time, haven't we, son?"

"Yes, we have, sir."

"Though we still have a long way to go. In three weeks' time, Black Moon and I are going off to Chicago Coliseum. Ever heard of it, Elegant? Chicago Coliseum?"

"Yes, sir."

"It's gonna be a step up for him. The fight up there's gonna mean a lot for his career."

Elegant was wondering where all of this was leading to.

"You're gonna outgrow the middleweight division one day, Elegant. B-but for now, you're stuck there. You won't outgrow it for at least another two years. No more than three. And by then, based on your record and Black Moon's and the excitement you two bring to the ring, there's gonna be a groundswell of interest from the boxing public for you two to fight each other."

Elegant envisioned this picture too, as Pee-Pot Manners and Black Moon had. It's one thing he knew Black Moon wanted more than anything in the world right now: to fight him in the ring.

"It's gonna be unavoidable."

Suddenly, Elegant needed assurance Pee-Pot was troubled by this.

"Ain't nothing that nobody's gonna be able to do about it. It's just one of those fact-of-life situations. I've seen it happen before, to other trainers. But it's gonna be the first for me."

"W-what have other trainers done, Mr. Manners? Solution they-they've come up with, sir?"

"Drop the reins. Bring new trainers into camp for them for the last few weeks or so. Trainers who still listen to them though. Carry out their plans—whatever strategy's necessary for the fight."

"I-I don't like this, Mr. Manners. Not at all, sir."

"Nobody does, Elegant—least of all me. But it's gonna be something we're gonna have to prepare ourselves for."

"Have you talked to Black Moon about it, sir?"

"No," Pee-Pot said matter-of-factly. "It ain't gonna bother Black Moon, only you, Elegant."

Mr. Manners' reply told you everything about the differences between his personality and Black Moon Johnson's, Elegant thought.

"You know that, right, Elegant?"

"Yes, sir."

"Black Moon just wants to fight you, so I hear. Was told."

"Yes, uh, Tommie, Tommie told me, Mr. Manners. Regarding Black Moon's feelings toward me."

"He'll fight you with no rules. In a back alley. Anywhere he can settle his dispute with, he's got with you."

"H-his, not mine."

"Look, Elegant, do you remember what I told you before? You boys are after the same thing. The same prize. Black Moon wants to claim. Ain't a day he doubts that prize is his. Belongs to him. Nobody else.

"This is boxing, Elegant. Son. Competition between men. In the worst sort of way." Pause. "You don't have to be decent, moral in a sport savage as this sport. Nobody's gotta make an excuse for their behavior. For what they do or say."

"But I want it too, Mr. Manners. As badly, sir. I want the prize too."

Pee-Pot was elated to see the fire in Elegant's eyes. And by seeing it, it'd made the conversation worthwhile, worth him sitting down to explain things to him.

There'd been a long pause between them.

"Last night—"

"I spoke to Tommie, Mr. Manners," Elegant said quietly.

"About his drinking?"

"His drinking. Yes, his drinking, sir."

"How did it—"

"I'd been trying all week to bring it up, Mr. Manners. Time it right. But—"

"It was Tommie, you mean who—"

"Who brought it up. Yes, sir, Tommie."

"Tommie ..."

"He doesn't see it as a problem."

"No, no, Elegant, they never do."

"But he doesn't, Mr. Manners."

Pee-Pot looked at Elegant, puzzled. "And so, what? You're gonna look at it through Tommie's eyes all of a sudden and not through your own, son?"

And suddenly, Elegant felt like a fish out of water.

"He's your friend, Elegant. Best one you've got, I would imagine ..."

"Yes, yes, you know he is, Mr. Manners. Best I've got."

"And when we first look at somebody we really, really like, we see the flaws in them, and then we feel bad 'cause we did and then don't want them to be there. Reverse all we saw around. Back off.

"Then ... so all we need is somebody to persuade us. Don't, there's no need for them to twist our arms but persuade us. Persuade us different."

"Tommie ...," Elegant said bowing his head.

"It's nothing for you to feel bad about, Elegant. Ashamed of."

Elegant lifted his head. "He said he likes the taste of alcohol, Mr. Manners. The, the taste of it, sir."

"Likes it," Pee-Pot said, shutting his eyes. "Likes it." Pause. "Tommie, Tommie Lathers Sr. didn't. Couldn't stand the taste of it ... the, the stuff," Pee-Pot said, opening his eyes. "Yet he let it kill him. Kept drinking it until it did."

"He knows you know he drinks, sir."

"Of course he does. Last Saturday when we talked, Elegant, I never said Tommie didn't know."

"No, you didn't. It's unavoidable not to in a small town like Longwood, Mr. Manners. Yes, I know that. Like any small town, sir."

"No, you can't enjoy secrets in a town small like this. Uh-uh—not when people are watching you."

Elegant thought about his reputation again, of going into Inwood on Friday nights with Tommie, of who was looking at him, compiling information on him, bundling it like he did the firewood from the woods this morning and then them using it as they saw fit.

"Tommie Lathers Sr., Elegant. Did, did Tommie tell you how much I tried helping him to, to stop drinking, but failed like everybody else—"

"Tommie has a theory on, on that, Mr. Manners."

Pee-Pot removed his cap. "Theory? Theory on what?"

"Why you haven't talked to him about his d-drinking, uh, sir."

"And Tommie says he has a theory as to why I don't?"

Elegant wasn't sure whether or not this would be painful to Pee-Pot Manners but, if anything, knew he was honest and what Tommie posited was more like truth than theory.

"It's because of Mr. Lathers, sir. That you couldn't stop his drinking at the time."

"Failed. Failed him. Damn, did I. Straight down the line."

"But Tommie didn't say 'failed,' sir."

"No, he didn't have to. Failed him when he needed me most. I do have that pain, Elegant. Carry it. For the life of me, I do. And if I looked at myself in the mirror, clear on, Tommie might be right. Maybe I'm afraid of failing again. Something I'm not used to."

Pee-Pot looked down at his hands. "Being the fighter I was, son." Then Pee-Pot relaxed. "I ruled the ring. These hands of mine. I was practically perfect inside the ring. Not accustomed to failure."

Elegant saw those brilliant days in Pee-Pot's face.

"With Tommie, why ... it feels like I would fail again," Pee-Pot said, looking directly at Elegant. "With him too, Elegant. That I would stand as much a chance with him as I did his father."

Pee-Pot stood.

"Excuse me, I'm going up to my room. Pardon me."

"Yes, sir."

Pee-Pot walked out of the room.

Elegant stood for no more than a second or two, only to sit back down. This whole situation with Tommie had deepened, Elegant thought. It'd taken on a brand-new character—not that it shouldn't.

"It always boils down to this vague, psychological matchstick. What's igniting our emotions." In Morgantown, his last fight there, at Fame Arena, he bought a book from a bookstore. He'd gone off for about a half hour by himself and dropped by the bookstore. He saw a book of good size and weight, worn, not on the shelf but in a cardboard box on the floor with other books in the same basic condition. It was a book on different schools of psychology, published by John Hopkins University.

Elegant bought the book, and when he got back to his room in the boarding house, Tommie was asleep, something he'd counted on. By now, Tommie knew he read Shakespeare. In fact, Tommie teased him good-naturedly about it. He didn't want Tommie to start thinking he was some kind of nutcase, looking at people through a high-powered microscope, in detail, so he snuck the book inside his suitcase, keeping it hidden from him.

But he couldn't deny he enjoyed studying the psychological dimensions and complexities of the mind. His mind had been advanced, autodidactically, to this point of maturation. He wanted to know more about human behavior, and the book he purchased in the Morgantown bookstore gave him hints. And Tommie, last night, gave him hints. And Pee-Pot Manners, this morning, gave him hints, Elegant thought.

Through their silence, Tommie and Pee-Pot Manners were dancing around each other, saddled with identical memories. Both were in Tommie Lathers's room when he died. Both there when he took his last breath on Earth—it's what Tommie said. The day before he died, Tommie Lathers Sr. got out of bed, and when they tried to stop him, he fought them off and got hold of a liquor bottle and drank it down— did it to kill himself. Nothing in the world could hide that "fact," Tommie'd said.

Just now, in the rocker, Pee-Pot Manners's voice quivered with emotion when he spoke of Tommie Lathers, as Tommie's voice had last night in the car. They were frightened by the same realities. They weren't able to sit down and talk honestly or truthfully about Tommie's drinking because of Tommie Lathers Sr. It's what his death had done to them, its lasting effect on them.

Elegant stood.

He was going outside to see if Gyp was back by the woodpile, lying in the sun. He would join her; sit next to her; look out to the tall, stately mountains; smell the clean, crisp air; and think of tomorrow, Sunday, when he would go back to the Body of Christ Church for church services and see Gem Loving for a second time in a week.

CHAPTER 10

Pee-Pot drove Elegant to church, but there would be no church service for him this morning. Pee-Pot wasn't in the mood for church but for spending the morning with Cora Manners at the grave site behind the church. It was a cheerful day, and there were wooden benches to sit on. And that he would do while listening to the choir, he told Elegant, as if he were listening to angels.

It's something he'd said he did periodically on summer days like this, make himself available to Cora Manners—feel her loving spirit.

Today, in church, Elegant was a few rows closer to the pulpit than on his first visit. For some reason, he began looking for Mr. Holloway, whom he didn't locate, which, of course, didn't mean he wasn't in church since he couldn't see everyone. It was a friendly, open-arms kind of church, as Mr. Whaley used to say. He felt at home even without Pee-Pot.

He was nervous, not the sweaty kind, because no sweat was visible atop his skin, but the kind that produces butterflies in the pit of your stomach. He felt like he was going to, at any minute, break out into a rash; and if anybody did look at him, it certainly wouldn't be Gem Loving, that's for sure!

During the week, he bought a new suit as if Gem Loving saw the one he wore his first trip to church—since she was away on her Christian retreat. Only, Pastor Loving had, and Francine Loving and her girlfriends had, so maybe if his name came up in conversation, however, whenever, one of them might make a comment to Gem Loving about his suit, and right away he'd lose his good standing.

He'd already thought this, Elegant thought, sitting in the pew—no matter how silly it all sounded!

Rapidly, The Body of Christ Church pews filled.

Where is she? Where's Gem Loving?

He knew where Pastor Loving was and Francine Loving was—he knew their responsibilities, but what about Gem Loving?

This has to stop! Right now!

But he said that last night and it didn't stop, not until he fell asleep. Up till then, for most of the day (once his mind got off the subject of Tommie), he thought of Gem Loving, what she was doing, doing that over and over again, and then trying to think of anything—the fight this week, fighting in a new town, a new arena—but his mind kept diving back to Gem Loving and only Gem loving.

Hearing rustling in the back of him, Elegant looked over his right shoulder, and there Pastor Loving stood in his plain, immaculately maintained black robe, smiling as if he were Jesus breaking a loaf of bread for the hungry of the Earth (as before).

The choir stood behind him, but Elegant didn't bother to look any further, not for Francine Loving, certainly not to find her, only Gem Loving.

"This is a call to worship," Pastor Loving announced. "We praise his name with *jubilation!*"

The congregants stood. The choir sang.

Pastor Loving proceeded down the aisle. Then, of course, trailed the choir; and looking to his right, Elegant saw Francine Loving. His head turned back to the front of the church, and then Elegant looked over to the aisle to his right, to the choir again, and …

There she was, Gem Loving, singing, marching down the aisle with the choir—a member of the choir!

It was a little later in the service, and Elegant had tried his best to concentrate on the church service in general, but his eyes continually sought out Gem Loving, even though she was off at an angle, where he'd have to awkwardly crook his neck in order to see her. And it wasn't much he saw of her, which only caused him further consternation.

Now he couldn't miss Gem Loving. She was heading for the microphone in front of the choir station. The congregation remained reverent and still.

She's going to sing! Gem Loving's going to sing!

Elegant's body froze, but his thoughts rammed him like a billy goat.

Can she sing? he thought. Or is she singing a solo because she's the pastor's daughter!

The organist, after Gem Loving's head nodded politely to him, indicating she was ready to sing, began playing the introductory chords for the song.

Please be able to sing! Please, Miss Loving! *Please!*

And when Gem Loving opened her mouth, Elegant heard a high, sweet, pure soprano voice; and he thought he was listening to an angel singing, not angels, certainly totally opposite to what was Pee-Pot's apropos description.

———

Church service was over, and Elegant was standing on Pastor Loving's receiving line. When Elegant finally got to Pastor Loving, he said, "Mr. Raines. Mr. Raines, how nice to see you again."

It indeed was a pleasant surprise for Elegant that Pastor Loving remembered his name.

"Good morning. Good morning," Pastor Loving said gleefully, shaking Elegant's hand.

"Good morning, Pastor Loving. Y-you remembered my name, sir. From my last visit, sir."

"A bad habit of mine after all these years, I would imagine, Mr. Raines."

"Pardon me, sir, but it sounds like a good, a very good habit to me, Pastor Loving, sir."

"It is. Of course it is, Mr. Raines. If you're going to take the time to remember my name then, I think, in all fairness, I should at least take the time to remember yours."

That makes perfect sense, Elegant thought—perfect sense!

"By the way, Mr. Raines, where's Mr. Manners this morning?"

"He's in the back of the church, sir."

"Visiting Cora Manners."

"Yes, sir."

Elegant knew it was time to move on since others were waiting on the receiving line.

"Won-wonderful sermon, Pastor Loving."

"If only I could preach like my daughter sings, huh, Mr. Raines?"

Stubbornly, Elegant gripped the Bible in his hand and then smiled at Pastor Loving.

Elegant was outside on church grounds. Looking around the grounds, he really didn't want to take flight, get to the back of the church, go to the grave site for Pee-Pot, but knew that'd be his next logical choice.

Weaving through bands of people out on the lawn, suddenly, Elegant felt his shoulder being tapped from behind.

"Elegant." Elegant turned.

"Mr. Holloway, sir."

Always neat, Mr. Holloway looked particularly neat in a three-piece striped seersucker suit with a gold pocket watch's chain running the length of the wide-mouth vest pocket. "Where's Mr. Manners, son?"

"I was just going for him, sir."

"Oh. Then he's in the back." Then Chadway Holloway's face bubbled. "So have you heard anything like it before, Elegant?"

"What's that, sir?"

"Gem, why Gem Loving sing!"

What's wrong with me? What!

"No, no, why no, Mr. Holloway!"

"She should be a music major. Music just pours out her. But she's not. Sadly. The great Marion Anderson is a contralto, I know, Elegant. But she could sing on the world stage, don't you think, and become the world's next great Negro singer?"

"Yes, I—"

"She's such a brilliant girl."

Elegant laughed to himself, seeing he wasn't going to get a word in edgewise with Mr. Holloway.

"Gem feels her calling is elsewhere. With children. Education. Educating our black children. Black youth. How she sees it. Hmm ..."

"That seems—"

"Noble, of course, Elegant. Noble. But you don't always know what

God's plans are. God does work in mysterious ways. We'll just have to wait and see on that. She's still so young. So many miles and roads ahead for her. For that sweet young lady to travel."

"Yes, sir."

"Well, let me get going then, Elegant. Let ... by the way, have you talked to her since you two met at the store Tuesday?"

"No, Mr. Holloway, I haven't, sir."

"So you ain't had an opportunity to tell her how much you enjoyed her singing this morning yet?"

"No, I, no, sir, I—"

"'Cause there she is—"

When Elegant's head turned, he saw her.

"Elegant. It's as good a time as any, wouldn't you think?"

"Yes, yes it is, Mr. Holloway."

"By the way," Chadway Holloway said, walking away, "I love that suit you got on this morning. Quite a dandy delight!"

"Y-yours too, Mr. Holloway. Yours too!"

Elegant watched Chadway Holloway repair for his car and then aimed his eyes back at Gem Loving, who was engaged, talking to four older women.

Nervous, still—but Mr. Manners will have to wait!

Elegant approached Gem Loving and the four churchwomen.

Gem Loving's head turned slightly.

"Mr. Raines. Good afternoon, Mr. Raines."

"Good afternoon, Miss Loving."

"Oh, excuse me, may I introduce you, Mr. Raines?"

Gem Loving commenced by introducing each of the churchwomen to Elegant; the women were friendly and accommodating.

So one of the women conversed with Elegant while the others conversed with Gem, and before too long, the women bid "good day" to her all at the same time and then smiled at him, bidding him the same.

Now, it seemed, it was just him and Gem Loving standing at the corner of the Body of Christ Church, even though there were still a number of people camped out on the church lawn.

"Your, your singing, Miss Loving, your voice, they were, it was, you were ..."

Elegant felt embarrassed.

"Thank you, Mr. Raines."

"But I didn't say anything, Miss Loving. Anything yet ...," Elegant said, his eyes dropping.

"Why of course you did, Mr. Raines."

She was wearing a blue-and-white poplin dress, white open-toe shoes, and a lovely cultured pearl necklace.

"They're my mother's pearls, Mr. Raines," she said, noting what Elegant's eyes addressed. "When she passed, they were left to me. Francine, my sister, wanted me to have them too. It's my most valued possession."

Elegant smiled.

"I saw you, by the way, uh ..." And then Gem thought, *Am I being too forward?* But she thought again, *The cat's already been let out of the bag, hasn't it?* "Practically everyone, in fact, from the pulpit."

Elegant didn't care, as long as she saw him. It really didn't matter who else she saw.

"I know about your mother, Miss Loving. Mr. Manners told me. I saw Mrs. Manners's headstone and your mother's during the same visit."

Gem smiled. "They truly deserve to be buried so close together. They were examples of mine. As a woman, I saw what I could be in this community one day, through them."

She was so beautiful, Elegant thought, this Gem Loving, inside and out. It was her physical beauty at first, but that didn't last long, not even in Mr. Holloway's store.

"I was just going to the back of the church. Mr. Manners is back there."

"Oh, he is!"

"Yes. Waiting for me, I would imagine."

"Do you mind if I join you, Mr. Raines? I haven't seen Mr. Manners in quite some time now."

Gem was wearing a white bonnet, and she adjusted it before taking her first step, Elegant stepping aside for her.

From the distance, Elegant saw Pee-Pot was sitting on the bench stiffly, with his arms folded and his legs crossed at the ankles. It looked a far cry different than seeing him in his rocker, how he normally relaxed.

"I hope Mr. Manners isn't sleeping, Miss Loving," Elegant whispered to Gem Loving.

"No, I don't think so, Mr. Raines. It's not happened on any previous occasion. When Mr. Manners's been out here."

And maybe ten or twelve yards later, Gem proved to be correct, for Pee-Pot's head whipped around.

"Gem!"

"Mr. Manners!"

It's when Gem lit off for Pee-Pot, and when she got there she began hugging him so spiritedly, Pee-Pot was forced to say, "Gem, Gem, now I'm not as young as I was yesterday!"

"It's so good to see you, Mr. Manners!"

Elegant had gotten to them.

"How was that trip of yours?"

"Mr. Manners, I always learn so much. I—"

"Gem, oh, you sang like an angel this morning. If I would've known what to expect, I wouldn't've skipped church service this morning."

"But you were out here."

Pee-Pot frowned. "It's not the same, Gem. Ain't. You should know that. By now. But I shut my eyes and used my imagi—so you two," Pee-Pot said, finally including Elegant, "have met. Know each other."

"Yes, Mr. Manners."

"Yes, sir."

"I told Elegant Pastor Loving had two lovely daughters. He did see Francine the first time he was here with me, now—"

"Pardon me, Mr. Manners," Gem said, shifting her eyes from Pee-Pot over to Elegant, "but I met Mr. Raines in Mr. Holloway's store on Tuesday, didn't I, Mr. Raines? We were introduced by Mr. Holloway."

"Tuesday. Yes it was, uh, Tuesday, Miss, right, uh, Miss Loving ... Mr. Manners."

"Oh ... I didn't know that ..."

"She, she does sing most beautifully, Mr. Manners. I did tell you that, uh, didn't I, uh, Miss Loving?"

"You did, Mr. Raines. And I'm most appreciative of your compliment," Gem said humbly.

Elegant looked at Cora Manners's grave site, and he saw the fresh flowers at the foot of the headstone, the ones Pee-Pot brought with him in the truck.

"Time to go, I suppose," Pee-Pot said, taking Gem's hand.

Elegant stepped aside for them.

Gem and Pee-Pot walked just a few feet hand in hand, and then together they stood at Helena Loving's headstone, both touching it. "God Bless you, Momma."

When Pee-Pot and Gem's eyes shut, Elegant followed suit.

They began walking hand in hand again. Elegant attached himself to them, to the left side of Gem. Gem was in the middle.

The three were at the truck. Gem bent forward and kissed Pee-Pot's cheek. This was at the back of the truck.

"And will I see you next Sunday, Mr. Manners?"

"Now, Gem, you know I don't make predictions—at least not that far in the future."

They laughed hardily, and then Pee-Pot excused himself, getting into the truck.

Gem and Elegant were alone again, and both seemed somewhat shy, tentative, this time.

"I ..."

"Thank you for such a pleasant surprise today, Miss Loving."

"I ..."

"Your singing. It was, after all, amazing."

"I'm so nervous before I sing. I suppose it's like your boxing, of which I know nothing about. The mechanics of it. But do you get nervous before you fight, Mr. Raines?"

What should he say? If he said no then he would seem somewhat a braggart, so saying yes was the safe, smart thing to say.

"Yes, I do, Miss Loving."

Pastor Loving came out of the church. He saw Gem and Elegant talking.

"But I always close my eyes and thank God for the gift he's bestowed upon me, and the opportunity," Gem said.

"I hope to see you again, Miss Loving."

"I do hope it too, Mr. Raines," Gem said, extending her right hand out to Elegant.

"Good day."

"Good day."

Pastor Loving was still on the church steps, and what he saw he didn't like—was not at all pleased by.

—⁓—

About a quarter of a mile from the church, on Barker Road, it's when Pee-Pot slowly, deliberately, turned to Elegant.

"So you didn't tell me. Was keeping it a secret from me."

"Oh, uh, Miss Loving, sir?"

"Yes, Gem Loving."

"I guess, uh, sir, my mind's been so occupied with the fight coming up this—"

"Now if you're gonna cook up a lie, son, it's gotta be a lot better than that. That malarkey you're about to hand me."

Elegant actually gulped like a big hiccup and looked at Pee-Pot with the innocence of a fallen angel.

"I ..."

"I don't blame you any, Elegant. I'd probably do the same if I was in your shoes."

"You, you would, Mr. Manners?"

"Of course. An old man like me doesn't have to know everything, you know."

"It wasn't that," Elegant said hurriedly, "Mr. Manners. Your age or anything like that, sir. I mean, if Tommie hadn't seen the look on my face when I came into the gym after, from Mr. Holloway's store, and knew Gem Loving put it there, she was back in Longwood, sir, I wouldn't've told him I met her either."

"Elegant ..."

"Uh, y-yes, Mr. Manners ...?"

"I never heard you put together such a long sentence as that one. But I guess there's always a first."

"Yes, sir. Always a first. Always, sir."

Everyone in Longwood knew about the effect Gem Loving had on the boys in Longwood, so Elegant's reaction to her was to be expected, Pee-Pot thought. But there was something about them together, something special, the aura they created, like him and Cora Manners, and Pastor Loving and Helena Loving.

"Oh, I got off the bench back there awful quick when I heard Gem begin to sing. Was gonna rush the church."

"You, you were, Mr. Manners?"

"But her voice just stopped me dead in my tracks. Besides, by the time I got inside, the way I move these days, her solo would've been over with."

Elegant laughed.

"Oh, you think it's funny, do you, Mr. Raines? If so, I'll see you in the gym tomorrow!"

"But, Mr. Manners, sir, I—"

"Save it, Mr. Raines. Save it—until I get my blood's worth!"

Elegant and Pee-Pot kept laughing.

———

Elegant and Tommie's winning streak was kept alive in Huntington, West Virginia, at the Radio Center Arena.

Elegant knocked out Fred "Mole" Moore in the second round. Tommie outpointed Edgar "Sharpie" Johnson—winning every round.

It was a Friday-night fight, so Elegant didn't have to deal with the Angel's Corner situation with Tommie, so in effect, it was a big relief. While his attitude wouldn't've changed anyway regarding going into Inwood for that kind of activity (dancing and sex), the personal reputation issue, once again, it did have everything to do with Gem Loving now, and he knew it.

Emotionally, he was in her grip—that plain and simple. He couldn't wait to see Gem Loving this Sunday, not having seen her in town all week. After church this Sunday, Pee-Pot had informed him there would be a social hour. During the summer, the social hour was every third Sunday of the month on Body of Christ's front lawn. He bought another new suit during the week, making it three new suits hanging in his closet. And along with the suit, a new tie and shirt.

The fight purse at Radio Center Arena was a little bigger than the purses at Fame Arena. Along with his job at the brickyard and picking up a few heads to cut from the brickyard (barbering them at the plant), Elegant was making more money than he ever made in his life. But what bothered him about staying at the farmhouse was his lack of monetary contribution to the household, something Pee-Pot refused to change—was tone-deaf to.

The fight at Radio Center Arena really pleased Elegant. It was one of his better performances, notwithstanding he knocked Mole Moore out in the second round and not the first. Pee-Pot felt the same. Mole Moore was a left-handed boxer (the toughest kind to figure out). And what made it worse was his style was compounded by an "ugly ducking" awkwardness. Elegant kept aiming hard, stiff jabs at Moore's midsection until one of those jabs turned into a perfect left hook that caught Moore square on the jaw, and Mole was doomed. He didn't drop like a mole but like a moose at 2:26 of round number two.

———

Long tables with white linen tablecloths were set out on the church lawn. Food was everywhere the eye could fathom: smoked turkey; thin, crunchy cornbread; buttermilk biscuits; Savannah red rice; glazed ham; catfish; salmon cakes; steamed cabbage; greens; peas; pilaf rice baked chicken; casseroles; potato salad; and pound cakes, apple pies, blackberry pies, mincemeat pies, et cetera.

There was a feast in front of the Body of Christ Church on Fowler Road. The church called it a social hour, but it took more than an hour for this extravagant church function to expire, typically starting at one o'clock and finishing at four o'clock.

Gem and Elegant had drifted away from the others. They'd found chairs off to the right of the church near a tall shade tree. They weren't sitting directly under it but a few feet away. The bright sun, they weren't looking into it, but it beamed off the back of their heads.

They'd eaten the main course but now drank from their cups of apple cider. Elegant had forsaken dessert (the pies and cakes and homemade ice cream), and so too Gem. Elegant because he was full. Gem because she was watching her weight.

"I'm glad things went well for you Friday night, Mr. Raines. Your boxing match."

Gem had looked at his face earlier and saw it remained unnicked.

All Elegant told her, when she asked, was that he'd won, nothing more, not the round nor how he'd won; no other specifics were discussed.

"I train very hard at it, and it's satisfactory when things go well for me, Miss Loving."

"Have you ever lost a contest?"

"No, I haven't, Miss Loving."

"Do you think about losing?" Pause.

"No, no, I don't, Miss Loving. I can't go in the ring with a negative mind. With negative thoughts."

The cup of cider was in Gem's lap. "May I say something to you, Mr. Raines, and not feel presumptuous or naïve in saying it?"

Elegant didn't know why such words as "presumptuous" and "naïve" were used by Gem Loving, but he was curious as all get-out to find out. "Of course," Elegant said, knitting his forehead and looking quite serious himself.

"It's all right …?"

"Yes."

Gem looked down at the cup of cider and then up at Elegant. "I know I'm not getting hit in the ring, what boxers do, so I have no illusions of that—but singing …"

"Of course. I see what you're driving at."

"It's okay?"

"Yes."

"All right to say that we, uh, singers, Mr. Raines, mustn't have negative thoughts before we sing. Negative, a negative mind … even though, I'm not always perfect," Gem laughed.

"I have to be. Must be, Miss Loving."

"What you do requires such courage, Mr. Raines. Being a boxer."

She was so smart, Elegant thought. So bright and intelligent—it burst right through her eyes and her smile and—

"I think boxing does build character."

That was the icing on the cake. He really liked Gem Loving—he really did!

Gem fell back in the chair and laughed. It was so sudden, it startled Elegant.

"Forgive me, Mr. Raines, for my impolite—"

"Forgiven, f-forgiven, Miss Loving."

"But every woman, young girl in Longwood, passes by Mr. Manners's gym, Pee-Pot's Pugilistic Paradise, the Pug, as it's charmingly nicknamed, as you well know, but doesn't know exactly what goes on inside there. Whatsoever."

"Oh," Elegant said, breathing a sigh of relief.

"It's a building for men only. Someone like me, a woman, has no idea what happens in there."

"A lot of sweat, I assure you, Miss Loving."

"Which most women have seen."

"I'm sure." Pause.

"Were you born in View Point, Texas?"

"No, uh, Miss Loving, uh … I was born in New Town, Oklahoma."

"Are your parents—"

"They're deceased. I was raised in an orphanage."

This saddened Gem, and it was all too transparent.

"But I'm okay, Miss Loving. R-really, I am."

"The state, it provided for you?"

"Yes, I was ten. Ten years old at—"

"Oh, Gem. Gem!"

Gem looked over to the corner of the church.

"Yes, Papa!"

"Oh, so there you are!"

Hurriedly, Pastor Loving walked toward Gem and Elegant.

Elegant stood.

"I wondered where you'd disappeared to," Pastor Loving said, getting to them. "But I see you're with Mr. Raines, uh, here."

"Yes, Papa. Mr. Raines and I thought we'd sit out here. In the back. Take up conversation here, sir."

Pastor Loving smiled. "And whose idea was that?"

Gem and Elegant looked at each other and then broke out laughing.

"Pardon me, Pastor Loving."

"Pardon me, Papa."

"Was … was it that funny, amusing, Gem?"

"No, no, Papa. But how did we get out here, Mr. Raines? Navigate ourselves to this spot?"

"I ..."

"You certainly didn't consider the shade tree, now did you? Because if you had, you'd be sitting, you and Mr. Raines, under it, wouldn't you? Not camping under this hot, unbearable sun?"

Elegant couldn't tell if Pastor Loving was being critical of them or not—or was just making a perceptive observation.

"Well ... you ... come along, Gem," he said, taking Gem's hand. "Sister Hattie Eastern would like to see you. She just got in from her sister's residence in Lakeland, Florida, and says she hasn't seen you all summer." Pause.

"You don't mind, do you, Mr. Raines?"

"No, no, I don't, Pastor Loving. No, sir."

Then Pastor Loving looked sternly at Gem.

"I knew you hadn't gone back to the house. And Francine said she hadn't seen you. And I knew you weren't inside the church, not for that period of absence," Pastor Loving said, walking away with Gem.

To Elegant, hearing what Pastor Loving said, his tone of voice, and witnessing his demeanor, it felt strongly that both he and Gem Loving were standing trial—had done something terribly amiss.

<hr />

Other than a few words exchanged between them once they got in the truck and early minutes into the drive back to the house, there'd been no verbal exchange between Pee-Pot and Elegant, and the silence was driving Elegant nuts, for there'd never been this kind of prolonged, sustained silence between them, and it seemed deliberate.

He was participating in it only because it seemed he had no other choice but to, that Pee-Pot Manners had created this vacuum and he in no way must upset it but be respectful toward it. Pee-Pot Manners was controlling it his way. But he had Gem to think about, Gem Loving he liked so much it ached his insides.

He couldn't believe the luck or the opportunity afforded him today, to have found time to spend with her, just the two of them in back of the Body of Christ Church, sitting, having apple cider, talking richly, expansively, as if an angel had planned it, had perched herself on his shoulder, or Gem Loving's shoulder—or maybe both their shoulders.

Last night, in bed, he didn't pray for this, but it felt like a blessing, a true one right now to have had a situation like this unfold, to open up to him so naturally, so fortuitously. They'd just drifted to the back of the church, didn't really "disappear" as Pastor Loving had put it, putting it in a category of design and intent where it didn't belong. They didn't have that much control over anything. They simply did not know each other that well to plan something out.

But just to sit with Gem Loving, Elegant thought. Just for him to be with her, to talk to her no matter how brief it now seemed, it was now the start of something, the beginning. It could be defined this way, how things had shaped up for them.

He couldn't mistake the power of love, Pee-Pot thought, not even at his age. He didn't think he'd get mixed up in this ever again, see it, be so intimate with it again. Why would he? Everything was kept at a remote distance, him living out on the farm, just him and Gyp and his occasional barber customers, the gym (where no women were allowed); so how could he become a witness to something like this: a Gem Loving and Elegant Raines? But he was. He had been exposed to them.

How did he know he would have an Elegant Raines in his life, these chain of events would occur, that his life would become better, enhanced because of Frank "Black Machine" Whaley's death, that it would offer up an Elegant Raines to him, someone like a son whose life was intricately entwined in his, where he had, for some time now, felt the emotional power of it, of a young man who had all but reawakened his life and given it greater content and purpose.

The territory he'd covered in his mind, Pee-Pot thought, was bumpy and tough. It was as simple and honest as the day was long. But it still had to be thought through, for if he didn't, he'd feel guilty, sorry for it. He couldn't be neglectful or careless, not when it came to this issue, Gem Loving and Elegant Raines. He certainly didn't want reality to come crashing down on Elegant, but what else is there in life, Pee-Pot thought, but reality and truth.

He wanted to look at Elegant while … instead, he was looking at the road. The road had no more deception in it than a rock or a tree. What you saw was what you saw, and what he knew was what he knew.

With discomfit Pee-Pot shifted his body's weight in the truck's front seat. He looked at Elegant.

"Elegant, Pastor Loving doesn't like fighters. None who might be interested in his daughters. In Gem or Francine. That's just fact, son. Pure, simple fact."

———

The Loving house, you could say, was inherited by Gem and Francine and Embry Loving from Helena Loving when she died. For in essence, it was her house from how it was decorated to how it was maintained, the everyday operation, attention and care to it, something which first fell to Gem, and then, when she left for Howard University, Francine's to uphold.

And maintain it Francine had, with great zeal, not unlike Gem when it was her sole province, something done with great devotion. The curtains were starched, and dust had no way of surviving in the Loving household; it couldn't survive a Francine or Gem Loving attack with a broom or mop or dust rag or dustpan.

When Gem got back to the house from the church's social hour, she retired to her bedroom. But it hadn't been a comfortable walk for her from the church to the house. After she'd spoken to Miss Hattie Eastern at length, she returned to the house. Maybe this, her talking to Hattie Eastern, would be construed by her father as a disappearance too, she'd thought at the time.

There was a doll on the bed, back against a sham, Flora, who she felt like holding but wouldn't, for suddenly she felt it'd make her look childish even if there was no one in the room but her—and she wasn't childish. But Flora was a constant comfort for her, especially when her mother died, not that she lost faith or didn't pray as hard or steadfast to God, but in certain trying moments, she did talk to Flora, she did share her feelings with her with a blinding, all-giving passion, sometimes isolating herself from the family, talking to Flora as if she were her mother incarnate, asking her why she had to die, why she and Francine and her father were left behind to grieve her, to suffer her death the way they had.

In fact, Flora was Helena Loving's creation, made by her hands—one of Helena Loving's many talents. She was six years old then when Flora came into her life, so it made Flora twelve years old.

"Flora, you're twelve years old," Gem laughed. "Did you, sometimes I for ..."

She was thinking of Elegant Raines. She couldn't stop thinking of him. She didn't want to stop thinking of Elegant Raines. They were delectable thoughts. Tall. Handsome. Elegant.

Gem laughed again. "Elegant. Elegant. Elegant Raines is so elegant."

In no way, fashion, did she want to degrade or insult boxers; but he did speak so well, so exceptionally well. It was atypical of a boxer—it really was. And she knew the backgrounds most came from, so it was of no surprise when she met a fighter for the first time—of what to expect in the way of speech and grammar. But not Elegant Raines, Gem thought. He was the exception to the rule, a huge cut above the grade.

Last night before falling to sleep, her last thoughts were of him. And she actually prayed to God he would come to church today (something she never did when she prayed to God, for her own benefit—not unless it was a college midterm exam!). She wanted to see him so badly. Her heart beat so wildly in church this morning before she saw him sitting in the pew, thinking, at the time, her heart might fly away.

Oh she'd had crushes on boys before, Gem thought. She had one on Malcolm Beecham Washington, a philosophy major at Howard University this spring semester, in fact. Only, Malcolm Beecham Washington was no Elegant Raines—not even close. She and Malcolm had one date, so she would know! Gem giggled. And with a crush, oftentimes, it hits quickly like a sun shower anyway, and then a week or so later it's gone, done, over with.

But this wasn't a crush she had on Elegant Raines but something much, much deeper. She just couldn't stop thinking of him now. Her mind refused to stop thinking of him, resolute and insatiable. She wouldn't exaggerate him or ...

"Papa, I think, was out of line with him. Mr. Raines. I just don't think it fair what he said now. Papa misconstrued our conduct in the back of the church."

She was a college student who was matriculating at Howard University, was on its campus alone, unchaperoned (of course). She had been trusted with at least this level of independence and responsibility, but you wouldn't think it by her father's tone of voice and actions. She was sure Elegant Raines caught it too, how condescending he was to them, treating them not like adults, mature young people, but like children—no better than children.

Gem walked over to Flora, picked her up, hugged her, and then laid her back against the shams, and this simple act did calm her. It did release her tension and some of her anger. And she was angry. She—

"Papa's home. Just came in the house."

She heard him enter the house. She knew it wasn't Francine. Francine was at Mrs. Etta Mae Taylor's home, reading to her (she'd recently gone blind), and wouldn't be back home so soon.

Her bedroom door was open.

She hadn't come upstairs to the bedroom to change her clothes, something, after church, was normal for her. And standing there in the room, suddenly, it was as if she had to get hold of her sensibilities, had to remember she was in the house, that certain things were expected of her by their routineness—what was customary on a Sunday when she got in from church.

"Gem. Gem. It's where I thought you'd be, darling. In your bedroom."

Gem turned to the door in response to her father's voice. Pastor Loving had yet gotten to the bedroom door.

"Gem."

Gem walked to the door; they hugged. They walked arm and arm to the wide window and looked over to the church, an unbroken sight line. They saw a smattering of the women of the church wrap the food's remains and then cart them off church grounds.

"The sisters of the church are such hard workers, aren't they, Gem?"

"Generous and giving, Papa."

"We're not rich in the pocketbook but rich of spirit and dedication."

And Gem knew all too well what her father was alluding to: that whatever foods were left over from the social hour would be donated to the local charities, in particular St Luke's Orphanage.

"It's testimony to the type of folk we have living in this community. This community's composition, Gem."

Pastor Loving angled his head to kiss Gem's forehead.

"The social hour's Christian fellowship, Gem. But what really binds the spirit, as you said, honey, is giving—the sharing of our small but infinite earthly rewards, of which there are so numerous. Are so bountiful in rewarding us."

These were the kind of words Gem grew up hearing from her parents: faith based, Bible based, a matrix of high-principled thoughts and deeds. They invigorated her spirit and gave her every reason to want to be alive, in love with life in Longwood, West Virginia.

She was going to mention Elegant Raines was raised in an orphanage but then thought better not to, not now. It's just that some of the food from the social hour was going to St. Luke's, and it seemed particularly relevant.

"You haven't changed out your clothes, Gem," Pastor Loving said, standing back from Gem, removing his glasses and taking her in.

There was a mystified look on her face. "You know, Gem, Elegant Raines is a very attractive young man."

The comment caught Gem completely off guard.

"I have been very impressed with him."

Gem didn't feel safe enough to say anything.

"Flora ..."

Gem looked where her father was looking, at Flora.

"There are certain things, Gem," Pastor Loving said, folding and refolding the stems of his glasses nervously and then putting them back on and then locking his fingers in front of him, "we never outgrow. I don't care how old we get. There're certain things we can't change. Just can't do it."

Pastor Loving was halfway across the floor when he stopped and turned back to Gem.

"He's a boxer. A fighter. Nothing's changed for me to change my opinion of them. Nothing, Gem. Nothing."

Pastor Loving left the room, leaving Gem heartbroken.

Sunday had come, and Elegant only saw Gem Loving in the choir, from the church pew. After church, he spoke to Pastor Loving at the church door, even though it was brief, not like on past occasions. He wasn't with Pee-

Pot; Pee-Pot and Black Moon had traveled to Chicago for Black Moon's Monday-night bout in Chicago Coliseum. Elegant walked the five-mile stretch to church that morning. During the week he'd looked for Gem Loving, hoping to see her in town; only, it never happened, and it was difficult for him to accept.

He didn't let any of it distract him, by no means disrupt his gym work, but at night it really sank in that he didn't see her that day, and it only raised his desire to see her the following day, that his luck would change.

After church Sunday, he did stand around outside the Body of Christ Church, hoping Gem Loving would emerge from it, but she never did. And he had trouble killing time on the church lawn since he really didn't know many of the parishioners well, even though they were all quite friendly toward him. Mr. Holloway was there, but then he ran off.

When he walked from the church, he began looking back over his shoulder, hoping, just hoping … And then he thought of going to the back of the church to visit Cora Manners's grave site, but how disingenuous and cheap would that have been, he'd thought, using Cora Manners as a ploy so he could stay on the church grounds longer, delaying his departure to the house, just for the sake … for he could see Gem Loving.

He was scared. All kinds of awful thoughts raced through his mind. Yes, all bad thoughts, negative thoughts, remembering Pastor Loving's voice's cold, flat tone last week (not this week at the church door, with Gem Loving not present) when he was looking for his daughter, when she was in his company, when all of this reached proportions he had no idea they could.

And then what Pee-Pot said in the truck, on the way home from church, Pastor Loving and fighters and his daughters. Were they doomed already, he and Gem Loving? He'd asked himself enough times to reinforce the question, strengthen it, for it not to limp like some nicked bird. He was already in love with her, out of count of any sane rationale why he shouldn't be. But Pastor Loving was already the obstacle—the one obstructing them.

He would've seen her today if not for Pastor Loving. She would've been the same person he met in Mr. Holloway's store and the two occasions in church. It would've been the same Gem Loving, except this time, they would've had even more to talk about, conversation between them more stimulating, eventful, and flowing.

But all he could do now was think about it, something there seemed nothing he could do anything about. He felt the pressure of feeling helpless, not being in control of anything, Pastor Loving controlling everything. He knew she liked him and that this was no game they were playing. He saw how her eyes sparkled, how sincere they were. How much they gave him hope.

He just didn't know where to go from here, where he was at this point. Hoping to see her in town again by blind luck, fate—whatever. Or just hope for next Sunday, that things had changed for the better, not for the worse—that, he couldn't stand. That would really, really hurt.

———

"Well, welcome home again, Mr. Manners!"

"Chicago's a great place to visit, Elegant. But not to live. But I say that about every place in comparison to Longwood, West Virginia, don't I?"

Gyp was up on her hind legs, her paws against Pee-Pot's chest, Pee-Pot bending over, Gyp licking his face.

"Gyp. Gyp. Oh, Gyp, girl. The more we stay at this, the more we love each other, don't we!"

Elegant had Pee-Pot's suitcase and put it at the bottom of the staircase.

It was a little after seven o'clock.

"Thought we'd get in earlier, Elegant, but looks like my timing's fine," Pee Pot said, his nose sniffing the air.

"Come right this way, Mr. Manners. Just follow me, sir!"

"Elegant, I know where the kitchen is. My way around my own house, son!"

Woof! Woof!

They'd eaten, and now they were relaxing, gabbing at the kitchen table.

"The second round, huh, Mr. Manners."

"Johnny McGibbons. A game white fighter. Black Moon knocked him stiff."

Elegant wasn't going to be afraid to inquire about the fight or Black

Moon. He was going to treat him as if he were just another fighter from the gym. For as soon as they sat, Pee-Pot told him about Black Moon's victory, about knocking out McGibbons in the second round, and he'd heard it at the gym too; but it didn't matter how many times he heard it—it was just another fight to him.

"Cold," Pete-Pot said with a certain sense of awe.

"Those Chicago fans really took to the boy."

"That's good, Mr. Manners."

"It is, Elegant. Like I tell you, son, you fight for yourself in the ring. But you've got to please the fans too. During the process. Give them something to cheer about. A good show for the money. It's only good sense." His arms folded over his chest. "It' why they want him back. Headline in September."

"Good for him, Mr. Manners."

"There's something about him. He's got all those muscles, Elegant, and he doesn't disappoint. A fan wants him to be what he is. Some of those body types like him badly disappoint. But not Black Moon. He lives up to the bargain. Delivers the goods 100 percent every time."

Even if it was Black Moon, his rival, it was still nice to talk about boxing, Elegant thought. It was such a romantic, heroic sport, where heroes abound, capture the public's imagination in fantastical ways.

"So were you at church Sunday?" Pee-Pot said, totally switching the subject. "Able to get off to church?"

Elegant didn't know how to answer without exposing his feelings. "Y-yes, sir."

"I ain't prying into this, Elegant. But I am concerned."

Elegant refused to be coy though, not with Pee-Pot Manners. "You mean me and Miss Loving, don't you, sir?"

"Yes, Elegant, the two of you."

Patiently, Pee-Pot waited for a reply but got none.

"I … what I said took the starch out you, didn't it?"

"No, it's what I didn't tell you, Mr. Manners, two Sundays past." Pause. "Pastor Loving already had made up his mind about me, sir."

"Yes, he was looking for Gem at the social hour. I know. And he found her with you behind the church."

"Even, even you are making it sound like …"

"No, it's not that, Elegant. Ain't—but Pastor Loving and me, Elegant ...
It's just there," Pee-Pot said. " You don't have to predict anything."

Elegant stood and then walked over to Gyp, who was lying down. He
pet her. He didn't know how to talk about Gem Loving, not even with
Pee-Pot.

"Elegant, did you see her, at least? Able to talk to her at church this
Sunday?"

"See her, yes, Mr. Manners. But talk to her, sir, no. She's in the choir,
after all."

Silence.

"But I didn't see her after church. She stayed inside. I hung around
outside the church as long as I could. As long as I could stand to, Mr.
Manners—without feeling foolish."

"This isn't Gem, Elegant. Gem Loving. This is her father doing this.
Pastor Loving who's in charge. This thing that's going on between you
two."

"I-I understand that, sir, Mr. Manners."

"Love—"

"You think she loves me!"

"Cora Manners. Cora Madison Manners. We knew, Elegant. Right
off. Everybody saw it. But me and Mrs. Manners saw it first."

Elegant had stopped petting Gyp. He walked over and hugged Pee-Pot
around his shoulders. Pee-Pot looked up at Elegant, surprised.

"Thank you, Mr. Manners. I thought I was going to go crazy, sir."

———

The news came lightning fast, and it came from Mr. Holloway while
Elegant shopped in his store that Friday. The cupboards at the house were
bare of specific foodstuffs again, and Elegant was doing his usual good
deed for Pee-Pot and himself.

"It's come, Elegant. It's finally come. The end of summer around
here."

Chad Holloway seemed serious, so Elegant took it in the same spirit
of his seriousness.

"But, but, Mr. Holloway, you're wrong, sir. With all due respect to you.
It can't be the end of summer, when it's only August 23, sir. It's not—"

"Gem's leaving Longwood next week. For college. P-pardon me, it's what I'm getting at. That university of hers. Howard University. It's the end of summer around here. Longwood. Might as well be when Gem leaves for school."

"Gem Loving is—

"Gotta leave sooner or later, Elegant. I know, at my age, it's the only way to take this. But it doesn't make it any easier for anybody. Nobody, son. Nobody. It's all the talk in town!"

"I-I—"

"She'll be singing her final solo in church Sunday. And then that's that. Wednesday, Gem's back to school. They'll have Gem back. All to themselves. Howard University. Washington, DC."

In Mr. Holloway's store, it hurt him so bad, hearing this about Gem Loving, that it made him feel hollow, and then his legs trembled—actually trembled. It was one church service he didn't want to attend but did. And after Gem Loving sang, he got up and excused himself, telling Pee-Pot he'd walk home (the five miles), back to the house, leaving him there; and Pee-Pot let him go, didn't try stopping him.

When he got home, he put on his sweats and boxing shoes. He loved Gyp so much. She knew this wasn't usual, what he was intending to do, jog into the woods on a Sunday, on a day off, on a day he didn't train, when the gym was a distant thought to him. So Gyp let him run without her, knew he wanted to be alone, feel whatever he had to feel privately, not even hear the swiftness of her at his side but let his anger boil, of him not being able to guide his life as he was guiding his footsteps through the woods on a known trail, not blind trails, impossible trails—trails there to defeat him. So Gyp let him go out on his journey.

That Wednesday, when he knew for sure she'd left Longwood, he walked out of the gym, out in the back of the Pug, and cried his eyes out, cried them out until they turned red. He went back into the gym, but it wasn't the same. It was the first time he wished he wasn't inside a gym but somewhere else—though he didn't know where. He felt lost, out of sorts; there was just no one who could save him.

He told Tommie about Gem Loving, how he thought they'd hit it off, but he, like it seemed every boxer in Longwood, knew Pastor Loving's position toward fighters—so he knew he'd struck out. His remedy for

Elegant was for him to step out with him on Friday night, head over to Angel's Corner in Inwood. Elegant turned Tommie's invitation down flat this time around.

Tommie, in his heart, at the time, knew something like that wouldn't work for Elegant—it was halfheartedly proposed anyway. Tommie's heart really wasn't in it, but he really felt for Elegant, and it was all he could come up with: Angel's Corner. He knew he'd really fallen hard for Gem Loving.

By Friday though, good news arrived at Elegant's doorstep by way of Pee-Pot: he was to headline at Fame Arena by popular demand. Indeed, it lifted Elegant's spirits temporarily. Wednesday was the bad day for him in the gym. Thursday, the next day, for those few hours in the gym, he dashed Gem Loving's having left Longwood out his mind, concentrating solely on the speed bag, the heavy bag, or who he was sparring with.

Now Elegant was as popular as any fighter in the Pug. Most of the fighters liked him. He'd won them over. Their affection. And there was an affection even in a boxing gym, even between hard, tough young men. Elegant still sought family as did a lot of them. It's what Frank "Black Machine" Whaley's gym gave him, and it's what the Pug was giving him: a sense of family.

Of course, this was what he was after from the start, from the time he set foot in Longwood from View Point, Texas—family. He was at home in Longwood. A town to drive his stakes in the ground and make it home. Indeed, no matter how famous he became.

CHAPTER 11

Elegant was in the gym from the brickyard. He was heading toward Pee-Pot's office when he heard Tommie (whom he hadn't seen) yell.

"Wouldn't go in there if I was you, Elegant!"

Then Tommie sprinted across the gym floor. Everyone in the gym seemed well aware of the situation.

"It's Black Moon and Mr. Manners," Tommie said, quickly skirting Elegant away from Pee-Pot's office.

"W-what do you mean, Tommie? Mean, Mr. Manners and—"

"Mr. Manners is in a snit. 'Bout to get down to business. Black Moon, for the past few days, ain't showing him no respect. And alla us in the gym know why." Pause.

"And it's just what he's doing now: holding Black Moon late. Talking things over. Sitting Black Moon down."

———

"Sit, Black Moon."

"I ain't sitting, Mr. Manners. I ain't sitting nowhere."

It was the second time Pee-Pot'd asked Black Moon to sit, and it was the second time he'd been rebuffed.

"At least you still say 'Mr. Manners.'"

"Ain't called for this today—you the one."

"What do you mean?" Pee-Pot said, not in the least pleased by what Black Moon said.

"Wasting my time, that what."

"And how's that, Black Moon?" Pee-Pot replied coolly.

Black Moon shuffled his feet.

"No, son. The past two days you've been wasting mine. And I wanna know why," Pee-Pot said, arching forward. "Your workouts have been sloppy. And you ain't listening to me or Mr. Moore. Paying attention to either of us. So you tell me 'cause I ain't in the game of … business of guessing."

"Who says I been sloppy? Who says!"

"Are you questioning me!"

"I been fine. Fine!"

"Hell you have!"

"Damn right I have!"

I'm the adult, I'm the trainer. I'm the wise man here, Pee-Pot thought. *This isn't getting me anywhere. Flaunting, asserting my authority. Fighting the boy—having a shouting contest with him.*

Pee-Pot got up out his chair.

Black Moon stood there tense, his fists clenched, not in his fighter's stance; but if Pee-Pot were somewhere near his age, there might be physical violence.

Pee-Pot looked into Black Moon's eyes. "Sit down, son. We've been at this too, far too long together."

After Black Moon looked at Pee-Pot long and hard, he shrugged his shoulders; his scowl vanished.

Black Moon looked down at the chair and then sat.

Pee-Pot stood behind him. He laid his hand on his shoulder. His hand stayed there a few seconds more. Pee-Pot returned to his desk. He sat.

Sympathetically, he looked at Black Moon. "Now what's wrong, Black Moon? Tell me?"

Black Moon was twenty one years old, and right now he looked sixteen without the scowl.

"I'm headlining that fight in Chicago …"

"Right …?"

"So, so how come that Elegant Raines boy got him a headline fight in Fame Arena? In Morgantown?"

"W-what does Elegant, what does Elegant Raines have to do with you, Black Moon? Your situation, son? Affect what you're doing in any way?"

"He ain't got no right headlining a fight. He ain't got no right. He ain't that good."

Now Pee-Pot understood what it was he was dealing with. Now he knew.

"The fans think so. Like the fans in Chicago think you're good enough to headline the show there. Asked for you back."

"Yeah, Mr. Manners. 'Cause I'm good. Best middleweight in the world!" Black Moon said. His fist pounded into his palm.

Pee-Pot wanted Black Moon to think like this, that he was the best. He wanted all of his fighters who were as good as Black Moon to think this way.

"And you can't say that 'bout that boy! You know you can't, Mr. Manners!"

Pee-Pot didn't respond.

"And why he been staying with you at the farm like he do? Since he been here?"

"Let's talk about your boxing, Black Moon. Uh, h-how sloppy your workouts have—"

"Ain't talking 'bout that!"

Now even Pee-Pot felt foolish in trying to shift the subject. In avoiding the deeper, more complex issues ground into his showdown with Black Moon.

"He don't deserve to stay at your house. How he deserve that, Mr. Manners? How come!"

"It, it was the circumstances," Pee-Pot stuttered. "Black Machine Whaley dying. Coming in from View Point, Texas, Black Moon. Here to Longwood to train. Out Mr. Whaley's gym to train with—"

"Why you treat him special?"

"Special, I don't—"

"Headlining in Fame Arena. In Morgan—"

"What was I to do? Turn down an offer from—"

"Hate ... hate that boy!"

"Why? Why do—"

"Hate him!" Black Moon said, smashing his fist into his palm again.

"Why do you—"

"C-can't be me and him. Can't be like that!" Black Moon said, leaping to his feet, his anger exploding.

"What, what do you mean by—"

"I ain't fighting for you no more!"

Pee-Pot charged to his feet and then restrained himself, his temper. He just stood there and stared at Black Moon.

"Ha. That what!"

Pee-Pot sat back down in the chair.

"Old man! Old man!" Black Moon said, taunting Pee-Pot.

"Very well, Black Moon. Ver—have it your … But, but what about the fight in Chicago next month? The, the Chicago Coliseum?"

"You don't see so good, do you, do you, old man! Seen people in Chicago talking to me. Got things to say. A promoter from New York. Abe, Abe Fein-Fein …"

"Feinstein. Abe Feinstein."

"Yeah, him. Him. Fein … Mr.—"

"Feinstein."

"Been calling me. To come to New York. Seen me fighting in New York and Chicago too. Mr. Fein … Want me to train under—"

"Duff Crawley."

"Promote my fights. Chicago ain't gonna be off the table."

"Of course. I'll break the contract."

Black Moon stared down at Pee-Pot. "See how easy I make it for you, old man. Since you don't want me no way. No, no goddamned ways!"

How much of that was fiction and how much fact, Pee-Pot thought. How do you separate the wheat from the chaff?

"So it over, old man. It over 'tween you and me!"

Silence.

"I'm sorry, Black Moon."

"I don't care, man. Don't fuckin' care!"

Black Moon ran to the door, flinging it open.

"And as for you! You!" Black Moon's finger was pointing at Elegant, who was in the ring with Gas and Juniper Davies, another Pug fighter.

And then Black Moon ran toward the ring.

Pee-Pot was running too.

Juniper Davies and Gas stood in front of Elegant, essentially shielding him.

Pee-Pot stopped running.

"We gonna meet! Meet! Gonna meet! And I'm gonna kill you, punk! Kill you! Fuckin' kill you!"

"Get outta here. Get outta here, Black Moon. Get the fuck outta here!" Gaston Moore said.

Black Moon turned around and looked at everyone he could find in the gym. "Don't 'long in this fuckin' place, no way. Punks you got in here … no fuckin' way!"

Pee-Pot turned and then walked back into his office, the door shutting quietly behind him.

Then Black Moon turned back around to Elegant.

"Ain't gonna be nobody to protect you the night we fight. Gonna be you and me, Elegant Raines. In, in the ring."

Calmly Black Moon began walking toward the gym's front door.

No one in the Pug moved.

Black Moon got to the door and then wheeled back around.

"Ain't nobody gonna be able to fuckin' save you, punk. Ain't gonna be *fuckin' nobody!*"

Gas had just left the office. He had come in the office to offer Pee-Pot his moral support. Pee-Pot was in the office alone, canvassing his own thoughts, thinking, guiltily, that Black Moon had done him a favor, had relieved him of a huge burden. He and Elegant were destined to fight for big stakes. Both were better fighters than the current reigning middleweight champion of the division, Gino Giannone. Even at this stage of their development, either one could beat him, wrest his crown. It was just a matter of who'd get to him first, or even if he was still champ by the time they climbed the middleweight ranks.

He was shocked by today's events, by Black Moon's actions. But how much resistance had he put up—how hard did he fight to keep Black Moon Johnson, retain him, try not to lose him? How guilty should he feel? Pee-Pot thought. Or should he have any guilt at all?

"Duff Crawley. He's a great trainer. And Abe Feinstein … if money was a disease, he'd be dead."

But Abe Feinstein could negotiate the important fights for his fighters. Sometimes his fighters took a "muffin" (dive) in order to get bigger fights, but Black Moon wouldn't do any of that, Pee-Pot thought. He'd rather cut off both his arms and legs than take a muffin.

Knock.

"Come in, Elegant."

Elegant stepped through the door. He was sweaty.

"How was your workout today? Under Mr. Moore?"

"Fine." Pause.

"Are, are you all right, Mr. Manners?" Elegant said, approaching Pee-Pot's desk. "I-I just want to know, sir."

The typewriter, Pee-Pot hadn't moved. He was sitting behind it as if it were shielding him. "No, Elegant. No. Black Moon and I've been together for six years. Since the boy was fifteen years old."

"I broke you up."

"Sure did. That you did. Uh-huh." Pause. "No sense in hiding the fact, Elegant."

"No, sir."

"Ain't nothing to hide when it's in plain sight. First time I lost a fighter because of another fighter. Him being jealous of him. If I've got two of the same kind, really good, and in the same weight class, one leaves because of competition. Leaves on good terms. Not because of envy ... jealousies."

Elegant smiled weakly.

"What it boiled down to, it-itself down to, was Black Moon's jealousy of you. Plain and simple."

"Yes, yes, I know, sir. Tommie told me."

"And what success you're gaining. The reputation you're carrying with you in the ring now. By coming outta this gym. The Pug. One you earned. Have established."

"Yes, sir."

Pee-Pot adjusted his cap and then folded his arms, looking away from Elegant. He messed with papers atop the desk. "But it goes deeper, even deeper than that, Elegant. Black Moon's got insecurities. And don't think for a second most fighters don't, 'cause they do, all over the damned place."

Pee-Pot turned his head and looked at Elegant as if to ask that question of him.

"Yes, I do, Mr. Manners." Elegant's eyes lowered.

"Elegant, you don't have to tell me what they are. Share them. In any way, son. I'll find out in due time and fashion."

But Elegant wondered if Pee-Pot Manners would ever find out the worst insecurity he was harboring, the one that had everything to do with his parents' deaths. The one he was scared of, frightened by, if ever he was confronted by it, had to look at it, and not run away from it like he'd been doing for most of his life.

———

Elegant recorded another knockout at Fame Arena, and now offers to fight in other fight arenas outside the state of West Virginia were pouring in. There was Miami Convention Hall, in Florida; Cleveland Arena, in Ohio; and Victory Arena in New Orleans, Louisiana.

Pee-Pot fielded all the arenas' offers and negotiated set dates. Also, during the process, he negotiated for Tommie. He wouldn't separate Tommie and Elegant. At this stage of their careers, it was like one was a good luck charm for the other. Pee-Pot was as superstitious as the next guy. And most fighters are superstitious. Most fighters bring into the ring with them all kinds of nutty, neurotic prefight rituals they must faithfully follow. Their fans know nothing about them, only their trainers or maybe family members—the ones who truly do understand them.

But it was not only that. Elegant's career was on an upswing, and sometimes Elegant would ride on Tommie's coattails (example: the Radio Center Arena fight) or vice versa. This was not only apparent to him but them too. It's why, for Pee-Pot, it was a dream come true to have both young men fighting in his boxing stable.

Without Cora, his life seemed in decline. But now with Tommie and Elegant, it'd taken flight. There would be big fights down the road. How he looked forward to them. He'd never trained a world champion, not in any weight class, but that could soon change. One thing Pee-Pot didn't have was a crystal ball. Nor was he a gypsy or a fortune teller. But Pee-Pot did like Elegant's and Tommie's chances. Each had a betting man's chance against all odds.

CHAPTER 12

It was Saturday. Pee-Pot'd just driven in from town. It was late September. The mail was on the truck's front seat, contained in a small pouch. But there was one piece of mail he didn't put in the pouch—it was sitting on top of it. By now the road's bumps had bounced it around a bit, but then Pee-Pot would straighten it out, and if jostled again, it'd be neatened again.

But Pee-Pot couldn't stop himself from looking down at the letter or smiling at it. If he looked in the mirror, he thought (he was about to pull the truck up onto the property on Hattersfield Road), his smile was so bright he might crack it and have seven years of bad luck on his hands, he chuckled.

To Pee-Pot, as for his opinion, the letter couldn't've come at a better time for Elegant. It's why he was looking at it, drawn to it—couldn't stop looking at it. Even as he parked the truck at the side of the farmhouse.

Woof! Woof!

"Gyp, wait until you see what came in the mail for Elegant, old girl!"

Gyp sniffed the letter and then walked off with Pee-Pot, following him from behind, wagging her tail.

―――

Elegant turned the page. He was reading Shakespeare's *The Two Gentlemen of Verona*. Whenever he wanted to just laugh out loud, he could always count on Valentine and Proteus and their two clownish servants, Speed and Launce. To follow their antics in Shakespeare's play was like following the antics of a puppet show, of who was pulling the strings on whom—the puppeteer or the puppets.

Spiritually, lately, he'd been down in the dumps—rock bottom. It was still Gem Loving. He still hadn't recovered from her departure from Longwood. He still thought, repeatedly, of the last day he spent with her in the back of the Body of Christ Church, the social hour that Sunday. He still worshipped at the church, and Pastor Loving now acted as if nothing had happened to come between them (certainly not his daughter, certainly not Gem Loving), and it was dishonest. But he wasn't a father who was trying to protect his daughter, so he went along with it—timid, nervous at first, but now doing it absent of the nerves and timidity.

In fact, he hadn't heard her name from Pee-Pot, Chadway Holloway, or, of course, Pastor Loving. He still saw Francine Loving, but she too kept her distance from him. But he still felt he'd done nothing wrong, and neither had Gem Loving. Yes, she knew about her father's attitude when it came to fighters, but their conversations were genuine and sincere. And it's what he most remembered about the time they spent together: their respect toward each other.

Elegant turned the page, for Speed was about to do something absolutely silly to make him laugh.

"Ha!"

"Elegant!"

"Yes, sir!" Elegant said, startled.

"I know you're reading that Shakespeare fellow, ain't you?"

Woof! Woof!

"To be laughing out loud like that!"

Woof! Woof!

Gyp walked over to Elegant. She stood up on her hind legs. Her front paws were up on his legs.

"I have to start reading that William Shakespeare fella for myself, son. I thought he just wrote tragedies. All he knew to write about."

"Not at all, Mr. Manners. He's known for comedies too, sir."

"Hmm ... why I didn't know that, Elegant. Had no idea."

"Yes, sir." Pause.

"A letter came in the post for you, son."

"F-for me, Mr.—"

"Come, Gyp. Come," Pee-Pot said, handing the letter to Elegant. And before Elegant registered even more surprise, Pee-Pot and Gyp left the room.

"Gem, Gem Loving! Gem, Gem Loving—I-I can't believe it! A letter from Gem Loving!"

He saw her name written across the envelope.

"I ..."

Elegant, not knowing what to say, said nothing—only rushed to open the letter.

September 24, 1946

Dear Mr. Raines,

I am back at Howard University pursuing my studies. Every year I look forward to returning to school so that I may complete my schooling so that I may one day step out into the world and bring what I have learned to fruition. What I mean is, to apply what I've learned in meaningful and practical experiences so that others may benefit from them.

But this year, I felt no urge to return to my schooling. And after a few weeks back on campus, unable to eliminate this feeling, all that was left for me to do was acknowledge it and express it. I am a young lady of repute, and this letter to you is remote to my cultural upbringing. But I had to write you.

I left from Longwood on August 28 filled with despair. This was because of what happened prior to my leaving and now what has transpired since. I have never been in the company of a young man whose company I enjoyed more, who I have liked so much, who is so intelligent.

I did not want to leave Longwood without saying good-bye to you. The lack of communication for those weeks after the church social hour, I apologize for. And, too, my total disappearance from view.

But I live in my father's house, and I both respect him with all my heart and love him with all my soul.

I am sure, by now, Mr. Manners has informed you of my father's feelings toward fighters. I offer no explanation for him, for it is not my place. I have written you only because I could do nothing else. I would continue to feel helpless if I did not.

Please accept my apologies for my actions. And please know they were not motivated by any unpleasant feelings toward you.

Sincerely yours,
Gem Loving

PS. Oh, and if we could stop with the formality and I could address you Elegant, and you address me Gem.

"Oh, I love you, Gem Loving! I love you!"
And now Elegant had to catch his breath and rub his dazed eyes, and he did feel dazed, goose pimply, in fact. It was why he was going to read Gem Loving's letter again and again until his eyes felt dead in his head.
And so pressing the letter down on the table, making certain no wrinkles affected it, already preserving it, Elegant's eyes cast down onto the letter, and off his eyes ran.
He must've been into his fifth or sixth reading (Elegant had lost count), when—Knock.
"Y-yes, Mr. Manners," Elegant said, hopping out of the chair to get to the door.
"Here, Elegant, you might need these."
Gyp wagged her tail.
"Thank you, Mr. Manners. Oh, oh thank you, sir."
It was an ink pen and an ink bottle and stationery.
"Figured you didn't pack any in your suitcase when you got in here from View Point. But you need them now."
"Yes, I do, Mr. Manners."
Pee-Pot shut the door for Elegant since his hands were full.
"Guess he'll be writing Gem right away. Huh, Gyp?"

Gyp smiled.

"Thank you, Mr. Manners. Oh, yes, thank you, sir!" Elegant said, hurrying to get back to the desk.

What a great, smart man Mr. Manners is, Elegant thought. A man for the ages!

Elegant sat back down. He was a bundle of kinetic energy, not until he slowed down, his heart stopped beating so frantically fast. Now he was looking down at the letter.

"What am I going to say? Put in the letter? W ..."

He'd read Gem Loving's letter so many times. But now he would have to read it in a way where he'd have to remove his heart from the equation and write a letter to Gem Loving that was intelligent but also calculatingly revealing.

Elegant rubbed the back of his neck. He did it a few times, his mind absorbing the letter, and then he took the sheets of stationery (at least ten), placing them together. *Gem Loving's letter was two and a half pages long, not that mine has to be, but at least Mr. Manners gave me enough stationery to allow for mistakes*, Elegant said to himself.

Elegant picked up the pen and then dipped it in the ink bottle. Suddenly, he felt calm, under control—as though this was old hat for him.

September 28, 1946

Dear Miss Loving,

I was honored to receive your letter in the post today. I am glad you are back at your studies, pursuing studies that will eventually benefit others, not only yourself. I have not enjoyed the benefits of higher education since I am mainly self-taught. In fact, I was reading William Shakespeare before receiving your letter, *The Two Gentlemen of Verona*, one of my favorite William Shakespeare plays. I do not know if you are familiar with it, but I suppose someone of your education is.

I did too despair when you left for your university. I did despair those Sundays when we no longer communicated and, it seemed, you had disappeared from view. That maybe you were a mirage. (Please forgive me for exaggeration, possibly, for my heart's beating too fast right now.)

I do know of Pastor Loving's feelings. Mr. Manner did tell me. I do understand but don't understand. I understand Pastor Loving protecting his daughter, but I do not understand him protecting you from me. You are the most intelligent young lady I have now met. Your company is splendid. I would just like to tell you this. There is nothing to apologize to me for. I am a fighter, and it is not something I would apologize to you for. And you are a young lady who is growing up, and there are certain expectations for you you need not apologize for. We were just caught in a trap. But by your communication, it no longer feels as bad. It feels as if there is hope.

I would like to end this letter by saying that not one minute of the day goes by that I do not think of you. William Shakespeare, my boxing, my other activities, they amount to very little now that I have met you.

The pen stopped. Elegant felt jittery and then took in a big breath. *My breath's always been good*, he laughed to himself. Roadwork. Roadwork. Rubbing the back of his neck again, he was going to reread the letter. When he finished reading through it, the first question he asked himself was "Have I said enough?" Pausing, he thought he had.

Picking up the extra stationery, it was time now to make his script more legible. And of course there were words scratched out, replaced by others, or scratched out for erasure. And there it was, another "scare," and now another "conquest." For deep in himself, his initial impulse after reading the letter, that he would actually have to sit down and write Gem Loving, did scare him.

But there it was, the two pages of stationery as tangible proof of him conquering that small fear. The confidence level he had not only in the ring but outside it. He told Gem Loving about his confidence going into the ring before a match but not outside the ring, how he was still striving to acquire it; and being put in this situation and feeling he had to respond quickly, unhesitatingly, helped.

He would walk the letter into town, the three miles. Or maybe he should run into town, do roadwork on a Saturday—jet the letter to Gem Loving as fast as it was humanly possible.

———

Exactly one week later, Gyp and Elegant sat on the front porch. Emphatically Elegant wrung his hands. He wanted it to get a letter from Gem Loving today. After all, he got one from her last week and he was spoiled. But it had to be today—he'd waited the week, pointing to today as reward for his patience. Both he and Gyp were looking up the road for Pee-Pot. He'd gone out to cut hair but would be sure to bring the mail in from the post office. Gyp was being as patient as him, but even she had begun whining a little, letting her feelings be known with little uncertainty.

———

A half hour later.

"There he is, Gyp!"

Woof!

"There Mr. Manners is!"

Woof! Woof!

"How's he driving, Gyp? H-how's Mr. Manners driving! I mean does it look like … Can you see his face?" Elegant's hand shaded his eyes. "Is Mr. Manners smiling, Gyp?

The truck hit its usual share of bumps on Hattersfield Road, and Pee-Pot's light body would bounce right along with the jolts.

"Gyp, we're in this together now. W-we have to be brave!"

Gyp didn't reply; she looked steady, looked like the great gun dog she once was, when she and Pee-Pot would wake at the crack of dawn to go out hunting, make a full day of it.

The Studebaker truck drawing nearer the house, Pee-Pot waved. That was nothing new for Elegant and Gyp, for he always did that—it being standard fare.

Woof!

And Elegant did the obligatory by waving. Then Pee-Pot pulled the truck up into the yard, and instead of chasing after the car, like he thought she would do as soon as she saw Pee-Pot, Gyp, instead, looked back at Elegant as if awaiting orders; and Elegant didn't move—so neither did Gyp. If ever he and Gyp felt in harmony, as one, never mind when they jogged, was now.

Listening for the truck door to shut, when it happened, it seemed Gyp's ears flapped, but really hadn't.

"Okay, Gyp, uh, we're prepared for better or worse, aren't we?" Elegant said after hearing Pee-Pot's shoes crunch down into the dirt, making his way toward them.

"What is it, Mr. Manners? What's the verdict? Yes or—"

"I got something behind my back, don't I?" Pee-Pot said, beaming, winking at Elegant. "Don't I, Gyp?"

Woof!

"Thank you, Mr. Manners. Thank you!" Elegant said, hugging Pee-Pot and then taking the letter out Pee-Pot's hand.

"Come, Gyp. Elegant doesn't need us now. Gem's letter's about the only thing that'll fancy him. All the way from Washington, DC." Pee-Pot chuckled. "Long distance. Across the Potomac."

They walked into the house.

Elegant looked around and then twirled. And unconsciously, completely unconscious, he began walking off the front porch and to the side of the house, passing the truck, and he just kept walking until he was in the backyard going down the gentle slope and off to flat ground as the October sun beat down on him and he stopped to smell the letter to see if Gem Loving had soaked it in perfume. It was wishful, but it was still as if he'd smelled perfume, for he felt afloat, lifted, something now carrying him other than his feet—maybe wings, Elegant laughed.

Easily he opened the envelope. And the letter, when he pulled it out of the envelope, was all he'd been waiting for for seven days.

October 5, 1946

Dear Elegant,

With glee I received your letter. I hoped I'd get a quick reply, and I was not disappointed. You do write splendidly and express yourself so well and accurately. I do know of William Shakespeare's *Two*

Gentlemen of Verona but have not read it. I will read it now since it is one of your favorite plays, and it has always sounded interesting to me.

You have found the hope I found. It did feel like a "trap" before. I had never experienced such a closed-in feeling, so claustrophobic. (And if this is exaggeration, I don't care either, for my heart is beating too fast too.) But am I stealing lines from you as William Shakespeare has been accused of doing from Christopher Marlowe? I don't know. But if I am, it feels wonderful.

There's not a minute I do not think of you. Even in my philosophy class with Professor Mayes, where my concentration is primary. Thinking of you frees me. I have never felt this free. My studies are going well as I know your training is under Mr. Manners. In the ring, I pray for your safety and that of your opponents. Nothing must happen to you. But please let me know when you fight next, even if it will worry me sick—it won't matter. I am not faint of heart. I'm fundamentally a farm girl: slaughter, pluck, and boil chickens.

I wish I could throw my arms around you. I wish so much for us. That there is this great sunlit future ahead of us. I really do. I don't think what we have is coincidence.

Lovingly,
Gem

"Gem, Gem …," Elegant said. Elegant pressed the letter to his heart and then started walking again, beyond the gym on the grounds.

Over the past few weeks, letters had been sailing back and forth between Elegant and Gem. If they, personally, could push the letters faster through the mails to get from one point to the next, they would. For both, it felt far too long between letters, which each had expressed more than once.

And there was so much to write about, that they were getting caught up with. He'd had two fights since their correspondence, both victories.

The Miami Convention Hall in Miami, Florida, he scored a second-round knockout over Enrique Salvador; and then in Cleveland Arena, in Cleveland, Ohio, he scored a one-round knockout over Greg "Boilerman" Bowers. Elegant had yet to be pressed, something that didn't worry Pee-Pot. But all great fighters eventually are tested inside the ring, when things aren't so easy and the fighter wins on guts and character, not just talent and skill.

For Pee-Pot though, it was always Elegant's composure before and during the fight. It was at his core. His superior intelligence would never pressure him to panic or show any signs of alarm. It was also his ability to correctly adjust to situations by absorbing them and then to find the best solution for them. He demonstrated this time and again no matter how brief the bouts. Not every great fighter had these gifts. Elegant Raines did.

They'd been deluged by fight offers. They came in from across the country. Elegant had a lot on his plate.

As for Tommie, he was keeping pace with Elegant—so he was still on track.

Their careers were blooming, moving on a fast track, and Elegant and Tommie's relationship was as solid as ever. Elegant told Tommie about him and Gem Loving, and Tommie encouraged it even though, again, he knew down the road Pastor Loving was sure to find out. Now using Gem Loving as a wedge, he told Tommie he could no longer go into Inwood on Friday nights with him, to Angel's Corner—that he'd feel guilty. Tommie understood and then laughed, telling Elegant, "Man, them babes still looking for you, Elegant. Shit, they is. 'Specially Tammi-Ray. Asks 'bout you all the damned time. Like crazy, man!"

Elegant was glad that that phase of his life was over. It was important his biological needs be met (his view of sex), but now it didn't matter. For him, it had no relevance. Sexually, he was going to save himself for Gem Loving and only Gem Loving.

He'd gotten the letter from Gem yesterday, and it's like he'd trembled like a leaf the whole day. In fact, he was afraid of his own shadow—it's how it felt for him. Yesterday he didn't know how he got through it without throwing off this tremendous worry in him, this situation Gem was throwing at him with seeming abandonment—throwing caution to the wind.

Yesterday, he thought he could handle it on his own but soon discovered it was impossible to. He needed guidance; he needed Pee-Pot Manners. It's why he asked Pee-Pot if he could meet with him in his room in five minutes. He said five minutes, for he still had to pull himself together, get a grip on himself. He wasn't to look at Gem's letter but still had the last section of it implanted in his mind.

This would be so important for us to do. Please let me know as quickly as possible. I do think this a perfect idea.

Love,
Gem

"'Love, Gem. Yes, I do love you, Gem. But …'"

"Elegant …"

"Yes, sir. Yes, Mr. Manners," Elegant said, hopping to his feet.

"Ha. Now calm down. It's only me. Pee-Pot Manners calling on you."

"Yes … yes sir, Mr. Manners, sir."

"Elegant, I take it, you're nervous," Pee-Pot said, sitting in the chair. "About something."

"It's this, sir."

"That's a letter from Gem."

Elegant was holding the letter in his hand. "It's what's in the letter, Mr. Manners, that troubles me. H-has been troubling me, sir."

Pee-Pot's forehead knitted.

"May I read certain, selective parts of the letter, Mr. Manners. Uh, to you, sir? N-now?"

"Of course, Elegant."

Elegant cleared his throat and then began reading "selective parts" of the letter aloud. When he stopped reading, he looked painfully at Pee-Pot.

"So Gem wants you to come up to Washington. To Howard University, the college campus to visit her?"

"Yes, Mr. Manners."

"And you don't know what to do? What to write Gem back to tell her?"

"She'd be doing this behind her father's back, Mr. Manners. Behind Pastor ... I would be too."

"I see," Pee-Pot said, shutting his eyes. "Uh ... uh-huh."

Elegant put the letter down on the table. Tears swelled up in his eyes. "I-I want to see her so bad, Mr. Manners. So bad ..."

"But you two write. Are writing each other."

This is not something Elegant wanted to hear: Pee-Pot Manners stating the obvious.

"Yes, we are."

Their eyes locked.

"But aren't you doing that behind Pastor Loving's back?"

Elegant hadn't thought of that—never saw it in that critical a light. "We, we are, Mr. Manners."

"But this is different, I know."

Elegant felt better, that his analysis was, after all, right—that this was far more significant.

"Elegant, going up there to see her. Gem."

"I know—it is, sir."

"It ain't letter writing, that's for sure. From afar. Ha."

"I'd like to laugh too, Mr. Manners. But I can't. I find this far too distressing." Pause. "What is Gem thinking of anyway?"

After all those letters, Pee-Pot thought, it's not "Miss Loving" anymore, but "Gem."

"Look, son, I knew you two were going to fall in love. That Pastor Loving wasn't gonna be able to stop you."

"And we are, Mr. Manners. Gem and I are, sir."

"Letter writing is wonderful. Is a wonderful way to communicate, but it's just not the same thing, Elegant. Of seeing that person's face or holding that person's hand. It's just not, and there's nobody to tell me or convince me different."

"I do agree, Mr. Manners."

"You have to agree, son. Ha!"

Elegant laughed.

"But I guess it is the honesty issue. All of that. Feeling you snuck behind somebody, another person's back. Pastor Loving's a minister at that."

"I respect him, sir."

"So does Gem. Far, far more than you do, you can imagine. And I know it must've been hard on her writing that letter of hers, no matter how clean it looks on paper." Pause.

"No, you've gotta go up to Washington, DC. The campus to see her. That's all there is to it. It's … this is too important for the two of you. This ain't do-or-die, mind you. Nothing like it. 'Cause nothing's gonna stand in the way of your relationship. But right now it needs this trip. It's gonna be the best thing for it, Elegant. Guaranteed."

CHAPTER 13

"See you now," Pee-Pot said, waving at Elegant. Gyp wagged her tail. Even Gyp got in the truck with them, came over to the train station, Five Hundred, in the County of Wetzel, to see Elegant off.

"Okay, Mr. Manners. Okay, Gyp!"

Elegant was on his way to Washington, DC, the nation's capital. He'd never been to Washington, DC. Of course, all the places east of West Virginia he'd been to was because of boxing taking him there. This, today, was to be different, brand new within the circumference of that experience.

He'd written the letter to Gem saying yes, he'd come to Washington, DC. And then arrangements were made. He'd just have to come to Slowe Hall, her dormitory (females only), and call on her, and she'd come down to the lobby to meet him. It had sounded so simple and he was hoping it'd be. He was in a suit, a new one, olive green. And since the weather'd changed, was quite chilly, he wore a trench coat. Today, in West Virginia, it was in the lower forties and would reach the upper forties—no higher. Pee-Pot told Elegant Washington's weather and West Virginia's weather were pretty much identical, and so that was good for him to know.

Now turning his attention back to Gem, he tried recalling her eyes and smile, which was easy for him to do whenever he'd shut his eyes—something he was doing in his train seat.

———

Gem and Elegant held hands.

Elegant had gotten to Washington safe and sound. He'd gotten to

Howard University's campus, gone to Slowe Hall, announced he, Mr. Elegant Raines, was the gentleman guest of Miss Gem Loving. He waited no more than two minutes, and there she was (voila!) in coat and hat and with woolen gloves in her hands. And they couldn't believe they were actually back together again—one looking at the other, enchanted.

They stood in front of the school's ornate library and then found a concrete bench and sat down looking out onto the campus and the other aged buildings.

"Oh, I can't believe you're here, Elegant. In Washington!" Gem said, turning to Elegant, hugging him. He didn't expect a kiss. This was good enough.

"Me either, Gem!"

"I'm used to the trip from Longwood, West Virginia, to Washington, DC, but how did you find it?"

"Uh, since I've been traveling lately, to fights, that is, uh, but of course it's with Tommie and Mr. Manners and Mr. Moore—but it was still, uh, a breeze, I-I guess ... uh, suppose."

"Such a long answer for such a short question."

"I know," Elegant laughed.

Then they looked back out onto the campus. It was Saturday, two o'clock, and Howard's campus, typically, was quiet.

"Elegant, your letter didn't indicate you had trouble with my suggestion or, should I say, request you come—but you did didn't you? In all honesty?"

"A lot."

"Don't worry, so did I. But ..." Gem squeezed Elegant's hand more. "I had to see you. I just had to."

Silence.

"May I ask you something ...?"

"Yes."

"Is this the first time you've done something behind your father's back?"

"Yes. Something as serious as this. Yes. And I didn't feel at all comfortable. But then anticipating seeing you from the moment I got up this morning until now, I do. I wouldn't change anything. S-second guess myself."

"Me, me either," Elegant said. "B-but I did need Mr. Manners to help me. Help guide me. I hope you don't mind."

"Mind … no, no, not at all." Pause.

"I hope you understand what I'm about to say."

Elegant was confident he would.

"My mother's my guardian angel. Since she died. I called on her spirit. She was sort of rebellious in her own way when she was young, she told me. Not reckless or disrespectful toward her parents, mind you, but thought certain conventional mores from past generations were ridiculous. In no way appropriate or fitting for her lifestyle."

"Really?"

"And she said she and my father took chances without her being specific about them. That got them into hot water."

"Ha."

"But not anything serious. Uh, she did make that especially clear to me though."

Elegant sobered. "Gem, do you think this is serious?"

"Elegant, I don't know."

And then they looked back out onto the campus. Because there was a sun and the wind had died down a little after noon, it didn't feel chilly to them on the bench, but they were young and passionate, and that, alone, kept their blood at a boil.

"Oh, by the way, Elegant, what was Mr. Manners's advice?"

"He was all for it. Me coming up here. It's good that Mr. Manners doesn't forget anything. That nothing escapes him."

"What? I don't know what you mean by that."

"When he was young, Gem. Him and Mrs. Manners. Young love, as Mr. Manners calls it."

Gem laughed.

They'd been sitting on the bench for well over twenty minutes talking up a storm. Elegant's body angled off to Gem's, him looking at her as well as her looking at him, possibly him memorizing every pore on her face and her the same. But then Gem caught Elegant looking rather intensely at her straight black hair more than what, she thought, he ought to—not that this was the first she'd caught him.

"I'm half Negro, Elegant, and half Shawnee Indian."

"Oh then that's what accounts, uh, explains your straight black hair and—"

"My father's hair too. He's half Negro and half Shawnee Indian. My mother was very light skinned. It's why Francine has a lot of her coloring, and I have all of Papa's—black.

"Yes, like me, Gem."

"Like you." Pause. "You, would you like to know the history of the Shawnee Indians and West Virginia? I'd—"

"You'll tell me?"

"Free of charge. I swear, Elegant," Gem said, crossing her heart. "Very brief ... though."

Gem cleared her throat.

"The Shawnees settled along southern Ohio, western Pennsylvania, and, of course, West Virginia. They settled in the village of Bull Town. Then, around the mid-1600s, were driven out of West Virginia by the Iroquois."

"They, they were?"

"And then we were scattered all over the country: Tennessee, the Carolinas, Oklahoma."

"That's terrible." Pause.

"Territory always meant a lot to Indian tribes. Just as it did to the whites. They all fought for it."

"I know."

"All the time, Elegant."

"So your family was able to stay in West Virginia?"

"Uh, no, not exactly. We were displaced. Uprooted too. But my father came back. He said he saw opportunity there. So returned. And there was something about being 'put on the run,' as Papa put it, that displeased him. So he worked his way back to West Virginia slowly."

"Gem, now I know the history of your hair!"

"Yes!" Gem laughed.

———

Forty minutes later, Elegant was walking Gem back to Slowe Hall.

"I really don't want this day to end."

Elegant said nothing but felt everything.

And then Gem stopped walking and stood in front of Elegant.

"Kiss me, Elegant! Kiss me!"

"Kiss … you … I …"

And then Gem shut her eyes and her lips hunted for Elegant's and then found them.

"Mmmm …," she said, her mouth closed.

CHAPTER 14

Tommie and Elegant were fighting in Duquesne Gardens in Pittsburgh, Pennsylvania, an old converted carbarn since streetcars, trolleys, snaked their way through a city of steel workers who got to the steel mills in just that fashion, as well as the fans to the fight this night. In fact, Pee-Pot, Gas, Elegant, and Tommie got to Duquesne Gardens by the same mode of transportation: trolley car.

This wasn't the first time for Pee-Pot or Gas to travel by trolley, and it wasn't the first time for Tommie and Elegant either since they'd experienced it in New Orleans—the first time for both.

It was a big fight house tonight. And Elegant was headlining the card, going up against a local favorite and one of the most feared middleweights in the division: Charlie Cohen. He was a battle-tested, two-fisted slugger, who was ranked number nine in the rankings. He was from what folk in Pittsburgh called The Hill. Pittsburgh had produced a number of great fighters, and this special locale had certainly produced its fair share.

Charlie Cohen was a Jewish fighter a lot of top fighters in the middleweight division tried ducking. He fought a lot to stay in shape and, like so many fighters of his day, for a meal ticket. Charlie Cohen was a fighter who'd take on any and all comers and now was taking on Elegant Raines in the Duquesne Gardens in Pittsburgh.

If Elegant won this fight, it would really open up eyes and ratchet up his career; Pee-Pot fully understood this. The strategy now was for Elegant to send a jolt through the middleweight division, for Pee-Pot Manners to offer up a fighter, Elegant Raines, who was so exciting and compelling in the ring the division couldn't resist him or get enough of him, for the fight fans and public wouldn't let it. By going nationwide, Elegant was beginning this campaign to attract this kind of attention, juice up the public with one electrifying fight after the other, in whatever arena he fought.

Therefore, Pee-Pot would be trading in on this strategy in the months to come when he'd turn Elegant over to a real, bona fide manager whose job would be to promote him, put him in the optimum position, for one day he could fight for the middleweight crown—the championship of the world.

"Set it up for you, Elegant. Got them fans all hopped up out there, man. Just listen to them!"

Tommie'd just knocked out Eddie "Lifeguard" Connors in round number six. Tommie's power was improving. In the past few months, he'd been hitting much harder.

"Can't wait for the main event!"

One more fight—that was on tap now—and Elegant would be out there in the Duquesne Garden arena.

"So how you feel, Elegant?"

"Why great, Tommie."

"Them fans come here for a show. And you gonna give them one, ain't you!"

Pee-Pot and Gas laughed.

"Now you don't have to cheerlead Elegant, Tommie, you know that."

"I know, sir," Tommie said while Gas cut tape off his hands. "But it's the first time Elegant's fighting with other things he got on his mind, Mr. Manners."

Pee-Pot's eyes squinted. "Uh, what you mean by that comment, son?"

Tommie looked up at Gas (who knew all about the situation and could be trusted) and then at Elegant, who was being rubbed down by Pee-Pot on the rubbing table.

"First time the boy'll be fighting while he's in love, sir."

Everybody cracked up.

"That's all!"

"Okay, Tommie, rub it in," Elegant laughed.

"Mr. Manners's doing a fine job of that, Elegant. From what I can see."

Elegant was out of the dressing room and marching down the garden's aisle. Needless to say, he was going up against a local favorite who created his own level of excitement, a banger, a tough-as-nails crowd-pleaser.

And surprisingly, at least to him, he was thinking of Gem. And it was the first he'd enter the ring thinking of something other than what lay before him, stepping inside a ring to fight a man, something as dangerous and daunting as that. But through their last correspondence, and therefore honoring her request, Elegant told Gem of this fight in Pittsburgh; and as usual, she wished him and his opponent safe going in the ring.

But now there was a new angle to his thinking, imagining Gem out in this ex-carbarn, in one of the ringside seats, cheering him on above the chorus of boos, that he had at least one other fan out there who came to the arena to see him win tonight—even if she knew absolutely nothing about boxing.

"Cohen's a crowder," Pee-Pot said.

Elegant nodded his head at Pee-Pot's piece of advice.

When the bell rang, cheers exploded for Charlie Cohen in the old carbarn.

Elegant sized up his opponent, someone who reminded him a lot of Black Moon Johnson, Cohen's shoulders and chest, just not as muscular in total as Black Moon's overall physique. Elegant saw Charlie Cohen wanted to set a good, lively tempo and that stiff jabs from him would keep Cohen off him.

Charlie Cohen's defense was terrific plus his reflexes. He didn't move with any particular grace inside the ring but with good, workmanlike purpose and, working behind his own jab, tried getting his off first, measuring distance well, but the jab not as effective as Cohen would like since Elegant's hand and foot speed seemed to, at every turn, frustrate him.

Elegant liked the round's peppy pace.

Now Cohen jabbed, catching Elegant's ear. It was a muscular jab. Now the next jab caught his cheekbone—another powerful jab. Elegant was going to let the guy crowd him. He wasn't going to jab to back him off since it was apparent Cohen wanted to utilize his strength to infight and, also, smother Elegant's punches. But this was all right by Elegant. This was something he felt he could do as well as any fighter in the ring: infight.

When Cohen hit Elegant with a body shot and then another, it's when his fans went wild, flew into a frenzy in the Duquesne arena. Then Cohen delivered another body shot. When Elegant tied him up, the fans booed. Stepping out a clinch, Elegant gave Cohen a clever head feint, and this time when he aimed his glove for Cohen's ribs, he hit him with a right-hand cross to the temple, dropping Cohen to the canvas.

Cohen didn't know what had hit him.

Twelve seconds remained in the round. Charlie Cohen struggled to his feet. He looked on queer street and then, suddenly realizing where he was, began retreating; Elegant let him.

Clang.

Charlie Cohen staggered back to his corner and his animated handlers.

Effusively Pee-Pot greeted Elegant back to the corner.

"Good job, son."

Clang.

As soon as Elegant got to ring center, he saw Charlie Cohen was still woozy from the first-round knockdown and that, in the second round, he was going to change the fight's pace, make it strictly defensive, not take any further chances for his own self-preservation—at least for now.

You could feel the tension racing through the big fight crowd, how unsettled it was, watching their local hero tentative, practically passive— certainly not the Charlie Cohen they knew and loved, who they came to see fight in the barn tonight.

Cohen still controlled the fight in this smart, intelligent, skillful way of negotiating time, negating any action by Elegant either by tying him up or moving away from him in order to survive the second round, stay clear of Elegant's perked-up offensive aggression. So for the final thirty seconds or so of the round, Elegant let Cohen off the hook by letting him continue to execute what, in boxing parlance, is called a survival mode and not further frustrate himself by chasing Cohen from ring post to ring post to net zero results.

There was a trickle of boos leaking out the fight crowd when the bell rang to end the round.

In the corner, Pee-Pot sensed the fight wouldn't go on like this, that it wasn't Cohen's fighting style, fighting a defensive fight, that it was employed by Charlie Cohen simply to clear away his head's cobwebs in order to stay in the fight, not get knocked out as surely he would had he opened up offensively and fought Elegant. If he'd made a fight out of it in the second round.

"Cohen's playing possum. But I don't have to tell you that, son."

Clang.

Elegant saw fire in Cohen's eyes, both clear as a chalk-blue sky. Cohen was setting round one's pace, not two's, and the crowd let out a monster of a cheer for him.

Charlie Cohen had a round, moon face. Again, it reminded Elegant of Black Moon's; only, it was a white face he was looking into, a Jewish fighter's face, not a black fighter's face.

Cohen was back attacking Elegant's body, with some of his body shots getting through. Cohen backed Elegant against the ropes, but it's when Cohen switched tactics by throwing elbows at his head, hoping to rough him up, Elegant ducking them as each elbow whistled past his ears. Cohen's body was badly off balance, off center, when throwing yet another elbow. Elegant felt this, so with his gloved hands, he pivoted Cohen until he was pinned tight against the ropes and then hit him with three pulverizing body shots, and down Cohen went.

At the count of six, Charlie Cohen stumbled back up on his feet.

In the center of the ring again, Elegant's fists hunted for Cohen's midsection and, when he found it, smashed it, Cohen not going down; he was simply rocked back on his heels, grunted, and then retreated off to the ropes, Elegant jabbing, jabbing, and then *bam!*—another hard shot to Cohen's gut, and Cohen dropped to one knee and then was up at the count of eight.

Cohen looked crippled in the ring as Elegant pressed forward. Cohen threw himself at Elegant. Elegant pushed Cohen off him. Suddenly, the bell rang.

Gas washed down Elegant's mouthpiece in the water bucket and then handed it to Pee-Pot, who stuck it back in Elegant's mouth after Elegant yawned open his mouth.

"Let's clean up this mess, Elegant," Pee-Pot said. "This round."

Clang.

Back out in the ring, Elegant now saw Charlie Cohen was clear-eyed but deadly hurt. He knew it was time to finish him off. Charlie Cohen was brave. He didn't want to show cowardice in the Duquesne Garden arena, the ex-carbarn, risk the chance of his fans booing him again, the faithful and loyal who really didn't understand he'd done the smart thing in round two, the right thing, not cowardly but sensible—what even brave fighters resort to when under great duress.

It'll just take a bunch of punches, a barrage of them now, Elegant said to himself. A series of hard, telling combinations thrown with speed, power, velocity, and accuracy at Charlie Cohen to end this.

But it took just two punches from Elegant, a straight jab and a crisp left hook; Elegant stepped back to witness Charlie Cohen's body hit the canvas, Elegant realizing then that Charlie Cohen wasn't rising back to his feet for a fourth time—that he wouldn't have to disappoint his loyal fans again, not after being knocked unconscious, lying flat on his back, his legs split apart from the brutal punishment that ended the boxing contest in the old carbarn arena in Pittsburgh, Pennsylvania.

———

Pee-Pot took his side trip from Pittsburgh to Martin County, Kentucky, to visit Biscuit. He'd been in touch with him but, physically, hadn't been in Biscuit's company for a few months. But this time, after the fight, he took the opportunity to visit him. The trip, of course, was of great value to both him and Biscuit. There were times (many) when he felt guilty that with Biscuit being so close, one state southwest of West Virginia, maybe he could do better—but his life was so busy. He spent two good, pleasant days with him. He was thinking about being with him Thanksgiving Day, of cooking a Thanksgiving turkey.

Pee-Pot had been back in the house for only an hour, but when he got through the door, he was bursting with joy. In fact, he told Elegant he had something to show him but, at the time, caught Elegant running out the door with his barber tools. For Manuel Dixon, who worked at the brickyard with Elegant, on his shift, had sustained a work-related accident, was laid up, and needed a haircut. He lived on Hattersfield Road, about three quarters of a mile up from the farmhouse, and in order for Elegant not to be late for their appointment—even if Manuel wasn't going anywhere anytime soon—he couldn't be delayed.

Now Elegant was walking back to the house, down Hattersfield Road, from Manuel's house, wondering just what Pee-Pot was so ecstatic about when he got in from Martin County. He already knew of his next fight in three weeks in the Cow Palace in San Francisco, California, against Jimmy O'Donnell. O'Donnell was once ranked number two in the world but, due to inactivity, had dropped down to number six.

"Mr. Manners said his manager told him he would box my ears off," Elegant laughed, slinging the bag of barber tools as he walked back to the house. It'd made him laugh when he read it, and even though he didn't have much trouble with Charlie Cohen two days ago, he was going to train for the O'Donnell fight harder than ever.

"You always have to prove yourself," Elegant said, walking a dark Hattersfield Road, minutes from the house. "Mr. Manners said you're only as good as your last fight. Tommie says, uh, keeps saying it too."

Tommie's drinking still hadn't affected his boxing performances. Now that he'd stopped going into Inwood and to Angel's Corner, it seemed Tommie's drinking had become a nonissue up for discussion between him and Mr. Manners, Elegant thought. There were no more eyewitness accounts from him to draw on.

Yesterday, as soon as Elegant got into the house and into his room, he dashed a letter off to Gem. He told her he'd won the Pittsburgh match in the fourth round and made certain she knew he nor Charlie Cohen were hurt. He knew how important it was for her to know this in accepting what he was doing as a profession. In his letters he was always sure to include this piece of information. He'd draw Tommie into the conversation too, remarking how he made out on the boxing card. Gem was the best thing to happen to him, and her letters conveyed the same sentiment to him.

When he got into the house, it surprised Elegant that Pee-Pot's suitcase was still at the bottom of the stairs.

"Elegant," Pee-Pot said from the living room.

"Yes, Mr. Manners, sir ...?"

"Would you please bring that suitcase in here with you."

Absentmindedly, Elegant put his bag of barber tools on the stairs.

"Yes, sir, Mr. Manners."

"Got something to show you."

Elegant's juices flowed again.

"Good evening, Mr. Manners."

"Good evening, Elegant."

"Here you are, sir, your suitcase."

Pee-Pot received the suitcase at his rocker and set it down in front of him. Elegant stood back.

"Don't go anywhere. Over to the ... What's in here," Pee-Pot said, opening the suitcase, "is for you."

Pee-Pot laid the suitcase flat on the floor, and on top of the rumpled clothes, he saw a newspaper. Pee-Pot got it and then handed it to Elegant.

"Pittsburgh Courier, page 15 of the sports section, son."

Elegant took the newspaper. He began thumbing its pages.

"You'll see the headline and the picture plain and clear."

Elegant saw the picture of Charlie Cohen sprawled out on the canvas, the referee standing over him, counting him out.

Cohen Knocked Out Cold in Four
Arnie Bessinger

Charlie Cohen, local middleweight sensation, didn't stand a ghost of a chance in Duquesne Gardens last night. In round four he was knocked out by a more sensational Negro fighter by the name of Elegant Raines. This colored boy beat Cohen, for whatever it's worth, as if he had other things on his mind (like catching a cross town trolley) but then became determined it was going to be a short but spectacular fight in the old carbarn for the lively throng rooting for Cohen. Elegant Raines punctuated the night by hitting Charlie with a left-hand hook that knocked him stiff as a fish.

Raines stands over six feet tall and is the most promising young fighter I've seen in any weight division that I can name in a long, long time. You can smell that kind of talent like you can smell a good cigar from the box seats at the opera. And this boy's name doesn't hurt him any: Elegant Raines.

Raines is elegant in the ring. And his power, prowess, and polish are undeniable, even though it didn't seem he hit ol' Charlieboy with his best shot, because I think if he had, maybe we'd be playing taps for the kid from "The Hill" in Pittsburgh, whom Raines made look over the Hill with his stupendous, lopsided four-round victory.

This Raines kid looks like the real McCoy. A fighter who could stir a beer and make it taste like a martini, or close to one, if left to anyone's imagination.

Elegant stood in front of Pee-Pot stunned.

Pee-Pot saw Elegant had finished reading the newspaper clipping. "I usually don't let my fighters read their newspaper clippings, Elegant. But you're different—you ain't gonna let it go to your head."

"No, Mr. Manners. Not at all, sir."

"Picked the paper up at the train station. Was hoping there'd be something in it about the fight. Spotted Arnie Bessinger in the arena that night so knew he was covering the fight for the *Courier*. Comes from a line of writers. His father was Bill Bessinger, another sports columnist during my heyday. About the best, fairest one on the fight beat."

Elegant folded the paper and handed it back to Pee-Pot.

"No, you keep it. That's yours. Maybe you can start a scrapbook," Pee-Pot chuckled. "It'll be the first article of many, I'm sure."

"Thanks, Mr. Manners."

"There's a long road ahead for us," Pee-Pot said, seemingly in a cautious tone.

"I know, sir."

"You're just so damned good you're making it look easy."

"But … but, uh, you know I work as hard as anyone in the gym, sir."

"The public wants the perfect fighter, but when they get one …"

Elegant sat.

"They love them until one day they don't. Nobody likes too much perfection."

Elegant didn't know what to say. This kind of blunt dialogue he was used to but was still too inexperienced in life situations to know anything about such human dynamics and personalities.

"But you can't worry about that, Elegant. Ain't your concern nor worry."

Elegant didn't understand that either.

"I-I won't, Mr. Manners."

Elegant figured he had to say something.

Then Pee-Pot looked at Elegant. He realized what he'd just done. "Forgive me."

Elegant looked at Pee-Pot wide-eyed.

"You know, I'm trying to prepare you for everything and, in so doing, protect you from everything—but I can't." Pee-Pot shut the suitcase. He stood. Elegant stood. "I know you've got scissors, Elegant, but do you need a jar of glue?"

"Yes, I do, Mr. Manners."

"I have a scrapbook."

"Y-you do, Mr. Manners!"

They were heading for the staircase.

"Has a lot of dust on it. But ..."

"I'd love to see it, sir!"

"And I'd love to show it to you," Pee-Pot said, slapping Elegant's back.

"You'll see I haven't aged a day in my life!"

Both broke out laughing.

Elegant fought Jimmy O'Donnell in the Cow Palace in San Francisco, California, and scored a three-round kayo. It was another devastating performance exhibited by him. And Tommie scored a fifth-round stoppage on the same card.

The middleweight rankings were out a few days ago, and for the first time, Elegant cracked the top ten, was ranked number eight. Tommie, in the welterweight division, was ranked number twelve. Black Moon cracked the top ten over a month ago, and he was still on track toward a title fight in the middleweight division. Black Moon went from a ranking of number seven down to five.

The division was playing itself out as Pee-Pot had predicted, so it was of little surprise to him. He'd said before that right now both Elegant and Black Moon were better than the reigning champ, Gino Gennaro, or any other top-ranked middleweight in the division—so it was just a matter of time and fate before Elegant and Black Moon fought. And once the boxing public got an ear of the history between them, it'd be the hottest-selling fight ticket in town.

During prefight hype, Pee-Pot knew Black Moon would issue every profane, malicious thing there was under the sun about him and Elegant and mean every word. Not only would the sportswriters pick up on his hatred of Elegant but the fans too, thus making this a promoter's dream. Consequently, dollar signs danced all over this match, fantastic gate receipts. Besides the heavyweight division, the middleweight division's popularity was due, in large part, one sportswriter theorized, to the basic fact that most middleweights represented the average American male in both height and weight; so there was a natural connection to the division on a profound personal level.

Elegant hadn't returned to Howard University to visit Gem. Neither, through their letters, had brought up the possibility of a second visit. He wanted to go back up to Washington, DC, to see her (you bet he did!) but, in the back of his mind, knew what he and Gem did was wrong and presumed Gem felt the same. There was Pastor Loving, and they couldn't, wouldn't forget him—he wouldn't let them. He still loomed large in the backdrop. And for him to be extricated from it, they needed his approval. For it, needless to say, was the only way they could establish a real relationship. Then and only then could they hope for a future together.

But now, in a few days, Gem was coming home for the Thanksgiving holidays. School would be out of session for a few days, and she was coming home to Longwood. Through their correspondence, neither knew how to handle the impending situation. Neither one had a plan as how to draw their relationship out into the open, of how to declare their love for each other to Pastor Loving, to tell him they'd been deceitful, writing and seeing each other in secret, behind his back, violating his rules—that they'd made a joint decision to do this on their own, through their own impulses.

Pee-Pot decided to spend Thanksgiving Day with Biscuit. He regretted he and Elegant and Gyp would miss out on, what would be, for them, their first Thanksgiving spent together, but thought it more important he be with Biscuit. He planned to cook turkeys for both households. He'd take a cooked turkey down to Martin County for him and Biscuit. He looked forward to it.

CHAPTER 15

It was Tuesday night, two days before Thanksgiving, shortly after eight o'clock.

Pee-Pot was down in the basement cleaning his barbering equipment while listening to The Dixie Hummingbirds on the Victrola. Elegant was in his room, reading. And Gyp was lying down in the living room, on the royal-blue throw rug.

Woof! Woof!

Gyp heard a car engine. Gyp jumped to her feet. Of course Gyp's barks alerted not only Pee-Pot but Elegant—neither expecting visitors to the house at this late hour.

If the back door were open, Gyp would've gone out the back and to the front of the house, but it wasn't due to it being November. Cold weather had set in.

Knock.

Knock.

Woof! Woof!

Elegant was out his room, and Pee-Pot was up from the basement. Both converged at the front door. Gyp was already there barking, standing guard.

"Quiet down, Gyp, quiet down. I don't expect it's trouble."

"I don't either," Elegant said, looking at Pee-Pot.

"Elegant! Mr. Manners!"

Pee-Pot flung the door open.

"Gem!" Pee-Pot said.

"Gem!"

"Oh, Mr. Manners, Elegant!"

And Gem was standing outside on the dark porch with a small suitcase in hand.

"Gem, what, what are you doing here!"

She looked cold and nervous and confused, practically disoriented.

"Come in! Come in!" Pee-Pot said, not waiting for Gem's reply to Elegant's question.

Pee-Pot grabbed hold of her, hugging her. Elegant stood there looking on. And then Gyp licked her hand greedily, as if warming it but more so to greet her, happy to see her, it seemed.

"I can't go home! I can't, I can't!" She burst out crying.

Pee-Pot led her into the living room.

Gyp was in front of them, Elegant behind them—now in total shock.

Before Gem sat, Pee-Pot took her small suitcase and then helped her out her long, cold overcoat.

Gem kept her head down, now nervously dabbing her eyes with the handkerchief she'd drawn out her pocketbook.

"I can't, Mr. Manners. I can't ..."

Both knew she was referring to going home again.

Elegant looked at Pee-Pot for direction, for he didn't know how to handle this, what to do in this foreign—to him—situation.

"You mean, you don't wanna go home, Gem?"

Slowly Gem lifted her head. "No. No, Mr. Manners. No."

She didn't look over at Elegant. He didn't expect her to; she was too emotionally overwrought.

"Why don't you, Gem?"

"I can't," Gem said plainly after clearing more tears.

"Why can't you?"

"B-because ..." It's when Gem finally looked over at Elegant. "Papa knows by now. About us," Gem said directly to Elegant. "I wrote him, Elegant. He must have the letter. It had to reach him today."

Elegant felt himself reeling, and Pee-Pot stood before Gem speechless.

"I- I couldn't hold it in any longer. I couldn't. I couldn't!" Gem was crying again, as hard and as painfully as before.

Absorbing this, Elegant understood Gem enough to know it was just a matter of time before the truth came out. He wasn't upset with her for doing what she did unless she wouldn't be Gem Loving.

"It's all right," Elegant said consolingly.

"It ... it is, Elegant? Is it?"

"Yes, of course it is, Gem. Of ... of course."

"But this isn't," Pee-Pot said, dashing a cold reality on the situation. "You coming here, Gem. And not going home to your father."

Silence.

"This isn't helping it any."

Elegant wished Pee-Pot hadn't said that but had.

"Surprised he hasn't called to talk to Elegant regarding it."

"No, Papa wouldn't, Mr. Manners," Gem said. "This is between Papa and me first, Mr. Manners. Not El-Elegant, sir."

Elegant knew what that was to mean: Gem was primary, he was secondary—but eventually, he'd be dealt with in the same strict way.

"Why didn't he meet you over in Five Hundred, at the train station?"

"I'm a day early, Mr. Manners. And I got a ride in from Mr. Jeffers who was at the station dropping off his cousin—"

"Lester Smith."

"Yes, sir. I told him I was a day early. I was going to surprise Papa. But I asked him if he would drop me off at Mr. Holloway's house. That I must see him about something. S-something urgent."

This was becoming more and more complicated, intriguing by the second, Elegant thought.

"I told Mr. Holloway I had to see you, Mr. Manners. So I asked him if he would drive me out here. To—"

"You getting in town fresh and with your suitcase, Gem? And Chadway, Chadway Holloway wasn't, he didn't show any interest, curiosity about, suspicions as to what you were doing? W-was so accommodating at this late hour of the night? Y-you coming out here to the farm?"

"Yes, Mr. Holloway did, Mr. Manners. I think he was. Was curious, suspicious. B-but I told him you would drive me home. But that I had to see you. It was important that I—"

"Chadway Holloway's a good man, all right, but I would've ..."

But then Pee-Pot felt foolish, for what did Chadway Holloway have to do with any of this, and who cared Gem was here and was on the verge of fighting the biggest battle of her life.

"It's … it's just, where do we go from here?" Pee-Pot asked.

"I know I have to go home."

"E-eventually," Elegant said.

"No, tonight," Pee-Pot said. "Tonight, Gem."

Gem agreed.

"You've gotta call home. Tell your father you're here. Come to the farm."

"Yes, sir."

Elegant felt awkward since he couldn't walk over and sit down and hold Gem to him like he wanted, not in front of Pee-Pot, not according to convention—two young people in a formal setting.

"But let me leave the room for the two of you can talk," Pee-Pot said, standing. "A few minutes won't hurt any—I don't think."

Elegant appreciated Pee-Pot's consideration toward them.

"Thank you, Mr. Manners."

"For you can catch your breath, Gem."

When Pee-Pot left the room, Gyp left with him.

"I'm sorry, Elegant!"

It's when Gem threw herself at him.

"It's all right, Gem. It's all—it is, it is."

Gem's head drew back. "A-about the letter, about this tonight?"

"Do you want water, a—"

"Yes, water. A glass of water. Thank, thank you."

When Elegant left the room, Gem felt her forehead. She was hot, she thought, and so very tense. The trip and the stops in between and the lies and partial lies—

"Here, Gem," Elegant said, handing Gem the cold glass of water.

"Thank you, Elegant," Gem said, trying to calm down, but her hand trembled badly.

He wasn't going to state the obvious, Elegant thought. He mustn't.

Hurriedly she drank from the glass of water. When finished, Elegant took the glass. "Be right back."

"Yes, Elegant. Y-yes."

How she wrote the letter to her father, she had no idea. Maybe it was the bravest thing she'd done in her life and maybe not, Gem thought. But it was something her father had to know. No, maybe she wasn't so brave, for to stand in front of him and tell him would've been a better act of bravery.

"The letter, Gem. The letter," Elegant said as soon as he got back from the kitchen.

"I told Papa everything, Elegant."

"Yes.

"That it was me who wrote you," Gem said, looking into Elegant's eyes. "I was the one who i-initiated first contact between us. Me, not you."

But a foundation had been built, and he was a coconspirator, Elegant thought.

"And that you came to Howard's campus to visit me. I had to do it this way. Send the letter and then, then come here tonight."

He took her hand. "Why?"

"B-because I had to see you. If I came home and told Papa, I would've been forbidden from seeing you. I wouldn't've seen you the whole ... entire, entire time I was home. If I told him as soon as I got ... I couldn't risk that. I couldn't, I couldn't—even if it's just for these precious, few precious minutes, it's worth it."

"Gem," Elegant said, holding her to him again. "What have we gotten ourselves into?"

"I don't know, Elegant."

"I love you so much. So much!"

"Me too. Me too. I love you too!"

Pee-Pot was out his room. He knew it was time. It was eight forty-seven, late, very late for this kind of circumstance Elegant and Gem were in, for Pastor Loving to have to drive out to the farmhouse to pick up Gem.

Gyp was outside Pee-Pot's door. "Come on, Gyp. We gotta go downstairs now and do what's right."

Gyp stood.

Gem and Elegant heard Pee-Pot and Gyp.

"Are, are you up for this, Gem?"

"No, Elegant. No. I've been a disobedient daughter."

Elegant squeezed her hand and shut his eyes; he felt a miserable pain in him.

Gem stood as soon as Pee-Pot entered the room.

Gyp walked off to the kitchen.

"Can you make the call now, Gem? To your father?"

Elegant stood too, standing beside Gem.

"Yes, Mr. Manners."

The telephone was across the floor, over by the room's entrance from the front door.

Tears had formed in Gem's eyes when she turned to Elegant, and then she walked to the telephone. She picked it up. After picking up the phone she was going to turn back to look at Elegant but, instead, stared blankly into the brown wooden wall.

She dialed. "Papa, I'm in Longwood. Yes, yes, I'm all right, Papa. I'm, I'm at Mr. Manners's house. I-I want to come home, Papa."

Gem and Elegant were alone in the living room. Pee-Pot had bid them good night. Gem was wearing a black skirt and bright green blouse with a multicolored, button-up cotton knit sweater. Knowing her father would be at the house any minute, she'd put her hat and woolen scarf back on. She would put her woolen gloves on as soon as she got out into the cold air.

Elegant was in a panic; he didn't know if he was looking at Gem Loving for the last time. They weren't talking right now, just waiting in silence, not knowing what their future was, would be, after tonight.

"G-Gem, we know we love each other."

"Yes, Elegant." Pause. "B-but what's going to happen to us now?"

"It's so unfair, Elegant. It's so unfair!"

She threw her arms around his neck. Elegant held her around the waist.

"I just can't think right now!"

"It's all I'm doing. It's going to be bad for us ... is-isn't it?"

"Yes," Gem said, breaking free of him.

"Yes," Elegant said, bowing his head.

"I live under my father's roof," Gem said. "I must complete college.

Find a useful profession. One as an educator—it's what's planned for me."

"Yes, of course."

"It, it just feels like everything's falling apart. Everything we have."

"Because I'm a fighter. It's, t-this is because I'm a fighter. Then I don't have to be one. I don't have to be a fighter, Gem!" Elegant said, springing to his feet as if he'd been freed.

"No, Elegant, you—"

Woof! Woof!

Gyp was in the kitchen.

"Gyp, you know who it is. Why're you barking!" Pee-Pot said from the bedroom, now in bed.

"He's here, Gem. He's here."

They were standing. Nervously, they held each other.

"I won't see you!"

"Don't say that, Gem!"

"Ever ... ever again, Elegant. Ever again!"

Honk.

They were at the door.

Gem turned to Elegant. She kissed him.

The house's front door opened, and Gem stepped out of the house and onto the dark porch. She was being guided only by the car's lights pointing at Hattersfield Road, not the house but the only light in the darkness.

Gem had yet to put on her woolen gloves.

Elegant closed the door as soon as Gem left the house. He was staring at the door when first he heard Gyp and then Pee-Pot behind him.

Elegant turned.

Gyp walked over to him and Elegant began petting her.

Pee-Pot was maybe halfway down the staircase in his solid-gray bathrobe.

"I was angry at you, Gyp."

Elegant looked up at Pee-Pot.

"She ... she did the right thing, Mr. Manners."

"I know she did. She always does."

"Gyp warned us, Mr. Manners."

"Uh-huh," Pee-Pot said, heading back up the stairs. "Warned you and Gem."

Elegant kept petting Gyp.

———

Gem was in her room.

Even Francine was forbidden from seeing her. Francine ran to Gem as soon as she got in the house. After that emotional outburst, Francine was sent to her room as well as Gem hers. Being away to college for two years, she felt more like a woman than a girl, but her father's punishment came swiftly.

Her first punishment was the silence from her father after, again, him checking to make certain, physically, she was all right. She'd interrupted Mr. Holloway's supper, so he had food for her; although at the time, she ate very little. But she had eaten, so that ruled out any consideration of Pastor Loving's. And yes, after that matter was settled, the ride provoked silence between them, not until she got to the house and he ordered her and Francine to their rooms. Now she had no idea of just how much Francine knew about her and Elegant Raines.

She was on the bed near Flora, and being so tired and somewhat bitter, she wanted to roll over and cry—but she'd done enough of that tonight. She just didn't want to do any more crying—she refused to. Sitting on the bed, all she wanted was to be strong. She wanted to do this for Elegant, for their love, to make her strong, not weak. They really loved each other. There wasn't any mistaking it.

And it was a love worth fighting for. She wouldn't run away from home; she wasn't thinking that. Elegant would never consent. She wasn't that impulsive or reckless. Love wouldn't push her to do that, to be out of character with herself. Elegant was too sensible to run away with her, and she was too sensible to ask him.

She'd already done the most impulsive thing, the most explosive, reckless thing: run off to Mr. Manners's farmhouse to see Elegant, she thought. Softly she lay down on her back. Her head was in front of Flora, and she reached back for her, laying her on her stomach. This act made her feel like a child.

"Maybe I am a child. Maybe I should be punished like this. Sent to my room. Francine and I ... Flora, Flora, this is real, Flora. This is real ..."

Gem shut her eyes. She was semiconscious.

Knock.

"Papa?"

"Gem, I want to come in."

"Yes, Papa," Gem said quickly, coming off her back.

The bedroom door opened.

When Pastor Loving came through the door he by no means looked pleased.

"Is this what you're learning at school now?"

Gem was standing straight as a ruler. "No, Papa."

"How to lie? Is that what's now being taught in the college curriculum?"

"No, Papa."

"You may think this rhetorical, what I'm saying, but it's not. For it is out of my house this happened. This deceit you have perpetuated and now have brought back to Longwood to not only suffer me embarrassment but embarrassment upon yourself."

Pause.

"You are a different daughter. You are a different person than the one I thought I knew. Gem Loving is lost." Pause. "But I am not going to stand idly by and let you lose yourself through this young man, through this person you think you're in love with. Am I right, Gem? You think you're in love with Elegant Raines?"

"Yes, I am in love with Elegant, P—"

"And it's gone this far, from Mr. Raines to Elegant, Elegant and not Mr. Raines—which is proper. Proper for young people of your ... Yes, it has. It has," Pastor Loving said, dipping his hand in his suit pocket, pulling out Gem's letter, the letter she wrote to him.

"There is deceit in this letter. Beguilement. Bewitchment. The way you have represented you and Mr. Raines in this letter," Pastor Loving said, looking down at it, "and the relationship you've come to develop in secret. Complete secret."

"I'm sorry, Papa," Gem said, her lower lip trembling. "I-I had no other choice, choice in the matter. You gave us—"

"Us? You are to blame in this, not Elegant Raines. You live under my roof. You are my child. I am your father. Elegant Raines did not disobey me. My daughter did."

No, Elegant shouldn't suffer blame, Gem thought. *No, he shouldn't be blamed!*

"But you are forbidden to see him, and he you. Do you hear me, Gem?"

Pastor Loving refolded the letter, putting it back inside his pocket. "Why should Mr. Raines be blamed? He's a man," Pastor Loving said quietly but emphatically. "He's done no real wrong. You wrote him. You invited him on campus."

"Yes."

Pastor Loving removed his glasses. The back of his hand brushed over his eyes. "I told Francine. I told your sister. I cautioned her. She's looked up to you, Gem. You've stood as a tall, shining beacon. So I let her read the letter in your own handwriting for there'd be no exaggeration on my part, overstatement of anything coming from me.

"Facts. That maybe, suddenly, I'm behaving cruelly, badly toward you. Something completely out of character for me."

"I-I accept my punishment, Papa."

"And that's to end it, Gem? It ends right here and now? What you feel for ... toward Elegant Raines. How you snap out of this, this delirium you're in ... have created?"

"And, and why must I suffer? Must, must Elegant suffer again, Papa—because Elegant is a fighter?" Gem asked. "A boxer, Papa?"

Looking at her, not being able to answer her, it was all Pastor Loving was doing: staring at her.

"He's a man, Papa. A man. Elegant Raines is a young man."

She was all but saying she wasn't going to fall out of love with Elegant Raines.

"I never thought I'd have to talk to you like this, Gem. Not you. But you'll never win. Not in my house."

———

"Francine!"

"Ssssh ... don't be frightened. It's me, Gem."

The door was cracked open, and everything was being said in the dark, just above a faint whisper.

Francine was through Gem's bedroom door, shutting it behind her. Then light-footedly, she scooted over to Gem's bed.

"Papa's sleeping," Francine said.

Gem and Francine giggled.

"And you know how he sleeps ..."

They giggled again.

"So he was snoring," Gem said, not giggling now.

"I heard him from my room. It's when I made my way down the hall."

Francine leaned over and hugged Gem.

"Oh ... Francine."

"I'm sorry, Gem."

Flora didn't sleep with Gem; she was in a chair by the bed. Francine saw Flora's outline.

"I guess you just had Flora to talk to. About everything, huh?"

They could see each other better now, less outlines, fuller figures.

"Come, get in bed with me, Francine!"

"Yes!"

Once Francine was in bed with Gem, they hugged again.

"Francine, your feet are cold!"

"I know!"

They began rubbing their feet together, laughing lightly again.

Then Gem seemed to expend all the air out her lungs.

"Yes, it was just Flora and me, Francine."

"Until Papa visited you."

"Yes."

Francine's beautiful light-brown eyes burned into Gem. "I read the letter, Gem."

"I had to start writing Mr. Raines."

Francine frowned in the dark. "Mr. Raines? But you call him Elegant, Gem. Not Mr. Raines. You wrote Elegant in the letter."

"I'm sorry, Francine. Yes, I did."

"You mustn't be formal with me."

"Now suddenly, Francine, you sound like my big sister. The older sister."

They giggled.

"Papa, he told me he let you read the letter I wrote him."

"I'm glad he did."

"Are you disappointed in me, Francine?" Gem said, taking her hand. "Behaving the way I have?"

"Do you mean that, Gem?"

"Of course, of course I do. Do you?"

"Why should I?"

"You know how we've been raised. The Loving sisters. The environment we're a product of."

"I think I'd do like you, if I met someone like Elegant Raines."

"You do?"

"Yes."

"Only, Papa wanted to make me feel ashamed."

"I figured Papa would. But you didn't do anything to the point where you should feel ashamed, I don't think."

"Me either."

"But you did lie to Papa."

"And I should be punished for it."

"Yes."

Gem tightened her grip on Francine's hand, and they stared out into the room, silently thinking.

"I wanted so badly to meet you in Five Hundred tomorrow, Gem. At the train station."

"I was looking forward to it too, but then—"

"You love him, Gem? Elegant Raines?"

"Francine ..."

"Do you? Do you ...?"

"I don't know what love is, but yes, I ..."

Francine giggled in her hand, and then looked over at Flora.

"Did you hear that, Flora? What Gem just said!"

"Of course she did!"

"He's so cute!"

"Handsome."

"Cute!"

"Handsome!"

"Jenny and Virginia and Elsie, when we first saw him at the church, standing outside the church, Gem, the first Sunday he came to church with Mr. Manners—we couldn't take our eyes off him. Neither of us could. And Papa caught us. He caught us, Gem. Ha!"

"Ha. I know Papa brought an end to that kind of foolishness right away. Broke it up."

"It was all right though. We still looked at him," Francine said, blushing red.

"I don't blame you," Gem laughed.

"Gem …"

"Yes …?"

"It'll be all right. It will. It will. Just wait and see!"

"Oh, Francine. I love you so …," Gem said, hugging Francine. Pause.

"I think I'd better get back to my room."

"Me too."

"You never know about Papa."

Both hopped out of the bed together.

"Good night, Flora."

When they got to the door, it was Gem who opened it, and both heads popped out of the door, and both cupped their ears.

"He's still snoring."

"Yes, he is," Gem replied.

"Good night, Gem."

"Good night, Francine."

"Prayers for everybody in the world tonight."

"Prayers for everybody in the world tonight."

And Gem watched as Francine began tiptoeing down the hall until she passed Pastor Loving's room, and then she turned back to Gem and giggled, covering her mouth with her hand.

Gem closed her door.

"Elegant Raines, I do love you. Now that everyone in the world knows," Gem said, picking up Flora. "At least Francine and Flora."

Gem put Flora back in the chair.

She didn't know the time, but now, at least, Gem thought, she could finally fall asleep.

Halfway through with his morning run with Gyp, Elegant was more contemplative than he'd ever been on the run—more so than what he was before leaving Pee-Pot and Gyp, figuring he'd made a mistake, not just him but Mr. Whaley too, that Pee-Pot Manners was not the boxing trainer for him, that they were looking at each other differently, through opposite sets of criteria, of a prism.

Gem, what she must be going through, was all he could think of though. It would be the same at the brickyard today (he just knew it), his mind trapped in her problem with Pastor Loving, trapped in *their* problem, in what was to happen to them. It didn't feel like an illicit relationship, one needing to be condemned, in any form railed against. He looked down at Gyp and again realized what he was doing. Now suddenly wishing he wasn't a fighter but someone else, anyone who would be acceptable to Pastor Loving.

"Gyp, Gyp, let's stop, Gyp. Let's just stop for a second, o-okay?"

Gyp stopped running as soon as Elegant did. Elegant had stopped before a distant hill, one just on the vista. He and Gyp, needless to say, were not breathing heavily—being just halfway through their morning paces. But Elegant was thinking romantically, poetically, trying to crush them, the thoughts he'd just had, that of a fighter. That of trying to be someone else, not who he was. Shakespeare so sure of the characters he created even if they weren't so often sure of themselves or happy with themselves—the skin they were born in.

But he was in a fighter's skin, bound up this way. He could romanticize eternal hills, the one in the distance, cold and unclouded, a refuge for animals who were wild and free. There was some of this in the boxing ring, as animal, savage, but also bound by rules like the laws of nature but free to sing the song in himself as a fighter, as a man, as a Negro, somewhere safe to unleash deadly blows to free himself.

It was a cold Longwood morning with abundant sun. Mittens were on each hand, and he was throwing punches at that hill in a straight trajectory with great power, with great satisfaction, aiming them at the hill as an object, as a way of expressing to Gem Loving how much he loved her. His heart so full of love for her, his fists could topple that piece of hill, knock it flat to the ground.

———

Pee-Pot had hung around the house this morning long enough to see just how disconsolate Elegant was. This was expected. But he wanted to be able to carry Elegant's feelings inside himself for the rest of the day or, at least, up to this point. He'd told Elegant not to come to the gym today, not after work—to go back to the gym at the farmhouse and work on whatever he chose.

Being Thanksgiving was pending, he'd be off. Friday he'd train and then was off on the weekend. Pee-Pot knew that sometimes in conquering your problems, mitigating them, you should be kept busy to keep your mind off them, but he thought it better Elegant relax. He knew his personality so well. He had to think, contemplate things thoroughly—that was the Elegant Raines he knew.

It was four twenty-one, and Pee-Pot was in his truck. So far, for most of the day, his mind had been distracted by Gem and Elegant's problem. He'd be off to Martin County tomorrow morning, first train out, with his and Biscuit's turkey. He'd spend the night there and then board Friday's first train back to Longwood. But this afternoon was going to have meaning and purpose. He wasn't going to stand idly by and do nothing for Elegant. For at twelve o'clock, he'd called Embry O. Loving and arranged a meeting between them in his home for four thirty.

Pastor Loving, he'd treated him respectfully—not unlike what was customary. Pastor Loving understood he wasn't poking his nose into something he shouldn't. He understood perfectly his relationship with Elegant Raines, that it went well beyond that of trainer/fighter. He told him the time he'd be free and if it was compatible to his day. And Pee-Pot had said, "Yes, four thirty's fine, Pastor Loving."

———

Pee-Pot knocked on the door and then waited.

Shortly, the door opened. "Good afternoon, Mr. Manners."

"Good afternoon, Pastor Loving."

They shook hands, and immediately, upon entering the house and Pastor Loving shutting the door, he reached for Pee-Pot's midlength coat and hat.

"Thank you, Pastor Loving."

Pee-Pot waited until Pastor Loving hung his coat and hat on a coat/hat rack near the house's entrance.

Together, they headed for the living room.

On many an occasion, Pee-Pot had been a guest in Pastor Loving's house, especially when Helena Loving died, offering his words and himself as comfort to Pastor Loving and his family as Helena Loving did for him when he lost Cora Manning.

Pastor Loving waited for Pee-Pot to sit on the paisley couch and then followed suit. When he sat, he crossed his leg and looked imposingly at Pee-Pot. "Well, Mr. Manners, we might as well get down to the why of you calling me this morning. Let us not beat around the bush regarding this most grave matter."

Pee-Pot felt Pastor Loving had, deftly, set the tone by using the word "grave," and there was no reason for them to "beat around the bush," as he'd said.

"None at all, Pastor Loving," Pee-Pot said, crossing his leg.

"Neither of my girls are home. They're over at the church, helping out. Preparing meals for, well, you know what the Body of Christ does traditionally on Thanksgiving Day, Mr. Manners—the number of folk in Longwood we'll feed by this time tomorrow in the church basement."

Pee-Pot smiled.

"Gem's not a prisoner. I did have her go straight to her room the minute we got in last night. Like any punishment. I, also, I hate using this word, but I did, under the circumstances, isolate her from Francine. But this morning, we were back to being a family. Conducting ourselves accordingly. Following our normal routine when she's back home from college."

"How much did Gem mope this morning, Pastor Loving?"

Pastor Loving didn't glare at Pee-Pot but held him steady in his gaze, much longer than normal. "I want this to be an honest discussion, Mr. Manners. One we both derive benefit from. I'm not a minister, a pastor, now but a man, a father. Also, if I need guidance, sometimes we do not know from whence it comes, Mr. Manners. Who God is using as his instrument." Pause.

"A lot. A lot, in answering your question, Mr. Manners. There's depression. Solidly in her."

"As well as Elegant."

"I would expect as much, wouldn't you, for the wound to be, still be open. Fresh. Neither able to heal or close it so quickly."

"You're speaking like you're—"

"In metaphors. Metaphors, Mr. Manners." Pause. "I'm shocked by this."

"Gem?"

"Yes, Gem. Gem. My daughter. Her actions. Violations. Disrespecting the principles she was taught and, in doing so, disrespecting me. Her father, Mr. Manners."

Pause.

"There's no hubris here ..."

Inwardly Pee-Pot chuckled. He wished Pastor Loving would speak English, plain English like he did on Sunday mornings from the pulpit but had a pretty good feeling he knew what he was saying.

"On my part."

"No, uh, certainly not, Pastor Loving. Certainly not."

"There's just, to be candid, no room for Elegant Raines in Gem's—"

"He's a fighter."

And it was as if Pee-Pot had punctured the air with those three words.

"Yes. Gem's told me she's dated on campus. A brilliant young man. A philosophy major, I believe he, he was. So ... yes, a fighter, Mr. Manners. A fighter, sir. Elegant Raines is a fighter." Long pause.

"You can kill a man in the ring, Mr. Manners. One fighter can kill another fighter. With one deadly blow. Am I not right?"

"Yes."

Of course Pee-Pot knew this was Pastor Embry O. Loving's position all along. That this was what he had to ponder, consider as a minister, as a moral pillar of his church and the Longwood community at large: one man possibly killing another man in the boxing ring.

Pee-Pot let Pastor Loving remove his glasses and shut his eyes, at once at peace with himself and, at the same time, in a struggle—a tug-of-war waging in him.

"My conscience," Pastor Loving said, his eyes still shut. "Oh, God, my conscience!"

Pastor Loving's eyes had popped open.

The discussion between him and Pastor Loving had reached the level of intensity Pee-Pot hoped it would. And now Pee-Pot saw it was time he seized this opportunity to get across what he thought were his most potent points of view, and relevant.

"What is poverty, Pastor Loving?"

Pastor Loving seemed fully engaged by Pee-Pot's question.

"What do you mean, Mr. Manners? Pov-poverty?"

"For a black man. What is poverty for a black man in this America? This country?"

Pastor Loving's head eased back.

"When a white man can cancel out so much he can't qualify for," Pee-Pot said. "To do."

"Are ... are, you are getting this discussion of Mr. Raines back on track, aren't you? You are talking about options, aren't you, Mr. Manners? Options for black folk. Black men in particular in this country. Ways and means of working their way out of poverty. The limitations. Economic restraints, limitations strapping us."

"Yes."

"Finding skills, no matter what they are. Where they come from."

"Boxing."

"An option, perspective of how to pull yourself up out of poverty."

"That's the story, Pastor Loving. A lot of my boys' stories. That come to my gym."

"Mr. Raines's story then—is what you're saying, Mr. Manners."

Pee-Pot's hands rubbed together. "He's an orphan. His parents died. No relatives helped out."

"He became a ward of the state. Is that it, Mr. Manners?"

"Yes. An orphanage took him in. He doesn't say much beyond that—and I don't ask him. Figure I'll wait for him to open up to me. Let him take his time at that. Felt that from the start." Pause. "Just know, Pastor

Loving, Elegant Raines is the finest young man I know. Have been around. Associated with."

"To be honest, he's certainly impressed me whenever I'm in his company. Intelligent. Well-spoken. Sincere."

"Oh, we love him. Gyp and me. Anyone who gets to—"

"Gem then?"

"Yes, Gem."

"Am I mistaken, Mr. Manners, but do you feel like a surrogate father, grandfather to him? The young man?"

"Ha. Uh-huh. Yes, yes I do, Pastor Loving. Grandfather though. Fooled myself in thinking father at one time too. Only, had to correct myself. Even I've gotta answer to age at some time or another."

"Yes, you do. Yes, you do." Pause.

"Uh, I'm leaving town in the morning."

"Oh, where to?"

"My brother, Biscuit Manners, over in Martin County, Kentucky."

"Yes, a former jockey," Pastor Loving mused. "Another method black men gained a measure of respectability—through horse racing. He was excellent at it," Pastor Loving said. He'd met Biscuit Manners at Cora Manners's funeral. Pause.

"Opportunity—"

"And taking advantage of it, Pastor Loving."

"Smartly. Intelligently, Mr. Manners."

"He's been ailing for a while. Isn't in the best of health."

"Oh, I didn't know that. Why haven't you … t-then I'll pray for him, Mr. Manners. By all means."

Pee-Pot stood. Pastor Loving did likewise.

"In church this Sunday."

"Thank you."

They began walking for the door.

"Carrying a turkey down there. Cook it tonight. Have it all ready for us for our turkey dinner."

"And what about Mr. Raines, Mr. Manners?"

"Oh, him and Gyp'll be at the farm. Theirs will get cooked tonight. Even though Elegant can cook. Quite well, I might add. Though I don't know about a big turkey.

The kind I bought. Cooking something big as that in a pot."

"Hmm ... and he's a good cook, you say, Mr. Manners?"

"Quite good. Before he started, uh, began training in the gym in town and working over at the brickyard, he'd make the meal for us. First time—"

They were practically at the front door. Pastor Loving removed Pee-Pot's hat and coat from the coat/hat rack, handing it to him.

"You can imagine my surprise the first time it happened. That's Elegant—thoughtful as ... just a fine, upstanding young man."

Pastor Loving stuck his hand out.

"Have a safe trip into Martin County tomorrow. Have a wonderful, blessed Thanksgiving. You and your brother."

"Thank you, Pastor Loving." Pause.

"We even lost our status in the sport of horse racing, didn't we, Mr. Manners? Our dominance there."

"Yes, we did."

"Over time."

"Imported white, uh, Irish jockeys over here," Pee-Pot said.

Pastor Loving opened the front door after Pee-Pot put on his coat and hat.

"Mr. Manners, you know I have a lot of thinking to do. Contemplation."

Pee-Pot just looked up at him. He said nothing.

He reached for Pee-Pot's hand again, gripping it firmer. "Mr. Manners, I'd like to call you sometime this evening, if it's no bother."

"No, not at all, Pastor Loving."

"Just let me clear my head." Pastor Loving looked around the house. "The house is ... it's certainly quiet enough without the girls around," he laughed.

He opened the front door for Pee-Pot. "Do you talk to your wife Cora sometimes when you have to make tough, difficult decisions, Mr. Manners?"

"Yes, oh yes, I do, Pastor Loving ..."

"Then we're alike. A lot alike, aren't we?"

"Good day."

"Good day, Mr. Manners."

"You did what, Mr. Manners!"

"I had to, Elegant."

It was how some of the conversation that transpired between Pee-Pot and Elegant when Pee-Pot told him what he'd done. Astonished, overwhelmed, Elegant did cry—it was a highlight in his life. It was paternal and loving, all the emotions he tried expressing to Pee-Pot but couldn't.

At seven o'clock the turkey's aroma in the oven filled out the big-roomed house. Elegant was waiting for Pastor Loving's phone call as well as Pee-Pot. But Elegant was on his bed, happy that Pastor Loving was taking a second look at his and Gem's relationship. While thinking, he'd open and close his eyes and would study each of their arguments. Pastor Loving's, that a man could be killed inside the ring. Therefore, a pastor having a moral issue with it, a moral stake in it. Most black men consigned to poverty post-slavery America, emancipated, but as allocation, not economically free but still feeling the redolent lashes of slavery and Reconstruction and Jim Crow. Black men seeking opportunity, education, trade, sports, boxing—something where they can make a living and earn honor and dignity and well-earned respect. And he was one of those black men. And now Pastor Loving had to consider him, Pee-Pot Manners's argument being that relevant and residually powerful. That much the centerpiece of poverty. What he, Elegant Raines, had brought to the table for thoughtful, thorough debate.

"Mr. Manners just continues to amaze me. He's done so much for me."

Tears filled Elegant's eyes, and all he could think of were his parents, how soft they'd make his heart feel when he could count on their kindness on bad days. In his youth. When they were alive.

By now, Elegant was sure Gem knew of Pee-Pot's visit. He was sure Pastor Loving wouldn't keep it from her. She was at the church (at least he knew where she was at four thirty in the afternoon), but his heart ballooned just by Pee-Pot's mentioning her name. It's how much he loved her. Being as nervous as he was, having the fear he had in him didn't matter while waiting for Pastor Loving's call to Mr. Manners, Elegant thought. Ironically, it was a relief. Ironically, his fears were producing hope.

Pee-Pot was basting the turkey with melted butter. He did his basting with a paint brush. This was the turkey for Elegant for tomorrow. Pee-Pot paused. By now, he had expected a call from Pastor Loving. He didn't know why, but he had. This was beginning to unnerve him. He was thinking optimistically, positively, not negatively—not targeting the worst that could happen to Gem and Elegant.

He only wished it didn't have to be like this, that life had to be this full of struggle. But it seemed the human animal needed it. The human animal's temperament, it seemed, needed highs and lows in order for it to function, release joy and pain, these opposite extremes.

Pee-Pot laughed and then went back to basting the turkey with the paint brush. He laughed at himself for digging into the human psyche, into the human soul. But it's all he did every day anyway, as a trainer, was work within that exciting, unpredictable area of the fighter. It fascinated him.

Ring.

Pee-Pot froze.

He took the paint brush and laid it down on the kitchen table. His heart was pumping lightning fast, so he could well imagine what Elegant's was doing.

The phone rang two more times.

"Yes. Good evening."

"Good evening, Mr. Manners."

"Good evening, Pastor Loving."

It was eight oh six.

"I, first, I'd like to apologize for calling your house so late. But a church problem arose, and it required my immediate attention as do most—as you can imagine." Pause.

"It does appear, Mr. Manners, that I did need your guidance. That you were a source of inspiration. That you did shine a light on a hidden but vital truth of being black in a country that wreaks with every one of our ancestors that's come before us. And what is our current reality today: economics. And our toehold in it.

"I want this relationship with Gem and Mr. Raines to continue. I had every right to feel as strongly as I did. My moral bearing. And I have a right, the freedom to change my mind. I will not shut myself off in a box of moral judgment."

"Oh, this is a …" Pee-Pot fell silent.

"For me, your silence says everything, Mr. Manners. You were my counsel, my teacher this time. I thank you."

Pee-Pot still didn't know what to say; he was so thrilled.

"And now, if I may, Mr. Manners …"

"Yes …?"

"Call upon your patience …"

"Yes …?"

"I imagine you've begun cooking the turkeys."

"Was just basting the second one, Pastor Loving." Pee-Pot looked over at the clock. "Oh, in about ha—another hour, I'll be sticking it in the oven."

"But I was going to ask that after the church Thanksgiving dinner, the girls and I have our own private dinner at the house, as I'm sure everyone in Longwood is aware of …"

"Yes," Pee-Pot said, shaking his head. "It's common knowledge in Longwood."

"Tomorrow, Mr. Manners, I'd like to pick Mr. Raines up from the farmhouse, and uh, five thirty tomorrow—and for him to have Thanksgiving dinner with us. Gem, Francine, and me."

"Y-you would!"

"Yes, if that wouldn't—"

"No, no, not at all, Pastor Loving. Elegant will just have his turkey Friday, Friday, that's all. The two of us when I get home!"

"I just hope," Pastor Loving laughed, "our turkey will be as tasty as yours."

"Ha!"

"So five thirty."

"Five thirty."

"Thank you for making this decision so easy for me. And again, have a safe trip to Martin County. And we will pray for your brother Biscuit this Sunday. He will be in our prayers."

"Thank you, Pastor Loving."

"Good evening."

"Good evening."

Pee-Pot hung up the phone and then stood in the vestibule.

"Elegant! Elegant!"

"Yes, Mr. Manners! Yes!"

And suddenly Gyp appeared.

"Oh, it's a great day, Gyp. It's a great day, ain't it!"

CHAPTER 16

To say Elegant was all thumbs would be putting it mildly. When you tie your tie eight different times eight different ways, that's proof positive. Or you mismatch your socks and don't know it until you put on your pants and then look down and see the fashion crime you've committed, then that's proof positive too.

Gyp stood by him throughout this entire shenanigan, patiently adjusting to Elegant's craziness like a wise old grizzled hen—even if she was a dog. The ride in Pastor Loving's car, now that was going to be interesting. It's something Elegant had been thinking of all day—and it still was.

He'd gotten advice from Pee-Pot: "Just be yourself, Elegant. Nobody else. It's all you've gotta be." And he'd taken it to heart. He wasn't going to be anybody else; he was just going to be Elegant Raines. He wasn't going to try to impress Pastor Loving now that the stage was his and he'd shifted his status from being a parishioner at the Body of Christ Church to an active suitor for Gem Loving's hand, in the eyes of Pastor Loving.

"So be it," Elegant said, looking at himself in the mirror in his gray, woolen, pinstriped suit. "So be it."

Now it was five twenty-seven, and Elegant knew Pastor Loving would be on time, so he was at the door in his overcoat (hatless), waiting.

"Gyp, three minutes. Three minutes, Gyp. T-to go. I hope I make it."

Elegant began petting Gyp. She rolled over on the floor and stretched out.

"I'm sorry I'm leaving you alone like this on Thanksgiving Day, of all days, Gyp."

Gyp yawned.

"I didn't expect this. No, not this."

It seemed he hadn't seen Gem forever. It's how it felt to him, when in reality it'd only been two days.

Woof!

Gyp was on her feet.

Elegant opened the door. Gyp ran out of the house.

Pastor Loving was out of the car.

"Gyp!"

Gyp dashed to him. She jumped up into Pastor Loving's arms.

Gyp was loping back to the house. She looked up at Elegant and then reentered the house.

Woof!

Both Elegant and Pastor Loving laughed.

"See you later, Gyp!"

Elegant shut the door.

"Mr. Raines, good afternoon."

"Good afternoon, Pastor Loving."

When Elegant got to Pastor Loving, they shook hands. Then Pastor Loving opened the car door.

"Thank you, sir."

Pastor Loving was inside the car with Elegant. He swung the car around on Hattersfield Road. It was a black Ford. It looked like a preacher's car (even if Pastor Loving's model was the most popular in the auto industry). But it took to the bumps on Hattersfield Road no better than Pee-Pot's Studebaker truck or Tommie's Ford Super Deluxe.

"Let me apologize for all of this, Mr. Raines."

Eagerly, Elegant replied, "Then, then your apology's accepted, Pastor Loving. Fully ac—"

"Now, now, not so eager, so fast, Mr. Raines. Let's not try to get ahead of ourselves too fast with this situation."

"Oh, uh, yes, Pastor Loving. Uh, no, no, we mustn't, mustn't, sir."

"Let me just say when I first saw you with Gem, I was afraid of what I saw. I saw the potential for this right away. It's what frightened me most. The attractiveness of the two of you together. It's … the danger." Pause.

"Just knowing you were a fighter, I saw no hope, no possibility, Mr.

Raines. That I would ultimately have to step in, intervene, crush this thing, and, therefore, break my daughter's heart. No father wants to do that."

Pastor Loving looked over at Elegant. "And as I said, this was something far too apparent that I would eventually have to do." Pause.

"So I did. And now we are where we are."

"And where's that, may I ask, Pastor Loving … respectfully?"

"A man has a right to be who he is. To choose his profession. To be as honorable in it as he chooses. To be a good man. A decent man. A charitable man. Isn't that what any moral person, uh, human being is, Mr. Raines? Based on that justification?"

"I … of course, sir."

"Are there any other qualifications you'd like to add?"

"No, sir. I think you've covered them all, Pastor Loving."

They were about seven minutes into the ride.

"Elegant, I'm not one to discuss boxing, but I hear you are quite good."

"Under Mr. Frank 'Black Machine' Whaley and Mr. Manners's tutelage, I've become quite good, sir. In the ring."

"Do you think your fists could kill a man, or is that a fair question to ask?"

"Yes, it is, Pastor Loving. Quite fair, sir." Pause. "I think any fighter who punches as hard as I do possesses the power in his punch I have, worries about this, sir."

"Well …?"

"Even before Gem prayed for my opponents not to leave the ring hurt, in anyway injured, I did too. I've hurt many fighters, Pastor Loving. But to kill a man in the ring, I could never command my fists to do that. Take part in that kind of savagery, sir."

Pastor Loving understood he'd asked a rhetorical question, for even he knew that some fighters, due to lack of conditioning or bad past beatings they suffered in the ring, had no say over their own fate. But he had to hear Elegant Raines's response; it was imperative.

"And Gem tells me you're a Shakespeare man."

"Yes, sir, I am. I've read many of his plays."

"Then we'll have to compare notes. I draw inspiration from his writings as well as other English poets and playwrights so dear to me."

Elegant knew they'd soon be at the house.

"Gem's happy."

That sounded so spectacular.

"But be careful, Elegant. Francine is too!"

———

Elegant pulled the chair out for Gem, and she sat. Then Elegant stood behind his chair, pulled it out, and sat. Pastor Loving had already pulled Francine's chair out for her.

Gem and Elegant sat next to each other at the dining room table. Francine sat across from them and Pastor Loving at the head of the table.

"May we bow our heads in prayer and bless the most divine, the most giving."

The prayer over, Pastor Loving stood and eyed the turkey.

"I bought it, but Francine and Gem cooked it, Elegant."

"Papa, I did most of the work!"

"Francine, don't let me tell the truth!" Gem laughed.

"If I may remain neutral, Elegant, I'm sure they both did their equal share. So that's settled, now isn't it, girls? It's how I settle all disputes in the Loving household, Elegant, whenever they're as serious as this."

They laughed.

Pastor Loving picked up the large carving knife and fork off platter. The turkey sat on the huge china platter; it was big, brown skinned, crisp, and beautiful. He sliced it into thin slices.

All eyes were set on the turkey, even though Elegant was thinking he'd rather be sitting in Francine's chair, across from Gem, not beside her, for he could look directly into her face as he did at the front door when he saw her, unashamedly, his heart on his sleeve, loving Gem Loving more than anything and anybody.

For Thanksgiving dinner, she'd chosen a black ankle-length dress with a black belt. But the dress had a rounded collar, her mother's pearls worn around her neck, and the contrast between her dark skin and the white pearls made her delicate face shine as beautifully and openly as ever he'd seen it.

"Hungry, Elegant?"

"Yes, very. Very, Pastor Loving."

Gem took his plate, and it's when they made eye contact, and he felt he was going to faint right there, right at the Lovings' dining room table on Thanksgiving Day.

—————

The unexpected had become so intrinsically a part of the past two days that he should not be at all surprised by him sitting in the car with Gem and her driving it, going over the same rough series of bumps in the road as Pee-Pot Manners and Tommie and Pastor Loving, Elegant thought. Gem shifted through a gear. Indeed, this was totally unexpected, Gem driving him home to the house, not knowing she drove, but Pastor Loving handing her the car keys and her taking them and Pastor Loving informing him, "Elegant, Gem will drive you back to the farm this evening, uh, won't you, Gem?" And you can well imagine his surprise not only by this fact of Gem driving but also of this big leap Pastor Loving had taken, of his acceptance and trust of him in such a short window of time.

They were no more than two minutes into the ride home. It was dark out. It was nine eleven and Gem was her usual bright self.

"Elegant, will you stop looking at me like that!"

"And how's that?"

"Strangely."

"How do you know? It's dark, and I'm dark. So what, you see my eyeballs?"

"Yes, no, uh—"

"Come on, Gem, make up your mind."

"Your head's been tilted, angled toward me for some time. Since you got in the car. Don't think I haven't noticed."

"Well, I am surprised—"

"That I drive?"

"Uh, yes."

"Papa thought it necessary. Francine drives too. You never know when there might be an emergency. Me or Francine c-could be of help to someone if Papa's not available."

There was so much charity in the three Lovings, Elegant thought. And they took that personal responsibility most seriously.

"Elegant, do you drive?"

"No," Elegant laughed.

"Then I'll teach you!"

(Of course Elegant was faking, but he was hoping it'd lead to this: Gem volunteering to teach him. The "fib" would be corrected later, he thought, grinning.)

He was full of turkey and stuffing and love and didn't want this day to end. It was happening all too fast.

"When?"

"How about tomorrow?"

"To—wait, no Gem, uh, I'm back to work at Mr. Miller's tomorrow and the gym—"

"Then when?"

"Saturday. Saturday. How about—"

"Fine. Ten o'clock. Papa'll be preparing his sermon, like always. Since I was born."

"Perfect."

"Perfect."

He could feel her bright smile on this dark country road, and it was infectious.

"Sunday, at church, I wish we could sit together, Elegant."

"But you'll be in the choir."

"Yes."

Suddenly Elegant was hit by something. "You're, you're singing a solo this Sunday, aren't you, Gem?"

"Yes, I … how'd you know? I was going to surprise you!"

"I know because, I mean, you're home, home from school. You have to sing a solo in church!"

"Says who?"

"Says everyone in town of Longwood. I think there'd be a riot if you didn't!"

Her first day home had been so gloomy, Gem thought. Running to Elegant first, Pee-Pot Manners's farm, before going home, gaining only a slight reprieve for her actions and being sent to her room by her father, told to stay there like a prisoner, at least for one night. And then in the morning, the storm clearing, things more reasonable, adjustable—Francine a comfort and the church's traditional Thanksgiving dinner preparations.

But it was Mr. Manners's visit, his intervention that clinched it, Gem thought. She'd be eternally grateful to Mr. Manners. She'd begun wondering if her father would've come around without him, taken such a huge, extraordinary leap.

"What are you thinking, Gem?"

"About us."

"It has been eventful, the past few days, hasn't it?"

"Exciting. Is this the way it's going to be for us, Elegant? From now on?"

"Gem, you're asking me?"

"Ha."

"I'm probably the wrong person to ask that question to. My life hasn't exactly, well …"

"Elegant, come on, you're a boxer. Everyone says boxing's exciting."

"Yes, yes, it is." Pause.

"If I attended one of your boxing matches," Gem said, shifting car gears, "I wouldn't be frightened by blood, like I told you."

"Maybe not, but you'd be upset by it, seeing it, wouldn't you?"

Gem calmed. "I would. I'd be sick. Sick to my stomach."

"Seeing another man hurt."

Gem looked at Elegant. "Who was I trying to fool, Elegant, just now?"

They were at the farmhouse.

Elegant didn't know how to end this evening, never mind Gem. They were holding hands, just sitting there in the cold car but seemingly unaffected by the cold, their bodies warm inside their clothing.

"I have to wait until Saturday to see you again, don't I, don't I, Gem?"

Gem didn't answer.

"It's going to seem like forever."

Gem said nothing. But her face drew closer and closer to his, and they kissed. They kissed again. He would see her eyes even in the dark while closed—it's how he remembered them tonight coming back from the kitchen and into the dining room with the sweet potato pie she'd baked, and looking down at him after cutting the pie with the pie knife, the loveliness of each eye, looking into his as if they no longer considered who at the table saw how much she loved him.

"I love you, Elegant," Gem whispered.

"Me too. I love you too, Gem."

Closing the car door and walking toward the house, the car hadn't moved. Elegant turned around, but in the dark, the moon not aglow, Gem didn't see this. He opened the door. The car turned on Hattersfield Road.

Woof! Woof!

Elegant turned the light on.

Gem had executed the U-turn.

Woof! Woof!

"Gyp! Gyp!" Gem screamed, having rolled the car window down, waving at Gyp, whom she saw but was not sure if Gyp saw her.

Woof! Woof!

The house was cold. And inside the house, it was short of firewood.

Elegant was petting Gyp's cold coat.

"I'll get the firewood, Gyp. Heat the house up."

He turned on another light. He and Gyp headed for the kitchen. He turned the kitchen light on. He was about to open the kitchen door for Gyp, when he stopped short of it.

"I really love Gem, Gyp. I really do. It feels great, Gyp. Great."

He opened the door and Gyp skipped out of the house with him. And it was dark in the back of the house too, needless to say, in getting to the woodpile.

———

It was 1947. February 18 was Elegant's birthday. It was on a Thursday. He turned nineteen; and he celebrated it with Tommie, Gyp, and Pee-Pot. Pee-Pot baked a chocolate layer cake, putting nineteen white candles on it, and Elegant blew all the candles out, of course.

The months had moved rapidly. And so too Elegant's, Tommie's, and Black Moon's boxing careers. In their divisions, they were taking on big-time contenders and beating them.

Each was causing a big stir, making it more and more difficult for other fighters ranked higher than them to avoid them. Suddenly Tommie was knocking his opponents out. He was becoming a more lethal puncher—even though he still had a reputation of a boxer, one of nonpareil skills.

But it was Black Moon Johnson and Elegant Raines who were capturing the imagination of the boxing world, the fancy of its fans and scribes. Because of their cross-country campaigns, plenty of fight fans had seen them fight live and had become excited by them. It was in the 1930s when the heavyweight division went through a dreadful drought, a dearth of white heavyweights with little talent or charisma, and black fighters stepped in to fill the void.

But the lower-weight classes always seemed to maintain a level of dynamic fighters regardless of race. But even now, in 1947, Black Moon and Elegant were providing the kind of power in the middleweight division the division had not seen.

And now, through Black Moon's interviews with the sports media, the story of Black Moon Johnson and Elegant Raines had been broached, discussed by Black Moon. He'd fed the media machine with his history with Pee-Pot Manners and Elegant Raines—his hatred toward them when he was a fighter in Pee-Pot Manners's boxing stable. He blasted Pee-Pot Manners, saying he held him back. That he kept him out of the big fights in favor of Elegant Raines, setting Elegant Raines up for he could eventually wrest the spotlight from him in Pee-Pot's Pugilistic Paradise gym.

Black Moon said he couldn't help but hate them, both of them, for they not only tried to take "bread off his table" but also tried holding him back from "fame and fortune."

The press wasn't interested in whether the story was true or not—it was great copy. The kind of copy sports reporters dream of. There was no investigation, no hard digging into facts, no reporters contacting Pee-Pot or Elegant. This was strictly a one-sided story, a one-sided headline. The media ran with the story like it was Man o' War storming down Churchhill Downs's renowned back stretch.

Pee-Pot sat down and pointed out the facts of life as they were to Elegant, that to deny the allegations would only add fuel to the fire, and they would take no part in that.

Instead, their strategy was that they'd let Black Moon be the bully, the bad guy, loudmouth; and when they fought (which was a certainty), they'd take the high road in all of this, the road they squarely wished to navigate.

They had no animosity toward Black Moon. Pee-Pot realized he was a troubled young man, one who wished to win at all costs and who wanted to wear the middleweight crown and would do anything in his power to wrest it. He always thought it'd be in the ring, not outside it too.

Of course Elegant had a series of problems with him. But in the end, it felt like all bluff and bluster to him even though it wasn't. But it was how he thought to handle it: give it puny value, estate, thereby he'd be able to defeat it. But his conflict with Black Moon struck at his Christian heart. Whether he could forgive him—which he had. Even though this feeling would be valueless in the ring when those few people from the gym who knew the real story might think differently after he defeated him, that he'd sought revenge when, in reality, he'd not.

For when they did fight, he was going to look upon Black Moon as just another opponent who wanted what he wanted. And he did want to win the championship as badly as anyone since he was just as hungry as Black Moon, just as eager. He didn't need fame and fortune but did need to feel fulfilled. He'd made the sacrifice to be great, and there were no illusions that he could.

Longwood without Gem was different. She'd been back for the Christmas holidays. But even with that visit, it seemed long ago. He confessed his sins to Gem that he could indeed drive a car the first time they got behind the car's steering wheel on that Saturday morning, when she began instructing him. They laughed and used it as time spent together for fun, merriment. She called from school. She had an allowance that allowed her to call him at the house twice a month. Between letters, the telephone (she called him on his birthday), her holiday stay, and his one trip back to Howard University's campus, it's how, generally, the relationship was moving along. They wrote once a week. There was a lot, from letter to letter, they talked about.

And one of the timely things he would talk about in his next letter to her would be his trip into Tulip, Tennessee, to visit one, Hancock Hollins III, a manager of fighters, along with other business ventures when it came to making money. Now aiming for the big fights on the horizon, the big pay days for Elegant, Pee-Pot wanted him to be promoted/managed by someone who had the clout to make those kinds of business deals available to them. It's why he'd gotten in touch with Hancock Hollins III, who had his finger on the pulse, knew all about Elegant Raines and his ring record. Hollins espoused his eagerness to sit down and talk to Pee-Pot and Elegant, arranging this meeting quickly, urgently, on his estate in Tulip, Tennessee.

At times Elegant sat down and took a long view of his life and what he came from. He wanted nothing to do with the South. Even if now living in the hills of West Virginia, at least it was on the northern tip of Pennsylvania and not the Mason-Dixon line. Also, during the Civil War, it was a non-Confederate state. Whenever he fought in Southern states, the old horrors manifested. In this way he was like Pee-Pot when he boarded trains. Pee-Pot stared into the past and remembered Cora Manners was murdered on a train by a Southern white man while traveling through the state of Alabama.

But unlike Pee-Pot, he couldn't show his horror or talk about it or give anyone any inkling it existed. What, at ten years old, he saw and heard in the South, in Saw Mill, South Carolina. It's why he hated traveling through the South's interior but had to learn to accept his circumstance. In a way, it's why he wasn't going to enjoy the trip into Tulip, Tennessee, with Pee-Pot to visit Hancock Hollins, although he understood full well the necessity of the visit and, therefore, grateful for what it might mean to his burgeoning boxing career.

But the South's psychological horrors still haunted him when physically encountering it, its white men, oppressors, not Ku Klux Klanners, not Southern white men wearing white hoods and robes. They didn't hide their faces nor who they were, act anonymously during their ride that day. They had to look straight into the eyes of the devil before they executed their brand of evil. It's how Elegant felt at ten and now nineteen. There'd been nothing he'd learned about white men to change his opinion of them.

CHAPTER 17

This was a typical Southern mansion defined by weeping willows and vast property and a huge white house and weather-beaten, dilapidated shacks, reminders of slavery and the families of slaves who lived in them from generation to generation. On the way in, on the long, narrow road populated by barren poplar trees, Elegant wondered how many slaves were hung from such trees, were lynched there—not to say it was there where they met their deaths, on Hancock Hollins's property, but poplar trees as symbols of the South and its bloody past.

The servant who answered the mansion's front door was black. He was dressed for the job. He was courteous. He was an older man with wire-thin, stooped shoulders who administered to their coats. After hanging the coats on a brass coat rack, he walked back to them.

"You may come with me," he said, motioning to Pee-Pot and Elegant. "This way, please."

The two tall white stately doors were shut. The servant opened the doors. He stepped into the room first.

"The two gentlemen are here, Mr. Hollins."

"Please show them in, Rupert."

"Yes, sir."

The two doors parted, and Pee-Pot and Elegant entered the grand-looking room, and the servant Rupert stepped out of the room when Hancock Hollins III said, "That'll be all for now, Rupert. Thank you."

"Yes, sir."

"Pee-Pot ..."

"Mr. Hollins."

Both Pee-Pot and Elegant approached Hollins's tastefully carved desk.

Hancock Hollins III was standing, and he was tall and full-bodied with a huge dome-shaped head with wisps of wild, tangled gray hair that gleamed with magnificence.

Right off he and Pee-Pot shook hands as Elegant stood behind Pee-Pot, to the right of Pee-Pot's right shoulder.

"So this must be Elegant Raines here. With you here, Pee-Pot. The young man."

"Yes, Mr. Hollins."

Hollins stuck his hand out and shook Elegant's hand when Elegant stepped forward, parallel to Pee-Pot.

"Impressive. You're quite impressive looking, Elegant," Hollins said.

Six handsome leather upholstered chairs ringed the desk.

"Why don't you sit then, gentlemen."

While Pee-Pot and Elegant sat, Hancock Hollins III stood in his three-piece woolen white suit and white shirt and solid red bow tie while he fingered the silver-plated pocket watch hanging loosely outside his vest pocket.

"How was the trip down, Pee-Pot?"

"Fine, Mr. Hollins. Quite nice to be back in Tennessee again."

"You just have to skip over Kentucky and here you are, in the grand state of Tennessee. Our lovely province."

The long drapes were open, and it was a dreary day. Pee-Pot and Elegant ran into rain on the way into Tulip, Tennessee.

"Now, Pee-Pot, how long's it been, the last time we engaged each other?"

"You know, Mr. Hollins, I was thinking that too—same as you on the way down. Thought it might come up in general conversation." Pause.

"Uh, the Dickie Williams and Ted Furman fight."

"So that had to be, what …?"

"Four years back."

"Four years back. Exactly. A long time for us, Pee-Pot. Between occasions. Glad my man won that night. Retired from the ring champ."

The door opened, and Rupert carried a tray with three tall glasses on it.

"Lemonade, gentlemen? What Southern gentleman doesn't like a glass of lemonade at noon day. Especially after coming in by train, to cool his thirst." Pause.

"Thank you, Rupert."

Both Elegant and Pee-Pot were pleased by the gesture. Both were thirsty, and so lemonade was in order. It was a little past twelve o'clock, and they were invited for lunch after the business meeting. The train trip to Hollins's estate was paid for by Hollins. They were picked up by his man at the train station and then driven by car to the Hollins property.

"I know about Biscuit. What his health generally looks like these days," Hollins said gravely, putting down his glass with a heavy, somber look.

"Thank you, Mr. Hollins."

"He was a great jockey like you were a great fighter, Pee-Pot," Hollins said genuinely. "Rode a mount as well as any man alive. Seen ride in the southlands. Had, must've had a clock in his head to control pace. I useta swear to the heavens. And his hands could steer any horse, big or small, just how—"

"But he's not dead yet. Not by a long shot."

"Oh no, uh-uh, I-I wasn't saying ... meaning to suggest that, Pee-Pot. Oh no. Heavens no!"

Elegant was glancing at rows and rows of books in Hancock Hollins's study. This was a white Southern gentleman's Southern trait: books. And like him, it would be Shakespeare, the great English poets, and of course religious books, the Gospel. They'd crowd out space on the book shelves.

And to the left of the bookcase was a huge brass-plated globe of the world you could spin, it appeared, to your heart's content, Elegant laughed to himself.

"I was with him for Thanksgiving and again for Christmas. He's always in good spirits."

"Remember how my daddy tried luring him over to our stables. Hoodwink him, my golly, into coming over here to the Hollins farm to ride for us. Do us good."

Pee-Pot laughed.

"But the Prescott farm ... Biscuit wouldn't ride for another soul but them. Was as loyal as a bloodhound to that family."

"And they proved worthy of his faith in them, Mr. Hollins. It's why

Biscuit doesn't have to worry about a penny to this day. A penny outta his pocket. The Prescotts made certain of that."

"Ain't that the truth," Hollins laughed.

Hollins's gaze switched over to Elegant.

"Mr. Raines, I'm an old man."

Pee-Pot laughed.

"Well, I am, Pee-Pot. Can't hide the stars, now can you? The moon either, at night."

"I know, Mr. Hollins. But since I'm pulling on the same rope, I thought you might be more kind," Pee-Pot said, lifting his glass of lemonade, drinking from it.

"Oh, no charity today, Pee-Pot. Ain't in the mood for it. I pray to the heavens though, but it can only spare me but so long."

Pee-Pot laughed, but Elegant's disposition was very composed, responsible.

"But honestly, Pee-Pot, it's my heart. What it is, is troubling me now. My doctor, well ... tells me, says it's not in the best of shape. Best condition for a man my age. It's estimated I've gotta year, year and a half. Two years, at most, I'll get out of it."

Pee-Pot's disposition changed.

"I'm not saying this to look for sympathy from you 'cause every man's gotta die in his own time."

"Of course not, Mr. Hollins."

"But you know what I'm saying, Pee-Pot. Trying ... getting at. Reading between the lines."

"Yes, yes. I am, Mr. Hollins."

"I want a championship fighter before I die. Dickie Williams was the last one I managed." He looked at Elegant again. "I want a champion before I die."

Elegant was looking at an old white man's cloudy eyes that had come alive.

"Elegant, can you do that for this old white man?"

Even if he had more questions than answers, he'd still respond the way he did.

"Yes, yes, I can, Mr. Hollins. Sir."

Hollins's body fell back in the chair. He shut his eyes. He clasped his large, weighty hands together, putting them down on the table like two big clubs.

"The South," he said, opening his eyes, "is such a magical place. This farm I inherited from my daddy. You saw the slave quarters on your way in, Elegant, on this ... uh, of course, Pee-Pot's been here before. Ain't his first trip through the grounds."

Pee-Pot shook his head.

"Daddy wouldn't destroy not a one of those dreadful shacks, and neither will I. Said he was gonna burn in hell one day for his sins. Multitude of them. For the owning of slaves. Another human being. Daddy thought that way for all slaveholders who enslaved black men, women, and children. Alla them was to burn in hell one day by the power and sword of the Almighty. God, Pee-Pot, God himself!" Hancock Hollins said it so loudly the study's walls rang from his hoarse, shrill voice.

"Till the day Daddy died he believed that as truth. He wanted to give the slaves up. Have nothing to do with them anymore—set them free, only couldn't. Was too weak of mind and spirit and filled with custom to set them free.

"Took the Civil War. Lincoln. The Great Emancipator. Abolitionists out the North to ... I wasn't born then. Wasn't around. Was born in 1867. Was raised up when the South was changing. When a white man no longer owned slaves but still had them as servants and nannies in his household to run things."

"Black servants and nannies, Mr. Hollins," Pee-Pot said. "You owned us, even though you can say you're free, go ahead and leave if you want—but where to, Mr. Hollins? Where would they go, any go, eventually, but wind up back working for the whites? For former slave owners? As property? Back on the farms—"

"Something they knew."

"Correct."

"It, it is why I won't have those shacks out there destroyed, Pee-Pot. Torn down. It's a lasting reminder and testament of human suffering. What it must've been for the blacks of the South back then. The old South. Not the new South. I'm not gonna be haunted by ghosts. I'm gonna respect them. Let those ghosts stay right out there on my property where they belong. So I can respect them every day of my life."

"What exactly do you mean, Mr. Hollins?" Pause.

"I can't atone for my daddy's sins, no father's son can, but I do wanna make a man's life better, whether he be white or black," Hollins said in answering Pee-Pot's question. "I'm not a benefactor. But I do wanna walk in the goodness and grace of God. Of the divine. Carry God's banner. Been trying to do just that for all, just about all my natural-born life."

Elegant was stunned by this kind of rhetoric on Hancock Hollins's part, coming from a white man, a Southerner. He wanted to think the South had changed but just how much? To what degree—to what lengths? Hancock Hollins wasn't saying that by fighting for him, under his management, he was making race relations between blacks and whites better, was he? That boxing provided this simplistic societal function, formula, healing for race relations when, in all practicality, money was the major player, the key factor. But he'd said he wanted a champion before he died. For what reason? For what purpose? To what end?

I must stand up and speak up for myself! I must say something!

"Par-pardon me, Mr. Hollins, sir. But if I may, sir ..."

Not only did Hollins register surprise by this sudden interruption from Elegant but Pee-Pot also.

"By all means, Elegant. By all means," Hollins said.

"Pardon, do pardon me ... but why must I provide you with a championship before you die, sir? For what purpose? To what end, Mr. Hollins, will it serve you, sir?"

There was this slow reaction from Hancock Hollins who looked well beyond Elegant's head, in fact, well above his head, but still, it was a distant look, pensive, quiet—rather magnetic and magnanimous.

"I suppose I must start this treatise by saying I always wanted to make the world fair. I, somehow, I never liked how it was." Pause. "It can be fair in the boxing ring. Between two men. Two men of distinction. White versus white. Black versus black. White versus black.

"I just want to see it one more time," he said, swallowing a fat lump of phlegm in his mouth. "For a young black fighter who deserves the opportunity. Or advantage, if you will. Is, is that some atonement? Atoning? I don't hardly know. But it's what I want for you, Elegant," Hollins said, bringing his eyes back down to Elegant's.

"I swear to you on my daddy's grave at the far end of this here mansion. It's all I want."

———

Home at his desk, itching to pen a letter to Gem, Elegant was just about to start. This was the morning after getting in from Tulip, Tennessee, with Pee-Pot. They'd gotten in late last night, and he wanted to write her but thought it best he sleep on it first.

February 28, 1947

Dearest Gem,

Mr. Manners and I just got in from our train trip to Tulip, Tennessee, to meet Mr. Hancock Hollins III. I'm so used to traveling by train that I am becoming quite an expert at it. It's my long legs, especially in sleeping berths, that I've had to overcome with some ingenuity. I always find it great fun and great joy to travel with Mr. Manners for whatever trip we take together.

Gem, I met an honest white man yesterday. Hancock Hollins is an honest white man. I had never in my life before sat down with a white man who talked so openly and honestly about race, the South, slavery, its past, and our black ancestry (as an Indian and Negro you and your family are so proud of being). This was a revelation for me.

I must admit. I was seduced by Mr. Hollins. The one thing he said that stood out that I'd like to share with you is when he said, "I'm not going to be haunted by ghosts."

Elegant stopped there in his letter writing, for he heard and saw his ghosts the moment he finished the sentence. They were still alive in him; Hollins's words hadn't done anything to erase them, liberate him of them. Steadying himself, Elegant chose to continue writing the letter.

This is a direct result of Mr. Hollins talking about his father's ownership of slaves on his plantation. Of not destroying the face of slavery existing there. There were reminders of that past, the slave quarters. The dilapidated slave shacks. They're still on the estate. Mr. Hollins said his father knew he was going to "burn in hell" because he held onto slaves. I'd heard a lot of slaveholders felt this way, but it was the first I'd heard a descendant of one say this in my presence.

I am Mr. Hollins's fighter now. He wants to win a championship with me and Mr. Manners. He is sure he will die in a matter of a year or two. I feel comfortable with this business arrangement. I didn't want to tie myself to the South through a Southern fight manager before yesterday, as I wrote you. I hope this is a degree of progress for me, Gem. I do not want to keep burying myself in the past.

And so, how are things going for you on campus? At the university?

And so Elegant continued writing the letter until he finally put his pen down, after signing off to Gem, saying,

Gem, I love you. I love you. I love you.

Rereading the letter, he had to study one sentence: I didn't want to tie myself to the South through a Southern fight manager before yesterday as I wrote you.

"Yes, I expressed it to you, Gem, but I didn't explain it."

He didn't know if he could explain it to Gem if Gem ever brought it up—or would he concoct a lie, a different version of his reality, an altered truth. For it's all she'd be asking, as anyone would. But it would be something he wouldn't deliver, the truth. He felt it necessary to even conceal it from Gem, the woman he loved.

"Mr. Hollins, I'm your fighter. I didn't know I'd ever be willing to trust a white man again. For no reason on Earth."

One month later, in March, the Black Moon Johnson and Elegant Raines bout was made. It was a big money fight, one that would be fought in the king-of-the-world boxing arena: Madison Square Garden, in New York City.

The fight between Black Moon Johnson and Elegant Raines was scheduled for the night of April 15, 1947, a Friday-night fight. Madison Square Garden outbid the other prestigious boxing arenas in the running. And following tradition, promoter Hancock Hollins and Black Moon's promoter, Abe Feinstein, wanted the match staged in the most famous boxing arena on the map.

For the fight's signing, Black Moon and Elegant were kept apart due to Black Moon's threats—nothing to do with Elegant's behavior. For Black Moon bragged he'd fight Elegant right there at the signing for free—nothing—just to "get me a piece of that boy." Both camps knew this had nothing to do with press copy.

Elegant had undergone a hard, vigorous camp. He'd increased his squats and sit-ups, and notched up his roadwork from five miles a day to eight. It was Black Moon's body shots again that loomed as both Pee-Pot's and Elegant's chief concern: they'd crippled other fighters. The ring was littered with cracked ribs coming from the end of Black Moon's sledgehammer fists. He knocked his opponents out all kinds of ways, body shots, head shots; and when they were out, they were out cold.

Black Moon, at times, could be a headhunter, but it was his body shots that made the biggest noise.

CHAPTER 18

Jimmy McClellan, the greatest boxing scribe in the business, was standing outside Pee-Pot's Pugilistic Paradise, gazing up at its dusty signage.

"Oh yeah, this is the place for me, all right. Paradise!"

Jimmy McClellan was in from New York City. He wrote for the *Daily World* and was in Longwood, West Virginia, this day to interview Pee-Pot and Elegant for the newspaper. He said he wanted to see what this part of the country looked like for himself, that it could produce Longwood and Monongalia two fighters of this "championship caliber."

"It's him!"

Jimmy McClellan'd entered through the Pug's doors. He smiled and then took a big breath as if breathing in the Pug.

Jimmy McClellan was a short, bowlegged, and bespectacled Irishman with thick silvery hair (quite dashing) and fit as a fiddle for a man approaching seventy-five. Gas had the honor of picking him up from Five Hundred and driving him into Longwood. He stood behind him.

"Okay, boys," McClellan gushed, "get back to work!"

The boxers laughed.

"Thanks, Gas."

"Mr. McClellan, Pee-Pot's right—"

Turning to his right, Jimmy McClellan saw Pee-Pot for himself. He was standing outside the office door with a sunny smile on his face. Jimmy McClellan's face was already cherry red.

"Pee-Pot!"

"Mr. McClellan!"

"Good to see you, Pee-Pot. An old friend."

"Same here, Mr. McClellan. Same here."

Pee-Pot led McClellan into the office. McClellan was carrying a brown fedora hat in one hand and a brown battered briefcase in the other. He put the briefcase down on the floor.

"So this is where you wound up, huh, Pee-Pot?"

"Back home, Mr. McClellan. Not that I ever left. My wife and home were here. My roots."

McClellan stood, picked the briefcase up off the floor, and put it atop the desk.

Pee-Pot shoved his Royal typewriter off to the right of the desk.

Then McClellan's briefcase snapped open. He pulled out a pencil and notepad. He left the briefcase on Pee-Pot's desk. He sat. "So I want the lowdown, Pee-Pot. All of it. Every last bloody drop of it."

"Sure, Mr. McClellan."

"Since I know the origins of how all of this began with you and the Elegant Raines kid. The kid coming out of Black Machine's gym and training here with you after he died."

"Elegant Raines came in from View Point, Texas, Mr. McClellan."

"Began as a beautiful story. A fairy tale. Until things soured on you and Black Moon. Went south on you."

McClellan flipped back the notebook's cover. "So go ahead, Pee-Pot. Shoot. Let's hear your side of the story. What Black Moon's omitting. Not telling the press. Us working stiffs about. All the vitals the kid's edited out."

Done with interviewing Pee-Pot, McClellan was with Elegant, finishing up on a new angle of his newspaper column

"Elegant, you're a person after my own heart, kid. Shakespeare. Shakespeare, I'm a world authority on Shakespeare."

"I haven't read all the plays—"

"Thirty-seven of them."

"Yet."

"Folios."

"Yes, sir."

"It's a wonder Willie Boy didn't go mad. Stark raving mad or blind, for that matter. You know."

"Uh, why, why's that, sir?"

Elegant was being interviewed while sitting behind Pee-Pot's desk (McClellan's brown battered briefcase was still anchored there), a new experience for him.

McClellan's hand brushed back his thick rug of silky gray hair, and he leaned forward, pluckily.

"You write that many plays, son, and lug around that many characters and plotlines in your head for that long ... who wouldn't go nuts, mad, crazy. Tell me? Would you? Come on ..."

"I never thought of it that way, Mr. McClellan. Quite like that, sir. Like ... no ... no ..."

"And using a quill pen, dipping it in an ink bottle, putting it down on parchment, vellum paper ... The eyes, kid, the eyes," McClellan said, removing his horn-rimmed glasses, stabbing his fingers in the direction of his eyes. "It's gotta be murder on the eyes. All right. Hard. Wanna quit on you. Exit stage right."

"I agree, sir. Ha." Pause.

"You know it's the details of creativity that interests me. His mind clicking off dialogue fast as an adding machine. And that damned pen of his running outta ink, and he's gotta take time, the time to refill it. How god-awful's that? Dipping the thing in an ink bottle sometimes, I know, when his creativity's racing like a racehorse for the finish line. Like when, me, at my typewriter, I'm banging away at it, not trying to forget a word of damned copy!"

Jimmy McClellan was back on his way to New York with his story and Gas having the honor of driving him back to the train station in Five Hundred.

Honk!

"See you two up in New York City, Pee-Pot, Elegant!"

"Sure thing, Mr. McClellan!"

"Right, sir!"

Pee-Pot and Elegant stood there waving as Gas's car puttered along, the speedometer's needle matching the speed limit in Longwood's business district.

"Well, there he goes," Pee-Pot said.

"Yes, sir …"

It was after four o'clock. Normally, Elegant would be coming in from the brickyard, but he worked half a day today in anticipation of Jimmy McClellan, of New York City visiting Longwood.

Pee-Pot patted Elegant's back.

"Some character, ain't he, son? Card?"

"You can say that again, Mr. Manners."

"There's a lot of them up in New York. Just pick any street corner you—but you know that, don't you, son?"

"Do I, sir."

"Sometimes I forget, Elegant, you're not a country bumpkin anymore. That you're seeing the world. Even though we haven't gotten overseas. But don't worry, one day that'll change too."

They were walking back into the gym.

"Mr. McClellan's gonna do right by us, don't you worry, Elegant. Uh-huh. Gonna give us a fair shake in that New York paper of his. What he writes is gospel. Pure gold. Always has and always will be."

⁓

Just in from Longwood, West Virginia

Jimmy McClellan

This kid, Black Moon, has been hogging every headline in town for the past few weeks—except mine, this time.

I just got in from Longwood, West Virginia, after paying an interesting visit with Pee-Pot Manners and Elegant Raines at Pee-Pot's Pugilistic Paradise (the Pug), where one drop of a fighter's sweat contains more truth inside it than one word out Black Moon's big, salty mouth. A kid who beat his way out of Monongalia, West Virginia, like he'd raided a chicken shack for lunch.

Black Moon is a bald-faced liar, and I'd tell the kid to his face (even at my advanced age), though he'd probably plaster my mug to the wall like a jar full of putty. Pee-Pot Manners did no wrong by him, nor Elegant Raines. This is William Shakespeare's *Othello* essayed by Pee-Pot Manners, being betrayed by Iago, essayed by Black Moon.

Scene setting: there is a bond between an old trainer and a young fighter who becomes jealous of another young fighter, Elegant Raines / Cassio, who seems favored by the old trainer, so he soon feels demoted, cast out, but neither is true.

This is not Shakespeare's play *Othello* in true version of replication but the jealousy of one person that has been driven so deeply into his innards it might as well be. For it is jealousy of one man of another. It does not have the wild mood swings of emotional jealousy that women's wounds carry between them but the searing jealousy between men. For Black Moon has said he would kill Elegant Raines in the ring if he could. That his fists could raise themselves with such temper and malice. And for what measure? As revenge for the common, equal balance of trust a trainer must exemplify to both fighters under his charge?

This is going to be a great fight between two great young black middleweights campaigning in the division for the middleweight crown, but one a liar and the other titled by gold. But both are Lord Talbots (no coward *he*) of William Shakespeare's *King Henry the Sixth*. They will fight heroically until the last drop of blood falls from their bodies, against all odds, if need be. They will be valiant and willful and able inside the ropes, stout in their endurance and persistence.

No fan will be cheated by Black Moon and Elegant Raines on that night of boxing. We are not modern men in our lust for blood; we are as dated as antiquity. But truth, sometimes, we let slip through the cracks in our fingers like oily thieves when big mouths claim themselves such slick purveyors of it.

PS. By the way, did you know Elegant Raines, this black fighter, reads Shakespeare? A kid, certainly, after this sportswriter's own heart.

———

Gem (with Pastor Loving's permission) had trained down from Howard University to Longwood before Elegant's fight with Black Moon. It was a surprise visit.

They'd chosen Lakeview Park for the afternoon picnic. Gem prepared a full spread of fried chicken and pickled potato salad. And there was a pineapple cake (Francine had baked) and juice in the picnic basket too. The blanket was spread out on the grass and the basket on the blanket. They'd eaten, and Elegant told Gem he'd more than likely have another slice of the cake before leaving the park; Francine's cake was so "good." This was a popular park for Longwooders, and there were people galore who were taking full advantage of the beautiful springlike temperature with as much gusto as Gem and Elegant.

They'd been sitting on the blanket but now were sitting side by side on a huge-sized rock. Gem was in a long, flowing pink cotton dress. Her hair was swept up in a ponytail with a pink ribbon bowed in the back. Francine was the topic of conversation.

"She so wanted to be a part of today's surprise, Elegant, but she's been tutoring a young lady at the church. Marjorie Fuller, who's excellent in all her school subjects but math and is trying to pull her grade up from below grade level. She'd like to go to college so badly."

"Francine, I still don't see her as much as I'd like, Gem."

"You're so busy though, Elegant. And so is she."

"Right. Right." Pause. "And so it'll be Francine's turn next to head off to college in the fall."

"But not Howard but Spelman College."

They were holding hands.

"I wouldn't want to follow in your footsteps either—if I were Francine."

"Elegant, I'm just another student at Howard University."

"I bet."

"Well, I am."

"Gem, I've been to Howard's campus, don't forget. I know your reputation."

"All right. All right. So my fame is spread far and wide, even though Francine would have no trouble exceeding my feats."

"Just try convincing Francine of that."

This was really an ideal day for doing a picnic, and Gem had already counted her blessings—that it'd turned out as it had.

Elegant watched a little boy dip his hand in a picnic basket and pull out a chunky leg of chicken and laughed.

Gem saw the boy too and laughed.

"He's so cute."

Elegant turned his face to her. "And so are you."

"I had to see you, Elegant. I just had to."

"Your father's incredible."

"He is." Pause.

"I suppose he was just responding to my letter. To plan this day for us."

"Is it … it's the fight, right, Gem?"

"Yes. The fight."

"W-with Black Moon."

"Yes."

Gem didn't want to say she was worried for him, not that, for she knew the great confidence Elegant had in himself and in his boxing abilities.

"It will be a difficult fight. It won't be easy, I know." Pause. "Gem, I've got great respect for Black Moon even if he doesn't for me."

"But …," Gem said hesitatingly, "you respect everyone you fight, don't you?"

"Yes. I respect all fighters, period."

She loved Elegant's humility and often wondered how he came by it, or was it just him?

"How does Mr. Manners feel going into the fight?"

"Ha!"

"W-what, so what's so funny?"

"Gem, you're beginning to sound like a sportswriter."

"I am?"

"Really, I'm not kidding."

"Then I'm making progress."

"You are."

Elegant looked around the park. He wasn't going to be too demonstrative; he didn't know who was looking, could be anyone from the church.

He kissed Gem's hand.

"Mr. Manners feels the same as me: Black Moon's going to be a big challenge for me. A major hurdle." Elegant sighed. "There's the champ of the division, uh, Gino Gennaro and Joey 'The Mark' DeMarco, who's ranked number one. But Mr. Manners feels Black Moon's much better than them."

And Gem was fretting again but aware she mustn't show it—no traces of it.

"You'll win, Elegant."

"Just don't worry about me, okay, Gem?"

"Then ..."

"It's okay to worry about me, Gem. It's, it's okay."

———

It was close to five o'clock.

Pee-Pot's truck was parked at the side of the house. Today, he'd visited Cora Manners's grave site.

Gem's car pulled up to the house.

Right off the bat she was upset.

"I don't hear Gyp, Elegant," Gem said, braking the car.

"You know Gyp's uncanny."

"I know."

"Mr. Manners has told her you're home. In fact, I wouldn't be at all surprised if she was in on the surprise."

Gem laughed. "Do you really think so?"

"I wouldn't put it past either of them."

Gem smiled. "I suppose she thinks she's doing the right thing by us."

"Our privacy, you mean ..."

"Yes."

"Thanks, Gem. You keep topping the experiences and pleasures we've enjoyed together. By today's fun time, of course." Pause. "Right after church you leave."

Gem's head yo-yoed. "Right."

There were plenty of people left in Lakeview Park when they left. They didn't want to leave, but they couldn't stay into the evening. They thought it would've been excessive.

"Don't expect a solo tomorrow. I'm not prepared."

"Gem, you must be reading my mind."

"It's what you were thinking, Elegant? Really? Really?"

"Really. Since you're back—"

"But just for a day and a half, if you add Friday night when I got in and part of Sunday."

Elegant looked at Pee-Pot's truck. It was back from Body of Christ Church.

"Mrs. Manners got her flowers a day early today."

Gem grabbed Elegant's hand and looked into his eyes. "Elegant, don't ever die."

Elegant kissed her.

"I don't want you to."

CHAPTER 13

Tonight was the fight between Elegant Raines and Black Moon Johnson at Madison Square Garden. It was April 15, 1947, and the fight sold out over seventeen days ago. Black Moon still captured most of the New York daily sports sections' headlines. This was attributable to Black Moon's relentless rhetoric and ferocious aura. He was as brutal as boxing, becoming the natural bully on the block. He'd become an acerbic, iconic figure among the average Joes out there in Americaland, who perceived him as the kid at school who beat them up regularly for their lunch money.

Only, after Jimmy McClellan's column in the *Daily World*, Elegant garnered some attention himself. Jimmy McClellan, it seems, had opened up a can of worms with his final paragraph: By the way, did you know Elegant Raines, this black fighter, reads Shakespeare? And it took only one writer to call Elegant "Kid Shakespeare," for all the stitching in Elegant's suit of armor to unravel.

Pee-Pot laughed over it. He told Elegant not to worry about it either (which Elegant did, worry), that the press would try getting any angle it could so just "roll with the punches."

Elegant didn't expect the pun and laughed like crazy along with Pee-Pot. Even though McClellan wrote more about the Manners / Black Moon / Raines situation in his column, saying there was no animosity toward Black Moon Johnson in the Manners's camp, the rest of the press didn't buy into it. The press was profoundly embedded in the fight's drama—was sold on that. It wasn't interested in any truth telling. It was still too heavily invested in the bad blood, grudge fight story, would not extricate themselves from it, the rancor—nor would Black Moon let them.

Tommie wasn't on this fight card with Elegant (something he chose not to do, said he'd be too nervous—unable to concentrate on his own fight). Fighting on the card would've been a great a showcase for his rising career. But Tommie brushed it off, saying he wanted to save all his energy for Elegant. Of course Tommie, pre-Elegant, never liked Black Moon. In fact, there weren't many fighters in the Pug who were still loyal to him, who wanted Black Moon to win.

Elegant couldn't approach this fight like any other fight, for tonight there was a lot at stake. For not only was Black Moon to be his toughest opponent to date, but Black Moon was also ranked the world's number two middleweight. But more importantly, a middleweight championship fight was scheduled for September between the champ, Gino Gennaro, and number one contender, Joey "The Mark" DeMarco. So whoever won tonight's fight, after the June title defense, would slip automatically into the number one slot. So grudge fight or not, the fight had great implications, rankingwise, in the middleweight division.

Black Moon was the betting man's choice at 5–3.

It was the first time Elegant had entered a fight as the underdog.

"Stop jumping around, would you, Tommie."

"Oh … sor-sorry, Mr. Manners. Didn't—"

"You're making me nervous. And I never get nervous."

"D-don't know what's wrong with me," Tommie said, looking down at Elegant, who looked calmly back at him.

Gas, Tommie, Pee-Pot, and Elegant were in the small dressing room. Any minute now, Elegant would loosen up by hitting the pads. Put sweat on his body.

Then Alton Timms came into the dressing room. He was a trainer from the Pug. For such an important fight, Alton Timms would be the third man in the corner, acting as Elegant's cut man—a top notch one at that.

"Al, you're back," Pee-Pot said as if he suddenly had to say something. "Uh, I see."

"Yeah, Pee-Pot, almost got lost in one of them crooked tunnels," Alton Timms said in his silky baritone voice.

Elegant was lying on a rubbing table. A towel was spread over his back. Right now, he was focused on what was ahead. He really liked how his mind and body felt today—especially his mind. It seemed particularly keen to everything around it. Pastor Loving said a prayer for him and Black Moon Wednesday before he left for New York. Even Gem had taken a backseat to Black Moon today, for he only thought about her a thousand times, not his usual six thousand.

"Gas, you wanna put the mitts on."

"Sure, Pee-Pot."

Of course Elegant knew what that meant, so he was up off the rubbing table. Then Tommie walked up and whispered in Elegant's ear, "Just pretend it's Black Moon's big, fat, crusty head, Elegant. All's you gotta do!"

Everyone was out of the dressing room but Pee-Pot and Elegant. Pee-Pot wanted to go over last-minute instructions with him.

Elegant wore a black robe with thin red stitching that spelled out his name; and set against his jet-black skin, his height, broad-set shoulders, and the oily sweat on him, he looked menacing. Elegant was sitting on the rubbing table.

"As I told you before, Elegant," Pee-Pot said, putting his hand on Elegant's right shoulder, "Black Moon can take a punch with the best of them. A combination of his jaw, chin, heart, and the boy's plain nastiness. I taught him defense well, but I hear he's lunging, is off balance a lot. But he, I'm gonna go with the fact he's still hard to hit with a good shot."

"Yes, sir."

"So like I've been telling you, we're gonna have to break him down round by round. Break him apart. 'Cause with your power, you're gonna hit him with shots he's never been hit with, with any consist—real consistency before."

"Yes, sir."

"The boy's gonna brush them punches off. But don't let it discourage you. Be persistent. He ain't gonna know what you're doing until it's too late. You've broken him apart. Uh, Black Moon's all aggression. All the boy knows. Wants to know. Only way he knows how to fight—just on natural instincts."

"Yes, sir."

"It's worked well for him up till now. But not tonight, Elegant. Not with you inside the ring with him."

It appeared they were set to join Gas and Alton Timms and Tommie in the tunnel just outside the dressing room, but Pee-Pot hesitated.

"By the way, Elegant, Black Moon ain't a dirty fighter," he said with respect and admiration. "Nothing's dirty about him. Boy's too vicious to be dirty. Ain't got time for it."

Pee-Pot already knew the kind of fight crowd that filled Madison Square Garden's seats: bloodthirsty. The fight's buildup shaped this result, not only the bad blood, this so-called grudge match, but the punching power of both participants, their potential for mayhem in the ring, producing ultimate devastation of one another.

This was the first time in the pit of his gut Pee-Pot felt this putrid. He was about to see Black Moon in the ring but under a different circumstance: not as his fighter but as his opponent. He never felt emotionally close to Black Moon but had understood the sociological/psychological troubles that had engineered Black Moon's personal background. But what he didn't know was what it would be in the ring, when he looked him straight in the eye in a setting where he was fiercely competitive too. The fiery fighter he once was when he campaigned in the lightweight division. Then he felt no pity for any man who stood in the ring with him. And any second now, it would be Black Moon, a young man who'd crossed the line of civility, decency, who made him strongly feel that old competitive fire he'd never lost. His feeling of beating another man unmercifully until he submitted to his will.

Elegant was the first fighter in the ring.

New York was a neutral site, and the crowd's response to him was generous, loud, enthusiastic. Elegant's feet danced in place, and as most fighters who have just entered the ring, Elegant limbered his muscles by firing off a series of punches.

It's when Black Moon and his cornermen—Duff Crawley, trainer; "Lefty" Leftwich, assistant trainer; and Frankie Crabtree, cut man— entered the ring and the applause and cheering from the crowd topped that of Elegant's. Upon hearing the crowd's response, Pee-pot was not in the least surprised, for it was Black Moon Johnson who sold this fight to the public, who wanted it on his side and not Elegant's, who now banged his gloves together and looked into Elegant's corner with a scowl. He rolled his head. He did not dance his feet but planted them to the canvas and threw one hellacious uppercut after the other as if silently crucifying the air.

Then Black Moon unrobed. And stitched across his trunks in big white block lettering was "BLACK MOON."

"I've dreamed of fighting here, Mr. Moore."

"Every fighter has, Elegant. But not every fighter gets a chance."

Elegant had kept his eyes out of Black Moon's corner.

But now, after ring ceremonies were cleared away, the corners were called to the middle of the ring.

When Elegant and Pee-Pot and the rest of the corner got to ring center, Black Moon ran in front of his cornermen—even if it was but a short distance.

It's when Pee-Pot and Black Moon made quick eye contact; it was vile.

Duff Crawley, a short, tough, bushy-haired, blue-eyed Irishman, smiled as if the sun had just set over Dublin.

Elegant was looking over the top of Black Moon's black shaved head.

It was at the end of the referee's instructions when Black Moon said, "It gonna be the last you see your boy standing alive, old man!"

And Pee-Pot felt the urge to spit in Black Moon's eye.

Pee-Pot removed Elegant's black robe with the red stitching: "Elegant Raines."

"Just fight him, Elegant. This is nothing personal."

"Yes, Mr. Manners."

Elegant's mouth opened wide for the mouthpiece.

"Elegant!"

Elegant looked to the right of him and it's when Tommie winked and then said, "Kick the boy's ass. For me!"

The bell clanged for round one, and when Elegant and Black Moon got to the middle of the ring, Elegant put his gloves out to touch gloves with Black Moon (which is customary sportsmanship), but Black Moon's gloves were swung wildly at Elegant's, falling a foot short, deliberately missing the mark.

The first thing Elegant did was judge his distance. He shot a jab that hit the top of Black Moon's bald head.

Black Moon grunted, smiling.

Elegant was determined to get his punches off first, to attack Black Moon, to be the aggressor—even more than what was usual.

He'd fought muscular fighters before but knew every muscle on Black Moon's body counted for something—was there for a reason. He was shooting jabs at him, hard, heavy shots, and then he'd drive powerful ones down to his midsection. But were blocked deftly by Black Moon's massive arms.

Black Moon got in a shot, a short one beneath Elegant's heart, and Elegant did have to catch his breath but didn't wince. Black Moon was trying to force him to the ropes. Successfully Elegant blocked him off by circling him and aiming everything at him hard and nasty. Elegant wasn't finding it difficult fighting Black Moon—he just realized how dangerous he was.

The bell clanged and Black Moon scooted back to his corner.

Pee-Pot, Gas, and Alton Timms attended to Elegant.

The bell clanged.

Round two.

"Game's over!" Black Moon said.

And Black Moon was pressing Elegant, picking up the already quick pace.

Elegant hit him with a sweet-looking uppercut, knocking Black Moon's head back; but it didn't deter him, derail him, for he pushed Elegant back with his bulked shoulders and then threw a crisp jab up the middle, knocking Elegant back, and then a short hook to Elegant's midsection as Elegant fired one back at him, doubling on it. Elegant was about to circle him, when Black Moon cut the ring off. He hit him with another rock of a jab, and Elegant was in the corner fighting for his life.

Elegant was trading punches with Black Moon, shooting them down at him, hitting shoulders, the top of his head—hitting anything he could hit—and Black Moon, whose head was moving beautifully, artfully, was countering with short, deadly shots, ones you heard echo off Madison Square Garden's old, venerable walls.

Elegant tied Black Moon up.

Elegant feinted and then unleashed another murderous uppercut from ring center that made the crowd gasp, and Black Moon's head flip back on his shoulders. And this time you felt the pain in Black Moon's body as it twitched, but quickly, he covered up by smashing Elegant with an overhead right and then exacting another as Elegant retreated, headed for the ropes again and then, using his quick feet, changed direction.

The bell clanged.

There was no panic in the Manners's corner.

After water from the water bottle and Vaseline applied to Elegant's face, Gas and Alton Timms working in tandem, Pee Pot said, "It ain't good to get hit by too many of those big punches of Black Moon's, Elegant."

Elegant nodded his head.

"But this is boxing. He is a great fighter." Pause. "Strong, ain't he?"

"Uh-huh!" Elegant said before Gas put the cleanly washed mouthpiece back in Elegant's mouth.

Round three.

Tommie was on the edge of his seat, and so there were times, to the dismay of people sitting near him, when he'd zip punches along with Elegant until, embarrassingly, he'd realize what he was doing, or had done, in effect.

"You fuckin' finished, Raines," Black Moon said at the beginning of the round.

"Ain't even—"

Elegant drilled Black Moon with a jab and then a heavy blow onto his left shoulder, and then his right, and then one straight up the gut. Yeah, Elegant said to himself, I'm gonna break him apart, all right. Break him down. Follow the strategy Mr. Manners laid out for me—the fight plan!

But Black Moon felt stronger, not weaker. Honestly, Elegant couldn't claim that he wasn't, but he set him back with a stiff double jab and then tripled it and then down to the ribs; and that one hurt Black Moon—it was visible.

And then Black Moon lunged forward, and Elegant peppered him with jabs and then finished it off with a raucous right hand, knocking

Black Moon backward. He hit him again, and Black Moon staggered back against the ring ropes. Elegant had him pinned there, and he sensed something. He sensed this could be the end of it, the fight, if he just stood his ground, stood in front of him peppering him more, really open him up, and then unleash the final blow.

Black Moon was on the ropes. He slid into his corner. Elegant lit after him, sliding his feet over to him, balancing himself. He hammered him again. Black Moon's eyes dropped; he looked dazed but then covered up like a turtle inside its protective shell. But Elegant repeatedly ripped one shot after the other. But suddenly, his back bouncing staunchly off the ropes, Black Moon hit Elegant with the most crunching, ugly sound of the night, a sensational shot to his rib cage, and you could hear Elegant shriek, scream out in pain like a wounded animal in the wild in Madison Square Garden's arena. He grabbed Black Moon, wrestled with him, tied him up until the referee broke them.

"Ha ha ha!"

Elegant limped back in retreat. Black Moon charged him. Black Moon bled from his nose, his mouth, the inside of it torn open, hanging loose as jagged fish flesh.

Elegant's right arm protected his ribcage.

The bell clanged.

Pee-Pot and Gas rushed out to get him. They helped Elegant back to the corner, to the boxer's stool.

"He broke it, didn't he, Elegant?"

"Y-yes, sir. I-I think so, Mr. ... Mr. Manners."

"Breathe, breathe, son. Get used to it." Pee-Pot wanted to say "the pain" but was going to negate it by not mentioning it. It was like an injury now, like Black Moon's busted nose and torn lip, and the blood splattered all over the top of his trunks and the ring canvas was part of the war.

But he also knew Elegant had never been hurt before (as he listened to his dodgy breathing) or in a fight like this before—had ranged over this territory, had never had to prove his courage beyond stepping into the ring to fight, which was brave enough.

"You're in great shape, Elegant. Remember that, son. Best shape of your life. You could go fifteen championship rounds if this was for the crown. Fifteen, Elegant. Fifteen rounds easy."

"Yes, sir."

Gas stuck the mouthpiece back in Elegant's mouth.

The bell clanged.

Round four.

"Broke it, Raines! And can't nobody fuckin' fix it!"

And so Black Moon came weaving at him, straight ahead, on his powerful legs. And Elegant was favoring his right side (plenty), and it's all Black Moon was doing, shooting punches at it until he clubbed Elegant with a right hand to the temple and Elegant stumbled to the side, but then when Black Moon led with a sweeping left hand, Elegant came over the top with a punishing left hand that stopped Black Moon in his tracks, and then another and another.

And then he closed in on him and hit Black Moon with a jackhammer left uppercut. Black Moon didn't fight back but, instead, ran away. And Elegant chased after him, jabbing him, jabbing him back into the corner. Black Moon's head was sticking up, unprotected, his eyes dusty, and the left hook knocked Black Moon's mouthpiece out his mouth, and his body was sent reeling across the ropes and out the corner. But Black Moon wouldn't go down. But his head was back against the ring ropes, sitting there as if dislodged from the rest of him. And Elegant still had so much power left in his left hand that if he hit him with it again, he could either scramble Black Moon's brains or, worse, kill him.

Elegant looked at the referee and then at Black Moon.

Black Moon motioned to Elegant with his gloved hand in front of him. "Come on, punk. Come on, punk. Fuckin' ... finish me. F-fuckin' ... finish me!"

And Elegant did, but not with a head shot but with a body shot. Not his best punch but enough to floor Black Moon, to spill his body onto the canvas and for the referee's count to ten.

It was the final blow that finished Black Moon Johnson off for the night in the Madison Square Garden arena before the roused crowd.

<hr />

This was the first time Pee-Pot really felt alone after a fight. And it was the first time in a long time he'd not shared a room with anyone while on the road. Ordinarily, he had a roommate on the road but not in this trip to New York City. Alton Timms was paired with Gas and, of course, Tommie with Elegant.

Pee-Pot'd just gotten off the phone with Hancock Hollins. Late last night Hollins called and now this morning. Because of his delicate health he, under strict doctor's orders, couldn't make the trip in for the fight from Tulip, Tennessee. He expressed his overwhelming appreciation and satisfaction of Elegant's win and how he'd won. Hollins and Pee-Pot talked about Elegant and how soon he'd be in line to fight for the middleweight championship. That at least one big obstacle was hurdled by the Hollins team.

All morning reporters had been after Pee-Pot, but he left a special list of names for the hotel's switchboard operator to patch through. There were only two names on that list: Hancock Hollins and Jimmy McClellan. It's who he was expecting any minute now in the hotel suite: Jimmy McClellan. He was to interview him and Elegant, in that order.

Pee-Pot had called for room service and eaten breakfast. It was ten twenty-eight. The interview with McClellan was for ten thirty. Suddenly, Pee-Pot thought of Gyp but knew she was all right back on the farm.

"I wonder if Gyp knows Elegant won—only, knowing her ... Ha ..."

Pee-Pot continued to chuckle, for Gyp wouldn't get credit in the newspapers today for Elegant's rousing victory last night, but she had covered a lot of ground with him over the past eleven months, for it'd been just short of a year the three had been together; and whoever said time flies, Pee-Pot thought, could not have been more right.

Knock.

In a flash Pee-Pot stood at the door.

"Good morning, Mr. McClellan."

"Good morning, Pee-Pot."

"Come in."

McClellan looked bedraggled and spent, but not Pee-Pot.

"Know, I know I look like someone the cat dragged in, Pee-Pot. So you don't have to make it obviously clear."

Pee-Pot laughed. They sat in the suite's spacious living room area.

"I had my deadline to meet. But boy oh boy, did I worry that I did it justice. The fight, that is. But I had to turn the damned copy in anyways. Editors don't give you any leeway. Not even at my age!" Pause.

"Damn, what a fight!"

"It was."

"Yeah"—McClellan's blue eyes were bloodshot—"I lost a lot of sleep last night. Wrote the same story ten times more in my head. T-the kid was a wounded animal, Pee-Pee-Pot. L-looked beat. Black Moon had done him in. Stopped him for sure ..."

Pee-Pot nodded his head.

"For chrissake, Pee-Pot, he fought that kid with one arm. Turned the tide of the fight. One goddamned arm!"

It was amazing to Pee-Pot too, but when Pee-Pot sent Elegant out in the fourth round, somehow he knew Elegant would do it, would find a way. He would perform the miracle he did—even though in none of his previous bouts had he been under any physical hardship, where his courage had to be tested so suddenly, so severely, by such a powerful and explosive opponent as Black Moon.

"There're no excuses in the ring, Mr. McClellan—you know that."

"Don't I, Pee-Pot. You live with them your whole life. They'll come back to haunt you."

It's why Pee-Pot could truthfully say he didn't have to live with any haunting regrets after his boxing career was over, and this would certainly hold true for Elegant too after what he did in the ring last night against Black Moon, looking into his heart and soul to try to find victory, not excuses.

"And for you, Pee-Pot," McClellan said, "how's it feel sending your fighter out like that? For another round in that kind of shape?"

McClellan didn't have his reporter's notepad out, for he knew he'd remember verbatim what Pee-Pot said.

"I don't know, Mr. McClellan, how it feels. I think I just look at it as another round. Another one my fighter's got to win and not lose to win the fight." Pause.

"Well, he won it all right."

"Yes, he did. Elegant sure did, Mr. McClellan," Pee-Pot said, satisfied. "I was proud of my fighter last night."

Elegant was in bed. He was not only banged up but bandaged up.

At the conclusion of the fight, he was rushed from Madison Square Garden by ambulance to St. Vincent's Hospital's emergency room to have his two cracked ribs bandaged. He'd had fun fielding Jimmy McClellan's questions, and now McClellan shut his notepad.

"What, no questions for me, Mr. McClellan?"

Tommie was in the bedroom the whole time during Elegant's interview.

McClellan turned to Tommie. "Don't worry, Mr. Lathers, your turn'll come. Down the road, son."

"Oh, so you coming back down to Longwood!"

"Now, now, I didn't say that," McClellan said cagily.

"Don't tell me you 'fraid of snakes, sir!"

"No, there're garden snakes in Brooklyn."

Elegant was enjoying this, but he could laugh but so much, hard, with his damaged, banged-up ribs.

Then with old, sweet Irish eyes, McClellan looked at Tommie. "But don't worry, Tommie, me lad, I know all about you. Been keeping an eye on you from my perch here in New York City."

Tommie looked at Elegant in the bed and then McClellan.

"Uh ... uh, you have?"

"Your last win over Eddie Martinez was a stunner."

Tommie stood and then let loose a volley of rapid-fire punches. "It was, it was, Mr. McClellan. Martinez don't stand a chance, a chance in hell, Mr. McClellan, sir!"

"I expect great things from you, kid."

Tommie's arms dropped. "Thanks, sir."

"You could become the next great welter. With your hand speed and sudden power surge of late."

"Don't know where the power's coming from. Guess I been watching Elegant here. What I keep telling myself, sir."

"Well, it's just a matter of which one of you grabs a boxing crown first."

"Gonna be Elegant. Gotta be, Mr. McClellan. Elegant. He's got the better ranking for now."

"True."

"Just gotta clear a few more logs outta them Virginia woods first, Mr. McClellan. What I gotta do, sir."

McClellan stood and then walked over to Tommie. He put his arm around his waist. "You're gonna make a helluva interview. Copy for me, son. What do you think, Elegant?"

"The best, Mr. McClellan."

McClellan turned back to Elegant. "You get some rest now—if this kid'll let you—"

"Ha."

"With those busted-up ribs."

"Yes, sir."

"You know, that fight's gonna go down as one of the greatest fights the garden's seen. What a fight. What a damned fight ...," McClellan kept saying, wagging his head. "From start to finish..."

Still wagging his head, McClellan was heading for the bedroom door. Tommie opened it for him. He led him into the adjoining room.

Tommie was back in the room. He looked sheepishly at Elegant. "Uh, maybe, Elegant, you oughta get you some shut-eye, man."

"Okay, Tommie. Uh, sure. I guess you're right."

"Black Moon, man, just wish you really bash him with that last shot you hit him with, Elegant. Done him in with." Tommie had been saying this repeatedly to Elegant. "Bashed his fucking face in!"

Elegant shut his eyes. "Yes, I know, Tommie."

"Got my hand all cocked. Shit, was waiting for you to, Elegant."

"Uh-huh."

"Be out there in the room if you need me." Pause. "Man, when you gonna pay me!"

Elegant laughed lightly.

Tommie, laughing too, shut the bedroom door.

"I just couldn't do it, Tommie," Elegant whispered under his breath. "Not even to Black Moon."

He couldn't hate him. He didn't want to. If only it was *him* in the ring and not Black Moon at the end of his fists. If only he could imagine *him* in that simple context: in the ring with him. Just the two of them. The man from the past who'd orphaned him. Who'd set him on the run until finally he was safe from him. But it took so long for him to finally feel safe. To finally feel he wouldn't get caught by him, dragged off. That no trace would ever be found of him. That this man would not face criminal charges.

But at least he could keep his hate alive. Not carry it in the ring where it did him no good even against someone like Black Moon Johnson. Someone who'd insulted and belittled him. But he could not, with fault, pretend it was him. For it was so small in comparison to what Black Moon did and said. It was so lean and pale and inconsequential. He could only hate whom he hated. Someone who would never step in the ring with him. Who now lived in a shadow world. Who wouldn't have the courage to if he could. Who could only fight outside the ring where a white man's law protected him. Where it offered him safe haven, comfort, and sovereignty after the depravity and atrocities and the pain he wielded onto the world.

—————

A little over an hour later.

Ring.

A minute later, Tommie burst through Elegant's hotel door.

"Elegant, wake up!"

"Tommie, Tommie ... y-you just woke me ..." Elegant looked frustrated, was trying to pull himself together. "I-I was dreaming ... But about what, I—"

"Well, you got you a phone call."

"Phone call? Why, I didn't hear the phone ring," Elegant said, looking over at the night stand.

"And it's gonna make you sleep better after you take it. Way, way better."

"It is ...?"

Tommie picked up the phone. "Well here he is, Gem."

"Gem? Gem! Hand me the phone, Tommie. Hand me the phone!"

"Hear him, Gem? Don't you? Huh? Well, Gem, guess that's the end of us. We done!"

"Gem!"

"Elegant!"

"Ouch!"

"Oh, Elegant, you musn't, you, you—"

"You know then!"

"Yes, Papa told me. Papa—your ribs—"

"Black Moon broke two of them."

"Oh, Elegant."

"It's all right, Gem. It's all right."

"It's the first time you've been hurt in the ring."

"Yes."

Elegant looked at Tommie as Tommie mouthed he was getting out of there. Elegant shook his head.

"I didn't want you to get hurt—not ever, Elegant. Not ever."

He would ride the wave, he thought. He wouldn't stanch her emotions, try to get in their way.

"I threw up. I'm sorry. B-but I did. I did—when I found out."

Silence.

"Black Moon …?"

"I don't know. I think he's all right. I tried not to hurt him. I could've, Gem. I really could've. He was practically helpless. I could've …"

It flashed back in his mind just how helpless Black Moon was, and maybe if he, if he'd been Black Moon, was on the ropes, their roles switched, he would've jeered Black Moon on by saying, "Finish me! Finish me!" Or by saying nothing, remaining blank faced, prepared for the execution.

"I thought I could attend a prizefight, Elegant. B-but now I can't. I really can't. That it was all talk. Bluff on my part."

It didn't matter her mood; he was just joyful to have someone like Gem love him like this. He didn't need someone to celebrate his victory, lift him on their shoulders, parade him around. He had enough of that with Tommie and Pee-Pot Manners and Gaston Moore and Alton Timms and, yes, this morning with Jimmy McClellan. It's not what he wanted or needed from her.

"I'm sorry."

"If you say it again, Gem, I'm not going to believe you."

"But I am, Elegant." Pause.

"It's painful?"

"A little."

"Then it is."

"A little."

"Elegant …"

"At least he didn't ruin my pretty face."

"Ha."

"Well, he didn't."

"And who said you have a pretty face?"

"You."

"No, I said handsome, if I recall."

"But you meant pretty."

"Who says?" Pause.

"Gem, it was a brutal fight. Reverend Loving's so right. He, he is."

"He admires you so much, Elegant."

"He does?"

"Yes."

"This has been tough on him, I know."

"But he's grown a lot because of it." Pause. "I think I can afford about another minute. Before my money runs out."

"Oh, Gem, I love you, love you, love you. I-I just hope you understand that things like this happen."

"Yes, I do."

"But, but I'll be more careful in the … What am I saying? What can I promise you?"

"Nothing. And, and it's how it should be. Nothing."

"I'll, I'll call tomorrow. You tomorrow. We'll be back in Longwood tomorrow."

"You know my schedule, classes, don't—"

"Do I!"

"Mmmmm … mmmm … mmmmmm …"

Elegant did the same into the phone, kissed Gem through it without feeling a stitch of pain in his two cracked ribs.

———

Gem was home from school for her summer vacation, and she and Elegant were having a ball, a great time of it, seeing each other practically every day. Even though Elegant had made a lot of money from the Black Moon fight, more than he ever could imagine, he still worked at the brickyard for the Miller Brothers. He'd gone back to work as soon as his ribs mended.

And there were big things going on in the middleweight division, for Joey "The Mark" DeMarco, the number one contender, four days ago, broke his hand during sparring; and it knocked him out of his scheduled fight with Gino Gennaro. It was to be a mandatory defense, and so Gino Gennaro wanted to fight, and Gennaro's manager was looking in Elegant's direction, and Hancock Hollins was as happy as pink, and in a few days they were going to sit down and work the whole promotional aspect of it out.

Indeed, this was much to Pee-Pot's satisfaction, for he'd been looking at Elegant carefully and cautiously, and what he was seeing was him physically filling out—that he was going to find it more and more difficult to fight at 160 pounds, that he would soon outgrow the division as was predicted when he first laid his eyes on him.

Elegant had become more acutely aware of this too so was watching his weight—but he still was at 168, 170 pounds now, even if he'd been inactive in the ring since the April 15 injury. So it meant, now, before the next fight, hopefully for the crown, he'd have to drop eight to ten pounds to make weight. He was a shade over six feet two, had grown an inch and a half since last year. He was going to be a heavyweight all right, unmistakably—without a doubt.

At Howard University, Gem had another honor's year spent on the dean's list. Sometimes you'd forget what a precocious student she was. She was a freshman who matriculated at Howard University at the age of sixteen, making academia, school, seem like a piece of cake for her—a legend of Longwood!

Francine would be attending Spelman College, and already, with it being July, Pastor Loving was crying the blues. He'd never been without at least one of the Loving girls in the household. He'd declared, from the pulpit, that there was "just no way I'll adjust." That if there "is any church family willing to take me in, I, indeed, would feel much obliged. Appreciative."

And even though it was said in jest, he'd gotten some offers, so at least it showed his parishioners were still paying attention to his sermons, hadn't tuned him out after twenty-plus years of preaching in the Body of Christ Church.

CHAPTER 20

Elegant looked at Gem, and even though she looked brave, he had to make sure by at least asking her, for she would be the one putting herself on the firing line, in front of the firing squad today, not him.

They were sitting in front of Helena Loving's gravestone, on the concrete bench, and Elegant knew why this site was apropos for what would unfold in sequence before this day was out. It was well after church, and Gem had invited him to the house for dinner. But it would be more than that, far more.

"Gem, you'll be all right?"

"Yes."

"You're sure?"

"I'm just glad Francine's doing all the cooking, not me. But she's still trying to impress you, Elegant, so it's okay—I suppose."

Gem leaned her head over on Elegant's shoulder and then straightened herself. Suddenly, she looked determined, ready, hyped up to press forward.

She stood.

Elegant stood.

"Are you ready? Papa should be in his study," Gem said, glancing at her watch.

Elegant hugged her and then released her. He didn't know what to say, so he took her hand and they walked off.

But then, without warning, Gem said, "Sorry, Elegant. Sorry!" And she ran over to the gravestone and was down on her knees kissing the gray-slate marble stone.

"Francine, you don't mind?"

"Mind? But Elegant," Francine asked with the spatula in her hand, "what's going on today? Really, Elegant." Her beautiful brown eyes had such gorgeous color in them.

Elegant sat at the kitchen table where the pan of dough for the homemade cake sat.

"There's so much secrecy. Mystery in the house."

Elegant leaned back in the chair and clasped both hands behind his head, apparently relaxed. "There is, isn't there, Francine?" Elegant said sagely. "Yes, I like that word 'mystery,' mystery you used, Francine."

"Oh, come in, Gem."

"I'm not disturbing you, uh, am I, Papa?"

"No, not in the least, honey. Just unwinding," Pastor Loving said, reclining on the leather couch. "Boy, do I need this respite after one of my earthy fire-and-brimstone sermons. Like I delivered today."

Pastor Loving smiled. "You know I plan one or two a year, in order to really rile them up. Light their fire!"

There was a chair at the head of the couch; Gem sat on it.

"Gem, where's Elegant? What did you—"

"Papa, may we talk?"

"Gem, it's what I thought we were doing, uh, talking, darling," Pastor Loving said teasingly.

"Seriously, Papa," Gem said nervously.

"Uh, Gem, what's wrong? What's troubling you? It's it in your face."

"It ..."

"Now what's wrong, young lady? Out with it. Talk to me."

"Nothing, Papa. I'm ... is it possible to grow more and more in love with someone, Papa?"

"Elegant, you mean?"

"Elegant, of ... of course Elegant."

"Then why didn't you just say it, and—"

"Papa, we're not getting anywhere."

"Oh, yes, yes, after all, this is supposed to be a 'serious' talk, isn't it?" Pause. "And about what, specifically, Gem? Or am I to confirm that one can love someone 'more and more.' It can be said about God too, that one can—"

"Papa, I want to marry Elegant."

It took but a second for Pastor Loving to swallow his words. "Marry, did you—"

"But first Elegant and I would like to become engaged."

"En-engaged, married ... why ..."

"Elegant's in the kitchen with—"

"Gem, Gem, my head's spinning. I don't think Elegant should come ... yes, he, no, what am I saying? I mean ..."

Gem leaned over and kissed her father's forehead.   "Papa—"

"But you're still in school, college, pursuing your studies. A senior this year."

"We'll be engaged, Papa. What's the difference between being engaged and dating? It just means more of a commitment, am I right?"

"Gem now, what, you're lecturing me? Your father?"

Gem blushed, embarrassed.

"Yes, commitment, commitment—it, uh, like I said, Gem, commitment."

Gem was laughing between her father's pauses.

"Let me get Elegant, Papa!"

"Uh, yes, you do that, you do that. You, you get him in here. Yes, get the young man in here!"

"I—"

"But, Gem, Gem, wait, wait. Wasn't Elegant supposed to do this? Ask for my permission, not—"

"He was too scared to, Papa. So we skipped with tradition."

"Gem!"

"Gem!"

"You first, Elegant," Gem said to Elegant, snatching his arm, dragging him out of the chair.

"Gem, why are you doing that to—"

"First things first, Francine!"

They'd cleared the kitchen.

"Did, did Pastor Loving say yes? Yes, Gem!"

They were at the study's door.

"Did—"

"Congratulations, Elegant. Congratulations to you and Gem!" Pastor Loving said, sticking out his hand.

"Congratulations for what? What are you congratulating G-Gem and Elegant for … a-about, P-Papa!" Francine said, perplexed after dropping everything in the kitchen, frantically tailing behind Gem and Elegant into the study.

"Oh, we'll tell you all about it, Francine. Won't we, Gem, Elegant!"

Gem and Elegant turned to Francine with the biggest smile ever seen south of Pennsylvania!

"So sit down, Francine. Have a seat!"

———

"Now to tell Mr. Manners."

"I'm afraid you'll have to do that one on your own, Elegant. I'm bushed."

"Yeah, the scary part is over."

They were sitting in the car outside the house on Hattersfield Road.

"There're different kinds of scared, aren't there, Elegant?"

"Gem, what do you mean by that?"

"The ring, and then this, real life. Or should I say, things outside the ring—like today."

"Yes, yes, but your heart still pumps like crazy," Elegant said, touching his. "When you were in the study with your father and I was with Francine, I was babbling like, like an idiot, Gem. With Francine."

"It just came out. And Papa was tongue-tied—and how often does that happen to Papa."

"Not when Pastor Loving's preaching, that's for sure."

"How surprised do you think Mr. Manners will be?"

"Surprised? Uh, just, uh, not for more than a second or two, probably. Since he kind of predicted this."

"He did?"

Elegant took her hand. "This finger won't be naked for long."

Gem looked down at her finger. "When will we look for an engagement ring?"

"How about next Saturday?"

"A deal!" Gem said, grabbing Elegant's hand, shaking it. "Oh, I'm so happy, Elegant. So happy!"

Gem's car was pulling away from the farmhouse.

Woof! Woof!

"Gyp! Gyp! Elegant and I are engaged, Gyp! We're engaged, Gyp!"

Woof! Woof!

"Now we have to tell Mr. Manners, Gyp!"

But the front door swung open.

"Did I just hear what I thought I heard? Was it correct!"

"Yes, you did, Mr. Manners. Yes, it was, sir!"

Pee-Pot and Elegant hugged and danced mindlessly.

When they stopped dancing, Pee-Pot put his hand on Elegant, looking up to him. "Pastor Loving's come a long way, hasn't he, Elegant? A long, long ways in a short time."

Then he and Elegant and Gyp walked into the house.

"Gyp, we're going to have a great run in the morning. The best we've ever had."

―――

Gem stopped the car on Hattersfield Road. This had been a dream day for her.

"Mrs. Elegant Raines. Mrs. Elegant Raines. Thank you, Momma. Thank you."

The car started back up.

"Thank you."

―――

The site cleared away, the money and date set, Elegant was to fight Gino Gennaro at Madison Square Garden on the night of October 22, 1947, for the middleweight championship of the world. Needless to say, Elegant was, literally, on cloud nine. Clearly, he'd rocketed his way through the middleweight division, but it was still done methodically (no matter how fast it was), fighting the top contenders, the best fighters in the division, and not even the color of his skin, being black, had impeded him, made the path more difficult like it had for other great black fighters of the past who'd campaigned for the crown.

The irony of the Black Moon Johnson fight was it catapulted Elegant into the fight fans' consciousness and that he was now being declared the most exciting boxer (young or veteran) in boxing. The fighting public was passionate about him; it wanted him back in the ring with Black Moon. The fight had been so scintillating, fight-of-the-ages kind of stuff. Yes, the fighting public was hungry for a rematch, but it had to be first things first for Elegant: after all, he was after a championship, not another grudge match shaped and styled and orchestrated by the fans and the working press.

In fact, there was as much excitement for this fight as a drum major could drum up, and it came from Gino Gennaro's camp, not Elegant's (of course not Elegant's). Gino Gennaro was a big talker, a character (he and Black Moon would make a perfect match, a promoter's dream), a big mouth, colorful; he made great quotes. He was cocky. He was someone who let his feelings be known on just about any subject at any time. He'd call the press; they didn't have to call him. In other words, if he sneezed, he wanted the world to know it—be an eyewitness.

Gennaro was a tough guy out of New York, the Bronx. He was twenty-nine years old. For the fight, he threw his age around, saying he was going to "plaster de young punk"—meaning Elegant Raines. He was "gonna knock him on his fresh ass."

He felt by Joey "The Mark" DeMarco breaking his hand: "It was Gawd tawkin' ta me. A gift from Gawd." That he'd have to beat the "livin' crap outta Elegant Raines sooner or later," so "it was good this here come up fur me ta fight de punk at de Gardun. In my home town—ya know?"

The bookies installed Elegant a 5–1 favorite.

CHAPTER 21

"Come on, Gyp! This run's for the championship!"

Gyp and Elegant were at their usual starting marker, in the back of the house, looking out to the hills, the woods. This was going to be their last morning run together before the Gino Gennaro fight for the middleweight crown. Gyp was busy wagging her tail, so she was up for it. Elegant had to express it, give the run more weight, currency—try to make it everything he thought it should be.

He felt if he won the championship, a big piece of it should be credited to Gyp, his first guide through the woods, his first adventure with her. Their first morning was storybook, her waking him up, getting him on his feet, him running groggily at first, but she stuck with him, didn't give up on him, let him find his rhythm; and then he caught the beauty of her pace, how she intended to weave him through the woods, take the air in in his lungs, feel the majesty of the short climbs that kept building into magnificence until he felt one with God and Gyp and how perfect nature is when it's you who follow its natural course, curve, lead, twist up through the hills in a steady stream.

Gyp and Elegant took off as usual with their fresh bale of energy, with a hunger for this morning, in their eagerness to take on the run.

They were racing for home now. Gyp was stretching easily and Elegant the same. Their chests were poked out as if the building had an invisible winner's tape strung lengthways across the dirt field, and their chests (the one that got there first) would snap it clean, make it explode as loud as a cannon shot to be heard around the world.

Oh, it was a great run all right. But now Gyp was winning. But Elegant kept pushing himself as hard as he could. Soon Gyp's tongue shot out of her mouth, and Elegant could feel this exquisite rise in himself, as if this run would define him as champ, even over Gyp, but it was competition; this was the run for the roses!

"Aaaaah … aaaah …," Elegant said, lunging for the invisible tape, tumbling, falling, winning, beating Gyp but not by much, Gyp atop him, now straddling him, licking his face clean with her sloppy, spongy tongue.

"Gyp, Gyp! Ha! Gyp, girl!"

Woof! Woof!

It was like they were dancing in the dirt even if Elegant was prostrate, lying on his back. But there was this packed action in their bodies, this suggestion of dance, of enjoyment, like a two-step or a twirl around a whale's beautiful, bloated belly.

Tommie was on the championship bout's undercard. He'd made it clear he wasn't going to duck the opportunity to expose himself, boost his boxing career no matter how on edge he was about Elegant's fight. Only, Pee-Pot wasn't mentally up to working two fighters' corners. He turned Tommie over to Gas and Alton Timms. He'd decided not to treat it like a routine night in the ring, when it wasn't.

Tommie won his fight against Jack "The Joker" Jenkins by TKO, in round six, on cuts. He'd cut Jenkins to ribbons. His garden debut was a smashing success. Yes, the New York crowd loved Tommie Lathers to death!

"I left them standing on their feet, Elegant!"

Tommie'd just come into the dressing room.

"I know you did, Tommie!"

Tommie scooted over to Elegant and hugged him around his neck.

"Man, I ain't had this much fun in my life, man. Fighting out there, Elegant. All them people. Fighting in a arena like that!"

"You'll get your turn again, Tommie. You'll be out there fighting Johnny 'Birdman' Bidman for the welterweight championship next."

"I know, Elegant. I know!" Tommie said, turning and then grabbing Pee-Pot. "Mr. Manners's gonna have two champions on his hands!"

Pee-Pot chuckled. "Well, let's get one first before we start talking about two, Tommie."

"Pee-Pot," Gas said, "you gotta let these young whippersnappers have some fun. Can't put a damper on things."

"Says who?" Pee-Pot said, toweling Elegant's glistening black skin (he'd loosened up). "The boy could slip on a banana peel going down the aisle tonight and break his leg."

"Hell, Pee-Pot, it's about the only way Gino Gennaro's gonna beat him: on a damned forfeit!"

⁓

And Elegant was standing before Gino Gennaro in the ring, this five foot nine, slope-shouldered, grizzled vet, with black hair dyed blonde (lots of it), and a six-o'clock shadow dark as West Virginia mud caking his olive-skinned face.

Before they touched gloves to fight for the world's championship, Gino Gennaro said, "I'm gonna finish off what Black Moon Johnson started, punk. Ha. Ain't you gonna look like a car wreck in da Bronx!"

It was the beginning of round four in this middleweight championship fight.

"This round, you finish him off, Elegant. Don't let him get outta this round. Okay, son?"

"Yes, sir."

Gas inserted the mouthpiece into Elegant's mouth. Elegant's front teeth chomped down on it.

Round number four.

The right side of Gino Gennaro's face looked like it'd been bashed by a hammer, and the left side, it was lumped too; but to Gennaro's credit, he came out for the fourth round. His right eye was shut, and his left one was closing, was cut inside the eyebrow. If Elegant didn't knock him out, then the the referee would have to stop the fight since Gennaro's corner wouldn't throw in the towel—Gennaro wouldn't let them.

Elegant circled Gennaro. He didn't like this, hurting a person like this, but Gennaro had a hard-as-a-nut-head, and he had paid the price for it. Elegant had busted Gennaro up with every shot in the book but could hit him harder, with more power, not all of it, if …

So he bunched his muscles and then relaxed. Then Gennaro threw a punch at him like a man practically blind, who had recognized the shadow of something real but then illusory.

The uppercut froze Gennaro like a rope. And then another sizzling uppercut rocketed his body backward, lifting him an inch off the canvas, and his head banged onto the canvas with a thud, and Gennaro lay on the canvas while blood spurt out of his mouth along with the bloody mouthpiece his teeth no longer gripped.

While the referee counted over Gino Gennaro, Elegant didn't know how to feel; only, spontaneously, he snapped out of it when Tommie burst into the ring. He heard Tommie's voice, and Tommie was lifting him, and Elegant was looking down at Gas and Alton Timms; and then the longest, widest, brightest smile he reserved for Pee-Pot, for the man who made him the new middleweight champion of the world tonight at Madison Square Garden in New York City and, what seemed, in front of the whole wide world.

———

Elegant was in Washington, DC, at Howard University, in its cafeteria. The students mobbed him like bobby-soxers. Oh, yeah, they all knew who Elegant Raines was. If they hadn't gotten an autograph from him before he was champ, they made certain they got one now that he was. Both him and Gem were unbothered by all the attention, for it was playful, done in great fun, even if their lunch had gotten cold; but a cafeteria worker took care of that, reheating the food.

And at least they had a corner of the student cafeteria that, by all appearances, seemed set aside exclusively for them. But this trip to the campus, a day after the fight, Elegant had to make!

They'd been laughing.

"But I did, Elegant. I did. I'd thought you'd be wearing a crown on your head."

"You did!"

"See how foolish I am. Unsmart, after all."

They were finishing off their homemade apple pie.

"It probably wouldn't fit anyway. My head's too big."

But Gem knew Elegant wouldn't let anything go to his head. He was just as humble as before. She saw it when he was signing autographs, the students' and teachers' (professors) autographs, how proud he was yet how humble. And he'd come straight from New York to Washington by train to be with her.

"Who got to you first?"

"Uh, Tommie. I was in a trance until then, Gem. A complete, total trance."

She'd won oratorical contests, math contests before, in Longwood, spelling bees too, but nothing that had "world's best" in front of it as a title.

"But Tommie, he snapped me out of it."

"I adore Tommie."

"Be careful, Gem. Don't forget, you're engaged."

"Here I've been flashing my engagement ring in front of your eyes all day, and you think I've forgotten?"

"You have, you have." Pause. "Gem, Mr. Manners said they're planning a parade in Longwood for me."

"Elegant," Gem said, dropping her fork, "what took you so long to tell me!"

"I, oh, I forgot, Gem. I-I forgot—uh, that's all."

"How could you? There're never parades in Longwood, not unless the baseball or football team win the state championship—which only happened one time, I-I think." Pause.

"Elegant, you're one of us now, a Longwooder," Gem said, leaning over the table, kissing him.

———

They were on their way back to Gem's dorm. Autograph seekers still hounded Elegant, nipping at his heels—but neither his nor Gem's disposition had changed.

"I want the years to sail by, don't you, Elegant?"

"Don't tell me. For—"

"We can get married."

Elegant turned to her. "Become Mrs. Elegant Raines."

"It's all I hope for. To be your wife. To have children."

"Gem, how many?"

"As many as you'd like," Gem said.

"I'm going to like that."

"Me too."

They were off to the side of Gem's dormitory, Slowe Hall, and Gem was looking at it like it was a fortress looming on the horizon.

"Back into my dungeon."

"Gem, I'm going to pretend I didn't hear that."

"I did love the college experience until I met you, Elegant. Now I love only you."

Elegant lifted her onto the short brick retaining wall with the two-foot-wide surface the students sat on.

"Last night was nothing compared to now. Right now, Gem."

"Elegant, d-do you mean that?" Gem asked, her face trembling.

"It wasn't, Gem. At one time, I thought winning the championship would be the greatest experience I'd ever have. But it isn't now that I have so much to look forward to with you."

The next day, Pee-Pot was in the basement, Pee-Pot's Parlor, cleaning a barber tool, when the phone rang.

It was ten in the morning.

"Yes, uh, hello?"

Pee-Pot's face was ashen.

"He ... he is!" Long pause.

"Thank you, Walter. Thank you."

"Yes, tomorrow. I'll be down there tomorrow. In the morning for, for the arrangements."

Pee-Pot hung up the phone.

He walked over to the barber chair and then sat. Then he stood. He was to go into the gym today after he cleaned the barber tools, return to his normal routine, the same as Elegant after they'd won the crown. Indeed, get back to his fighters and his barber customers, take them off the back burner.

"But now this," Pee-Pot said grimly.

He knew Gyp was in the backyard. But he would go up to Elegant's room first, where he'd left him.

"Elegant …"

"Yes, Mr. Manners," Elegant said, sitting up in bed.

"My brother died this morning," Pee-Pot said, reaching out for Elegant. "Biscuit, Biscuit Manners is dead."

They were back from Biscuit Manners's funeral, from Martin County, Kentucky. Once Elegant and Pee-Pot got there, everything went well. Pee-Pot took charge of things. Elegant was there assisting him in any capacity he could. In fact, Pee-Pot called him his right-hand man, not that Elegant had much to do.

It was good for them to see Gyp. She was right outside the farmhouse wagging her tail and barking, Gyp being glad to have them back like they were coming in from a fight off the road, not a funeral. But she'd made it feel like a regular road trip by deluding them.

The one single light was on in the living room, and Pee-Pot was in an old, hole-filled sweater, sitting in his rocker. Gyp was on the rug, her head down on her forepaws.

"Thank you again," Pee-Pot said, looking over at Elegant. "You made the trip for me bearable."

Quiet.

"No matter how prepared you are for something like this, when it comes … It can hit you so hard as to numb you. Your senses, Elegant."

For this was the most Pee-Pot had opened up to Elegant since he was at his door four days ago, telling him Biscuit Manners was deceased, reaching out to him for emotional support and comfort. But after that, everything had been matter-of-fact, straightforward, transferring all of his trainer's skill and talent into a new arena, where it could be skillfully utilized for the management of a loved one's death.

"Just to fight as hard as he did … I guess if you keep your attitude strong as Biscuit did, begin to think you can even keep dying on hold for a little while longer. On a long leash."

Pee-Pot smiled. It was another light in the living room. It seemed to lift the gloom.

"When he got those big rides, oh, Elegant, son, what a time it was for him. None was better. When he talked about it, it was like he was choking back the tears. He was so damned happy. Proud of himself. I guess it felt like he was riding for nobility. Before all those rich white folk."

Some were at Biscuit Manners's funeral, rich white folk, Elegant thought. They hadn't forgot Biscuit Manners, it seemed.

"Meant something to a black man then. Not so much now, but back then it did, during my and Biscuit's day. Looked for respect in any corner we could find it. Was always the reflection of a white man. A black man."

Those words stung Elegant.

Pee-Pot stood.

Gyp stood.

"I'm gonna go down to the basement, finish off cleaning my barber tools. Finish off what I'd started. I was halfway done before the call came."

Elegant hadn't moved.

"Got a whole lot of heads to cut. To catch up with in Longwood the next couple of days."

Elegant smiled.

"What are you gonna do, Gyp, now that you're up on your feet with me?"

Gyp looked at Pee-Pot with sheepish eyes and then plopped back down on the throw rug.

"Thought so!" Pause.

"Roadwork in the morning, Elegant?"

"Roadwork, sir."

"Get rid of some of that rust you've got!"

"Yes, sir!"

"You and Gyp." Pause.

"Well, Biscuit had a good sending off, didn't he? To his Maker. It's what any man would want."

———

There were so many new developments that had transpired over a span of many months. One was another tragedy: Hancock Hollins's death. It was another funeral Pee-Pot and Elegant attended. But this one, of course, in Tulip, Tennessee. And though you would think it might create a vacuum for Pee-Pot and Elegant managerially, it didn't, for a smooth transition was paved over to his nephew, Collingsworth Hollins, Hancock Hollins's deceased brother's sole surviving heir, one that had been consummated just weeks before Hollins's death.

Collingsworth Hollins was in his late fifties. He was of the same stripe as his uncle. He was a man of heart and character who backed words up with deeds. By no means did Hollins's death leave the Hollins/Manners/Raines team floundering—there being no costly interruption.

The only problem now *was* Elegant's weight. Pee-Pot kept looking at Elegant's body versus the scale. Undoubtedly, they were in direct contradiction. Elegant was nineteen and a half years old. All the ripeness of potential had now fully flowered to the point where it no longer could be reversed.

It's why Pee-Pot hastened for a quick defense of the middleweight title between Elegant and Joey "The Mark" DeMarco. DeMarco broke his hand in April, but it'd mended, and he could fight for the title against Elegant that he was supposed to fight for against Gino Gennaro.

The fight was made, and on December 19, at Madison Square Garden, Elegant knocked DeMarco out in the second round. The following day Elegant announced, at a press conference, he would vacate the middleweight division by relinquishing his crown and move up to the light heavyweight weight class. He said, "I regret this turn of events." Et cetera, et cetera.

Black Moon greeted the announcement with scorn, derision. He insisted Elegant Raines had run out the division to duck him. He'd called Elegant a yellow-bellied coward, for starters. That he'd chase after him in the light heavyweight division in order to fight him again. Only, Pee-Pot saw it as an unrealistic threat. He knew Black Moon's body well enough to know it couldn't carry 170–175 pounds, not with an overmuscular frame perfectly suited for 160 pounds—not one pound more.

It'd take just two or three wins in the light heavyweight division for Elegant to prove himself, to take on the champion of the division, Harold "Haymaker" Gaines. Elegant posted two fights and recorded two knockouts, rounds two and one. Pens were drawn and the dotted line signed, and on March 3, 1948, Elegant, at twenty years old, won the light heavyweight championship of the world over Harold "Haymaker" Gaines in his hometown of Chicago at the Chicago Coliseum in a thrilling one-round knockout.

At 175 pounds, Elegant's power was even more terrifying. Three title defenses by Elegant had produced three victories.

Wedged between these exciting developments was Gem, in May, graduating from Howard University with full honors. Gem was the valedictorian of her graduating class and back living at home. She was a teacher. But her school, Longwood High School, had bigger plans for Gem Loving. They wanted her, at her young, tender age, to take over as principal of Longwood High School when next year, June of 1949, Miss Grace Atwood planned to retire from Longwood's school system after thirty-five years of dedicated service.

Gem was flabbergasted by the magnanimous offer. She had to seriously consider whether this was what she wanted. It'd take her out of the classroom and away from teaching students—something she loved. It was why she became an educator in the first place. It was where her heart and soul was.

———

The days were long. After all, it was July in Longwood. Elegant was sitting on the blanket in the grass in Lakeview Park, and Gem was heading back to him, walking quite determinedly with each step as if gaining momentum. He wanted to say, "Slow down, Gem (she was about eighty yards from him)! You'll break out in a sweat in this hot sun walking like that," but then again, he felt this spark in her that was just too exhilarating to try to snuff.

Now Gem was standing in front of him with both fists balled on her slender hips.

"Now what, Gem?" Elegant said, Gem's shadow draping him.

"I don't have to be a June bride, when I can be a March bride instead, Elegant!"

"Oh no!"

"Oh yes!" Gem said, pulling him by his hands and up to his feet.

"You're going to have to carry me across the threshold!"

Gem then, without warning, jumped into Elegant's arms.

"You might as well get practice!"

Both sitting back down on the blanket, both comfortable, Elegant and Gem seemed in no rush to leave the park. He was holding her from behind. Her head lay back against his chest.

"Don't worry, I'll face your father this time. Sit down in the study with him.

Not you, Gem. Not this time around."

"You mean, we'll follow with tradition, convention," Gem said, turning her head up to Elegant, winking.

Then Gem's hand reached for a blade of grass at the blanket's edge and then put the tip of it in her mouth (not the dirt part), which stuck out.

"It'll be a cinch this time."

"I know."

"Papa's going to be busy, isn't he, Elegant? Our wedding day."

"You can say that again."

"First, he'll have to give me away and then administer the vows."

"Maybe he'll have Assistant Pastor Green perform the—"

"No, not Papa."

"No," Elegant said, "I suppose not. Not your father. No … uh-uh. Not Pastor Loving." Pause.

"And Tommie'll be my best man!"

"And Francine my maid-of-honor!"

"March it is then!"

Elegant rushed to his feet. "Come on, Gem," Elegant said, now pulling her by her hands and off the blanket. "We have to see your father!"

Serenely Gem folded the blanket and then burst out laughing. Elegant swept her off her feet and carried her out of Lakeview Park.

"Married!"

"Married!"

"Married!"

Elegant didn't know who said it louder—Pee-Pot or Tommie.

"March!"

"March!"

"March!"

"Mr. Manners, what did you and Tommie do? Plan this, sir?"

When he and Gem got not only Pastor Loving's permission to marry Gem but also his blessings too, Elegant rushed out of Pastor Loving's house, hopped in his car (a 1947 Ford sedan), and sped (thirty miles an hour) over to the Pug to tell Tommie and Pee-Pot the excellent news. Elegant, when he saw Tommie on the gym floor, dragged him into Pee-Pot's office with him.

"And Tommie will be my best man!"

"Damn!" Tommie said, looking at Elegant and then at Pee-Pot and then back at Elegant. "Damn!"

"Now," Pee-Pot said, leaning back in his chair, "whose idea was this anyway?"

"Uh, Gem's, sir."

"And what about Pastor—"

"Just came from the house. Just got his blessings, sir."

"Oh, so it is official then."

"Oh is it, Mr. Manners. As official as it can get."

"Aaah, you know Mr. Manners just teasing you anyways, Elegant. Pastor Loving's a lucky man. Gonna have you for his son-in-law."

"And just to think how it all started off, huh? All began for you two, Elegant.

The beginning of all this."

"I know, Mr. Manners." Elegant sighed. "Not very, at all promising, was it, sir?"

"It's why, boys, you never know about life. And the only way to know is by living it."

"It's why I know things gonna get patched up soon, Mr. Manners. For me. Uh—is, sir, is."

And Pee-Pot and Elegant knew what Tommie was alluding to.

"Things will, Tommie. They will," Pee-Pot said reassuringly. "Gonna turn the corner for you. Just give it time, Tommie."

"Well, gonna get on back out there, finish off my workout," Tommie said, looking Elegant up and down suspiciously.

"Come on, Tommie. So I have today off. One day off. Y-you had last Thursday off, so—"

"But least I ain't made no wedding plans to get married on my day off, Elegant. Not like you!"

"Go, Tommie. Go. And leave the boy alone!" Pee-Pot said, pointing his finger to the office door.

When Tommie sped out of the room, all Pee-Pot could do was break out laughing.

"You know, Elegant, ha, Tommie's right."

"I-I know, Mr. Manners."

"March, but no date yet, uh, you and Gem?" Pee-Pot said, looking up at Elegant.

"Yes. Yes, with Francine, it seems, in school, we'll make it as convenient for her as we can, sir." Pause. "You know, Mr. Manners, I can't wait to tell Gyp."

"So you're off to the house to tell her?"

"Yes, sir."

"Don't let me stop you."

"I'll see you at the house then."

Elegant opened the office door and was about to close it when he heard Pee-Pot say, "And don't ask for any days off anytime soon, Elegant! It's no telling what you'll do next—on your own!"

On November 2, 1948, there was another announcement regarding Elegant's boxing career: he would vacate the light heavyweight division, relinquish his crown, and step up to the heavyweight division and campaign for the crown, the one the hard-hitting Domenic Botti held for one year and two title defenses. No one in the boxing world was taken aback by Elegant's announcement, for it was predicted by practically every newspaper man who had "sports columnist" written in front of his name and covered boxing as his beat.

The plan for the Hollins team, was to start with the fifteenth ranked fighter in the division and then for Elegant to work his way up, workmanlike—needless to say. This wasn't to be an easy entry into such a cherished, worshipped, and prestigious division as the heavyweight division. There would be no short work for Elegant. This wouldn't be anything like him coming out of the middleweight division and stepping up to the light heavyweight division to bring attention to a lightly regarded weight class and create a big stir, a big money fight for the division in the process by name association.

Elegant's new campaign would begin with Steamroller Jankowski and then Oscar Hernandez and then Ernie "Sideways" Morton and then on and on, Elegant moving through the division until he reached the top. By all indications, it appeared Dominic Botti could become a dominant heavyweight, one who could hold onto the crown for a long time, considering what the division currently was offering him in terms of competition.

As for Elegant, still a shade over six feet two, he would, from now on, bring a comfortable 198–200 pounds into the ring. Pee-Pot portended that eventually, Elegant would hit the scales at between 208–210, no higher. It was a new challenge for them, Pee-Pot and Elegant. A challenge both welcomed with open arms. To be the heavyweight champion of the world was as big a prize as any fighter could dream of.

CHAPTER 22

April 5, 1949

"Ain't supposed to kiss him yet, Gem!" Tommie said.

"No, not yet!" Pastor Loving seconded.

"Saturday, Gem. Saturday!"

It was Thursday night, and the wedding rehearsal was just about to end. Tommie had kept it all lively, having the time of his life. He'd stood in for Francine (maid-of-honor) at one time during the rehearsal—as if she had to be stood in for—and had been a general cutup. Francine would be in from Spelman College tomorrow night. The wedding was for noon. An accommodation was made for Francine, an April wedding, not March.

Pee-Pot and Cora Manners were married in Body of Christ, and Pee-Pot was sitting, reminiscing about it, the wedding rehearsal, the fun. It was Francois Baptiste who was the cutup then, kept everyone on their toes and in stitches at the wedding rehearsal. And it was Pastor Lawrence P. Moreland who officiated, was the pastor of the Body of Christ Church. Of that group, all had passed on.

Now his life would pass into a new phase, or would it go back to what it was before Elegant came into his life, Pee-Pot thought, his and Gyp's? Pee-Pot twisted in the pew. It was a good life, him and Gyp, but Elegant had enhanced both their lives. He had no idea of how his life was going to be without Elegant in the farmhouse, down the hall from him. This was a time when he'd have to call on the sage advice he'd given to Tommie so freely, so easily, yet so earnestly: "That's why, boys, you never know about life. And the only way to know is by living it."

Now to Pee-Pot, it sounded pompous, pretentious, not wise, sagacious, now that he was facing this crucial turn of events. He'd predicted this love affair between Gem and Elegant, but little did he know they'd spin their wheels so fast, make Saturday come so soon.

After their honeymoon, they'd be renting out a room in town—even though he knew something they didn't, was a big, big surprise.

"Mr. Manners, Mr. Manners," Elegant said, motioning to Pee-Pot.

"Uh, yes, Elegant?" Pee-Pot said, snapping out of his contemplations.

"Tommie, sir, Tommie's about to take pictures of us."

And so Pee-Pot saw Tommie with the Polaroid camera.

"For their grandkids, Mr. Manners!"

Pee-Pot was up out of the pew. "I'm all for that!"

"For they can show them they was young at one time."

Pee-Pot was about to step into the picture frame.

"Don't, don't mean no offense by it, Mr. Manners."

The wedding party laughed.

"Don't worry, Tommie, at my young, tender age, none's taken!"

"Now, Francine, let Gem get some rest tonight. You know she's got a big day ahead of her tomorrow."

"Yes, Papa."

Then Pastor Loving waited for them with his arms outstretched, just outside Gem's door. When they got to him, he wrapped his arms around them as Gem kissed his right cheek and Francine his left.

"My wonderful daughters!"

Francine and Gem looked at each other and, as if on cue, said, "Our wonderful father!"

"How many times haven't we said that, girls? Celebrated it just between ourselves."

Then Pastor Loving just held them to him lovingly. He kissed their foreheads.

"I won't be long with her, Papa. I promise."

They'd turned to go back into Gem's room.

"How would I know?" Pastor Loving asked, yawning once and then twice. "When you know I'll be fast asleep once my head hits the pillow."

They laughed.

He yawned a third time. "But, Gem," Pastor Loving said, stopping her, "I might as well confess one thing to you, with this, uh, being your last night in the house. You and Francine and I together ..."

"Yes, Papa?" Francine said, seemingly taking more interest in what her father had to say than Gem.

"I know all about you two," he said, wagging his finger at them.

"About—"

"I might as well confess, like I said. Your mother—"

"No, she didn't, Papa!"

"Oh yes, she did, Gem. Yes, she did!"

"But Momma wasn't supposed to—"

"Now, Francine, your mother was an honest woman, could be trusted, but you expected too much out of her, honey."

"Then ..."

"Yes. I know all about what you two'd do when I fell asleep. Started to snore. Your nocturnal habits when my eyes were shut. I just don't know how often it happened!"

"Ha."

"Since ... I'm asleep, when it does!"

"Ha."

"Good night, girls."

"Good night, Papa."

"Good night, Papa."

They heard Pastor Loving's bedroom door close.

"Well, the myth of Helena Loving has just been destroyed," Gem laughed. "Hasn't it, Francine?"

"I wonder how many other secrets Momma told Papa," Francine said, her forehead knotting.

"We'll never know, Francine. Will we?"

"Not unless we twist Papa's arm!" Pause.

"Gem ..."

"Yes ...?"

"Gem, what are you going to do with Flora?" Francine said, picking Flora up off the bed. "Now? Now that you'll be married tomorrow?"

"Why, take her with me—what else?"

"I'm sorry, I know that. Uh ... but do you think Elegant, she'll wind up on your bed like—"

"He knows about Flora, of course he ... Now, now that's a good question, is-isn't it? And, and it's one I hadn't thought of before. Not ..."

Francine handed Flora back to Gem, and Gem looked at her fondly and then put her back on the bed, against the sham.

"There're going to be a lot of new things you'll have to get used to, right, Gem? Beginning tomorrow."

"Uh, right, Francine. Yes, you're right."

"But Elegant's so easy to get along with. I'm sure he'll make things easy for you."

"But Flora ..."

Suddenly, Francine felt sorry for Gem, for she was looking down at Flora as if she were a child, as if she were about to abandon her because of something now bigger and more important than the two of them.

"Is it time for me to grow up, Francine? Starting tomorrow? On my wedding day?"

"Gem, I'm sorry. I shouldn't have—"

"Brought it up? But I'm glad you did. I'm—"

"Then let's change the subject."

"I do have to grow up, Francine. And this might be a part of it. Do you think I should be afraid of it?"

"No. I've never known you to be afraid of anything, Gem."

"There. Then that solves it. I'll just work it out with Elegant when the time comes. It's what I'll do."

Francine didn't feel so bad now. If there was a crisis, Francine thought, Gem had all but swept it away—clean.

"The bridal gown—"

"You want to see it again, Fran—"

"I want to get married in it too, Gem!"

"It is Momma's, Francine. After all. An heirloom. Momma wouldn't have it any other way!"

"I've already told you about Brandon—"

"Lancaster. The one and only Brandon Lancaster," Gem said playfully, swooning.

"I mean, he's no Elegant Raines, Gem, but—"

"He's stolen your heart." Pause.

"Well … it's just a matter of whether I've stolen his. Brandon's so shy," Francine said, brushing her hand over her finely braided hair.

"You know sometimes, Francine … you have to take the bull by the horns. How do you think I got Elegant to—"

"Move so—"

"Fast?"

"Yes."

"Yes. At times I had to assert myself. Become more aggressive."

"Gem, you did!"

"I did!"

"Then maybe I'd better get a move on when I get back to Spelman's campus."

"I told Elegant I didn't have to be a June bride. And I also—"

"Gem, I hope Brandon Lancaster's prepared for the new Francine Loving when I get back to school," Francine said, her skin flushed, red. "You and Elegant are going to have a beautiful wedding tomorrow, I'm sure. But wait, Gem, wait until you see our wedding. Mine and Brandon Lancaster's!"

April 7, 1949

There were the usual trappings, the rice thrown onto the church grounds, bouquets, colorful streamers, the car with the sign JUST MARRIED splashed across the trunk, and the black automobile speeding away from the church like a bank robbery was just committed in broad daylight, not two young newlyweds who were being waved to wildly by a throng of well-dressed well-wishers standing out on the dirt road, Fowler Road.

"Well, they're off. They're off," Pastor Loving said, drawing Francine closer to him.

"Yes, Papa."

"I don't know if I can go through this again, Francine. With you, darling."

Francine smiled bravely.

Gyp was barking in the road, looking up Fowler Road at the car.

"Go ahead, Gyp. Go ahead. Keep barking. Get it out ... all out of your system, Gyp," Pee-Pot said.

Tommie rubbed the knuckles of his right hand with his left.

"Damn. They looked happy. Damn," Tommie said, standing off, away from everyone on the road, alone.

———

They were on a train and on their way to New York City for their honeymoon. Gem had never been to New York City, and Elegant was going to show her around. By the number of times he'd been to New York, he knew it pretty well. Gem was looking forward to touring it and taking pictures of it. From out of the blue, Gem had become a camera buff. You could find her taking pictures all around Longwood with her Kodak camera.

It was to be a three-day vacation. They were staying in the Charleston Hotel in Harlem. Why such a unique name in the heart and soul of Harlem was that the hotel's owner, Eli Dawkins, was from Charleston, South Carolina; so why not the Charleston Hotel in Harlem?

As soon as Elegant and Gem stepped foot into the Charleston, Elegant gained celebrity status. He was addressed as "champ" by the entire hotel staff. Elegant and Gem were whisked off to their honeymoon suite, room 511.

Room 511's door had just shut, and Harold, the bellhop, had just been handsomely tipped by Elegant for carrying the bags into the extravagantly styled bedroom suite.

"No wonder you picked this hotel, Elegant—'champ' this and 'champ' that," Gem said, turning to him.

"Now, Gem ... no, no, it wasn't that. Honest, I swear it wasn't," Elegant said, crossing his heart. "You know I have no ego."

"I love it though!" Gem said, grabbing Elegant's hand, walking excitedly over to the expansive window in front of her.

They looked down onto 125th Street at Harlem at night like they were looking up at sunbursts in the sky. There was this hustle and bustle Gem had not seen before, not even in Washington, DC—the radiant stream of cars, the street's lamppost lights shimmering off them bright as gems or diamonds worn by the richest of the black Harlemnites partying the night away in clubs, the extravagances and indulgences of the wealthy.

"It seems everyone's going somewhere, Elegant, doesn't it? Right now?"

"You're right. But that's Harlem for you, Gem," Elegant said as if boasting about it. "It seems like everyone's got somewhere to go, no matter the time of day."

"But why did I know it'd be like this. Just how I imagined it." Pause. "Hungry?"

It was after seven o'clock.

"How'd you guess?"

"Your stomach, uh, Gem. It ..."

"Oh ..."

"Just now."

"Don't tell me I didn't hear it."

"I don't think you'd hear anything right now."

"No," Gem said, calming down, "I-I suppose not."

"Now don't let me ruin it, "Elegant said, worried he had.

"No, Elegant. Not at all. B-but I am behaving like a schoolgirl."

Elegant placed his finger beneath her chin. "No, you're acting like Gem Loving, my wife."

"Yes, yes, I, I am."

"So room service, or do you want me to escort you down to—"

"Room service, Elegant. Let's stay in the room. It's so private here. The way it is."

"It is ...," Elegant said, looking around the room.

"And," Gem giggled, "I don't think I could stand to hear another 'champ' come out of another person's mouth tonight."

"Me either."

———

But they heard it again when Lloyd, their waiter, came up to their room with their food and belted Elegant with "champ" enough times so as to knock him silly. And it was a dinner eaten under candlelight with expensive silverware and a canopy of romance covering it.

They'd been out of their wedding clothes the minute they'd left church. Each, after the wedding reception, went back to the house. They'd changed in separate rooms (even if they were man and wife) and then got back over to the church for their grand send-off.

Gem and Elegant had never really discussed sex. They'd hinted at it by talking about children, speaking on that subject, parenthood—but it's as far as it'd gotten. She'd seen Elegant stripped down to his trunks, but that was only in newspaper photos, not in person, not standing in front of her, his chest fully exposed to her. This was not something that had ever happened between them.

And as for Elegant, what did he know of Gem's body but her eyes and lips and hands and the small of her back. What did he know of her skin but the light, gentle, smooth touching of it—not flesh in passion or want or need. He was not a virgin; she was. And he was sitting at the table wondering what fears she might have and how they might manifest, and how would he silence them or, at least, help her to control them when they came.

"Elegant, I think I'm going to burst!" Gem said, putting her glass down on the table.

"You, you did eat a lot, Gem. Were, are you nervous?"

"About sex? Yes?"

"Oh, Gem, don't be," Elegant said, taking her hand into his.

"Not, no, not"—Gem frowned—"about sex, having sex with you, Elegant ..."

"B-but what, Gem!"

"About, but about pleasing you. Satisfying you sexually."

Elegant let go of her hand. "Oh."

"Not, not about having sex with you. But afterwards. How you'll feel afterwards. After we have sex."

She was this smart young lady, this intelligent young lady, worldly without having seen the world, of opening its every lid. It's what was said about the young Shakespeare, Elegant thought, someone who had lived in Stratford-upon-Avon in England, in a room, but knew how the human world (its soul) worked.

But then Gem stood, and Elegant didn't know why. His eyes trailed her off to the window, but he'd been caught off guard because of his brief but profound thoughts, thinking, but now sensed Gem was being Gem, that she'd walked over to the window and had looked down on 125th Street to contemplate, not among nature this time (Longwood) but among the city's glare, the night lights and Harlem's folk in full view, tilted motion, their activity inspiring thought or poetry or wherever your passion led you.

Walking back over to him, looking down at him with smoky eyes, Gem said, "Let's go into the bedroom, Elegant."

Elegant stood to take her hand, and they walked over the living room's carpet, off from the living room's table with its glasses and silverware and dirtied plates, and into the bedroom the living room led seamlessly into.

When they got to the front of the big, sprawling bed, Gem said, "I'll undress first in front of you, Elegant. And then you can undress in front of me. All right?"

And so Gem began unbuttoning the front of the white straight-line dress until she stepped out of it. There was a fashionable backless bench at the bottom of the bed, and she turned and laid her dress on it.

Turning back to Elegant, she smiled. Then she looked at the spaghetti-thin straps of her slip, sliding them off her shoulders; and with her help, the slip came off and Gem stood there in laced panties and bra.

Elegant knew she was tall and slender, but now he saw she was shapely, that her legs blended wonderfully, beautifully in tune with the rest of her.

Gem stood on one leg and kicked the other leg back, allowing her to slip off her shoe. With the other leg, she repeated the action.

And on cue, Elegant knew it was time for him to take off his clothing. And he took off his jacket, pulling a short chair to his right a foot from him; and then removing his shirt (his chest bare), he then unbelted his pants, removing them along with his shoes and socks.

Standing before her in boxer shorts, Gem was amazed by Elegant's body, for it was nothing similar to what she saw in the newspaper photos, not now, not at this time as her eyes ranged over him and she felt the delicate power in him, why it was that way when he held her, when she anchored herself to him so desirably and receptively.

Elegant walked up to her and touched the flesh of her waist. Her waist was warm.

Looking into each other's eyes, each sensed it was going to be a good night for them in the honeymoon suite in the Charleston Hotel, the hotbed of Harlem just outside their bedroom window.

Three cars were out on Fowler Road.

Pee-Pot's truck hid behind a batch of bushes. Tommie's souped-up Ford did too.

Pastor Loving parked his car off on the side of the road, visible to the world. The three had plans for the newlyweds today, big ones, once they arrived in Longwood!

"Gyp, Gem, and Elegant will be here soon enough."

Woof!

Gyp sat up on her haunches on the car's front seat like she was sitting on a queen's cushioned throne. Her ears were perked.

It'd been rough on Pee-Pot and Gyp with Elegant out of the house for the past three days. It had the character of the pre-Elegant days. While they tried for it not to show, it was a strain on them, like competing with a phantom or the past, something no longer natural—now totally adverse to them.

Cora's death had put them through this before. But this was different: Elegant was not dead. He'd still be accessible to them, just not like before. Pee-Pot had tried a clear approach to this new life by thinking logically though all its facets. But contemplative thoughts can't cloud feelings, not when Pee-Pot concluded that they were some of his and Gyp's best days that were now behind them. So he dwelled on them far too long and far too much. To try to toss them away too quickly would be far too foolish and clumsy, Pee-Pot thought.

"After three days in New York, it does feel a little odd being back in Longwood, doesn't it, Elegant?"

They'd just passed the Earl's place.

"Think so?"

"I feel like a big-city girl."

"Come on, Gem," Elegant said, taking a sideways glance at Gem. "You're just teasing, right?"

"Of course. But it was thrilling."

"It was. Especially with you."

The car was aglow.

"But Harlem—"

"I was there before, granted …"

"Yes, granted. Uh, go on …"

"But it was the fights, do you know what I mean?"

"Yes, I do," Gem said, touching his arm, wanting to put her head on his shoulder but knowing he was driving the car.

"It was, this was a brand-new experience for me."

Gem felt she could curl up in his arms—but again, Elegant was driving the car.

"We have so many pictures to remember our honeymoon by, Elegant."

"I know."

"We're going to have the biggest photo album. I'm going to make sure of it."

Gem's hand was on Elegant's leg. Suddenly, it'd tensed, and she knew why: how would her father look at her now that she was no longer a virgin? For some reason, as soon as she got into Longwood, it's where her mind darted off to, of when she stood before her father as a new woman, one who was now sexual, who knew now how beautifully a man and woman can make love together and also knew her father and mother must've had this kind of passion between them, inside them, as well as Pee-Pot Manners and Cora Manners.

Yes, she thought about this now that she was no longer a virgin, now that she and Elegant had made love over the past three days in Harlem. Now that she knew what the feeling of having sex was like for any woman who was in love.

"I—"

"Gem, look, look, it's Pastor—"

"Papa!"

"Gem, Elegant, stop the car. Stop the car and follow me!"

Pastor Loving's body was halfway in the car and halfway out. The black Ford sedan was at the intersection of Fowler Road and Amber Road.

"Elegant, what's gotten into—"

And then Pastor Loving sped off in the car.

"Follow him. Pastor Loving said we should follow him, Gem!"

And follow him Elegant did.

Neither Elegant nor Gem could figure out what was happening to them, this strange behavior coming from Pastor Loving on their first day back in Longwood.

"Where's Papa taking us?"

"He, he was actually waiting for us, Gem, on Fowler Road!"

Elegant was about ten yards behind Pastor Loving, neither gaining nor losing ground.

Pastor Loving's arm shot out of the car window as if communicating something to them but getting lost in Gem's and Elegant's translations.

Suddenly, they were on Garland Road, a road not as bumpy as Amber Road, the jolts to the spine on Garland Road less severe.

"Look, Elegant, look, it's Mr. Cleveland Parson's old place!"

Elegant didn't know Mr. Parson so offered no comment.

Pastor Loving braked the car in front of the Parson place.

Honk!

Elegant honked back and then pulled up behind Pastor Loving's car.

Pastor Loving hopped out of the car and so did Gem.

"Papa! Papa!"

"Gem!"

Honk!

Elegant turned, and Tommie and Pee-Pot bore down on Cleveland Parson's place too.

Gyp was the first out of the truck and ran to Elegant, leaping into his arms.

"Gyp, Gyp!"

When Tommie got out of the car, he totally ignored Elegant but ran over to Gem, hugging her.

"Did you and Elegant behave yourselves in New York?" Tommie whispered in Gem's ear.

"Now what do you think, Tommie?"

Pastor Loving was hugging Elegant.

Pee-Pot was bringing up the rear.

"If I ain't always late for the party!"

"Mr. Manners!"

"Elegant!"

They took their time before they hugged, but when they did, it was special.

Coming to their senses, Gem looked at everyone but Elegant. "We were coming to the house as planned, Papa. And then go off to Miss Cambridge's boarding house."

"I know, Gem, I know," Pastor Loving said, taking Gem's hand. "But haven't you, don't you see—"

"The house, Mr. Parson's house looks brand new."

They still stood in the road, not on the Parsons' property.

"New clapboards," Gem said, "new windows, a porch—"

"You name it, Gem. It's county property though since Cleve Parson died intestate."

"Come again, Pastor Loving, sir?"

"Oh, that means without a will, Tommie."

"Oh, gotcha. Gotcha, sir."

Woof!

"Don't tell me you knew what that big word meant, uh, uh—"

"Intestate," Elegant said.

"Yeah, uh, that word, Gyp?"

"So what do you think, Elegant.?"

"It's nice, Pastor Loving, sir. Quite."

"It's up for sale."

"There's no For Sale sign in the yard, Papa. At least I don't see—"

"It's going to be sold through private hands."

"Why that's a shame," Gem said.

"It is," Elegant said. "It should be up for public sale. A house like this."

Pastor Loving entered onto the property, everyone but Gem and Elegant.

"Come, let's take a better look at the place."

"Papa, Elegant and I are, we are tired, aren't we, Elegant?" Gem sighed. "We'd like to get to the house and then go off to—"

"Yes, Gem, but …"

"Gem, your husband has spoken," Pastor Loving laughed.

They all laughed.

Gem walked up to Pastor Loving and let him lead the way.

They were on the new porch.

"Hmm … let's see what it looks like inside."

"Papa, I-I don't think—"

"Since we all here, Gem. Seen what the county done with the outside, might as well find out what they done to the inside," Tommie said.

"Come on, Gem, you're outnumbered on this one."

Gem broke out into laughter. "Yes, I certainly am, aren't I." She looked down at the doorknob and then reached for it, turning it.

"It's locked. Good, Papa!"

"But not for long, Gem," Pastor Loving said, sliding his fingers down into his vest pocket, and when they came out his pocket, out came a set of keys. "Not so fast … Not when I have a set of keys to your new house!"

"New house, Papa!

"New house, Pastor Loving!"

"Step aside, Gem, and let me do the honors!"

"This is ours, Papa!" Gem said, jumping up and down. "Elegant's and mine!"

"I can't believe this! I can't believe this. This beats staying in Miss Cambridge's boarding house any day!"

Pee-pot slapped Elegant on the back.

Gem turned and grabbed Elegant's hand.

As soon as they got into the house, it shined from head to toe, from the beautifully shellacked oak wood floors to the brown-stained mahogany banisters to the clean, finely finished ceilings.

"Now for the grand tour!" Pastor Loving said appetizingly.

"But, Pastor Loving, how did—"

"We'll discuss it all later. The details of it later—how about that, Elegant?"

"Yes, sir. Of course!"

"Some place, huh, Elegant? Some place, wouldn't you say, son?"

"It sure is, Mr. Manners."

Woof!

After having combed through the house from top to bottom, it was bare except for a few essentials, a bedroom set that both Elegant and Gem loved and Pee-Pot bought for them (wedding present, of course), a kitchen set that they too loved (a wedding present from Tommie), and washcloths and towels (courtesy of Gyp, so Pee-Pot claimed). Also, there was an icebox and a stove and a kitchen table in the kitchen and food in the ice box. It was a nine-room house, perfect for grandchildren, Pastor Loving had remarked in passing.

But even more amazing to Gem and Elegant was all their clothes were moved into the house, Pastor Loving and Francine (before going back to Spelman College) doing the honors. And Pee-Pot and Tommie doing the same for Elegant.

———

"Gem, can, I mean, can you believe any of this happened?" Elegant said, brushing his teeth at the shiny porcelain bathroom sink. "The scheme, how it played out? The exquisite timing of it?"

Gem entered the bathroom wearing a robe. Her hair was down, lying across her shoulders. "Mama, and especially Francine, would be proud of Papa." Pause.

"We owe the men of the Body of Christ a lot."

"It took them three weeks, Elegant, after Papa bought it to do all the work on the house. If you only saw it before, how Mr. Parson kept it. After all, he was elderly and lived alone for many years before he died so …"

Elegant spit the toothpaste into the sink.

"I love this community, Gem. We'll never move from here," Elegant said, rinsing out the toothbrush and then putting it inside the wall medicine cabinet.

He held her and then let go of her limply. It was Gem's turn to brush her teeth at the sink.

"What's wrong, Elegant?"

"Now I have to get back to the business of boxing. Of being a boxer again."

"Elegant, after all, you are a fighter."

"I know. The honeymoon's over." Pause. "It's what Mr. Manners reminded me of—boy, did he ever."

"Thought so," Gem laughed.

Gem put the toothbrush away and then joined Elegant, sitting partially on his knee.

"I'm about to begin fighting as a heavyweight. My next bout, in fact."

"I know."

"I have to prove myself all over again. In a brand-new division."

"And you're nervous," Gem said, lifting Elegant's chin. "Aren't you?"

"Somewhat. A lot's expected of me. Two world titles, going for a third."

"You'll do fine," Gem said, kissing Elegant's forehead.

"That's all you've got to—"

"Elegant, I'm going to do it!" Gem said, springing off his leg.

"Do, do what!"

Elegant stood.

"I just decided."

"Okay, now, let's—"

"Miss Atwood's job. Principal. That's the new challenge for me."

"Oh, right. Right, Gem, r-right."

"I can fight for the students that way. Have a say, voice in curriculum. Books, materials, perceptions of our students. It all meshes, Elegant. Me being the voice for our black children in the county."

"You'll do a great job, Gem!"

"Papa talks about a calling. I guess this is mine."

They were making their way into the bedroom. When they got there, Gem headed straight for the bed.

"A new bed," she said, patting it with her hand. "Hmmm ..."

Elegant's right eyebrow arched.

"Looks like we have to break it in, Elegant, don't we?" Gem said, removing her bathrobe, standing there in her slip. "Slowly ..."

"Gem, I can't believe how—"

"Irresistible I am?" Gem said, slipping into bed.

"No, naughty. A preacher's daughter."

"But a fighter's wife ..."

"Oh, so you're going to blame it on me now?" Elegant said, removing his bathrobe.

"Flora, move over," Gem said, taking Flora off the bed. She'd been lying back against the sham. Gem put her in the chair.

"I'm glad they didn't forget her, Elegant. When they moved everything."

"Me too."

He was in his boxer shorts.

"Elegant, uh, you are going to turn off the lights, aren't you?"

"Right. Right. The lights!"

"Sex is sexier that way, I've discovered"

"Gem, we're going to have to talk … really …"

"But not now, Elegant."

Elegant rushed across the bedroom floor to turn off the lights.

———

Elegant rolled over in the bed.

He kissed Gem's neck.

"Mmmm …"

Then she became fully conscious.

"Roadwork?"

"Roadwork."

Of course it was five thirty.

Elegant hopped out of bed and into the dark morning. He'd put his gear on a chair (on his side of the bed) with his boxing shoes beneath it. He gathered everything in his arms, walked into the bathroom, and popped on the bathroom light and then washed and dressed.

He couldn't wait to do his roadwork. But then without warning, he got a sharp prick in the pit of his stomach, for he'd be doing it without Gyp under this new arrangement.

"Gyp."

Was this going to be new? Elegant thought. He'd traded Gyp in for Gem. He didn't want to think of it this way, in such stark, poignant terms—but he had. He really had. Gyp had now been substituted for, in a way, in the process—in this new life of his. He didn't want to feel sad. Why should he feel sad when waking up to Gem, her knowing his routine, even though he no longer worked at the brickyard, for the Miller Brothers, since his fighting now had made him wealthy.

"Just do your roadwork. Just do your roadwork!"

But he had to wonder what Gyp was doing, he had to. It would be unfair to Gyp, to who they were and their times and memories together, if he didn't.

Back in the bedroom, he kissed Gem a second time.

"I'll have breakfast ready for us when you get back, Elegant."

"Gem, you don't—"

She kissed his lips.

"Don't worry about me. Just go!"

"Okay. See you when I get back."

He was out of the room, and Gem was out of the bed.

Jogging down the hall and then down the staircase and then into the kitchen, Elegant opened the back door and was greeted by a beautiful gray moon and bright stars. It was going to feel odd without Gyp to run with, Elegant thought, taking his first short steps down the back porch stairs.

"All right, here—"

Woof!

"Gyp, Gyp," Elegant said, astonished. "Is, is that you? Is it, girl!"

Gyp rounded the corner of the house.

"Gyp! Gyp, it's you, Gyp!"

Elegant scooped Gyp up into his arms, and Gyp lathered his face with her tongue. "I can't believe this!"

Gyp squirmed out of Elegant's arms.

"Okay. Okay. Okay, Gyp!"

Gyp was back on the ground.

Both looked out onto the grounds, onto the hills, out onto what they would have to discover, conquer together, as if it were pristine, untouched, no one the wiser or more knowledgeable as to where trails were plotted out for the run. Gyp not to lead to teach Elegant the way this time around but Gyp and Elegant sharing equal responsibility for creating new paths, the breaking of new ground, as if destroying, demystifying old ones, tossing them aside, to the wind, while creating new stories, myths, for themselves on a morning that seemed open for overripe adventure.

The eggs were just right. The sausage, the grits—Gem Raines could cook!

As soon as Elegant got into the house, there Gem was to towel him off. She wasn't surprised by what Gyp did. Pee-Pot had pretty much hinted to her that she would do what she did this morning—that Elegant wouldn't "get off the hook that easy." So when she heard Gyp in the backyard, she wasn't in the least surprised, even though she'd told Elegant she was just so not to dampen the excitement of a very exciting morning for them: waking up in their new house her father bought them.

"I don't know who stumbled more in the woods, me or Gyp, Gem. Honestly."

"I bet you and Gyp will do much better tomorrow."

Elegant stood and collected the plates.

"Thanks," Gem said.

"It was a lot of fun though. I think we got seven miles in." Pause.

"But Gyp and I will figure it out."

"Why don't you clock yourselves, Elegant?"

"Good idea." Pause. "Why didn't I think of that?"

"It's just that you and Gyp are so conditioned to the old run—"

"Right. Right."

"That you want everything to seem natural, I suppose," Gem said, looking back at Elegant with what seemed a question mark on her face.

"Natural. You're absolutely right."

The water was pouring over the plates and glasses and silverware.

"Now for the gym, in a few hours. After my layoff."

"Honeymoon, you mean."

"I stand corrected: honeymoon. But I have a feeling Mr. Manners isn't going to care, that it's not going to matter to him one way or the other what it's called. He's still going to rake me over the coals."

Elegant, since he no longer worked in the brickyard and Black Moon was long out of the gym, began his workout at eleven o'clock.

Elegant felt Gem's arms snake around him.

"You miss him, don't you?"

"Yes, uh-huh," Elegant said. "What about you?"

"Papa? Yes. But you see how, by a stroke of luck, we're planted right in the middle of them."

"Right, Gem."

"Divine intervention?"

"Could be," Elegant said. Then he said more affirmatively, "Why not?"

"Yes, why not?"

There was a lot to feel good about today besides Gyp showing up for the morning run and him going off to the gym later.

"And so, it'll be furniture hunting for the next few weeks."

Gem was back sitting at the kitchen table, Elegant still over at the sink.

"I wish you'd come along with me."

Elegant's finger wagged. "Now, Gem ... we decided."

"I know," she said glumly.

"That you would—"

"Surprise you." Pause. "But what if ..."

"But what if what?"

"I fail miserably. You hate what I buy."

"You!"

"Yes, me."

"Now that's funny. You know I have every confidence in you. Whatever you buy."

"Me too!" Gem said, clapping her hands. "I can't wait to get started!"

Strangely, Elegant stared at her.

"Oh, I was just feigning modesty before. That's all."

"Uh, right, right."

"It's going to be so much fun. A joy. Yes, it's probably better I work alone. There'll be less fuss that way."

"Oh, what you really meant to say is interference from me. Your husband."

"As long as you don't make me send anything I buy back."

Gem walked over to Elegant. "You promise?"

"I promise," Elegant said, crossing his heart.

"How about we seal it with a kiss?"

"Mmm ... I'll start with the living room, of course. Of course ..."

"By the way, Gem, what are you singing in church this Sunday?"

"Oh, 'This Little Light of Mine.'"

"Would you, would you ... uh ... uh ..." Elegant's hand was encouraging Gem.

"Sing!" Gem said incredulously. "Elegant, it's too early. Sing? No, no!"

It was six forty-nine.

"I'd probably sound like I have a frog in my throat."

Gem's school day began at nine. She always got to Longwood High School at eight fifteen. In the past, her father drove her; now Elegant would. The two days of school she'd missed were awarded to her by Principal Atwood for the excellent work she was doing. And this morning she would inform her she would step into her shoes as principal for the new school year beginning in the fall.

"Gem," Elegant said as Gem was about to leave the kitchen, "I didn't know life could be like this. This good."

And it made Gem take quick account of what Elegant just said to her with such total, complete conviction and sincerity, for she still didn't know that much about Elegant's life, the one before he got to Longwood, West Virginia, from View Point, Texas.

"I love you, Gem."

"I love you, Elegant."

But there would come a time for him, not her, Gem thought as she walked through the bare-roomed living room, when Elegant would bear his soul, all his scars. And this was how she must always express her love for him on a much deeper level, was to be patient, silent, accepting, wait for him to lift the curtain on his life for it could be examined in vivid detail, truthfully—thoroughly convinced that that time for him and them had finally arrived.

CHAPTER 23

Everything was clicking beautifully together for Elegant and Gem. Gem had started with the house's living room, furnishing it elegantly (pardon the pun) for her and Elegant. On the ground floor, there was a room for a study. A sofa—that would be next on the shopping list.

And now Gem was going through a crash course program on becoming a principal, all the administrative details of the job—its responsibilities. And as usual, her attitude and brilliance made everything look like a breeze, not work.

And Elegant had stepped back inside the ring as a heavyweight at 198 pounds. Again, yes, he would have to prove himself to the fans and media. And as it always was from going from a lighter division to a heavier one, was his power, its effectiveness, and the opponent's power, its effect in the transition.

Well, the fans and the media never got to see if Elegant could take the power of either fifteenth-ranked Joe "Steamroller" Jankowski or fourteenth-ranked Oscar Hernandez, for he left Steamroller's body spread out on the canvas in 2:27 seconds of the first round. And as for Oscar Hernandez, he quit after the second round from two extraordinary body shots delivered to the same, identical spot. Oscar Hernandez simply held onto the ring ropes, took a knee, grimaced in great pain, and said damned if he was going to continue.

So chinwise the book was still open on Elegant, but powerwise, he'd quieted any critics he might have with his two impressive and decisive wins. He would fight every two months in his march, until he was solidly positioned into the heavyweight picture. This was the plan the team of

Hollins formulated. This was the ultimate prize for Elegant, to become heavyweight champion of the world and hold onto the crown for as long as he was able.

But as well as Elegant's career was going, Tommie's was its antithesis. He was still fighting and still splendid and was ranked number five in the welterweight division. But suddenly no one wanted to fight him. He'd hit a roadblock, a blockade: he was too good, so everyone was avoiding Tommie Lathers, the higher-ranked fighters in the division. But far more sinister was, as a sportswriter wrote in his daily column, talent isn't rising in the welterweight division but corruption. Fixed fights. For the article pointed its accusatory finger at the mob, the syndicate, the "unofficial ruling body," when there was a lack of a ruling body, a jurisdiction with any power, muscle, or will when the polluters of the sport—the article continued—controlled it with iron fists.

Tommie was now fighting for Collingsworth Hollins, not just Elegant. He'd become his manager for his past four fights, and even his clean money couldn't break the stranglehold the mob forced on the division. It was, literally, sucking the blood out of it and, more directly, out of Tommie.

Tommie had been out of the ring for three months, something, to him, that seemed an eternity. There were no more exciting boxing cards with him and Elegant twin billed, headlining the show. This stopped, this routine, this ritual, a few fights back. There were rumors (all true) that he was drinking heavily and more often. Only, it still hadn't impacted his training or conditioning. But Tommie was souring on the fight game. When he was drunk, it poured out of him through impetuous, uncontrollable verbal ramblings. But feelings that were shorn and laid out all too emotionally bare: coherent, forceful, lucid—how he hated his life that suddenly had slumped, slowed down to a crawl.

It's why tonight Tommie was at Gem and Elegant's house. It's why Pee-Pot was there in the house too. It's why Gem had cooked dinner for them. And she was out of the dining room, and the three sat at the brand-new dining room table Gem ordered by catalogue two months ago and received three days ago.

Pee-Pot said they had to boost Tommie's confidence back to where it'd been, and needless to say, Elegant agreed. It was their number one priority,

Tommie. He was Tommie Lathers Sr.'s son to Pee-Pot and a brother to Elegant.

Elegant was at the head of the table (man of the house), Pee-Pot to his left, and Tommie to his right. Gem had sat at the bottom of the table.

Tommie, who'd been cracking jokes up till now, picked up the buffed cake knife, viewed it, and then laid it down on the table. Then he looked at the uncut lemon cake Gem left on the table for dessert for Elegant to cut. Then unconsciously, it seemed, Tommie picked the cake knife back up and began twirling it.

"I know why you got me here at the house," Tommie said, looking over at Pee-Pot and then at Elegant.

"You know why, Tommie?"

"Yes, sir, Mr. Manners: things ain't going like they oughta. I'd like, sir. Ain't going so tough for me. With things in my life. Me getting down, sir."

"I know, son."

"Right, Tommie."

"And you and Elegant, sir, you don't want me to. Ain't for it."

"No, Tommie," Pee-Pot said. "It's the worst thing that can happen to a fighter."

"Just don't know no bastards could do this to me. Like this!"

"I know, Tommie. It's when the fight business stinks. You wanna heave up your guts," Pee-Pot said disgustedly. "I've ... I've seen it all too much."

"Corruption, Mr. Manners?"

"Corruption, Elegant. Poison the whole fight game. Stink it up from top to bottom." Silence.

"Tommie, listen now, son," Pee-Pot said, leaning forward, "Mr. Hollins and I want you to fight."

"Who, Mr. Manners? Who?" Tommie asked eagerly.

"R-Ron Darcy."

"Him! That bum! I beat him twice! Twice already!" Tommie said, irate. "Twice, Mr. Manners. Twice!"

"Now hold on, Tommie, listen, listen to me ... You-you've gotta stay active, you've—"

"But I ain't gonna learn nothing from the fight, Mr. Manners. You know I ain't. I-I fought that boy twice, knocked him out in the fourth round both times. What you want, Mr. Manners? Me to knock him out in three, t-two this time!"

"Tommie, Tommie, I'm sorry," Pee-Pot pleaded, "but they won't fight you right now."

Tommie clenched his fist, lifted it up, and it looked like he was about to bring it crashing down onto the dining room table but didn't. But there were tears building in his eyes. "But what'd I do, Mr. Manners, Elegant, I do …?"

"Nothing, Tommie. Nothing."

"Aint, ain't did nothing to deserve this. For them, them people to treat me like this," Tommie sobbed.

For Pee-Pot, it was like sitting at the dining room table, across from Tommie, and seeing a dream destroyed. How many times in his life had he seen this scene play itself out with a fighter? And no matter how many times he saw it, it didn't matter; it was still heart wrenching to see someone who put so much of himself into something suffer as Tommie was. It harkened back to the days he was active in the ring. The fights that should've been made but weren't. The fight contracts that should've been signed but weren't. All the fixes and dives that were "in." All the cowardly men smoking the top-dollar cigars, burning the fighter's career up in flames.

He knew Tommie's stomach was burning, was flaming. It's how it feels, Pee-Pot thought. You don't cry out of self-pity but out of self-realization that something is being taken from you. That something will never be the same again. That you've lost trust, faith in so many things. So many things. So many things.

"I'll fight him, Mr. Manners … I'll fight him …"

This practically broke Pee-Pot's heart hearing it.

Pee-Pot was leaving the house. He'd said good night to Gem, kissing her. Gem had gone back into the study to prepare tomorrow's school lesson.

"I think we did some good, don't you?" Pee-Pot said, tugging on the bill of his checkered cap.

"A lot, sir."

"The psychological dimensions, range of this are amazing, Elegant."
"I know."
"No, I'm sorry, you don't, you don't," Pee-Pot said avuncularly. "Not until you've experienced it. It's happened to you. You can only imagine how it feels."
"Yes, yes, sir."
Pee-Pot hugged Elegant and then stepped off the porch, making his way to the Studebaker.
"Gyp told me to tell you she'll see you in the morning."
"Yes, she will, Mr. Manners."
"And, oh, Elegant, that dining room table of Gem's was sure worth waiting for, wasn't it? A beauty. Gorgeous wood."
"Yes, sir, it was."
On Garland Road, Pee-Pot honked.
They'd moved out of the living room and into the dining room, so it's where Tommie was.
"G-gonna do my best, Elegant," Tommie said, punching his fist into his hand.
Does Tommie mean it? Elegant thought.
"G-gotta take what comes. Comes along. Even if I gotta fight a bum like Ron Darcy a thousand times. Fight me bad fights."
It's what Tommie was calling a lot of the fighters ranked below him lately: bums. Ron Darcy was ranked ninth in the welterweight division.
"Can I say something …?"
"What, me stop you? Ha. Man, what, you crazy!"
"It's all going to change for you. It will."
"So, what, keep my chin up, huh?"
Elegant didn't know if Tommie was being sincere or not, but it had nothing to do with him, their personal situation, he was well aware of that, but instead the other things.
"So it don't get hit."
Elegant sat down on the classy chairs Gem purchased.
Tommie was on the couch and clasped his hands together and then laid back. "Ha."
"What, Tommie?"
"Ha."

"What? Let me in on the joke, would you?"

"Ha. Would move up to the middleweight division if I could put me on some weight. Ha. More steam in my punches."

"But ..."

"Yeah, Black Moon, he's ruling the division now. The champ. Shit. Can't kick that boy's ass. Not on a scare, man. Not on Halloween night with a damn bat in my hand, Elegant. Can't."

Gem entered the room.

"What's so funny," Gem asked cautiously. "I heard you two all the way in the study."

"Oh, nothing, Gem, noth—"

"Gem, you inviting me by for dinner tomorrow night too? Heck, seen all them leftovers you got."

"Tommie," Gem said sweetly, "you're invited by every day of the week."

"Gem, I ain't that hungry!"

Now Tommie was out on the house's front porch with Elegant, having bid Gem good night with a hug and a kiss.

"You and Mr. Manners ... thanks. B-but it ain't been easy, Elegant."

"I know."

"But I gotta get back in the ring. It's been killing me. Bad, bad."

Elegant recalled his first few weeks in Longwood, working out on the farm, in the gym, how it'd killed his spirit, not sparring with anyone, not hitting them. But for Tommie, it was the crowd, missing the crowd and the winning.

"I'm a fighter, Elegant. A fighter. Ain't nothing else. Like, like my daddy was. How Daddy was."

There was more implied. His "daddy," Elegant thought. Why was he inserted into the conversation?

"Thanks," Tommie said, turning and hugging Elegant. "Thanks."

Tommie moved off the porch.

He took a few steps away from the house and then turned back, recovering those steps. "You lucky, Elegant." Pause. "Y-you got Gem."

Elegant smiled mildly.

"Look what you got."

Elegant was at a loss for words.

"Look, man."

Elegant felt at a disadvantage now that Tommie had all the advantage in this thing that was going on.

"Man, I should, oughta slow down, Elegant. Oughta, oughta slow down, man."

Elegant still didn't know how to respond.

"Angel's Corner, all them girls—getting tired of it. That shit. Every Friday night. Don't enjoy it like I useta. L-like b-before."

"You can, you can do something about it, Tommie. I know you can."

Tommie kicked the dirt like he was kicking at a tin can in the road. "What I was thinking, Elegant. How I was trying, trying to refocus my thinking and all." Pause.

"Start living a clean life, a good life. Look for a girl. Pardon, uh, young lady like Gem, Elegant. Know it ain't easy to find one like her, but if I don't try, man, never gonna find her. Ain't never, Elegant. Shit."

———

Elegant walked into the study where Gem was.

Gem turned. "Elegant … how's Tommie?"

Gem knew what tonight's dinner was about—Elegant had told her.

"He's my best friend, do you know that, Gem? Tommie's my best friend in life, Tommie Lathers."

Many times her father had told her of people like Tommie Lathers, who tried bearing their pain, their suffering alone, not as some martyrdom but so not to burden others with their burden.

"You got Tommie to talk. Talk out his feelings."

"Yes."

"That was important."

"Yes."

Elegant walked over to her. He put his hands on her shoulders. He rubbed them, what proved to soothe her.

"Tommie's looking at our lives and envisioning it as his, his own."

Gem's forehead cropped.

"He envisions it as ideal, Gem."

"Do you think that's healthy?"

"I don't know," Elegant said, shaking his head. "Really, I don't."

Gem's hands were holding Elegant's as Elegant continued rubbing Gem's shoulders from behind.

"But it's a positive image. Tommie needs to put positive images in his mind right now."

"Agreed," Gem said.

"I love the guy so much."

Then Elegant looked down on the top of the desk to see what Gem was doing, or wasn't doing.

"That's not schoolwork that you're—"

"I'm writing Francine. Do you mind?"

"Writing Francine, but Francine just left for school."

"So?"

"Gem …"

"Francine and I still have a lot to talk about."

"Like what?"

"Elegant, remember, you're my husband, not my warden."

"Right, I'll try to remember that—for the future."

"Do. Please do."

"By the way, Mr. Manners said the dining room table, it was worth the wait. It's a beauty."

"He never ages, does he, Elegant?"

"Gem, how can I say that when I haven't known him as long as you."

"Well, believe me, he hasn't."

"Nor will he," Elegant said.

"Nor will he," Gem said.

"At least, finally, we agree on something!"

———

Tommie fought Ron Darcy, and instead of pasting him in four rounds, he pasted him in two. It was the only clear challenge Tommie saw for himself, the challenge to surpass his two previous performances against Darcy. But the fight did nothing to nourish his spirit. He was still in the same rut as before. The fight did nothing to improve his ranking, change the picture in the welterweight division, the corruption, its malaise.

Pee-Pot nor Elegant would question their motives to get Tommie back in the ring, but it'd done him no good. In preparation for the fight, there were the occasional glimpses, flashes of the old Tommie Lathers, but it was just fighting Darcy ("a bum"), pretending it meant something for him when all along he knew, in his heart, it didn't. It's what sank the effort.

Currently, it was at the point where Pee-Pot was afraid for Collingsworth Hollins to arrange another fight below Tommie's ranking. Surely it would be another fighter he had fought and defeated. Surely it would spell gloom for Tommie, catapult him into a new melancholy, make him feel as if he were treading water. Would cause him to call his next opponent a bum, not show the kind of respect Tommie always showed another fighter up till now. Up until his career was stalled, subjected to this bad period in his life no one was changing.

CHAPTER 24

Pee-Pot and Elegant were on the road in New Orleans's Victory Arena to fight Bad Henry Barnes, the eleventh-ranked heavyweight in the division. Barnes was a young black heavyweight like him who showed great promise. He was a two-fisted slugger who moved well inside the ring, much better than most heavyweights his size: six foot four, 226 pounds. In fact, this was the test fight fans were looking for to challenge Elegant Raines. Someone, they felt, who punched just as hard as him since the one blemish they'd cite when they spoke of Elegant Raines, when they picked out a chink in his armor, was the Black Moon Johnson fight, when Black Moon cracked two of Elegant's ribs in their violent four-round tiff.

That was the fight when Elegant had to hold on for dear life for his survival. Black Moon had damaged him. He'd hurt him, and it had taken all his bravery, heart, guts, and survival skills to beat him—finally punish him and knock him out. This was what the fight world expected tonight between Elegant Raines and Bad Henry Barnes, an all-out war, a survival-of-the-fittest kind of contest between two heavy hitters. Elegant was entering the fight in the best physical and mental condition of his life. The training, the home life—him and Gem. He'd never felt better, more complete, more satisfied, more ready to fight a man.

He was at the top of his game. He was coming in at 205 pounds, and Barnes could hit him with a wrecking ball, and he'd still be standing as tall as the Empire State Building.

Bad Henry Barnes was 22–0: twenty wins by knockout.

It was round three of the fight and Elegant had let Bad Henry Barnes do to him what no fighter, other than Black Moon, had ever done: pressure him into a corner and trap him there. Barnes's booming jabs had actually put Elegant there, in that precarious position, and Victory Arena was going wild, insane, for Elegant had decided to fight his way out of the corner, not hold on, not try to grab and clinch the bigger, taller, stronger fighter but go toe to toe with him. And while Bad Henry was trying to find openings to deliver his blasting, telling body shots, Elegant was selective, meticulously picking out openings of his own by throwing snappy, clean uppercuts, punches going straight up the middle gut, one followed by another and then another until he heard Bad Henry grunt, groan, and then begin backing off him. Barnes's body shots had become less effective, less damaging. Elegant had rallied himself. He'd worked himself out of the corner and now was driving Barnes backward with one meaty jab after the other until he'd trapped him in the opposite corner.

Bad Henry's eyes dampened, his breathing became scant, waning. His gloves dropped slowly down to his waist. His torso bent forward too, but occasionally, Barnes's right hand pawed feebly at Elegant.

It was the hard short shot to Barnes's liver that did the damage. It sailed Bad Henry's body off the ring ropes. It made him stumble a few feet from the middle of the ring. The short referee's body shadowed Barnes. Bad Henry had fallen prostrate onto the canvas with a clamor, a thud, with the authority of a man of his size, strength, and great overall length.

Elegant had spoken to Gem by phone. It was after eleven o'clock. Pee-Pot hadn't been in the hotel room long.

"So you weren't worried, Mr. Manners?"

They'd been reviewing the Barnes fight.

"We've done enough of these things together, Elegant. The boy was dangerous, but there's nobody as smart as you, son, in the ring. Don't know if there's ever been—to my knowledge."

"He was tough though, sir."

"Good and tough. I don't see anybody in the top five as good as him.

It's why Domenic Botti's got no worries for now. He can just coast. Can rule over everybody till we arrive. Can take the crown from him."

Elegant was sitting on the bed and then laid his head back on the pillow. He was lying on the bedspread; the bed was still made.

"Miss him, don't you?"

"A lot, Mr. Manners. I can't get used to him not being with us, sir. In the boxing arenas."

"Me either, Elegant. But Mr. Hollins said he's gonna try to fix that for us with the next promotion he does. Get you and Tommie back together on the next fight card again."

"I hope so, Mr. Manners. I really do, sir."

Pee-Pot stood. "I wish I was God at times, Elegant. Guess we all do."

"Yes, sir."

"Fix things the way they oughta be fixed in the universe. So people don't have to suffer so much."

"Yes, sir."

"Good night."

"Good night, Mr. Manners." Pause.

"But it'll be a new year—"

It was December 2.

"Soon. I believe in a new year, Elegant. A fresh start. New horizons."

This was the dark side of Tommie Lathers.

He had fornicated with three girls tonight. It was the Moonlight Motel in Inwood, three quarters of a mile from Angel's Corner. It was just him and them and booze. He didn't have to talk them into a foursome, a four-way—they wanted it. All he had to do was pay for the room and supply the liquor.

He was in a 1948 burgundy Ford Super Deluxe convertible (not the 1941 one or the 1945 one he traded in last year), driving home drunk. He was in the car alone, feeling every drop of liquor in his gut. Tommie wanted to puke, but he never puked. He was too good at being drunk. He was still in Inwood but slowly was making his way into Longwood, would cross into it before long.

"Ought ... oughta be in New Orleans. Oughta ... oughta be in New Orleans ... Victory Arena ..."

One hand was on the steering wheel, the other grabbing at his stomach.

"W-with Elegant, Elegant ... Mr., Mr. Manners. Oughta be ... oughta be, man ..."

But he wasn't, and it was killing him. The world he knew had been shaken, and not for a day or a month but for hundreds of days it felt, for more months than he could stand, than he—

"Can ... can ... can beat alla 'em. Alla 'em. B-beat the hell outta alla 'em t-top f-fighters. B-but they ain't gonna fight me. Ain't ... ain't gonna let me. No-nobody, them, them people ain't gonna let me ... let me ... lay ... lay a glove on 'em, lay ... a fucking glove on 'em ..."

A crippling pain was in Tommie's head. Tommie felt like his head was splitting open. The dark out on Castle Road looked darker. From inside the car, Tommie's eyes looked hard into the front windshield.

"I ... I can make it, can ... I ... I can make it ... I ... I can make it home. Shit, I-I always do ... always ... always ..."

Elegant had it all, championships, belts, fighting for another one, Gem, a wife, a life outside the ring, not just inside it, Tommie thought. He was thinking straight; as long as he thought of Elegant, he was thinking straight.

"I ... I gotta keep thinking of Elegant. Elegant ... Elegant and Gem ... Gem ... Mr. Moore, Mr., Mr. Manners ... Elegant ... They gonna get me home, man, h-home ..."

Not him, he mustn't think of himself, his messed-up crazy life, what he did tonight in the Moonlight Motel's room with those three girls, whores, skanks, no Gem Loving Raines, no girl to make his life special, to make it work like a charm, illumine it, even if he fell down flat on his face, that special girl would prop him back up on his feet, keep doing it until she won and he lost, and then he could beat the hell out of anything, out of life—out of any damned thing!

He was in Longwood.

"Ha ... know this shit like the fucking, fucking palm of my ... my f-fucking hand now ... Ha. Yeah, yeah, yeah ... ha ... ha ... Swing at me, you, you motherfuckers, swing at me ... g-go ahead, swing at ..."

The car was weaving on Moreland Road, and so was Tommie. He sat up straight in the car seat now, gripping the steering wheel stiffly with both hands; he was alert, as if he'd talked sense into himself, made himself sober, that the empty bottles of liquor lying on the motel floor had disappeared, vanished, and it was a new day, and last night was really over, cleaned up, washed away, the cheapness of it.

"Ha. I-I ain't never gonna be champion. Of t-the world ... the world ... I ain't never gonna be one, Mr. Manners, sir ... Them hoods ... h ... mobsters ain't gonna let me be champ, champion of the world. Give me a c-chance. Fucking ... g-got all that fucking money. F-fucking money, man. Man. R-robbing me. Robbing me blind, Mr. Manners ... Blind, blind ...

"Ain't gonna, gonna let Tommie Lathers ... 'come ... 'come champion of the world."

Abruptly, sharply, the car sped up on Moreland Road. Tommie's foot had mashed down on the gas pedal, accelerated the car, and he laughed and then giggled like a kid, not someone who was twenty-two years old trying to get back home, to his house, safe and sound.

"Ha. Ha. Motherfuckers. Motherfuckers. T-they can all go to fucking hell. Fucking hell. Fucking hell. Alla 'em. Ha. S-straight to hell. Hear me, Elegant. Hear, y ... hear me. Ha ..."

And the car, it weaved off Moreland Road; and even in the dark, the big oak tree still stood there, silent and still and solid.

"Beat the hell out the world, Elegant. Beat the hell out the fucking world, man. Man. Shit! Shit! Shit!"

Tommie's foot mashed down on the gas pedal again; the car jumped, accelerated, and then darted.

"No! No! No!"

Tommie saw the oak tree's dark outline in the car's windshield.

"No, Daddy ... Daddy ... No!"

—⁓—

It was 7:27 a.m. New Orleans time.

Pee-Pot was in his hat and robe and slippers. He'd just crossed the hall, and his head fell into the door, and he could barely lift his hand, but did, and rapped on Elegant's door and waited with his head still pressed to the door.

The door opened, and Pee-Pot practically stumbled into Elegant's room.

"Mr. Manners, what's wrong, sir? Mr. Manners!"

Pee-Pot took to the first chair he saw.

Elegant continued to look down at Pee-Pot's hands that covered his face. Pee-Pot's fingers dug into his face. Pee-Pot kept doing it.

"P-please sit, Elegant. You, you gotta sit down, son. Gotta ..."

Elegant was in a bathrobe and slippers. He'd been up. Pee-Pot hadn't awakened him.

Pee-Pot's hands flashed back up to his face, covering it again, and he went back to digging his fingers into it.

"I'm sitting. I'm ..."

Tears ran out Pee-Pot's eyes. "I got the worse news. Worse kind of ... be the bearer of the ... oh, oh ... Elegant," Pee-Pot said, his heart burning.

Elegant was scared.

"It's Tommie. Tommie. It's Tommie. Tommie's dead!"

Elegant's body flew out of the chair.

"Dead! Dead!"

"This morning. This morning. Four o'clock this morning!"

"No, Mr. Manners. No. Tommie's not dead. Tommie's not—he can't be dead!"

"His car hit a tree. Broke ... Tommie broke his neck!"

"No, sir, sir, Mr. Manners. You're mistaken! Mistaken, Mr. Manners!"

Pee-Pot couldn't help him. He simply couldn't.

Elegant fell to the floor. He was prostrate.

"Just got the call. Alton Timms. Just got the ... On ... was Moreland Road. Oh, oh. Oh. I—"

"It can't be, it can't—"

"Somebody heard it. Ran out there. Say they, Alton Timms. Al just called. My room ... Alton Timms ... El-Elegant ... Alton ..."

Gas entered the room. He walked over to a chair and sat down. He was in robe and slippers too.

"Damn ... damn ... damn ..."

Elegant rolled over on his back.

"Damn ...," Gas had said it again.

———

Pee-Pot and Elegant were pallbearers for Tommie's funeral. Ceremonially, they and four other pallbearers lifted and carried Tommie's casket into the Body of Christ Church. They did this with four other pallbearers entering into the church and four different ones leaving the church for the burial. Pee-Pot's Pugilistic Paradise was in shock. Tommie's death had put a chill in the gym's spine, and everyone, it seemed, wanted to be a pallbearer—everyone.

Both of Tommie's parents were buried behind the Body of Christ Church. But for a long time now, this burial ground could not accommodate another plot. So Tommie was buried in Sunrise Cemetery, a few miles south of the Body of Christ Church. Naturally, the gym was shut down for Tommie's funeral. Now there was a pall hanging over the Pug. Pastor Loving, in eulogizing Tommie's life, tried his best to bear witness to the emotional wreckage of a community losing a young person with a great gift, a great talent, and who was well loved by all Longwooders.

It was a long funeral service.

Gem sang.

Elegant cried a lot; he couldn't help it. He openly wept in the church pew.

———

Gem kissed Pee-Pot. Then Pee-Pot turned to Elegant, hugging him warmly. He took their coats. Gyp greeted them as soon as they entered the house and then slipped out into the evening's damp, cold air. There wasn't the usual spark between them: the air was dead. Pee-Pot asked them to come by the house. It was seven thirty. They weren't there for dinner. There'd been no mention of dinner by Pee-Pot, so Gem and Elegant had eaten beforehand, and so too Pee-Pot.

Elegant and Gem had walked into the living room while Pee-Pot hung the coats. Pee-Pot paused before going into the living room. He took full account of himself, it seemed.

The chimney corner, with the wood burning, crackling, heated the room. Elegant's mind, while sitting on the cushioned bench with Gem, traveled back to the first time he sat on the bench when he first came in from View Point, Texas, suitcase in tow, of how nervous he was sitting before Pee-Pot Manners, this man he was coming to as a fighter of Frank "Black Machine" Whaley, the Whaley Gym, and how much he wanted to fight for a man Mr. Whaley revered, exalted, opined as saintly, his heart in his mouth, his hopes strung out on a thin string.

After sitting in the rocker, Pee-Pot smiled, taking everything in and then shutting his eyes, easing back his head, relaxing, seeming to bring the whole tenor of his body into alignment.

"We have to talk, don't we?"

Gem looked at Elegant.

"As family."

"Yes, Mr. Manners," Elegant said.

Gem smiled.

"Have you two done much talking?"

"No, Mr. Manners, we haven't," Gem said.

"With death, you go off in a corner sometime. With it. To be by yourself. To whimper."

They'd all experienced the profound effect of losing loved ones in their lives, grief, and the remedy was always time, which they never thought they could give it, be able to give it, time, time ... And now Tommie's death had that, such brutish impatience to it, as if the pain would never leave them.

"Do you want to talk about Tommie's drinking, Mr. Manners? The guilt I-I still have about ... about it, sir?"

"You weren't gonna be able to stop it," Pee-Pot said frankly. "And I wasn't either."

"W-why, Mr. Manners? W-why not, sir?"

"Because Tommie wanted to drink. He didn't see anything wrong with it. Never did he."

"I-I can't accept that, Mr. Manners," Elegant said, shaking his head from side to side. "I can't accept that, sir. I just can't."

"There're, there're things you've just got to accept, son. Can't turn your eyes from. Accept—"

"Until it kills them, sir!"

Pee-Pot fell silent.

Gem, since Tommie's death, didn't know how to penetrate Elegant's feelings. She'd felt, the past few days, that only Pee-Pot Manners could. And here was their time together, she thought, to push through their emotions with panic and maybe fear but also with the intuition of one helping the other in bringing why Tommie had died into better focus.

"Did he want to die, Mr. Manners? Did Tommie? D-did he want to die!"

Alertly, Pee-Pot straightened himself in the rocker. "What do you mean, Elegant? Suggesting? Suicide!"

"Yes, Mr. Manners. Suicide, sir, suicide." Pause. "You mean you haven't thought it?"

"No. No, uh, I haven't … haven't …," Pee-Pot said, lowering his head. "And, and you have?"

"It's all I've thought, sir. Since it, this … this so-called accident happened."

"Suicide …?"

"Yes, suicide. His career, Mr. Manners. T-Tommie's career. Bums, bums. He'd begun calling the fighters he fought bums, sir. What they were … became to him, Mr. Manners."

"No, no," Pee-Pot said spiritedly. "I can't believe that, Elegant. Not about Tommie. I can't."

"Why not, sir!"

"I won't!"

"Didn't his father? Didn't he, Mr. Manners?"

Gem couldn't believe the sadness she saw in Pee-Pot's eyes.

"Oh … oh … that. That was different. So much different than this. What happened here. To Tommie."

"How, Mr. Manners?"

"Mr. Lathers, Tommie Lathers Sr. was an old fighter, Elegant. An old fighter who didn't know how to quit the ring. L-leave it, that's all. Who had old glories in him. You see. Old wins … victories."

Hearing something spoken like this saddened Gem: it made her feel a fighter's soul.

"But, but Tommie, he, he saw no future for himself in the division …

the welterweight division, Mr. Manners. He didn't, sir," Elegant said forcibly.

"But I told him to wait, Elegant. To wait. That his time would come."

"I know you did. Tommie told me."

"I-I think he was drunk. It's what I think. And, and the car spun out of control. Think … what I think. That, that Tommie didn't see the tree. Or, or if he did, Elegant, it was too late. There was nothing at that point he could do."

Elegant rose out of bed.

Gem felt him. She realized it wasn't five thirty but much earlier (her body knew this by now). Elegant's gear was on the chair, and he went there and took it off the chair and stooped to get his boxing shoes.

Elegant darted into the bathroom.

Once finished dressing in the bathroom, Elegant darted back into the bedroom.

Elegant kissed Gem's forehead.

Gem opened her eyes. "You're going to run early this morning, Elegant?" she asked, for she wasn't going to pretend she was sleeping.

"Yes, Gem."

"Have a good run."

Elegant kissed Gem's lips.

He darted out of the room.

All night in bed he'd been restless, Gem thought. He was still convinced Tommie had killed himself, had committed suicide, that Mr. Manners, no matter how hard he tried, couldn't convince him different.

"Elegant's going to run without Gyp this morning."

She knew he really wanted to be alone, do whatever he had to be alone.

Gem looked over at Flora's outline in the chair suddenly, as if Flora could help her, but then she shut her eyes. She said nothing to her.

Elegant was out in the cold morning air, and he wanted to feel free, free of worry, free of pain, free of any earthly chains binding him, clamping him in. He had to be a part of life but wanted to feel separated from it for now. But this morning he had to seek out the future, what had been ground in his bones that even the months without it couldn't change, slip him out of some past he held so sacred, sacrosanct, that he cherished it with every stride he now took toward that place, toward that element, toward a destiny he wanted not only for himself, but once he and Tommie had combined to become what they'd become, for Tommie too.

It was the running of the hills, the land, the sacrificing that must be made to become a world's champion in the ring. It was the honor in it when you go to the gym and are among other fighters who've done the same daily roadwork, miles, too. There was the honor in sweat, Elegant thought. There was the honor in words, as in Shakespeare. There was honor. Tommie's life was honorable. Tommie's life had nobility. He tried his best, Elegant thought. He wanted what was best for himself and others. He was the one who made him feel at home in Pee-Pot's Pugilistic Paradise. He was the one with the big smile and big heart—who made that first day in the gym a good one for him, manageable, memorable. He was the one who rooted for him in the boxing arenas they fought in, the fight towns, who cheered him on to victory, who wanted as much for him as he wanted for himself.

This morning's run had to be about this, about honoring Tommie not through words but through sweat. Honoring him through some kind of imperishable, invincible sweat that only fighters like him and Tommie know about and work up somewhere deep in their spirit, giving almost everything a purity, a worth, a tangible dignity, with genuine, stalwart effort.

Gyp heard him no matter how silent he thought he was fleeting across the field but was back on the farm property. Gyp got up off the living room's royal-blue throw rug, her ears pricked by his movement. She knew Elegant would be back. She was awake and was waiting for his return, to run for the building without her but to still run for it as if she were with him.

Gyp whimpered and then made her way up the narrow stairs like she did on any other morning when the back door wasn't open, because it wasn't warm but cold, and Pee-Pot had to let her out of the house so to go off to Elegant's house.

In bed, Pee-Pot had been tossing and turning. This evening's meeting had done some good but not enough to quell the ugly mention of suicide, of Tommie taking his life—which he hadn't considered, only Elegant. Elegant had gone, possibly, deeper, far deeper than he had in trying to figure out Tommie's psychic condition, what actually happened out on Moreland Road. Tommie drunk behind the car's steering wheel at four o'clock in the morning. Every day a trainer looks into a fighter's eyes to look sometimes into his soul, and other times into his mind. It was only that he thought he had this whole thing figured out, yet how clear was it, or how murky. How much of Tommie Lathers didn't he see? Did he miss when he looked?

"G-Gyp."

He'd heard her whimper outside his bedroom door.

Pee-Pot knew it wasn't time for him to let Gyp out of the house to go over to Elegant's.

But Pee-Pot got out of the bed. He was in his long johns and thick woolen socks. He searched for his slippers.

"Okay, Gyp. I heard you."

Gyp had whimpered again.

Pee-Pot opened the door. "Why, Gyp? Why? Why go out for Elegant so early, Gyp?"

Pee-Pot stooped over to pet Gyp, but Gyp turned and walked away.

"What's troubling you, Gyp? What's wrong?"

Pee-Pot couldn't make sense out of it, none of it, so he followed Gyp to the staircase, where she already had made her descent down the stairs but wasn't at the front door, the door Pee-Pot let her out of to get off to Elegant's.

Pee-Pot turned on another light. "This is strange. Y-you're acting strange, Gyp, this morning."

Pee-Pot was in the kitchen. Gyp was at the back door. Pee-Pot stooped over again and pet Gyp this time. Gyp couldn't elude him. Her body was against the door.

"It … it's four thirty-five, Gyp," Pee-Pot said, looking up at the kitchen clock.

Pee-Pot reached for the doorknob. Gyp scooted back from the door. And then Pee-Pot opened the back door and he heard something, like some distant thunder echo in his ears.

Gyp ran off, but to the back of the house, and Pee-Pot saw her, and he stepped out onto the cold porch and saw the building was lit.

"Elegant, Elegant. Elegant's in there!"

Quickly Pee-Pot ducked back into the house.

Gyp was at the building but didn't go inside. She just lay down on the ground to the right side of the door.

Pee-Pot came out of the house in a robe, a heavy coat, with boots on. The farther he got, the more he could see. The moonlight creased the sky, one side brighter than the other until he saw Gyp. But what led Pee-Pot was the sound of thunder, of pent-up anger, of Elegant hitting the heavy bag with all his might, ferocity. It's what it had to be—it was the only thing it could be: Elegant's fists as he'd never heard them before.

Gyp looked up at Pee-Pot, and Gyp felt a power in Pee-Pot, and Pee-Pot felt a power in Gyp, for both understood well why Elegant was in the building, why it must be here where his fury must be unleashed, not on the jog, not in the Pug, but here, on this property, where it could be just between the three of them, intimate, uncensored, and violent.

Quietly, Pee-Pot stepped into the building, and he saw Elegant banging the heavy bag from behind him, stripped down to his trunks, sweating, his ebony body glistening. He hit the bag with one powerful punch after the other, prompting Pee-Pot to say in the door's dark shadow.

"Elegant could kill a man with those blows."

Tommie had unleashed this in Elegant, but it was being aimed at something else. It had to be, Pee-Pot thought. With that kind of pure anger in him.

CHAPTER 25

August 1951

"I don't believe it, Gem. I don't believe it!"

"Well, start, because I'm pregnant!"

Elegant started the car. He glanced over at Gem. Tenderly his hand patted her stomach.

"Just think a baby's inside here."

"Not just any baby—it's our baby."

"Our baby. Our baby."

They were in front of Dr. Maxwell Glover's red brick building. Gem had all the definitive symptoms necessary to be pregnant. All she needed was confirmation—a doctor's confirmation, that is.

"Who do we tell first, Gem?"

"Papa, of course!"

Elegant's hand was still on Gem's stomach. She lifted his hand from her stomach and then kissed it, looking into Elegant's eyes that were looking as intensely into hers.

"You were thinking about Mr. Manners and Gyp, weren't you, Elegant? Tell me the truth."

"Yes," Elegant laughed.

"Thought so."

"You look so beautiful, Gem," Elegant said, now holding Gem's face in his hand. "So beautiful, pregnant."

"I feel it too."

"And you'll grow even more beautiful as our baby grows inside you ... You'll have this glow, special glow, then."

Gem's school year was in a few weeks. But being a principal, she was still engaged with many administrative duties during the summer, vacation time—it was just the students weren't back in school, that's all.

"I hope Papa's home."

"Me too!"

"It's hard keeping up with his schedule these days."

"It's funny ..."

"Elegant, what?"

"How we all must adjust, find our way ... You know what I mean, Gem?"

"Yes."

"Pastor Loving, when we married. Adjusting. Finding a way. Mr. Manners—"

"Right, adjusting."

Now there was silence.

"Tommie would've been really happy for us today, Gem."

———

Gem sang in church this morning, and Pastor Loving had said from the pulpit, "Two people sang this morning: Gem and my grandchild!" And he'd said it like he really believed it—that it wasn't just an overzealous grandfather-to-be who, already, was overindulging his grandchild.

"Gem! Gem!"

Gem was startled out her sleep.

The night lamp popped on. Elegant had turned the light on.

"Is, is the baby all right? Is the baby all right!"

Gem's shocked face startled Elegant.

"Oh, I'm sorry, Gem. I'm sorry ..."

Elegant sobbed. He laid his head across Gem's stomach. Gem still hadn't recovered but began caressing the top of Elegant's head.

"The, the baby's all right. The baby's all right."

"Yes, it is, Elegant. The baby is."

Their bodies were under the heavy quilt, being late February. But

Elegant was sweating, his back and forehead specifically, a blotch of sweat in his long johns, was fresh and damp.

"Gem, I-I had a horrible nightmare."

Elegant came up to her, his head, since Gem had propped herself up, shifted the pillow to her back.

"There's been so much loss in my life. I-I don't want to lose anything else, Gem."

This nightmare had its origins in the past, a past Gem knew so little of, where Elegant Raines really came from (for she always had her doubts). Who Elegant Raines really was, not as a person but what had shaped him. And she was still waiting for answers, for him to finally confess his past (for it's what it felt like it must be: a confession), to shine light on it.

"We won't lose the baby, Elegant."

"I-I can't say that, Gem."

"God's will be done."

"After what I've been through, I can't say that."

Maybe it will happen tonight, now, Gem thought. Right now.

"I love God, I have faith ... but I can't say that, Gem. I can't, just can't ..."

His head was on her shoulder. She kissed his forehead and wiped his sweat, sweat that continued to moisten it.

"I haven't had that nightmare in a long time. In ... Why can't I tell you my past, Gem? Why is it so restricted? Off-limits to everyone?"

"I don't know, Elegant. Why—"

"I want to ..." Pause.

"But I can't. It's not like I don't know what I'm doing. I'm not conscious of it. It's just that I can't tell anyone. You or Mr. Manners, the people I love. It's too horrible a past. Too violent. I couldn't explain it. Know how. My heart's too full of hate."

"Hate?"

"H-hate and revenge. Hate and revenge. I ... I ..."

Gem's eyes were teary. Relatively speaking, they were newly married, and their courtship hadn't been long, not like customary courtships in Longwood. And during most of it, she was in Washington, DC, at school, and he was in Longwood or fighting in another town, city, boxing arena, Gem thought. Tommie's death was their first crisis together, and now

Elegant's past, something left unresolved, their second. And tonight, it'd awakened him in the form of a nightmare to question their baby's health, whether or not it could live, successfully survive in her womb for the next three months, not die there, not be lost through a repulsive act, cruelty, as if the past could reach the baby to suffer it mortal harm, kill it, take away its chance to live.

"I can wait, Elegant. I can. As long as you know the baby will be all right."

"I'm haunted, Gem."

"I can wait, Elegant. Don't think I can't."

"Haunted."

On May 1, 1952, Tommie Embry Raines was born to Gem Loving Raines and Elegant Raines. He weighed in at seven pounds seven ounces. He looked like both of them—Gem's eyes, Elegant's features. And then if you took different looks at him from different angles you'd say Tommie Embry Raines looked more like Gem, or he looked more like Elegant.

Of course he was named after Tommie with no opposition from Pastor Loving, who said his name, Embry, had to appear somewhere on his grandson's birth certificate. He got his wish. Pastor Loving wasn't banking on Gem and Elegant having another boy—if they were "blessed enough" to have another child—so he was taking full of advantage of his first grandchild.

Throughout Gem's pregnancy, Elegant was fighting, still waging his campaign through the heavyweight ranks. He was ranked seventh in the division, all stoppages, remaining undefeated in three weight classes: middleweight, light heavyweight, and heavyweight. The public was clamoring (practically demanding) for a championship fight between Elegant and Domenic Botti for over a year now, but Elegant wanted to do it the right way, the ethical, honorable way, by knocking off all contenders in front of him in the rankings one at a time, pretty much in a row. Much like a row of ducks at a carnival.

Pee-Pot and Elegant were going to play by the rules of the game, not by someone else's.

"Today he looks like me," Pastor Loving said, looking down into the baby crib. Then he actually stood back and repeated the same thing.

Elegant, Pee-Pot, and Gem laughed.

The baby crib was set up in the dining room. It was a Sunday gathering at the Raines's home. It was near becoming habit since Tommie's arrival, something that began organically and was following the same course.

"My grandson likes to sleep, all right," Pastor Loving opined, still looking down into Tommie's crib. "He's showing off his brain power."

Gem got up and walked over to her father, taking his arm as Pastor Loving put his arm around her waist.

"I remember when you and Francine were that tiny."

"Me too," Pee-Pot said.

"And if you say anything to suggest the same," Gem said, turning to Elegant, "then please, Elegant, bite your tongue!"

"Gem, don't tempt me!"

"I'll tell you one thing," Pee-Pot said, "they were gorgeous though, you two girls. And it had nothing to do with you being the preacher's daughters either."

"No, Mr. Manners, I still would've prayed for you, no matter—for anyone who said they weren't."

"Talking about Francine though, I can't believe she'll be graduating college in two weeks, something you mentioned before, Pastor Loving."

"You can say that again, Mr. Manners. Really …," Elegant said.

"Says she's going to give Gem a run for that principalship job of hers at Longwood High School soon," Pastor Loving said, winking at Gem.

"She can have it now that I have Tommie!"

"Y-you don't mean that, do you, Gem?"

"No, no, Papa. I was teasing. Being, just being flippant. But Tommie has been a joy and, at the same time, a revelation."

Elegant stood, walked over to the crib. "I hope no one takes this the wrong way, and I know you won't, Mr. Manners, sir," Elegant said, standing on the other side of the baby crib from Gem and Pastor Loving, looking at Pee-Pot sitting at the dining room table, "since this, at one time, did come up in conversation between us quite some time back, sir, if I recall."

"Now you're expecting a lot outta me. My memory, Elegant. Just how far back, son, was it, because—"

"It's what you said, Pastor Loving."

"Me, Elegant?"

"About … regarding Francine, sir. As some sort of aspiration … And then it struck me …"

"Yes, Elegant …?"

"Our son can't aspire to be like me, a fighter. To take up my profession."

"It is honorable," Pee-Pot said. "But no, you're right. And I do remember that conversation between the two of us in the front room. Quite well."

"I won't let him become a boxer."

"This, then—this saddens you then, Elegant?"

"Yes, it does. In a way, Pastor Loving."

"Of course it does. And in no way am I minimizing this. Marginalizing your feelings, son."

"Yes, I know that, Pastor Loving. I understand that."

"But the one important thing," Gem said, "is that he'll probably look up to you as proudly as anyone. As any son can to his father."

"After all, Elegant, how many sons can say their father was the heavyweight champion of the world?"

"You're right, Pastor Loving. You, yes—how many."

Gem was glad it came up, that Elegant shared his feelings so openly with everyone in the room. That he hadn't guarded them.

"Cake?"

"No apple pie, Gem?"

"Next Sunday, Mr. Manners."

"Oh … oh, I thought it was this Sunday." Pause. "Guess I'm getting my Sundays mixed up. See, talking about my memory …"

It was five thirty and Gyp wasn't at the house.

Elegant stood on the house's front porch, waiting for her. This was the first this had happened, but there was always a first time for something, Elegant thought.

He let a few more minutes pass, and then it's when he began to worry. He looked around and then lit off the porch and onto Garland Road. Elegant knew what route Gyp took to get to the house, so he followed it, precisely.

He was running, not jogging but running. He had this bad karma in him. It's why he didn't go into the house, pick up the phone, and call Pee-Pot, for if there was something wrong, Pee-Pot would've telephoned, told him Gyp wouldn't be running with him this morning.

This was a May morning, and the air was light, and Elegant was dashing through it like never before. He was probably less than a mile between the two houses when he heard a whimper and saw the outline of a dark lump at the side of the road, maybe fifty yards in front of him.

"Gyp! Gyp!"

The whimpering continued.

"Gyp!"

He ran to her and fell down on his knees in the dirt in front of her.

"Oh no! No!"

Gyp's eyes were open and her tongue licked his face. Elegant scooped her up in his arms and then ran off with her down the dark road.

———

"Mr. Manners! Mr. Manners! It's Gyp, Gyp!"

Pee-Pot was at the kitchen table.

"Gyp!"

"I-I don't, don't know what's wrong, what's wrong with her!"

Gyp whimpered.

Elegant laid Gyp down on the kitchen floor. Pee-Pot was down on his knees.

"What's wrong, Gyp? Tell me!"

"I'll call Dr. Brewer, Mr. Manners!"

Elegant ran into the living room.

"Even though," Pee-Pot said looking into Gyp's eyes, "I already know what's wrong with her."

This was said under Pee-Pot's breath.

Pee-Pot and Elegant were driving back from Dr. Brewer's house in the truck.

"I knew what it was all along: a respiratory problem."

Gyp was lying on the truck's flatbed. A blanket covered her. It wasn't that she needed a blanket, but before leaving the house, Pee-Pot had spread a blanket over her anyway.

"It's always gotta be something," Pee-Pot said. "Something we gotta die from."

Die, Elegant didn't want to hear that word. "Die!"

Stonily Pee-Pot looked into the truck window. "W-what do you think's going on, Elegant? Ain't you ... what do you think's happening to her?" Pause. "How you think it all begins to unravel for us?"

Elegant didn't want to believe how far things had gotten in such a short space of time. Him getting up to do his roadwork, Gyp coming to the house at the usual time for him, not arriving, her slumping in the road, him finding her by the side of the road.

Elegant stole a glance at his watch, and knew Gem must be wondering where he was. She'd more than likely called the house.

Pee-Pot saw what he'd done. "I can drop you off, Elegant. Gem must be wonder—"

"You don't have to, Mr. Manners. I'll call from the house."

It was six fifty-two.

"I just want her last days on Earth to be comfortable, that's all I want. All I can do for Gyp. Ain't nothing more to do for her."

Having spent the entire morning and afternoon at the house, Elegant cancelled training. Pee-Pot let him. But Pee-Pot kept to his schedule; he had to—his responsibilities hadn't stopped because of Gyp's condition.

"I can't take it, Gem. I can't take any more of this!"

Elegant bolted off the bed.

Gem had just come into the bedroom.

"I can't go through this again!"

He was back on the bed, on the edge of the bed, bare chested. He'd been lying atop the bed disrobed down to his waist.

Gem sat in a chair.

"I don't know what I'd do, Gem. I don't know what I'd do …"

It was seven twelve. Elegant hadn't eaten. When he got in from the house, there was dinner for him, but he'd excused himself by saying he wanted to lie down and rest. Even Tommie, frolicking in his crib, hadn't altered his mood.

When he called her from the house with all the details, she was on the verge of breaking down and, at times, panicked. Elegant said he was staying at the house. She called twice during the day.

Elegant fell back on the bed.

What kind of day had it been for him? One of talking to Gyp, just talking to her as often as there was opportunity. At times she was up on her feet but walked slowly, tiredly, weakly. She left the house in order to defecate and urinate. And there was a brief walk both took. And then Gyp stopped and recuperated. And it seemed to Elegant as if their lives were frozen in time. She lay down. He sat beside her, looking out on Hattersfield Road, the woods, the hills they used to climb, and knew instantly, in a snapshot, that it was over for them.

She drank a lot of water today but ate little solid foods. Gyp did little of that during the day. Pee-Pot did get back from the gym earlier than usual. He said he called on Gas to step in for him. Plus, a few barber customers he cancelled, didn't tell them (his customers) about Gyp; only Gas knew the situation.

When he got in the house with Gyp lying on her royal-blue throw rug in the living room, Elegant and Pee-Pot stood over her, looking down at her with no conversation generated between them, until Pee-Pot finally offered.

"Elegant, I'll take over now."

"Yes, Mr. Manners. Sir."

Then Elegant got down on his knees and kissed Gyp's forehead and then stood, knowing Gyp knew what he'd done even while asleep.

———

"Are you going to call the house? Tonight?"

"No, Gem."

"I am."

Elegant came up off his back. He was on the bed in the bedroom. "First Tommie, now Gyp. L-let me get over Tommie first, Gem. Let me get over Tommie's death first."

There wasn't any door open for positive thought for Elegant, Gem thought. She could go over there and take his hand and then say, "Let's pray, Elegant. Let's pray"—since everything's in God's hands. But she wouldn't. She didn't have the impulse to. It was another time she had to let Elegant struggle on his own terms, without interruption or interference from her.

She would call the house, check on Gyp. It's all she could do for now. She hadn't spoken to Pee-Pot yet. Maybe he was seeking comfort, words that might help. And she was having great difficulty too. This wasn't one-sided; this wasn't just in two people's favor.

"I'm going to call the house, Elegant."

"Oh … yes …"

Gem stood.

"I'll just lie here." Pause.

"Tommie …?"

"He's resting."

Elegant smiled. "Good. Good for him."

———

Elegant was doing his calisthenics when he looked around the gym. Pee-Pot's Pugilistic Paradise seemed to be on a death watch since four days ago, when Pee-Pot told the fighters of Gyp's condition—that she was nearing death. There'd been lethargy in the gym ever since. There was this feeling of dread. There was, palpably, this feeling of loss. It's what Elegant was staring into the face of when he looked around the gym, fighters waiting for the worse possible news to come, like he was.

He had to keep training. He was to fight in nine days, in Convention Hall Arena in Philadelphia. He was to fight the fifth-ranked contender in the heavyweight division, Johnny "Bank "On It" Banker. He was a real gritty fighter who slipped down in the rankings when Domenic Botti knocked him out in a championship match over two years ago. He'd been inactive for a long time (thus, his current ranking). But he'd had two strong outings in the past six months. Elegant would be his third.

Today Pee-Pot wasn't in the gym. Neither was he yesterday. Elegant was working with Gas. This was no time for Pee-Pot to be in the gym, not with Gyp dying—he was devoting all his time to her.

After his training sessions, as usual, Elegant would rush out of the gym and over to the house to be with Gyp. He'd get there a little after two o'clock and then stay for dinner. During dinner, he and Pee-Pot sat at the kitchen table and not do much talking, but it was company for both, even if it did give them a false sense of security, of well-being. And then Elegant would leave just before seven thirty, for he did have to think of Gem and Tommie and the house—Gem going through her own vigil, her own private pain.

<hr />

Pee-Pot had gone up to the bathroom and was back downstairs. In a little over an hour, Elegant would be by the house. Pee-Pot walked over to Gyp. He checked on her. He removed his checkered cap and rubbed the back of his neck and then bent down over her.

"I could let Dr. Brewer put you to sleep, Gyp. But I won't. Ain't gonna do that. I know you don't want me to. You wanna be with me. To the end, Gyp. Right to the very end of this."

Pee-Pot straightened himself.

Maybe it wasn't fair, Pee-Pot thought. Maybe it wasn't fair what he was doing to Gyp, but she wouldn't want it any other way. It was the pact they had with each other, unwritten, unsigned, but it had been fourteen years of trust between them; and she trusted him now no matter how sick she was, that he would let her die in the house.

Pee-Pot walked into the kitchen. Most of the meal was cooked. All he had to do now was shuck the boiled corn. Pee-Pot sat down at the kitchen table. The pot with the corn in it was to his right. The empty pot was to his left. Pee-Pot sighed, grimly, and then began shucking the corn.

She was the best gundog there was in Longwood. He wasn't the only one who declared it—it was said by consensus. He and Gyp were proud of that. When there were hunting parties, Gyp was the standout, the star, pointing her black tail proud as a peacock. It was always her spirit he most loved, her willingness, not just the instinct of a Labrador, but that's what her station was, her breed, and she was going to show it off as if she were born to the manor.

"Ha."

She belonged around fighters, among them, her fighting spirit. Her setting was perfect, and she had a special, unique understanding of it. Before Elegant, she loved fighters, Pee-Pot thought, but not like Elegant. Right away, Elegant swept her off her feet. Pee-Pot laughed to himself. He could tell. After, initially, she'd sniffed him to make certain it was him (the letter, the scent—who knew? Maybe both were fooling each other), for them, it was wine and roses.

And the first morning, taking him out on the trail, up and through the—

"Guess that's enough. It's just me and Elegant, and some left over for leftovers."

Pee-Pot left the five remaining corn to be shucked in the pot. He picked up the pot with the water in it and then lit a flame under it.

Pee-Pot wiped his hands clean in the towel.

"Let me see how Gyp's doing."

He walked into the living room, and the moment he did, he knew Gyp was dead. He could smell it.

He walked over to her and then began sobbing and shaking. There was a blanket he'd put on the rocker. His hand reached for it.

He looked at Gyp again; she looked peaceful, he thought.

Pee-Pot spread the blanket over her.

"The corn. The corn. I-I put it on a high flame."

Pee-Pot walked into the kitchen and turned the stove off. Then he walked back into the living room and sat in the rocker and then just stared blankly at the blanket.

Forty-five minutes later.

The doorbell rang.

Pee-Pot got up from the rocker.

He opened the front door.

"Gyp's dead, Elegant."

The tools were down in the house's basement. The hammer, the saw, the chisel, the bench plane. The unused wood and shavings were down in the house's basement too, along with wood dust, the fine particles from the filing down, smoothing out of the pine wood.

Pee-Pot carried the casket he built for Gyp last night in the basement. She was upstairs on the floor. He hadn't moved her, not even touched her. He'd kept the blanket spread over her. He got the strength to go down into the basement forty to fifty minutes after Elegant left the house.

It was more like he was in a daze, that he must do something other than stare at the blanket with Gyp lying beneath it, knowing she was dead. It was like Cora when he went down to Montgomery, Alabama, to recover her body, knowing she was under the sheet, lying there, and she wasn't going to get up, come alive, rise from the dead—and it was the same with Gyp, at the time.

After building the casket and staining the wood and shellacking it, he called Elegant at three in the morning, knowing neither he nor Gem would find the time objectionable, maybe agreeable, under the circumstances. But he called to prepare them for this morning's burial of Gyp at ten o'clock.

After doing that, he felt much better about things, and he sat down in the rocker and shut his eyes, for he was exhausted. He didn't get much sleep in the rocker, but it helped. He didn't want to sleep in the bed. When Cora died, it was really hard for him to.

When he went down to the basement again, the pine wood was dry, and carrying the casket upstairs, into the living room, he laid it beside Gyp.

Now Pee-Pot was carrying the casket with Gyp inside it. He was at the back of the house, out in the field. He held it in both arms horizontally. Gem and Elegant flanked him. No one knew yet that Gyp had died, not Gas, not anyone but Gem and Elegant. The burial of Gyp would be just for them and them alone. Tommie was being babysat, so Gem took care of that duty.

They were approaching the mark where the shovel was (it's where Pee-Pot had put it), equidistant to the house and the woods.

The walk was solemn for all three. It was a solemn greeting at the door, a solemn ride over to the house in the car by Gem and Elegant. But after the initial greeting, Pee-Pot did what he had to do, walked in the living room, pulled the blanket off Gyp; and as soon as he had, Gem said, "Gyp ... oh, Gyp ..." Pee-Pot placed her in the casket, and the three took long, long looks at her smooth black coat, and then Pee-Pot shut the casket and began carrying her to where they were, a matter of twenty to twenty-five feet from the shovel.

Next to the shovel were rocks. Those rocks would be arranged to mark Gyp's plot.

Elegant grabbed the shovel and then began digging. He was crying. Gem was crying. Pee-Pot put the casket down on the ground.

Elegant had finished digging. He didn't know if he'd dug six feet down or not. For him, right now, it didn't matter.

Pee-Pot handed the casket to Elegant.

Elegant climbed out of the deep hole.

Gem took Elegant's hand and then Pee-Pot's. The three looked down into the hole at the casket.

"May she lie in peace," Pee-Pot said. "She lived a good life. May she lie in peace."

Elegant sobbed.

"You wanna just go ahead and throw the dirt over it, Elegant?"

Elegant didn't know if he could lift the shovel.

"Y-yes, Mr. Manners."

Elegant grabbed the shovel. He looked back down into the hole.

"Good, good-bye, Gyp."

"Good-bye, Gyp," Gem said.

Slowly Elegant began throwing the dirt down into the hole and then stopped.

"I can't do it!" Elegant shrieked and then began running across the field, toward the woods.

"I'll do it then," Pee-Pot said, releasing Gem's hand. "I should've done it all along."

Gem was looking at Elegant as he fled across the field.

"Yes, Mr. Manners."

Pee-Pot picked up the shovel off the ground and then looked up at Gem. "Gem, you go after him. Elegant, Gem."

"No, Mr. Manners. I'm going to stay with, here with you."

Pee-Pot looked at Gem again and then bent, digging the shovel into the dirt and then tossing the dirt into the hole.

Elegant wiped his eyes, but the tears wouldn't abate. He was at the edge of the woods, not at any far distance inside it.

"I just couldn't."

It was bad enough he had to dig the hole for Gyp, but to throw dirt over the hole, over Gyp's casket, he couldn't do it. He felt badly that he'd run off, deserted Pee-Pot and Gem, but this suffocating feeling overcame him, and he had to be freed of it. It's the only way he could describe it: it felt like it was suffocating him.

How many times had he thought about the morning runs? How many? And right now he was where he wanted to be, in the woods, in the sacred place, the sanctuary that belonged to him and Gyp they'd claimed together with nature, nourishing it with their spirits, longing to be one with it, silent, faceless, indistinguishable, making it impossible to see them on the landscape, the skyline, without seeing the grandeur of nature in them, the sparkle, the thrust, the sweat dripping when days were hot, humid, say July and August (especially August), not winter, the frigid months, when the cold stifled their breaths—not sweat them to a boil.

"It's done, Gem." Pause. "You'd better go off to him. Find him."

"Yes, Mr. Manners."

Gem made her way from Pee-Pot, and when she got to a certain point in the field, she waved to him.

Pee-Pot waved back.

Pee-Pot struck the tip of the shovel's blade into the dirt. Then he removed his cap, took a handkerchief out his pocket, and wiped his forehead and then the back of his neck.

"You'll always be here, Gyp. You'll always be right here, Gyp. With me."

"Gem." Elegant rushed to her, holding her. "How's Mr. Manners!"

"Fine."

"It's done then. Over with."

"Gyp's buried. We arranged the stones."

"I couldn't do it. I was strangling. It's like the air had been cut off. How, it's how it felt."

"It was awful. Just awful, Elegant—the whole time, wasn't it?"

They walked over to a tree, and Elegant leaned against it as Gem leaned into him. It was the first time Gem had been in these woods, in this setting. It was the first she and Elegant had shared it together.

"Y-you're sure Mr. Manners is all right?"

"Yes. He needed to be alone. Like you were."

"What about you, Gem?"

"I think I need people around me. I do, Elegant. Tommie was a comfort for me. Holding him. Talking to him around the house. A baby's a spark of life, don't you think, think? You can actually feel it."

"I'm sorry, Gem, but all I feel today is tragedy. First Tommie and now Gyp. Tragedy. I'll never read another Shakespeare play!"

Elegant broke away from her.

"Why do I like to read them, those tragedies so much for? Why Gem!"

"Why are you questioning yourself, Elegant? Why, why do you need to question yourself?"

He walked farther from her.

"Because, because, I'm trying to understand myself. Trying to know more about myself. My attraction to tragedy."

It was Elegant's past again, Gem thought. There could be no other reason for his emotional outburst.

"Maybe it's your intellect, Elegant, your—"

Elegant's eyes looked at her uncompromisingly, bruisingly.

"Oh, Elegant, forgive me. I'm, for being so, so intellectually dishonest."

"You, you know why I'm burning like, inside like a flame, Gem."

"Yes, I do, Elegant."

Elegant walked farther off. When he stopped walking, he just stood there as if he'd planted himself there.

His breathing was hard, sweated.

Gem froze in place too.

Elegant turned to her. "Gem, let's go back."

Gem stuck out her hand.

"I'm sure Mr. Manners needs us. By now. He has to."

———

Convention Hall Arena, Philadelphia.

"What's Elegant doing, Pee-Pot? What the hell's the boy doing in there!"

It was round six.

"You know what he's doing, Gas. Ain't no secret."

Then Gas nodded his head. "Of course. But if ... if—"

"Things were normal?"

"Yeah. Banker would've been knocked out in two—two rounds."

Pee-Pot nodded his head as he watched Elegant throw listless, ineffective jabs at Banker, hitting him but not discouraging him or in any way backing him off, something, at short range, at such perfect range, his jab normally did.

Tonight, Elegant was scoring just enough points, hitting Banker just enough times to win each round. And it was not only him scoring just enough to win each round but employing his defense to do so, as if he were in the gym sparring with defense his primary focus, tightening it up, sharpening it, improving it—but not in front of fight fans, a full house in Convention Hall Arena where most had come to see Elegant Raines, this great heavyweight, this great knockout artist with grace and flair and charm and history in the ring, who'd controlled weight divisions like kings control kingdoms.

Elegant came back to the corner and sat on the boxer's stool.

"You're winning, Elegant. Beating him."

Gas looked at Pee-Pot practically cross-eyed.

When the minute was up, Pee-Pot sent Elegant out for round seven.

"That's all you had to say? Tell him, Pee-Pot? Nothing more than he's winning the fight!"

"That's all, Gas," Pee-Pot said, pulling the boxer's stool out of the ring.

"Hell, I, I thought you'd say, might, might say more."

Pee-Pot watched Elegant as he let "Bank On It" Banker press him.

———

Pee-Pot, Gas, and Elegant were back inside the dressing room.

"Elegant, look, you won," Gas said, his arm on Elegant's shoulder. "But if Mr. Manners isn't gonna—"

Pee-Pot stepped in. "Let me talk to him, Gas," Pee-Pot said, wedging himself between them. "In private."

"Of course, Pee-Pot. Of—I'll be outside."

Gas cleared the room.

Elegant removed his robe and then sat on the rubbing table.

"I know what you're going to say, Mr. Manners. I do, sir."

"Do you, Elegant?"

"Yes. That I was lousy tonight, sir."

"Yes, you were, you—"

"And I'm sorry for my bad performance. I apologize for—"

"I wasn't going to say so much that you were lousy, Elegant, but that Gyp wouldn't like that. What you did tonight. Gyp wouldn't approve of it, at all what you did in the ring tonight."

"I couldn't fight, Mr. Manners. I-I just couldn't," Elegant said, crying.

"Why couldn't you?"

"I-I just couldn't," Elegant said stubbornly.

"I'm grieving too. We're all grieving. All of us."

"Yes, I know, I know," Elegant said, picking up his robe, using the sleeve of it to dab his eyes.

"It's dangerous in the ring, Elegant. Son. It's always dangerous in the ring. With any fighter …"

Elegant's eyes were expressionless.

"I-I ain't gotta remind you. You can't take chances out there, Elegant. You just can't do it. It ain't safe. And don't ever think it is. Not with any 220-pound man."

"I couldn't hurt him. I didn't want to."

"And you think you're honoring Gyp, respecting her this way—her memory this way, by doing what you did tonight?"

Elegant was stunned.

"Well, you're not. Ain't at all. Not Gyp's memory. The Gyp you and I knew."

"I'm so confused, Mr. Manners, sir. I'm …"

Pee-Pot was nonresponsive.

"I wanted you to, to beat on me out there, Mr. Manners. Berate me. Push me, since … since I couldn't push myself. Do it myself, f-for myself. G-get me angry."

"You know I'm not like that with you, son. Never been. For somebody else but not you. Somebody as intelligent, sensitive as you."

"I let Gyp down, myself, the fans."

"Uh-huh. The fans, Elegant. The fans—always remember the fans, son. The folk in the seats. Who pay their money to see you fight."

"I'm still learning, Mr. Manners. I'm, I'm still learning."

"Of course you are," Pee-Pot said, cutting the tape from the bottom of Elegant's glove, untying the laces, pulling it off Elegant's hand.

CHAPTER 26

1953

Elegant was the number one heavyweight contender, having dispatched of the number three and two contenders in that order. Botti had fought the number one fighter in the heavyweight division, Raiman Greer, knocking him out. Elegant was back in top form, having Gyp and Tommie as his guardian angels, having learned his lesson in the Banker fight, something he vowed to never repeat again inside the ring.

Boxing, the heavyweight division, was hungry for this fight, and it would happen September 3 at Yankee Stadium under the lights and bugs. It was a big, big money fight, the biggest of its era. Two men with incredible power who'd proved themselves the best in the division, Domenic Botti, by seven title defenses and wins, and Elegant Raines, by sweeping through the division for the past three and a half years.

The fight's buildup between these two champions would be incredible, right up until fight night. But not a great deal of buildup had to be done. This was the fight that had to happen, was inevitable, would add luster, polish to the game, in a bigger picture.

Gem was in the car and on a mission. It was a Saturday morning. She was in the car without Tommie—he was at home with Elegant. Elegant knew what her mission was this morning, why her car was aimed in Pee-Pot's direction, his farmhouse. He knew why—completely. He was all for what

Gem was doing now but had had his reservations. Gem suggested it before, four months back, but he was against it, not strongly opposed to it, but enough to make Gem weigh matters more judiciously, until she began feeling uncomfortable with the idea, and then abandoned it entirely.

Over the passing months, since Gyp's death, Gem and Pee-Pot had become extremely close. There were frequent phone calls and dinners at the house. There was Pee-Pot watching Tommie grow, his attachment to him. But through it all, she still saw this certain distinct sadness in his eyes, and it was Gyp.

It was especially there, he saw it, Elegant told her, when coming in, home from a road trip, an out-of-state fight, knowing what wasn't at the house to greet him, Gyp. Indeed, this was hard on him. He intimated it to Elegant a few times, but since the last time (some time back), the subject had been dropped but not forgotten by Elegant nor Gem.

Even Elegant, after a year, still had bad moments; and it didn't have to be when he was at the house, out in the field, the gym out there—it was in bed, pensive moments, dreams. It was just missing Gyp with all his heart and soul. Old days, it seemed, that were not replaceable by new ones, not when it came to Gyp—to what they'd had.

Gem's smile seemed to brighten by degrees the nearer she got to the house. She did look beautiful in a white blouse, the black of her jet-black hair, her high cheekbones with a tint of red, and her black eyes pearl-like, gleaming. Tommie hadn't done anything to alter her shape, so maybe she had been lucky—supported by good family genes.

"Okay, prepare yourself, Gem Loving Raines."

Gem pulled the car off Hattersfield Road, up onto the property. And as always, she parked her car next to Pee-Pot's dark-green-avocado Studebaker truck (the same one; nothing had changed).

"Okay, wish me luck!" Gem said, crossing her fingers.

Gem rang the doorbell.

"Gem."

"Mr. Manners."

"Right on time," Pee-Pot said as Gem walked into the house.

"Yes." Gem sighed. "Right on time."

It was eleven o'clock.

Together they walked into the living room. Nothing had changed in the Pee-Pot Manners household—furniturewise, that is: the rocker, the bench seat with its cushions, Gyp's royal-blue throw rug remaining down on the living room floor.

"My, you look beautiful, Gem. Hope Elegant said the same as me this morning. He did, didn't he?"

"No."

"Oh, then it must've been Tommie. He's quite a distraction, uh, can be at times. At his age."

"I'm glad you're Elegant's trainer, Mr. Manners, and not his alibi artist," Gem said, breaking out laughing.

Pee-Pot chuckled.

Gem felt at ease now but knew before entering the house that she and Pee-Pot would find something amusing to laugh about.

"You know, Gem," Pee-Pot said, fingering the bill of his trusty checkered cap, "you had me thinking about this morning last night."

Gem cleared her throat.

"You were awfully mysterious."

"I ... well I had to be, Mr. Manners."

"Had to be?"

"Why, yes, of course."

"Now, Gem, you gotta slow down, 'cause I couldn't get my grip on this thing before, and now it's really—"

"I'll be right back, uh, then, Mr. Manners. If it's all right."

"Right back? But, Gem, you just got here. In the house, I mean—"

"You just stay put, Mr. Manners, where you are, and I'll be right back."

"The last time I was bossed around by a woman," Pee-Pot said under his breath, "was Cora Madison Manners. Of course it was Cora. Ha. Cora ... who else ..." He mused, "Now Gem Loving Raines. Not too bad, huh?"

"Mr. Manners ..."

"Oh, you're back, Gem."

"Mr. Manners, you'll have to close your eyes, sir."

"Close my eyes? Now what kind of foolishness is it that I've gotta close—"

"It's a surprise."

"Oh, why didn't you say that? Who doesn't like surprises?"

Gem waited.

"They're shut, closed. Since I knew what was to come next."

Hesitantly, Gem approached him.

Pee-Pot heard her hesitancy. "Come on, Gem. Come on."

Then Gem stood maybe ten feet from Pee-Pot and put what she had in her hands down on the floor.

"Gem … I heard that."

"Y-yes, Mr. Manners. I-I expected you to. To."

Pee-Pot waited as he heard, what he knew, Gem opening something but decided to remain quiet this time.

"Mr. Manners, it-it's all right to—"

"W-what's that? What in God's name is that!"

"A dog, Mr. Manners. A dog. A miniature fox terrier."

Yap!

Gem had removed its muzzle. The dog was frisky.

"Who's it for!"

"You, Mr. Manners. You, sir."

Pee-Pot stared coldly at the dog. "I don't need a dog!"

Yap! Yap!

"I don't need a dog!" Pee-Pot said, getting up out his rocker brusquely, agitated, walking away from Gem, the rocker, going over to the window, looking out it angrily, fuming—and then turning back to stare at the small, slight dog as coldly as before.

"I don't want a dog!"

Gem was holding the dog in her arms and then put it down on the floor. The dog's tail was docked and wagging, and suddenly, it scampered over to Gyp's royal-blue throw rug and her nose began sniffing it.

"Get away from there! You get away from there!"

Frightened by Pee-Pot's voice, acrimony, the dog scampered back over to Gem and then turned back to Pee-Pot and looked at him with ears perked, fearlessly.

"You don't belong over there! Stay away from there!"

Pee-Pot's head turned back to the window.

Gem lifted the dog off the floor.

"You shouldn't've done this, Gem." Pause. "You have no right," Pee-Pot said, his back turned to her. "You and Elegant."

"Elegant was always opposed ... against it, the idea, resisted it, not until recently."

"Then he should've stayed that way!"

Now Pee-Pot seemed to be wrestling with himself. "I don't mean to be so angry. Upset. Have never been angry at you and Elegant before, Gem, but this ..."

Yap!

"It doesn't even bark like a dog!"

"He's six months old, Mr. Manners. Only, only six months old."

"I don't care, Gem. I don't, just don't care," Pee-Pot said, shaking his head. "And nobody can make me."

Pee-Pot turned and then sluggishly walked back to the rocker and sat, not looking at either Gem or the dog but down at the floor. "You have no right interfering with me and Gyp, Gem. Nobody has the ... that right."

"No, I don't, Mr. Manners."

"I can't replace Mrs. Manners. I can't replace Biscuit Manners. And I can't replace Gyp."

Yap!

"Why's it gotta bark that way? Why!" Pee-Pot said, now staring at the dog.

Gem had prepared herself for resistance, but now she felt she'd made a bad mistake, had used bad judgment. That it—

"I apologize, Mr. Manners. I overstepped the boundaries of good taste ... Far ... far too personal, Mr. Manners."

"Personal? But you-you're family, Gem. You and Elegant and Tommie. The only real family I've got."

"What I meant to say," Gem said, the miniature terrier sitting up on her lap, "is that I became far too intimate, personal with your feelings."

Pee-Pot shrugged his shoulders. "You just can't replace something that easily, Gem. You know that," Pee-Pot said gently. "I don't have to tell you that. Not, not you, Gem."

"No, you don't, Mr. Manners."

Pee-Pot still wasn't looking at the dog.

Yap!

"I'll take him back, Mr. Manners," Gem said, standing, putting him on the floor. The dog stood on the floor brazenly.

"You're gonna put him back in the box. The portable dog box then."

In fact, Gem was bending over, picking him up.

"That muzzle's not gonna go back on it, is—"

"Of course not, Mr. Manners. That was a part of the surprise. To keep him quiet. From the house to the car. When I entered the house."

Pee-Pot was embarrassed by what he'd said. "Oh, oh ... of course it was, Gem. Uh, of course ... I just ain't thinking straight—right now."

Gem turned around to the dog.

"Do you think he wants to get in, back in, now that he's out?"

"Ha," Gem said, turning back to Pee-Pot with a glint in her eyes. "He's going to have to. He has no other choice, Mr. Manners. He's frisky. He'll be all over the car or me on the way home."

Gem picked up the dog.

"He's frisky, all right. Full of life." Pause.

"Stop, Gem. Stop."

Pause.

"Don't put him back in the box."

"But ..."

The dog and Pee-Pot's eyes had made contact.

"Life. There ain't much life in this house but me, is there? Not much else. Any other kind of life breathing through the house."

Gem sat back down on the bench, and the dog in her lap curled his body.

"You're not out to replace Gyp, Gem. I see that now."

"It was just ... well, companionship, Mr. Manners. It was the long view I had, sir. I was taking."

"Of course." Pause.

"Six months old."

"You remember, Mr.—"

"And he's got a sweet face, even though he's a male. Might not like me saying, take to me saying so. To his way of thinking."

"No, I don't think he minds, Mr. Manners."

Yap!

"No. I guess not, Gem. I guess not."

The dog and Pee-Pot were looking at each other; it seemed they couldn't take their eyes off each other.

He was a tricolored miniature fox terrier: black, white, and tan.

"Must weigh twelve to thirteen pounds," Pee-Pot said, using his trainer's eyes to size the dog up.

"Twelve pounds to be exact, Mr. Manners. I had him weighed by Mr. Bryers, in his store," Gem laughed.

"Said twelve first."

"You sure did."

"Mr. Bryers's pet store in town. Old Ed Bryers, who else. Hmm …"

"He keeps the store so clean."

"Does."

Pee-Pot pushed forward in the rocker. "No, don't take him back in the dog box, Gem. I'll look after him."

"You will, Mr. Manners!"

"If he can stand an old man like me."

"Let's ask him, Mr. Manners."

They both looked at him.

Silence.

Both laughed.

"Well, at least he's got an independent mind and spirit, Gem. It's all I can ask for."

———

Gem had left the house and it was just Pee-Pot and the dog.

The dog was frisky, barking and growling, being a menace one minute and then a saint the next. But Pee-Pot didn't mind. He wanted it to get everything out its system. After all, it was a brand-new environment for him, so it was expected. He'd been talking to it off and on, but in time, the little dog would adjust, he thought, and then the rules set, implemented. He'd be ready to learn then, like any smart animal, which he knew, by reputation, terriers were. He knew, also, they were fearless hunters, a strong breed, a strong constitution, and longevity. He also knew now he'd have to buy toys for him, something Gem suggested before leaving.

She was smart all right, Pee-Pot thought at the time. She could've bought the toys at Ed Bryers's store today and then brought them with her;

only, she wanted him to involve himself more with the dog—its needs. And he hadn't fed him yet, something the two of them would have to work out to each other's satisfaction.

Yap! Yap!

It was funny, Pee-Pot thought, looking at the dog. He was a terror, was all over the place but didn't bother Gyp's rug, didn't even go near it … But Pee-Pot got up from the rocker, walked over to the royal-blue rug and took it up off the floor.

The dog stopped its activity and stared at Pee-Pot.

"Just in case you forget your boundaries."

The dog looked bemused and then went back to its belligerent antics.

Pee-Pot had to admit he was really enjoying the dog, his company. He didn't have anything planned for the day except cutting Roscoe Jane's hair (who forgot his appointment and called) at the house, so this wasn't bad, seeing the little guy take a go at the house, literally attacking it at full force, his tiny teeth bared.

Suddenly, the dog calmed down.

Pee-Pot chuckled.

"So you're tired now. All pooped out now."

The dog had tipped ears.

"I let you have run of the downstairs."

Pee-Pot looked over at Gyp's throw rug folded up at the side of the rocker.

"Come, boy," Pee-Pot said, flicking his finger out at the dog.

The dog ran to Pee-Pot, hopping up into his arms. Pee-Pot held him, and then he squirmed out his arms and nestled in his lap. "Ha. You are a lapdog, after all, ain't you?"

The dog shut his eyes, and Pee-Pot began petting its short head, the short fur between its ears.

"Cozy, ain't you."

Pee-Pot began rocking the rocker back and forth.

"Was thinking … I've gotta come up with a name for you, don't I?"
Pause.

"I guess so. But don't worry any," Pee-Pot said, looking down at the dog, "I've come up with one."

The dog hadn't opened its eyes.

Pee-Pot squirmed and then grinned.

"No sense in complicating things any. You're a Jack Russell terrier breed. So we'll just call you Jack!"

Jack's eyes popped open.

"How's that?"

Jack's eyes closed.

———

Jack was out in the yard. Pee-Pot figured he'd gone out there to do his business.

Pee-Pot was at the phone. He dialed.

"Gem …"

"Mr. Manners." Pause. "How's—"

"Thank you, Gem. I've had a great day."

Gem's hand covered the phone. "Elegant, it's Mr. Manners."

"Jack's doing fine."

"Jack?"

"I'll explain it to you later. Right now, I gotta go out in the yard and see what he's doing. What kind of mischief he's been up to. Ha. He's been out there for an awful long time now."

———

Elegant was in the most intense training grind he'd ever put himself through for a prizefight—never mind a championship fight. This was the championship, the prize he'd probably been after his entire life since he began boxing: the heavyweight championship of the world. He was to be called the king of the sport. And while it wasn't for him an ego fixation to own such a title, it would mean for him that he'd reached the pinnacle, the top rung of something; and afterwards, the test would be to continue to sustain it, stay on top, hold onto the championship belt by fighting all contenders, thus creating this realized, rich body of accomplishment and self-fulfillment.

It's how Elegant perceived it, through this kind of prism, in a context created to sustain his self-worth, something, when he began with Frank

"Black Machine" Whaley, the Whaley Gym, he was in desperate need of, self-worth. His past crisscrossed him, the deep, horrible wounds inflicted; and he had to find a salve, a balm, some kind of rescue, relief from the past. And it was through boxing, the ring, with all its history and lore and legacy and tradition and heroic proportion and manifest glory. This was the place to find himself, to make real an Elegant Raines, to turn him into a person, to mean something, to have some legitimate, authorized value and description.

And he had the gifts, the talent for boxing. He had the heart and mind and soul and courage for boxing. He had the chin, the fists for boxing. He could uphold boxing's tradition and legacy, these precious things Frank "Black Machine" Whaley taught him in the Whaley Gym about boxing, and then Pee-Pot Manners furthering the lessons, the education in Pee-Pot's Pugilistic Paradise gym, the Pug, and at the farmhouse. The things the great fighters used to dominate the ring. And he wanted to emulate them—be like them, one with them, matching his spirit with their spirit. And up till now, he had. Up till now, Elegant had felt the glory of the enterprise. He felt himself lift himself up to a different level, a brand-new rung.

Boxing had lifted him out of chaos, out of wanting, out of poverty, out of a conflicted soul. It'd taken him beyond wishing for something, hoping for something, not having the opportunity for something significant. He was a black man in a white man's world and had to find out where he belonged in it. He'd adopted the philosophy of the poor to find opportunity, to scratch, claw until he saw a visible, clear path, option—something that could reasonably change, resonate, reform his economy for the better. And he found it through boxing.

And now the heavyweight championship of the world was in the offing. And to wrest it, make it his own, to claim it on September 3, 1954, in Yankee Stadium, he would fight Domenic Botti for the heavyweight crown. It's how far Elegant had gotten with this enterprise: onto the glory road that feted course toward a bigger-than-life prize as grand reward.

Elegant was running over to the house now as routine, for he had, by now, encouraged Jack to at least run across the field with him and into the woods, but maybe fifty yards in and then wait for his return. It took Jack a few days to figure all of this out, but once he warmed to it (as pupil), it was as natural to him as fish taking to water.

Jack was a tree climber though and was perched on a tree branch, looking for Elegant with three feet planted and his forepaw lifted, his mouth open, his ears attenuated, and his tail still, not until he saw Elegant weave back to him, sweating, oily black.

Yap! Yap!

"Okay, I'm back, Jack!"

Elegant cut around another tree, and then he was close to twenty-five yards from Jack.

Yap! Yap!

Then Elegant was under the tree, and it's when Jack took a flying leap at him, and Elegant caught him in his arms.

Yap! Yap!

"Ha!"

They were back in the gym. Elegant was toweling himself. He never felt better. This marked his final workout in Longwood. Next stop: New York City. In three days, Monday, he'd set up camp. He'd chop wood tomorrow, so it wouldn't be a workout, and Sunday, church. Pastor Loving, as a matter of course, routinely prayed a special prayer for him and his opponent (Botti) before his fights. Gem would sing.

Yap!

"Elegant …"

Elegant hadn't heard him, but Jack had.

Jack jumped up into Pee-Pot's arms.

"Good morning."

Jack leaped out Pee-Pot's arms.

"Was listening to the radio, Elegant, and I don't know what they're gonna talk about around here for the next week while we're gone. Since it's all they talk about, is the fight."

"I know, Mr. Manners."

"I keep looking for the odds to change in our favor, but they're still—"

"Three to two in Botti's favor, Mr. Manners."

"Been that way four weeks steady."

"He, after all, is the champ, Mr. Manners."

"Guess so, Elegant. He's defended the crown well. Hasn't ducked anyone. Taken on all comers. Got all that championship experience tucked under his belt."

Elegant picked up a grooming brush, and of course, Jack knew who it was for. He walked over to Elegant, looked up at him innocently, and then lay down in front of him.

Pee-Pot chuckled.

Elegant got down on the floor with him and then began brushing Jack's tricolored coat.

"There's no secret to Botti. You know that. He's got raw power and can take a punch with the best of them."

"Yes, sir."

"Our strategy then is to hit him enough times, for he'll fall. And that'll come with your speed. But he's gonna try to hit you with every punch—"

"Elbow—"

"Ha. No, son, Botti's not the cleanest fighter in the ring. Elbow. The kitchen sink. Everything in the book. Anything to win. Beat you."

Elegant paused with the grooming brush. "I've felt that way, Mr. Manners. But I couldn't fight dirty."

"I don't know, Elegant … maybe 'cause you know they wouldn't let us fight dirty."

"You mean …?"

"Yes, a black fighter. Not with a white fighter. But the opposite's true. The case."

"L-like life, Mr. Manners."

"Yes," Pee-Pot said. "Uh-huh."

Yap!

Jack had broken the silence.

Later.

This was so sentimental, but it had to be done, Elegant thought. He had to stand before the stones, look down at the dirt, see the casket below it—let Gyp know he was there. And Jack was beside him, used to the stones by now and why they were propped there at this particular spot.

"She was great, Jack. A great lady, Gyp, Jack."

He had to thank Gyp for what was to come. He had to give thanks and praise to Gyp for all the years of her love and devotion to him. What it meant to her as it meant to him to be a champ. A middleweight champ first and then a light heavyweight champ and now the opportunity of repeating it on September 3.

Every morning Gyp was beside him—without fail. She hadn't missed a morning's run with him once he regained his mental state, his lungs were able, cleared to breathe fresh again—after the Banker fight. It's when he became a different person, had learned another lesson about life—about the "eternal well," how it replenishes itself even when, by all appearances, it appears empty but isn't. There's still beauty to be drawn from it, opportunities, things you carry into victories and defeats.

It's what Gyp's death taught him, and he was sure there'd be more she'd teach him because he was going to keep himself open to her teachings, feel her strength, draw on it whenever he could, know it was always there for him.

Looking down at Jack, he was wagging his tail.

Elegant threw a hard rubber ball about eighty yards in distance.

"Jack, fetch it. Go fetch it, Jack!"

Yap! Yap!

Jack scampered after the ball, his ears pinned back to his head, his legs spinning.

Jack loved it when Elegant threw the rubber ball for him, especially that far out.

—

Elegant was in the bedroom. Gem was packing for him.

"Want to get rid of me that much, huh, Gem?"

Gem pressed the tie down with her hand.

"You know, Elegant, I don't think I'll ever get used to this …"

In his heart, he never expected her to, not Gem, not someone who never thought, not even in her wildest dreams, that she'd marry a fighter.

She had turned to look at Elegant for an answer, a reply, but Elegant sat in the wicker chair blank.

"I want to win so badly, Gem," Elegant finally said.

What else should he say? Gem thought—but only, it's the way he'd just said it.

"Any, is there any reason why, Elegant?"

"I did say, just say what I ... that passionately or desperately, Gem, which?"

"Both."

"For our economic well-being, may-maybe that was it."

Gem stopped what she was doing by walking over to Elegant, sitting on his lap, and then kissing him. "Mmm ..."

"Do you think, Gem?"

"No, it goes further than that, is more profound. It's what it sounded like to me."

"Then drive, Gem. My drive. My ambition."

She would accept that explanation, Gem thought. She would, but then it would be a matter of how much should she accept, not question, reject, but accept in order to give a percentage to it, rate it on this scale she'd fixed in her mind of Elegant's true psychological makeup, of what, just how much all the other components, dynamics, added up to, but were small, percentagewise, to the whole of the equation, of what really was at the root of anchoring him down with seemingly unjust, unresolved burden.

"I just wish it hadn't come out that way."

"Then you would want to stifle yourself, Elegant."

"Stifle myself? Sti—"

"Elegant, I don't want to push this."

Elegant frowned. "You mean to make me feel upset with myself, don't you?"

"Yes," Gem said.

"I want this over with. I do."

Gem refused to say the obvious or repeat "I know you do, Elegant" like a parrot, as if she really didn't want this over with, this dimension of Elegant Raines that still remained a puzzle to her, an enigma, gaining momentum and then dissipating, petering out, and then pulsating, throbbing—obsessively urgent and restless, with no resolution.

"But it's my state of mind right now, Gem, with the fight looming. On, on the horizon. Emotionally."

Gem kissed his cheek; only, this time, Elegant's arms wouldn't let go of her. They held her much tighter. Elegant seemingly not caring one way or the other about words or feeling obligated to them, just raw and naked feelings. And it's how this felt to Gem, a rawness in him that was trying to express itself without words, without making more excuses, creating more delays for what she knew one day, ultimately, inevitably, would shock her, his story—would push her back into his past, his world, inside that experience, or experiences, that could make the ugliness real, fresh; and all he was asking was for her to be prepared for it, to be strong, steady, reliable, not cower when the worst of that world was yanked off, revealed to her in all its venality, fury, something he would need her to help him finally escape.

Realizing it was all right now, Gem said, "Now may I get back to packing your suitcase?"

"And I'll see, uh, go and see what Tommie's doing. How's that?"

Both stood.

When Gem got back to the suitcase on the bed, Elegant said, "Thanks."

And Gem didn't know if it was for packing the suitcase he was thanking her or for what had just transpired between them, but either way, she smiled.

Elegant was in the house's hallway. He looked back at the bedroom. He stopped. He was protecting himself just now, in the room with Gem, his mental well-being. And he was trying to rise above the moment, to find a magic moment.

He was in Tommie's room and knew the second he got to the door that Tommie was napping. He was looking down on this dark-skinned bundle of joy tucked away in his small bed, who now favored Gem more than him. His face had formed, taken on its permanence. Tommie was stretched out, indulging in himself without really knowing it, understanding it at two and a half years old.

But it's how he'd think when he'd see a child unencumbered by the world, how he had to be, at one time, lying like Tommie, indulging sleep.

"Magic moment."

Saying it aloud in the room, it sounded hollow, as if he'd lifted it out a book, out of a piece of ordinary, pedestrian literature. But he was looking down at Tommie's tiny body and knew Tommie's life would be protected by him. He'd never have to suffer as a child what he'd suffered. He'd never be ripped away from his family. This Raines family in Longwood, West Virginia, would survive anything thrown its way. There was no fear for the future for him on his part or Gem's. Just looking down at him, reassured him of this, Elegant thought. It made the future realized.

Money, economics would play a factor in him winning the heavyweight championship of the world. In the bedroom with Gem, he wasn't being totally dishonest with her regarding that: money and security for Tommie. And what about love? What about the love Tommie would have—his, Gem's, Pastor Loving's, Mr. Manners's, Francine's—even Jack's, Elegant laughed. And yes, even the community of Longwood.

"You're lucky to be alive, Tommie."

And he was lucky to be Tommie's father, Elegant thought. Of providing a future for his son lying peaceably in his bed. This was the real magic moment before setting off for the fight in New York City in a couple of days. This is what he had at one time in Saw Mill, South Carolina. This was how his father, he imagined, looked at him when he was a tot, not with the same hope, of course not, but with the same love and affection—the same desire to keep him safe, away from evil men.

Elegant stood there as if he'd passed on a truth to a new generation.

September 1, 1954

This was like they were on honeymoon again, Gem and Elegant in New York City, Harlem, to be exact, staying in the Charleston Hotel, in the same honeymoon suite, room 511, except there would be no hanky-panky, sex—but of course, they knew this.

Early this afternoon, Gem had gotten into New York City for the fight (Elegant there three days prior to her). It'd be the first time she'd, in person, see Elegant fight in the ring. This fight for the heavyweight championship of the world in New York City, Yankee Stadium, against Domenic Botti. Gem thought it important she be there, in attendance the night of the fight in what she hoped would be the crowning moment for Elegant, and she wanted to share in it with him. He didn't ask her to come, but he didn't have to, for as soon as the announcement was made, it's when she made her vocal declaration. Needless to say, Elegant melted into her arms upon contact.

They were eating dinner.

Gem dropped her fork.

"Now, Gem, you mustn't be nervous."

Quizzically Gem looked at Elegant. "I am, aren't I?"

Elegant got up, picked her fork up from off the floor. "Yes, you are."

"But that's natural, isn't it?"

Elegant handed her the fork. "Yes. Even two days before the fight. Yes, it is."

"But I won't be around you Friday, will I, Elegant?"

"No. Not Friday."

Elegant sat back down.

"This is new to me," Gem said wistfully. "All, all new to me."

"I know."

Then Gem looked around the hotel room. "But it's worth it, Elegant. Being back in this room. Reliving—"

"Great moments."

"Wonderful, fond memories."

Elegant studied her. "You'll be at ringside, Gem. I-I must warn you …"

"Of what …?"

"It's where it's the worst at a fight. The most brutal and violent. At ringside. On, on—you'll be on top of the ring."

She wasn't going to think about it, feel intimidated, Gem thought. And she hadn't up till now. All she wanted was to be there, at the fight, in two days. She was just nervous about that.

Elegant leaned over the short table, taking her hand. "You do understand, don't you?"

"Yes, perfectly. Perfectly, Elegant." Pause.

"You'll see me differently."

You're not an animal. Primitive. You have a skill. You have a gift.

"You'll see a different me, Gem."

"It will still be you, Elegant."

Elegant teased the food on his plate with the fork. "I guess." Pause. "I could never hurt a man," Elegant said, looking intently into Gem's eyes. "Really, really hurt him, Gem."

Gem was looking as intently at him.

"I only want to win. Not hurt anyone." Pause. "It's just these fists," Elegant said, raising them, forming them in a big, tight ball. "They have power in them. Immense, amazing power."

Gem wondered how they got so powerful. She knew they were even with her naiveté toward boxing—that they knocked out big men, strong men, knocked them unconscious.

"Maybe I'll be the one hurt Friday night. Not Domenic Botti."

Yes, she thought, he was testing her reaction.

"Suppose it's me, Gem? Then what?"

"Don't say that, Elegant. Ask, ask me that!"

She threw the napkin down onto the plate of food and ran out of the room.

"Don't!"

Gem was in the bedroom. She had thrown herself onto the bed, taken the bedspread and buried her head in it, sobbing.

Elegant was on the bed, taking her in his arms, holding her, trying to console her.

"I'm sorry. I don't know why I said that. What I said. J-just said."

"You, you've been so confident, Elegant. You've never said, thought about being hurt. Hurt before. In, in the ring before … Before a fight."

"But you'll be there, Gem," Elegant said, turning his face from her. "You'll be at ringside. It'll all be different tomorrow night."

"Then I won't go. I won't be there!"

Elegant held his head in his hands. "I don't know what I'm saying!"

She didn't know her attending the fight was putting this kind of mental pressure on him.

"It's … it's just that I'm trying. I'm, I'm attempting to try to prepare you for something I can't prepare you for …"

She was holding him.

"I know you can't, Elegant. That you can't do."

"Two men fighting to prove what? What, Gem, what?"

What was happening to Elegant? Gem thought. Talking like this so openly, so philosophically about something he loved, she knew he loved.

"What, Gem? What?"

"Would you talk like this to Mr. Manners?"

Knocked back, Elegant's eyes began hunting through Gem's. "No, no. No. I wouldn't."

"Then why are you talking to me like this?"

"I …"

"Please don't say you don't know, Elegant."

"Because I think it'll make you laugh, if I do. If I should … do say that."

And then suddenly, Gem began laughing, and so did Elegant.

Both got up from the bed arm in arm.

"I hope my fish isn't cold."

"Gem …"

"Okay, it is."

Elegant seated Gem at the table.

"Thanks."

Elegant sat. "I was worried, Gem. About you."

"I'm not pretending to be brave, Elegant. I don't want to feel I am. In any way pretending."

"On my account. But y-you're vulnerable. Just say your vulnerability—"

"That's enough!" Gem said, throwing her hands in the air, laughing. "No more psychological analyses, please!"

Gem went back to eating her cold fish. Actually, she was picking at it with her fork like she just found it dead on a beach.

"I wonder how Tommie's doing. Or what he's doing right now."

"I'm ready to call the house whenever you are."

"Then let me hurry up and eat!"

"Me too!"

Just because Tommie was in the loving care of Pastor Loving and Francine until Gem and Elegant got back from New York City didn't rule out him being in the loving care of every female member of the Body of Christ Church too, right about now, in Longwood.

CHAPTER 27

The day of the fight, September 3, was a seventy-six-degree day with fight time temperatures expected to hover in the low sixties or midfifties. It would be a perfect night for boxing, for the biggest fight of the decade. There was no doubt in any fans or sportswriters' minds (or pens) that Elegant Raines and Domenic Botti would put on a fight for all time.

And Elegant had been secluded, isolated from Gem for the day. He was in a Manhattan hotel. Geographically, Gem was closer to Yankee Stadium than Elegant. Gem was to be chauffeured by limousine to Yankee Stadium, given the red-carpet treatment—something, in and of itself, she thought exciting.

Of course she was a country girl, but this was another day she would pin big memories to, another day (even though she wouldn't take pictures before or after the fight) she would taste and feel along with Elegant. The only problem was she didn't know how to dress for the fight, but Elegant convinced her her taste in clothes was so impeccable there'd be no problems. But Pee-Pot helped her out. He said there'd be diamonds and jewels and glitter, but she would stand out in something red—a red A-line dress and her mother's pearls.

Gem agreed, adding a light wrap for her shoulders to further compliment her look.

Now that the fight was about six hours away, Gem no longer felt nervous. Undoubtedly, she didn't know just how she'd feel once she got to the fight. Once she entered Yankee Stadium, she sat down with only one person she knew, had had some brief contact with: Collingsworth Hollins. This didn't trouble her, but it was odd, strange, indeed. In Longwood,

West Virginia, of course, there was no contact with whites. It was strictly an all-black community, one which was planned, designed, cut out to fit this paradigm. And Howard University, it was an all-black university. It was founded for that purpose, with that educational mandate.

And so for Elegant's fight, she would be sitting next to a white man who made this night possible for Elegant, a black man. Gem was progressive enough to acknowledge and comprehend progress, but this would be the first time she'd experience it to this proportion, on this scale, where all the world saw it glaring at it. But what the world wouldn't see was what Elegant thought of Collingsworth Hollins: Collingsworth Hollins's integrity, his goodness. Since his uncle Hancock Hollins's death, he'd guided Elegant's boxing career ably, with no feelings of advantage or privilege. At one time Elegant had said, "I'm treated as an equal under Mr. Hollins." And it was all Elegant said he could ask for in a business arrangement of this importance.

Not living with white people as neighbors in Longwood, not mixing with them, all she really knew about them was what they'd done to separate the country, the races, for black people to have to create a Longwood, West Virginia, out of necessity. Race relations was not something she and Elegant talked about. Not too many people in Longwood did: their lives were an accepted fact of life.

But tonight, at the fight, the two worlds would collide in all its thunder and lightning: black and white. Gem had thought this through this afternoon after coming back to the Charleston Hotel from taking photos with her Kodak camera of changed sites she saw in Harlem, different from her past visit. A Harlem of black people, the exception being white store proprietors and police to run it.

It would be a stark black-and-white contrast there, beneath the stars, in the open air arena in Yankee Stadium. Domenic Botti and Elegant Raines would really be fighting, with no pretense or deception on anyone's part, for their race, for its superiority in the boxing ring in the year of 1954 in the United States of America.

Even Gem was smart enough to know what tonight's fight was about, what was at stake, how both races felt this way, where their loyalties and faith lay—the one thing neither race was yet willing to forfeit or forget.

Botti, in the press, bragged, up to the start of the fight, how he was going to "moida" Elegant Raines. And a heavyweight champion who had successfully defended his crown seven times—who had a ring record of fifty-one wins (forty-seven by knockout), three losses, and one draw—could brag, one presumed. He would do this before a fight, it being common knowledge, but once in the ring, all talk stopped. They say Domenic Botti was as silent as a church ghost. It's when he let his fists talk for him like most champions do when the microphones are turned off and the ring lights turned on and all that's left for a fighter is to face another fighter, look him square in the eyes, and then try to destroy him with the subtleness of overt physical gestures, not verbal taunts.

September 3. Yankee Stadium dressing room. Six o'clock.

"You're leaving the hotel now, Gem?"

"Yes, Elegant. This very instant."

Elegant's hand covered the phone. "Gem's about to leave the hotel, Mr. Manners."

"I was paged."

"Then the limousine's outside the hotel, waiting for you."

"This is all new for me, Elegant. I'm excited."

"I'm glad."

"All right then. I'd better get downstairs to the lobby."

"And they'll bring you straight to the dressing room when, uh, once you're here, don't worry."

"I love you, Elegant."

"I love you. Oh ... how I love you, Gem!"

The limousine had whisked Gem from the hotel. There was a wall of traffic (of course no one knew who she was; her limousine was just one among a herd of many on its way to Yankee Stadium), but once she got to Yankee Stadium and saw it she marveled, not believing its size. Since the car slowed on its approach to the stadium, she grabbed her Kodak and took pictures from the car's backseat. They'd be the last pictures she'd take tonight, she'd told herself, even if she had to tie both hands behind her back. But it was the ecstasy and stature of Yankee Stadium's construction she couldn't resist, how it stood as a brick and steel monument for Elegant. Of how he built each brick in him to get to here tonight. And the Yankee Stadium did look charming, with its great girth of body, so she snapped pictures at will.

Finally, the limo was parked in the stadium's reserved section, and Gem could feel an adrenaline rush. She was looking at a throng of people, and never had she seen this number of people gathered together at one time, certainly not in Longwood or in her father's church or at Howard University football games, but there they were, this crush of humanity coming together, filling up areas of the stadium, ringing it, and—

"Mrs. Raines, if you would come with me, ma'am."

"Yes. Of course."

She was out of the car, and the silver silk wrap she didn't need, but laid across her shoulders as if she did. She was being whisked into the Yankee Stadium through a side door, by the chauffeur's official pass.

"Eddie O'Connor?"

"Yes, Mrs. Raines's chauffeur."

"Mike Llewellyn. I'll take over from here. Thank you."

"Right. Okay, Mrs. Raines. Pleasure's been all mine."

"Thank you. Thank you for getting me here safely."

"Like I said, my pleasure, ma'am. And I hope those pictures you took on the way in come out okay."

"Mrs. Raines, Mike Llewellyn. If you would step this way, please."

"Thank you."

Llewellyn waited for her.

Gem joined him at the top of a long hallway that was unattractive, unspectacular, more like an underground tunnel—and maybe it was.

Gem and Llewellyn began walking down the narrow tunnel.

"You get used to this dingy part of the stadium," Llewellyn said, looking up at a naked, dim light bulb. "Ain't as glamorous as what's outside, that's for sure."

Gem laughed good-naturedly. "No, no, it's not."

"But nobody sees this part of the stadium anyway but special guests like you."

Gem laughed more.

There was another hallway/tunnel ahead, and then another.

"We're almost there, Mrs. Raines. I guess you never expected this though."

"No, it's all right, Mr. Llewellyn."

"You need a map."

"Ha."

It was like a jigsaw puzzle, Gem thought.

"Mrs. Raines ..."

"Yes, Mr. Llewellyn?"

"Everybody just calls me Mike. But with that guy, Eddie ... uh ... Eddie—"

"O'Connor."

"Right. My memory's not so hot. I tried to impress the guy by using my last name. Being formal and all. After all, Mrs. Raines, this is a championship fight tonight. And I have the honor of escorting one of the combatant's wives to his dressing room, don't I?"

Down another tunnel they traveled.

"There, there it is!"

And everything looked bright and finished, the painted walls, the painted floors, giving it an aura of being a part of something of far greater significance.

"Through that door, Mrs. Raines, is your husband."

Gem's heart leaped.

Knock.

"Mike?"

"Mike, Mickey."

"Come in, Mrs. Raines."

"Thank you."

"Mickey'll take care of you from here, Mrs. Raines."

"You can come with me, ma'am."

"But I got you back when you get back out. Show you to your seat."

"Thanks, Mr. Llewellyn."

Mickey looked oddly at Mike.

Off Gem and Mickey went, just through another door, another knock on that door, Gas opening it.

"Gem!"

"Mr. Moore!"

"Thank you," Gas said to Mickey before shutting the door.

Elegant turned.

"Gem!"

"Elegant!"

Gem ran to him. Then she saw Pee-Pot come out of the men's room.

"Mr. Manners!"

"Don't let me stop you, Gem!"

Elegant and Gem hugged and then kissed.

"Do you need the wrap, Gem?"

"Oh no, Elegant. Not yet."

"Then, uh, it's still comfortable out."

"Yes."

"Good."

"Good," Pee-Pot said, echoing Elegant.

"Got all the royal treatment of a queen, huh, Gem? All the trimmings, huh?" Gas said.

"Yes sir, Mr. Moore," Gem said. "Oh, hello, Mr. Timms."

"See, I always get the short end of the stick. Second handler in line."

"Don't worry, Al, I was a bucket boy too, until Pee-Pot found one."

Pee-Pot took Gem's hand. "Are you worried, Gem, 'cause don't be. Elegant's gonna do fine. Just fine for himself out in the ring tonight."

Gem sighed. "I haven't been all day, Mr. Manners. But when I get out in the stadium with Mr. Hollins …"

"Well, if we don't pray while you're here, Gem, I guess we'll all be sinners in the eyes of Pastor Loving and the Lord's. I don't know which could be worse."

The prayer prayed, the circle broken, Gem knew it was time to leave the dressing room.

"I won't disappoint you, Gem. I promise."

"Elegant, I know you won't."

"See you after the fight."

They kissed.

"After the fight," Gem said, lowering her eyes.

The door opened and then closed. As soon as it did, Pee-Pot walked up to Elegant.

"This is hard on you, ain't it, son?"

"Yes, it is, Mr. Manners. Gem's first fight, sir. And it has to be tonight. With so much at stake. On the line for me, sir."

<center>~~~~~</center>

"Mrs. Raines."

"Mr. Hollins."

They shook hands.

Hollins was tall, wiry, and with a shock of gray-blond hair.

He waited for her to sit. His party of six hadn't acknowledged her.

"I'd like all of y'all to meet Mrs. Gem Raines here. Elegant Raines's wife, it's safe to say," he said in a smooth, sophisticated Tennessean drawl.

The party of six stood, and in so doing, so did Gem.

"Pleasure to meet you," Gem said to one and all.

Then everyone sat.

"I know this will be your first fight, Mrs. Raines. This evening."

"Yes, it will."

"And that you are a preacher's daughter."

"Yes, yes, I am ...," Gem said hesitantly.

"The language can be quite rough, crude in a boxing arena. At, at a boxing event, ma'am."

"Oh, yes, I'm sure, Mr. Hollins." Pause. "But can it be any cruder than trying to wash a pig, a stubborn, contrary pig at that, Mr. Hollins, who doesn't want to be washed. The words you can use under your breath ..."

"Oh, that ... No, no ... not that. Ha!"

But after recovering from his lighthearted laughter, Collingsworth Hollins said, "But they are unsavory words at times, ma'am. Are quite unkind in nature and tone and import. Can be quite racially charged and injurious."

<center>~~~~~</center>

Pee-Pot and Elegant stood off in a corner of the dressing room.

| 419 |

"Elegant, this is gonna be a great night for you, son."

Elegant nodded his head.

"But we really worked to get here, didn't we?"

"And I've enjoyed every moment, every second of it, with you, Mr. Manners."

"Even when you ran off?"

"I did leave a letter for you though, Mr. Manners."

"Hoped like hell you'd come back, Elegant. Did I." Pause. "Well, you did, and now look at what we have. Have now. In front of us. A heavyweight championship fight."

"Gem, she doesn't miss anything, does she, Mr. Manners?"

"Uh … sure—just like her father."

"You don't know what I mean, do you, sir? Am, uh, just what I'm implying, sir."

"No, Elegant. No, I don't."

"Tommie and Gyp, sir."

"Yes. Yes. Of course. Of course. Tommie and Gyp. It's just as much their night as ours, Elegant."

"My guardian angels."

"Gem's prayer for us tonight, it stimulated that."

"My father and mother too," Elegant said, the words coursing out his mouth.

Pee-Pot looked baffled.

"My guardian angels, Mr. Manners."

"Oh … yes … yes …"

Minutes later, there was the knock on the dressing room door.

Pee-Pot opened the door.

"It's time for the walk, Mr. Manners."

"Thanks, Mickey."

Elegant's body gleamed with sweat.

"You heard that, Elegant?"

"Loud and clear, Mr. Manners."

"I love hearing that. Only in New York," Gas said, clapping his hands. "Only in New York City do you hear that!"

The Raines entourage was heading toward the ring with the buzzing building from the Yankee Stadium crowd. With Elegant's hands clasped onto the back of Pee-Pot's lean shoulders and Gas and Alton Timms keeping in step with Pee-Pot and Elegant, the sun over the outdoor stadium painted a fading, orangey tail in the sky, fitting for September, for summer, for a heavyweight championship fight that a creeping darkness—after all the introductions are made and the national anthem sung, all the ceremony cleared out of the way—the bright ring lights would knife through to sculpt the ring glittery and new for this sold-out fight.

The entourage now in the ring; the buzz died down. Then it was recharged when Dominic Botti was spotted exiting the Yankee Stadium's dugout. He was crossing Yankee Stadium's infield, advancing toward the ring. The fans were close to hysterical. The applause became deafening, even in this outdoor, cavernous, electric place.

Elegant looked down at Gem, and they winked simultaneously at each other, something he had promised he'd do. But he was really looking at her to ascertain if she was all right. He felt she was.

Pee-Pot, when Elegant's concentration broke, looked down at her too; but she didn't see him since she was still looking up at Elegant.

The prefight ceremonies drew to a close. But before the referee's instructions to Elegant and Domenic Botti began, the sun had slipped from the sky, and darkness had pervaded the field. The ring's lights broke through the darkness like heavenly light.

"This is it, Elegant."

"Yes, sir, Mr. Manners."

Fritzie Lehman, the short-statured balding referee (the best in the business), who was precise, artful, and light of foot but potent of mouth, called the corners together to ring center.

When Elegant got to ring center, he faced a man, Domenic Botti, who was four inches shorter than him, at five feet ten. Botti had a tough, tugboat of a body. He was short armed and barrel chested. His chin was stout and his chest hairy. His satin red lips had twisted into a hard scowl. He was cross-eyed. Botti was the reigning heavyweight champion of the world. He looked it.

Elegant looked above his head. And how did he feel right now? Exhilarated, privileged to be fighting for the world's heavyweight crown.

"So just follow my instructions to the T, gentlemen. And good luck tonight. Let's put on a good show for everybody. Keep it clean. God bless you," Fritzie Lehman said.

And how did Pee-Pot feel right now? He'd never had a fighter of his, in all his years as a boxing trainer, fight for the world's heavyweight championship.

"This night we won't soon forget, Elegant."

"No, Mr. Manners."

When Gas inserted Elegant's mouthpiece, it's when Elegant looked down at ringside at Gem, now sitting to the right of Collingsworth Hollins. She looked petrified.

"Just stay on top of him, Elegant. It's all. Relentless. Relentlessly."

Then Pee-Pot hugged Elegant like he was hugging him for him and Gem and all of Elegant's guardian angels.

Clang.

Gem had never heard a bell clang like this one did in Yankee Stadium.

Round number one.

Domenic Botti was a clumsy fighter but effective.

He charged straight at Elegant at the opening bell but was met by a whistling jab and excellent footwork that moved Elegant out Botti's path but created a new one, a better one for himself, while banging Botti, making target practice out of his butcher block body.

Botti slowed his attack but then accelerated it. He was a silent assassin. His awkward movements were muscular as he pressured Elegant into the ropes and then winged wicked shots at his head, ramming him with big blows Elegant's elbows blocked.

And in between Botti's battering blows, between his gloves, Elegant was content to hit Botti, to jolt back his head with explosive, well-timed uppercuts, until Botti held onto him, tying Elegant up, falling heavily on him and doing heavy breathing.

Elegant was back working from the middle of the ring, controlling Botti, Botti weathering the storm, but then he'd return to his wild rampaging, taking those blistering jabs of Elegant's, trying to smother

Elegant, infight him for he could deliver his crushing head and body shots. And a few got in, and Elegant felt Botti's power on the tip of his jaw and in the pit of his stomach. The kind of strength and power that had knocked out forty-seven of Botti's fifty-two opponents.

But Elegant was confident he was in the best shape of his boxing career. Only Black Moon Johnson had cracked two of his ribs when they fought as middleweights, and he didn't want a repeat of that. Not tonight, not—

Clang.

"Are, are you all right, Mrs. Raines?"

"Yes, yes, I am," Gem said. "I-I am, Mr. Hollins."

"Are, are you sure, ma'am?"

"Y-ye-yes," Gem said, her voice trembling. Actually, she felt like throwing up.

Elegant was sitting on the boxer's stool.

"He's a bull, ain't he, Elegant?"

"Yes, you, you can say that again, Mr. Manners."

Pee-Pot instructed Elegant to take in a deep breath.

Then Elegant drank from the water bottle Gas tipped into his mouth.

This could be a long night or a short one for Elegant, Pee-Pot thought. For there was no quit in Botti, even if he'd breathed heavily in the first round. But that was only nervous energy, tension, Pee-Pot further thought—something every fighter has in a big, important fight like this.

"He's a fighter who won't quit—until you make him, Elegant."

Clang.

Round number two.

Gem sat back in her seat, shut her eyes, and then reopened them.

Neither fighter's strategy or style had changed. Botti was eating leather, still stalking Elegant; and with a savage body shot, he backed Elegant across the ring and then roughhoused him by grabbing him around the waist, swinging him. But before Fritzie Lehman, the referee, could warn him, Elegant was against the ropes, and a panicky elbow from Botti flew at Elegant's head (changing his tactics), which Elegant ducked.

"None of that roughhouse crap with me, Botti. This ain't no fucking back-alley brawl between these here fucking ropes!"

Botti grunted, his crossed eyes were dark as coal, and sweat flew off his hairy arms like seeds hurled to the wind.

Fritzie Lehman waltzed out of range of them, off to neutral ground.

Elegant caught Botti with a short, chopping right hand, with Botti responding by flailing at him with overhand rights, Elegant slipping then. Botti had backed him in the corner. Trying to get out of the corner, Elegant sidestepped Botti. But Botti bashed him in the back of his head simultaneous to Elegant's foot being pinned to the canvas by Botti's foot, and Elegant stumbled forward, tumbling when Botti, chasing him, clubbed the back of his head with three more hard, vicious overhand rights.

Elegant fell face first into the canvas.

He was down on one knee, unhurt, listening to Fritzie Lehman's booming count above the crowd's cacophonous roar reach three. He was about to rise, when he heard this laugh, this hideous, craven laugh he'd heard before in Saw Mill, South Carolina … And it froze his left knee to the canvas.

"Five …"

No, he never heard anyone's voice in the ring but Pee-Pot's, but his trainer's, up till now, not—

"Six …"

And Elegant was on his feet. He stood there solid, upright, Lehman still blocking him off from Botti. Elegant still hearing that laugh, the chilling, sickening, evil laugh he'd never forget … that'd been in him what seemed all his life—at least from the age of ten.

Gem was scared, for she didn't recognize Elegant, the look that deadened his eyes.

He was there! The man from the past! The man from Saw Mill, South Carolina! Out there somewhere in the crowd!

Botti was on a rampage, running at Elegant (but for Elegant, through his eyes, practically in slow motion, in a slowed down version of reality) to get to him after the second-round knockdown.

And Elegant felt both insane and merciless as he smashed Botti, stepping inside the shorter man's reach. He used his right shoulder to bull him back against the ropes. His fists ripped into Botti's liver and then another. And then a crunching blow to Botti's face, pushing it in. And then more of the same until Botti was knocked through the ropes.

Botti was half conscious. His body hung halfway in the ring and halfway out, over press row, the typewriters and the press's paper clutter.

Fritzie Lehman slipped between Elegant and Botti. His hands waved frantically in the air, signaling the championship match was officially over.

Pee-Pot and Gas and Alton Timms charged into the ring.

Only, Elegant ran away from them. Quickly, spontaneously, he hopped over the ring ropes and onto Yankee Stadium's infield and into the crowd.

Gem and Collingsworth Hollins thought he was heading for them, but he wasn't.

Elegant realized where the laugh came from, that hideous, sickening shrill of a laugh. It came from the tall man in the white, Southern suit, with all that mop of hair on his red, pockmarked head and face. Someone who was pretending to be a gentleman in Yankee Stadium in New York City. Someone who was respectable, civil, law-abiding—a human being.

But he was a murderer. Really a murderer. A man who'd killed everything in Elegant's life.

And Elegant ripped off his boxing gloves and taped hands. And bare fisted, he began beating this man with all the power and rage in him.

Gem screamed and so did the man.

"No! Elegant, no!"

"Yes! Yes! I killed him, Gem! I killed him! *I killed him!*"

CHAPTER 28

The next day, September 4, Elegant killed Rube Nash.

Elegant's fists mangled his face. They crushed every bone, including each eye socket. They broke his neck. Elegant's arraignment was tomorrow. Last night he'd been cuffed by the New York City Police and led out Yankee Stadium. He was driven in a patrol car to a local precinct in the Bronx where he was stripped naked, fingerprinted, and photographed after winning the heavyweight championship of the world and then killing a white man. This person by the name of Rube Nash.

Elegant and Pee-Pot and Gem were sitting at a long, narrow wooden table in a private room in the police precinct. The room was poorly lit. There was a guard at the door and one on either side of the room, all three armed but no guns drawn but holstered.

Gem had stopped crying.

Elegant was on one side of the table and Gem and Pee-Pot the other. Gem and Pee-Pot sat side by side.

Gem's arms stretched across the table. She held Elegant's hands.

Conversation had already begun. About two minutes of it after the initial sad, gloomy greeting, marked by nervous, anxious exchanges.

"With Tommie's death, I knew you could kill a man."

"Then … you saw—"

"Gyp led me down to the gym that morning. Uh, I saw you hitting the heavy bag. It's the hardest I ever saw you hit something. I saw anger in you, Elegant. Buried away."

"Yes … I unleashed it," Elegant said, looking at Gem. "That morning. When I came onto the property, Mr. Manners. Went into the building." Elegant's eyes had a cloudy, faraway look in them.

"I know his name. But who was he to you?" Pee-Pot asked. "Ex-exactly, son?"

"Yes, who, Elegant?"

Elegant's body didn't move. "Rube Nash was the man who killed my parents. Momma and Daddy. Selma and Austin Lacy."

Gem gasped.

Pee-Pot's eyes stayed fixed on Elegant and Elegant alone.

"He was the son of Dowd Nash. I—my father killed him."

"Your father—"

"Yes, Mr. Manners. Shot him. Killed him in Saw Mill, South Carolina."

"Then you were born in Saw Mill, South Carolina, and not—"

"No, sir, not Camp Town, Oklahoma. My father was a sharecropper. We were sharecropping, Gem."

"Yes, Elegant."

"And Dowd Nash was cheating us out of everything my father worked for. And, and my father … he got fed up, Daddy … just … He shot Dowd Nash. With his rifle. He killed a white man in Saw Mill, South Carolina. In 1938."

Pee-Pot saw the scenario unfolding.

Gem's stomach ached as if bleeding.

"My father rode back to our farm, Gem, after he killed Dowd Nash, and he was near mad. Crazed, Mr. Manners. And my mother, Momma, she screamed in pain, in such pain when Daddy told her everything. What he'd done."

"Elegant, Elegant …"

"Let me finish, Gem. Please. Say, say what I have to say …"

Elegant took his hands, the heel of his palms, and began rubbing them over his forehead.

"Daddy ran out into the yard, Momma running after him, and, and me too, with the rifle he killed Dowd Nash with and, and stood in the middle of the yard and said, 'Run, Selma! Run! You and Elegant get outta here! Out this place!'

"And … and then, then he raised the rifle to his head, w-with Momma screaming, looking at him, and fired the rifle!"

Elegant's body sagged, folded over. And his head fell forward onto the table and he cried along with Gem.

But then Elegant's head rose up off the table with tears in his eyes.

"But that's not all … it, it's not all, the end, Gem … Mr. … Mr. Manners," Elegant said, looking at them. "It didn't end there …"

"Momma gathered me. She … and the few things we had, we were going to … but she heard them coming, and there were woods, and she told me to run, and Momma opened the back door.

"'Go, Elegant!' *Momma said,* 'Go!'

"And I ran in to the woods, out the back door. Y-yes, into the woods!"

Elegant was looking into both Pee-Pot's and Gem's eyes.

"I ran … but not into the woods, deep inside, or away … but the edge, r-rim of it. And what I saw were eight men. There were eight of them. Eight white men with rifles and guns rode up to the house.

"Rube Nash was the first to … off his horse, then the others.

"'Nigga! Nigga! A dead nigga done shot hisself!'

"He spat on Daddy. A-and then took the butt of the rifle and split Daddy's head open. And then he turned to the others.

"'The nigga woman Selma an' his son, Elegant. Git 'em, goddammit. Git 'em!'

"They ran into the house, all of them but Rube Nash. They dragged Momma out the house. And, and then, then …"

"No! No, Elegant!"

"They raped her, Gem! They raped her next to my daddy. N-next to his body. By his brains and blood. Momma screaming. Screaming. While one by one they raped her. Eight of them!

"And, and I wanted to run out the woods and, and t-to save Momma. Save her—die for her like Daddy, my father died for us, b-but …"

Even Pee-Pot didn't know how much more he could take. He didn't expect this, not this graphic horror. But then he thought soberly, woven in it, was Cora Manner's blood too, her life and her death, and the South and its justice, and the reaping of revenge from one generation to the next.

"But they took her. Rode off with her. And when they rode off I heard this laugh, this shriek from Rube Nash. The one I'd never forget—not ever. I couldn't free myself of. Ever, ever …"

A long silence ensued.

"My life was a series of running after that. Living from hand to mouth. Meeting people who trusted me that I wouldn't steal from them, take anything from them. Who were good enough, kind enough, Christian enough to house me. Take me in. Take care of me.

"Eventually I made my way out of South Carolina. Headed west. Years passed until I finally wound up in Oklahoma. Then Texas."

"Frank 'Black Machine' Whaley, Whaley's Gym, Elegant."

"Yes, Mr. Manners. Mr. Whaley. Whaley's Gym. But with a new name."

"Last name—it's what you mean, Elegant."

"Yes, Gem. Last name. From Elegant Lacy to Elegant Raines. I changed it the first night I was on the run. Alone—when it rained, and I … Just put an *e*, added an *e* to it … later …"

Gem knew there was a God but didn't feel him inside her now. Not that her faith, the foundation of it, had, in anyway, been shattered or shaken, but she felt empty inside. Dead.

And Pee-Pot knew the larger prize was never the heavyweight championship of the world for Elegant. Clearly, he saw that now.

"I'm a murderer, Gem. I'm a murderer. Tommie's father is a murderer!"

"No, no, you're not, Elegant. No, you're not!"

"Rube Nash has torn our family apart again. I was supposed to protect Tommie from him. This generation from him. My family from evil white men like him!"

"We'll, we'll be all right, Elegant. We will, Elegant."

"No, you won't. No, you won't, Gem. No, you won't!"

Silence.

"I read so much. Read and read so much—so not to be alone. Why, why I read so much. So many books." Pause. "Was determined to read. All the time," Elegant sobbed.

Gem was aware Elegant was looking back into his life again, in his mind.

It was Shakespeare, Gem thought. Shakespeare soothed him. He was able to see tragedy through Shakespeare's eyes, that it just wasn't him who saw it, his father kill himself, his mother raped by crazed, cowardly men—for him to not see how they killed her when they rode off with her (or was she already dead?) on their horses, the eight white men.

The room door opened.

The desk sergeant entered the room. "Mrs. Raines, Mr. Hollins is outside. He said if he isn't disturbing you, he'd like to see you. Said it's about Mr. Raines's defense lawyer."

"Yes, the lawyer. Thank you." Gem stood.

Elegant looked up at Gem.

"I won't be long, Elegant. I promise."

"Yes, of, of course not, Gem. Of course not."

Gem walked out of the room with the desk sergeant.

"How will she do it, Mr. Manners? How will Gem be able to handle this, sir!"

"She'll have her father, Pastor Loving, and Francine and Tommie and me. And all of Longwood behind her, Elegant. There to support her. The whole Longwood community will be there for her."

Elegant sat back in the chair. His hands hid his eyes.

> *Are in the poorest things superfluous*
> *Allow not more than nature needs,*
> *Man's life's as cheap as beasts ...*

"King Lear, Mr. Manners. King Lear."

"What, Elegant? What ...?"

"It's who I was thinking of. Of right now: King Lear, Mr. Manners."

Pee-Pot's head rocked.

Elegant looked down at his powerful hands.

Now he was a tragic figure. But maybe, like Shakespeare's characters, he was always a tragic figure, Elegant thought.

"Don't worry, Elegant, we're gonna win this. I know it's gonna be the fight of our lives, but we're gonna win this legal fight in the court that's ahead of us," Pee-Pot said, his fingers tugging rigorously at his checkered cap's bill.

"Like we always have in the ring together," Pee-Pot said. "No different, son. This w-will be no different for us."

Elegant's eyes looked over toward the door, and he hoped Gem would get back to the room soon, back from outside. Suddenly, it's all he hoped for in the room where, even with Pee-Pot sitting there with him, he felt alone.